Old Bones Old Ways

OLD BONES OLD WAYS

THE MANTICORE'S SHADOW
BOOK TWO

GREYSON BLACK &
E. SCOTT CLEVENGER

SAINAN
Books

Cover Art/Design: E Scott Clevenger
Typography: E Scott Clevenger
Cover Copyright: © 2025 by Sainan Books
Maps by: E. Scott Clevenger

Sainan Books, LLC
Bolingbrook, IL 60440
United States

Originally published in Paperback, Hardback, and eBook by Sainan Books in November 2025

ISBN: 979-8-9906012-7-7 (Trade Paperback) | ISBN: 979-8-9906012-8-4 (eBook) | ISBN: 979-8-9906012-6-0 (Hardback)
Library of Congress Control Number: 2025918135

AI usage statement - No generative AI was used in this novel. All finished text is the original creation of the authors.

My mother may have begun my obsession with reading and with fantasy, but it was honed through the stories I read. My inspirations came from Terry Brooks, Orson Scott Card, Poppy Z. Brite, and Anne Rice, among others. This book would not be possible without the support of my good friend Derek, my cheerleader Johnny, and of course, my co-author Scott.
--- Greyson

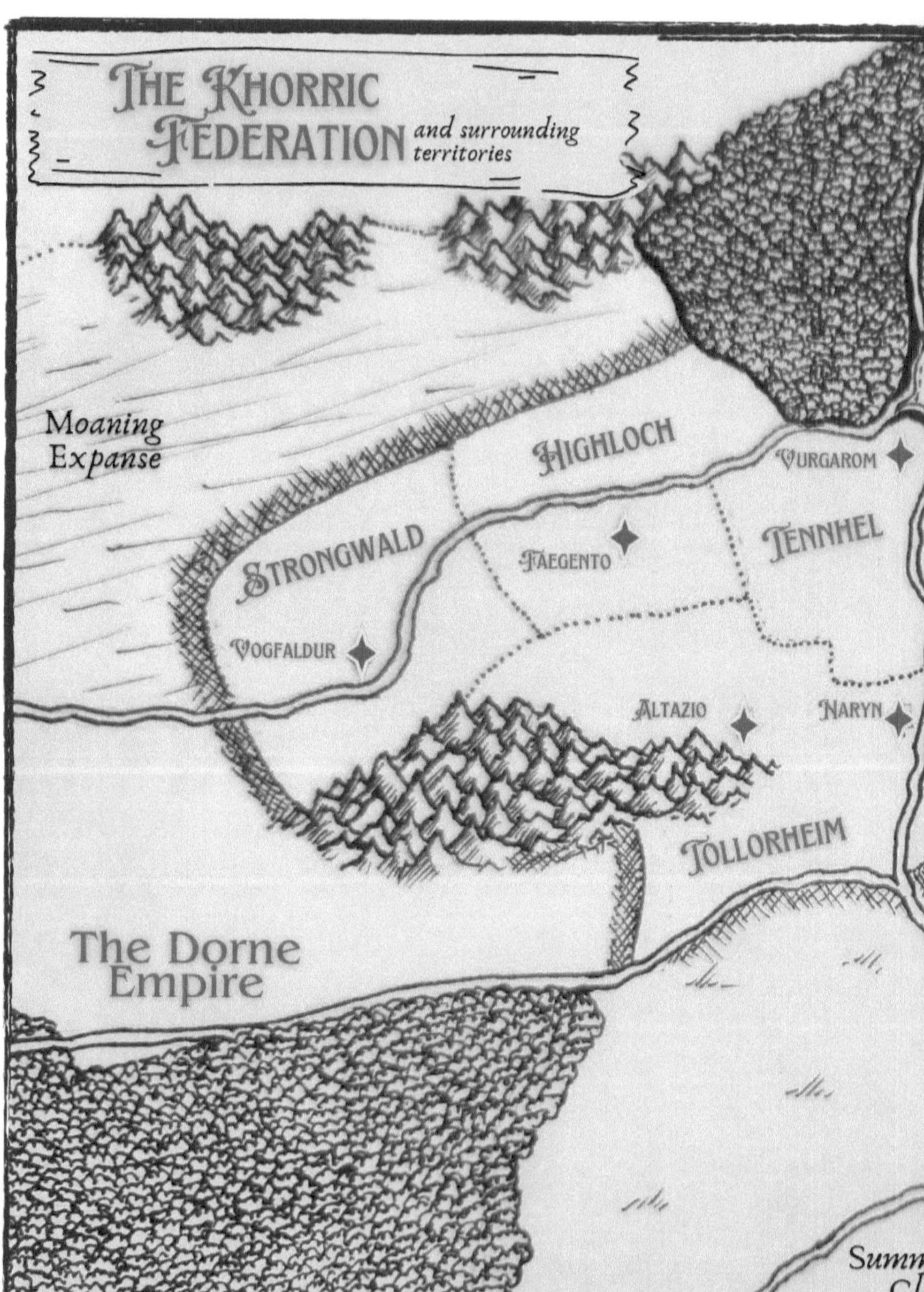

THE KHORRIC FEDERATION and surrounding territories
Moaning Expanse
HIGHLOCH
VURGAROM
STRONGWALD
FAEGENTO
TENNHEL
VOGFALDUR
ALTAZIO
NARYN
TOLLORHEIM
The Dorne Empire
Summ
Gla

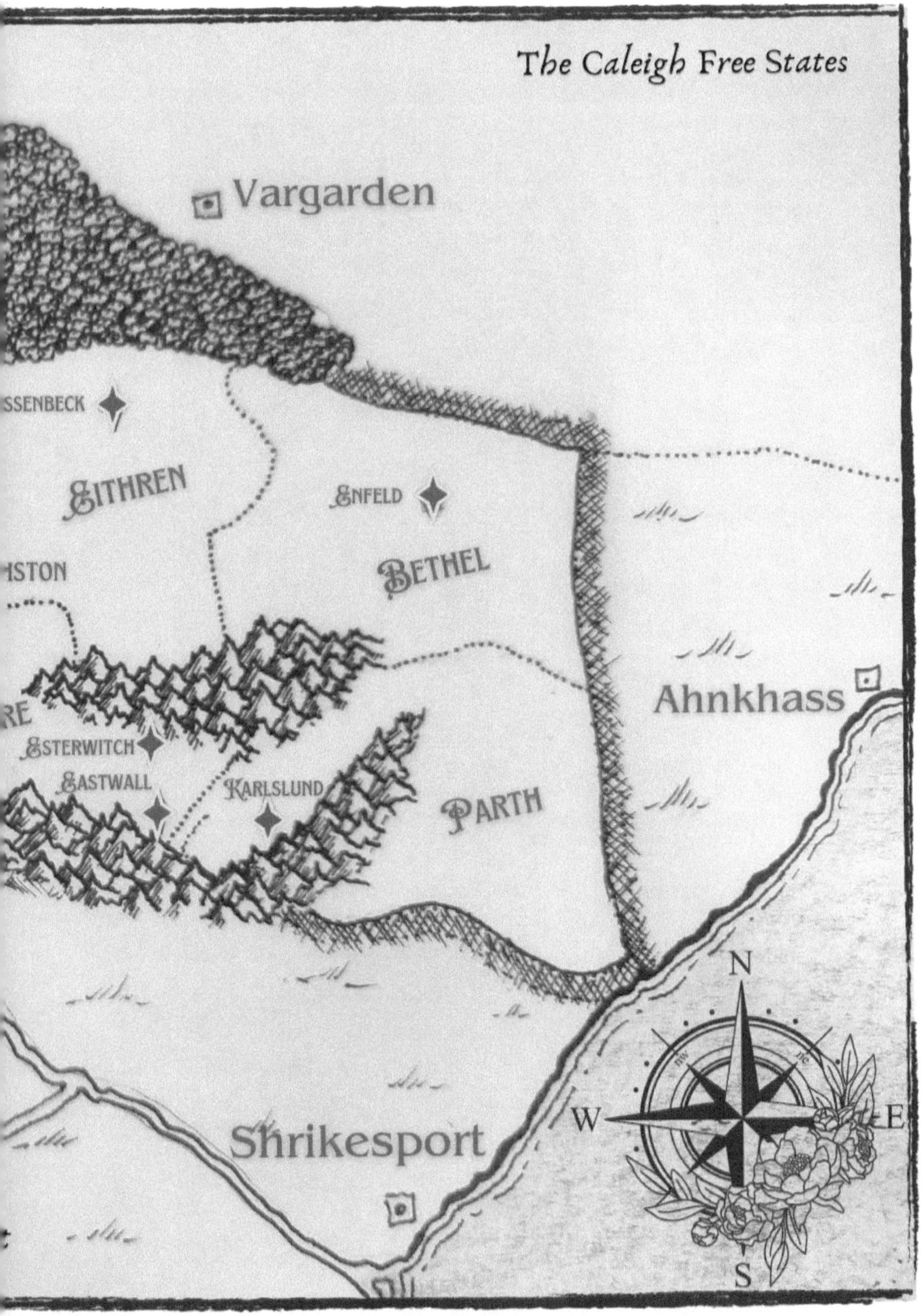

The Caleigh Free States
Vargarden
SSENBECK
SITHREN
ENFELD
BETHEL
HSTON
RE
ESTERWITCH
EASTWALL
KARLSLUND
PARTH
Ahnkhass
N
W
E
S
Shrikesport

Table of Contents

APPENDIX

Old Bones Old Ways

1

Ghosts

It should have been a great night for camping. The light of the moon in the clear sky should have provided comfort and solace to the small group of campers huddled together. But the open plains made them feel isolated, exposed, and alone. Nearly a month had passed since the fall of Highston, and the travelers were still uneasy. The travel was slow, and their desire to hide was thwarted by the open landscape of the Eithren province of the Khorric Federation. It was an arduous journey, fraught with peril, towards a land they knew nothing about.

While there was plenty of light, the chill in the air meant that they needed a fire to keep warm. It was springtime on the plains, and the Khorric Federation was still trying to shake off the last vestiges of winter. They had located their camp in a rare copse of trees, and nestled their fire deep in the little grove, blocking it from the view of passersby. Every precaution had been taken, but the fear of being hunted remained.

Road weary and exhausted, the four travelers were an unusual group to be sure, but they had survived much together and had been forged into something special. They had survived the resurrection of the War of Night, battled Investurants, and escaped the clutches of the Bright Guild, Manticore. Four unique individuals, all with their own tales, bonded in friendship and committed to each other.

The smallest two figures were nestled closely, sleeping soundly. Jesse, the Isnashi, was laid out in his bedroll, his small arms and his wings wrapped around Thorn, his tiny Goblin friend. Of the group, these two thieves had known each other the longest. Jesse had been betrayed by Manticore, and now was on the run. Thorn, as always, by his side.

Curled up on the other side of the fire was Symon. His feline heritage kept him warmer than Jesse or Thorn, but even he kept a blanket wrapped around him to hold off the chill. An aristocrat, a blacksmith, and a budding sorcerer, Symon had found himself caught in the center of a plot between Manticore and the Investurants. Former friends had risen to power and proven to be devious and selfish, selling him out. Now, he ran for survival to a place he knew nothing about, hoping for answers.

The only one still awake was the large, quadrupedal figure who stood watch in the night. Argyle had walked the perimeter of the campsite, taking in all that they had seen and encountered since the fall of Highston. His former master, Grendel, had been the man who had betrayed Jesse and Symon. Leader of Manticore and an up and coming Noble, Grendel Montrell's plot had been to overthrow Highston and give it to the "New Nobles", which had reignited the War of Night. Investurants were in the Federation for the first time in forty years, and controlled the city until the New Noble Council could establish their dominance.

Now, Argyle sat watching the camp. Frost coated his rocky skin. He sat motionless, that stillness that only Gargoyles can achieve, his eyes locked on the horizon, looking for threats. The cold air didn't bother his kind, and his keen eyes cut through the darkness with ease. For this reason, Argyle often held the middle watch, where the night was deepest, and protected them on their travels. A string of quiet nights had only intensified their alertness, so the Genbu stood silently waiting for trouble.

As if bidden, Argyle watched a shadow portal open off the edge of the woods. A few hundred yards away, they could only hope it was a scouting party, and their camp was hidden well enough to remain undetected. From the portal, Investurant scouts stepped onto the plains, looking for quarry.

It was a small squad of lower Shadows. A Lightning Cult of scouts and trackers, shorter ears and less graceful than their high-blooded counterparts. Moonlight danced on their blue skin, and their swords gleamed darkly in the night, and the night shadowed their feral faces. Eyes intent, the scouts scanned the area searching for their prey.

Argyle cursed as the squad leader pointed towards the campground.

"*Natse sol'el a'hi,*" the scout leader said. *There they are.* Simple words, but the intent was clear. The Investurants had found their targets, and they wouldn't be there much longer. It was not in them to fail.

"*Take the boys, kill the rest.*"

"*We should wait for the whole squad,*" the second said.

"*Yes,*" the leader said. "*You are right. They are more than they seem.*"

The Genbu hesitated. Dealings with the Investurants were familiar to him. Under Manticore, Argyle had brokered many offers with them. Low-born squad leaders were often overly ambitious. Perhaps he could negotiate their survival if he offered some of the secrets he still possessed.

A low growl formed in his throat as a half dozen additional scouts emerged from a second portal. Then a lanky Highblood with a long face, pointed ears, and thin eyes stepped out. All eyes turned to him. The mood of the Lightning Cult changed to abject worship. This Highblood was their patron. He would guide them in this mission. Argyle abandoned his hope of resolving this without violence.

"*Rel'day'sainar,*" the scout leader said, bowing his head. "*You have come to help?*"

"*Yes, I am here to make sure we succeed. General Rhon wants them brought to the Ombramaes directly. If we retrieve them, we'll be rewarded with great honor.*"

Argyle glanced at the three sleeping figures, but held his focus on the Investurants. It would be too easy to lose them in the shadows. Such an advantage would prove fatal to his companions.

"*Fan out! Flank them. Kill the big one first. The rest, we'll drag back to—*"

The voice of the Highblood was cut short as a blade emerged from the portal and struck his neck, nearly severing his head. Blood sprayed across the field, and the scout leader barely raised his eyes above the noble in time to dodge a figure leaping from the portal beyond.

The new warrior was adorned in a variety of weapons, wrapped in a ragged cloak, and moved with a savage speed and grace. He exploded into action, his blades a blur, slicing through the Investurant scouts before they could even draw their weapons. Twin knives, almost long enough to be shortswords, with flat backs and broader curved tips, sliced with deadly precision through necks, thighs, and arms, raining blood into the night. Three dead soldiers before the body of the Highblood had even hit the ground.

Argyle watched as the shadow scouts looked at each other nervously. Even at this distance, he could see the fear dancing in their eyes. They looked, for all intents and purposes, as if they were facing a nightmare come to life. Slowly hands reached for blades and they took defensive stances. The Genbu didn't know the origin of this mystery killer. Be he from Sainan or the Shadow Realm of Mumvuri, the only thing Argyle knew was that he was saving them now.

"Don't break!" the squad leader cried. *"Tactics! We fight as one. Communicate! Destroy him, then we take the boys. We shall not be taken down by this broken figure. We shall not fear—"*

"The Ghost," the figure said. "You will fear the Ghost."

Argyle smiled at the beauty. This "Ghost," wherever he may hail from, at least spoke Mumvuri and was delighting in the terror he was causing. Two scouts approached the Ghost from opposing angles. Though they were attempting to split his defenses and overwhelm him, the Ghost stalked forward, waiting for their strikes. Without breaking stride, he twisted his blades at the moment of their attack, deflecting the warriors and redirecting each of their attacks into the body of the other.

The last three warriors ignored the signal of their captain to circle out. They were breaking. All hope of preservation was abandoned. Only thoughts of escape remained. The warriors ran through the trees, leaves, and branches brushing through their bodies as they phased between solid and shadow. The Ghost pressed through the woods after them. He nimbly jumped and ducked over obstacles without pause.

Driving ever nearer, they arced through the edge of their patch of woods, returning to their entry point. Realizing they were not going to be able to lose their pursuer, the final three scouts turned to face the Ghost, hoping to buy enough time for their leader to escape. Before they could even stop and gain their bearings, their mad attacker barreled through one of the scouts, leaving the Shadow's belly laid open in his wake. The final two had barely turned before they went into sheer panic. The Ghost relentlessly pursued them, all the while, his eyes remained locked on the squad leader. He would not be turned. He would not be slowed.

The scouts made a turn, taking a hard run, attempting to get an angle and make a push towards escape. The Ghost ran them down with ease, his pace seemed almost lazy as he cut the distance between them. He took the last in line with a quick slash of his left hand, jumped on the second, dispatching him with a strike from the right. Standing over his victim, the warrior threw his short blade and split the last remaining scout's skull. The force of the blow threw the Investurant warrior from the ground and he slid down the pathway. The Ghost turned silently on his heel and began walking towards the leader. Steady, methodical, and ominous the figure walked through the night. Argyle could barely hear the words *"Osival,"* the Ghost said and extended his hand. The blade wriggled free of the fallen scout and flew into his hand.

The leader dashed and leaped through the portal. His hands flailed wildly as he gestured to dismiss the portal, closing the gate between worlds. As the portal shrunk, the Ghost glanced quickly at the campers, one final sight, and Argyle locked eyes with the man. The shadowed figure nodded once, just briefly, before taking off at full speed. The Investurant squad leader continued to gesture violently, trying, in vain, to encourage the magic to be released. The portal was nearly closed, only a pace wide as the Ghost leaped through after his prey. The portal snapped shut behind him, and sliced through the tip of his cloak, leaving a hand-width scrap of fabric that floated in the wind.

The wind carried the fabric past the woods and tumbled over the knee-high grass that stretched out in all directions. As the fabric blew in the wind, it turned and cleared to the flattened area where the camp was. Argyle caught the scrap in his paw as Symon, bleary-eyed, walked up from behind.

"Argyle, is everything okay?" he asked. "I thought I heard something."

"No, there is nothing," Argyle said. "Go back to sleep, I've the watch."

The Ennedi sniffed the air, and his eyes tightened. "Are you sure?"

"A brief conflict. Nothing that concerns us."

The big smith shrugged, and returned to his blankets. Within moments, Symon had returned to sleep and left Argyle to his thoughts. Another night, another obstacle averted. The path to Vargarden still lay ahead. Fulfilling their arrival in Vargarden was the only thing that mattered. Argyle would not fail.

Symon was lost. Flames danced all around him. Smoke and ash hung in the air stinging his eyes and nose. Jesse's dead body lay at his feet. His flesh began to melt and peel away from the bone as the boy's lifeless eyes stared back at him.

"Why?" Jesse asked. His voice was twisted and decayed. The voice of the dead. "Why do you keep getting me killed?"

Symon awoke with a start.

Small bones crunched under his fingers as he pushed himself up from his bedroll. A half dozen skeletal fragments collected beneath his hand, all small woodland creatures, as if pulled to him in the night. He covered them with dirt, and rose. This was the second time it had happened since leaving Highston.

Having nothing to do for it, Symon explored the direction of the disturbance the night before, to satisfy his curiosity and take his mind off his nightmare. Not much remained, likely being removed by scavenging animals in the night, but evidence remained. Blood smears were visible on the trees, and the sole body of an Investurant scout remained. They had been close, too close, to being found, but still remained safe.

He sniffed the air, hoping in vain that any of the scents would reveal more, and found it too muddled for any information. Too much time had passed and the animal scents covered much of the original source. Symon walked back to the camp and gave Argyle a quick, calculating stare. "What happened last night?"

"A small raiding party appeared," Argyle replied. "I was keeping with the hope that they would pass beyond us and leave us undeterred. By the time I realized they had located us and were a threat, the situation had adapted. A malevolent force in the night dispatched them. At that time, I ascertained no benefit to rousing you."

"Well," Symon said. "Next time, wake us. We need to be careful."

"Of course, Master Cylkas."

Symon gathered his things, pushing his friends to get underway and put some distance behind them. The travel was difficult, as the trails were muddy, and they could not afford to be seen on the main roads. Still, the group slogged through the fields and trees, ever forward, on their journey.

Mid afternoon saw them passing a moderately sized village of Vaettir. Realizing that the group would be hard pressed to remain incognito and hide a six foot tall lion-like Ennedi, a Goblin, and an eight-foot-tall, quadrupedal Gargoyle, the group agreed to let Jesse handle supplies.

An hour later, Jesse returned with home cooked meals and news.

"The old man in the orchard today said it's another week to Essenbeck, at least," said Jesse. "Vargarden could be twice that length on the other side. At least the roads are easy to follow and lead right there, so there's little excuse to get lost."

"Lost," said Symon dryly. "I feel like we are all lost. What are we doing?"

"We're doing what your dad said," answered Jesse. "We're going to Vargarden."

"Right. 'Take my blade, return to Vargarden. You have much about your heritage you need to know. Train your Gift, and make me proud!'" Symon said, sighing. He remembered his father's words, but still did not know how to feel about them. Sarcasm and pain crept into his voice. "That is our only option, right?"

"Maybe yours!" interjected Thorn from Jesse's other side. She slapped Jesse on the shoulder and said, "Me and this punk bitch here could disappear into Essenbeck, no problem."

"Hey!" Jesse said. "Let's cut the guy a break." Jesse gazed back at Symon, his friend, and his eyes softened. "What's up? Something feel off, or are you just punking out?"

"No," Symon said. "I mean, I do not think so. Nothing feels... off. But it is Vargarden, correct? The Land of the Dead."

"Yeah, but your dad was from there, too! It can't be ALL bad. Your dad seemed like a good guy."

"I thought he was."

Jesse shrugged. "At least he wasn't Grendel. Could have been worse."

"Grendel was a villain for sure," said Symon. "But at least you knew he was a villain. You could trust him to be a villain. You knew where you stood with him, and how far you could trust his word."

"Perhaps," interjected Argyle. "But what point do you bring?"

"Only that it would seem my father could be as much a villain," said Symon. "But all the worse, because he disguised his true self from me as thoroughly as Lord Grendel Montrell hid his nature from my father. Hidden armor and a sword? His hatred of the *Ombramaes* and hers for him? Who was he?"

"Well—" Jesse started.

"And to top it all he was a magic user! A Necromancer! The entire time, he was hiding his true self and spouting hypocrisy every time he told me that magic would not aid us. That my magic was not welcome to our home or our business!"

Symon was yelling now. Emotions had boiled to the surface that he had not expected. He still had not unpacked the betrayal he felt from his father, and it was obvious that he would struggle to do so.

Silence surrounded the group for a moment, before Symon added, "Truthfully, who was the real villain?"

"Shit," Jesse whispered, putting his arm around the Ennedi. "It will be okay. Life is nothing but a collection of villains," sighed Jesse. "I guess the best we can do is choose the lesser bad guys to get used by."

"So we follow the path behind those walls of living death? To the necromancers. Hundreds of them, they say, all dressed in black robes, their flesh pale and undernourished as if they were near dead themselves?"

"Is that true?" Thorn asked.

Symon shrugged. "I'm not sure how much of all of that was true, and how much is propaganda, but it sounds true. The Academy instructors also spoke of their homeland, about how the citizens are ruled by their own dead, toiling under the watchful eye of their own re-living ancestors. If that is even close to the truth, this will not be a pleasant visit."

"The Academy has been known for its penchant for exaggeration and misinformation," Argyle said, curtly. "But it would be wise to expect danger and trouble. Vargarden is a necessity, however. Even Master A'Dynell agreed."

"Fu-uck," said Jesse under his breath. "Remind me why we are friends again?"

Symon chuckled grimly and answered, "Because you appear to be just as hopeless and desperate as myself?"

2

The Essenbeck Job

"We have coin, Thorn."

"We have LIMITED coin," said Thorn, a mischievous smile on her face. "You know we can stretch that coin with a little hand waving."

It felt good to be in a city again. After all the time on the road, alone and unprotected, the comfort of thousands of people all jumbled together felt cozy and familiar. So much about the moment brought a level of nostalgia. The two friends were browsing a market remarkably similar to areas they haunted in Highston, arm in arm down the aisles between stalls and carts. The sights, sounds, and smells were so familiar that Jesse felt a wave of homesickness.

Those feelings alone brought a level of danger, however. He had to remind himself that they didn't know the easy marks here. They didn't know the guards or the good areas of the city. And most importantly, they didn't know the underworld here.

Thorn, it appeared, was more comfortable. Jesse had caught her pocketing a small supply of dried meat as they left the previous shop. The unnecessary risk was what had prompted him to call her out.

Jesse sighed. "We can also stretch Symon's coin by sweet talking people into better deals. We don't always have to be stealing."

"That's it though," Thorn griped, "anything we are paying for, even if you use your honeyed tongue, is still coming from Symon. All I'm saying is, there's nothing wrong with a little honest theft."

"I'm not going to win this, am I?" Jesse asked, watching out of the corner of his eye as Thorn pocketed a pair of apples. He hissed, glancing around to see whether someone may have made them.

"Nope. But do you really want to?"

"Kind of," said Jesse.

"Why?" asked Thorn, somewhat surprised. "You've never had a problem with it before."

"Yeah, BEFORE," Jesse stressed. "When it was the only way. Survival, necessity, life or death." He grinned and added, "Or when goaded by a certain best friend!"

"You are just jealous that I am better at it than you."

"Yeah, yeah. You're also better looking," Jesse laughed. "But still, if we don't have to be thieves, then should we? What's wrong with being honest?"

"Sweetums? Jes? Are you trying to grow a conscience on me?" she asked. "Is the blacksmith rubbing off on you that badly?"

Jesse thought about it. Symon had changed Jesse's life in many ways. He had gotten used to being around a man who took care of things legitimately. It didn't hurt that Jesse was enamored by the big Ennedi. While they hadn't broached the topic of romance, the two had grown quite close over the past months. Jesse wondered if something could have happened if Highston hadn't fallen under attack and forced them to flee. Jesse had to admit that Symon was a big reason for his shift in mindset.

He gazed down at Thorn. "Would that be so bad? Can we not change? Are Street Rats all we are good for?"

"Fuck that!" Thorn yelled, stopping in the street. "What in the Thirteen Hells is wrong with being a Street Rat?"

"Maybe nothing," replied Jesse. "Maybe everything."

"You think he's better than us?!" she continued. "What? Because he's never been hungry? Because he doesn't steal? Because he had a house and family?

"So what!" she said. Her tone was serious, but not angry. Jesse had offended her, but she wasn't attacking him, just proving her points. "Lucky maybe, but not better. He had all those things, and now they're all gone. What happens when his money runs out? How good will he be then?"

"Symon would find a way," Jesse said. "He's good. Upstanding. But not... not pious." Jesse was stumbling to find a way to explain it. "When the Friars say we should be 'good people' it sounds wrong. They tell us to give back, but take it all from us. When Symon says it, it makes sense. So, what do I think about being a good person? Is it wrong to want more? Does nothing the Friars say matter? Or do they have a point?"

"The Friars?" Thorn laughed. "You are suddenly worried about the fucking priests?" Thorn asked incredulously. "When in the Shining Court did you ever worry about what a Friar has to say about anything outside of their price tag?"

"I don't know," moaned Jesse. He waved his hands in frustration. "What if there's more? More I could do. Like help rather than take. It's just, magic teaches that everything has a cost, and a right way to do it. It's just that it's had me thinking."

"Our way has a cost, too," said Thorn. "We just pay it up front in training, and after in risk."

"I suppose," said Jesse.

"Look, if you want to help people or 'do more', then do that. Take an apprentice. Be a mentor, take them under your wing..." she smiled toothily at her joke. Then in a snarl, "Just don't be like... him."

"Xerian?" Jesse asked. He flinched at the sting of that name being brought up. He almost couldn't say it, himself.

"Yeah, you know the life can be hard. You want to make it better, help those people."

"What about the rest? Shopkeepers, citizens, and them. Stealing from them doesn't bother you?"

"Hell no! As far as I'm concerned, it's just another payment method to be evaluated. You can beg for freebies, barter for trade, pay coin, or if the opening is there, steal it."

Thorn wrapped her arm around Jesse's waist, and he draped his arm over her shoulders. As they continued on, Thorn added, "Besides, places in the Khorr want to be robbed. They practically ask for it."

"How do you figure that?" asked Jesse, grinning.

"When the government wants a location absolutely left alone for a particular moment, what do they do?"

"Easy," said Jesse. "Go to a Bright Guild, and pay them enough to enforce discipline on the area."

"Exactly! So the Bright Guilds are actually performing a service. If they weren't in place, everyone would be stealing and killing randomly and indiscriminately."

"You really believe that? That the underworld is necessary and stealing is valid?"

"Well," hesitated Thorn, looking for the logic trap. "From places that deserve it, or in need, absolutely."

"So no stealing from orphans or widows?"

"What do you take me for?" asked Thorn in mock outrage. "Some stinking Goblin?"

"So if, say, we were in some little innocent village, and some nice old lady gave us lunch out of the goodness of her own heart, you wouldn't steal a shiny new blanket from her, right?"

Thorn laughed. "Absolutely not! Unless we needed it more than she did." She turned to him once again, eyes alight with curiosity. "That smith still has you smitten, though? Got in your head to 'be worthy of him?'"

"It's not like that."

"Oh, I've heard that before."

The two of them continued to laugh as Thorn led them to another part of the market. Both of them had noticed markings for the Bright Guild named Beckoning, and wanted to avoid rival territory. As soon as they were clear of the market stalls and headed down a new street, Thorn took out an apple, polished it on her sleeve, and tossed it in the air in Jesse's general direction. Always alert to his surroundings, the movement did not catch him unaware, and he caught the fruit with ease. The small Goblin then took out a dried fish that Jesse had not even noticed her pilfer, and began to chew it thoughtfully.

Jesse had wanted to gather information about home. Twisting and turning their way through the unfamiliar city, they finally saw their first territory markings for Manticore. It took another fifteen minutes before they stood before Houndstooth Mercantile, a dry goods shop that would not only get them the supplies they needed for the road, but was also a contact point for the branch of Manticore in Essenbeck.

"You sure about this?" asked Thorn. "Poking this beast? We are on the run, after all. We should just get the supplies, and then disappear. Send Symon away and start over. New guilds, new life."

"We're fine," replied Jesse. "I'm just going to find out what I can about Highston. Besides, Grendel's dead. We're running from Investurants, not Manticore."

"Even so... you don't know THIS Manticore!"

"Why do you think that? Manticore is Manticore. I know the signs, I know the calls. I should be able to get at least a little information."

"Um, Jes? I think you are forgetting something. We aren't Manticore. Why should they help us?"

"Hey, sweet talking silver tongue, remember?" said Jesse with a cocky grin.

"Right," Thorn deadpanned. "Until you find out there's a bounty on you. Or that you've been black-listed. Or, fuck, any other thousand reasons that they could make money off your corpse!"

"You're worrying too much. We didn't do anything to the Brights. Besides, even if Highston Manticore is pissed about us fighting Grendel... New city, new rules, girl. They may not have even had time to reach out to Essenbeck. We're fine."

"Yeah, that Distant Message spell takes, what, two or three whole minutes?" Thorn muttered under her breath.

Jesse shook his head and crossed the street.

Opening the main door, he stepped into the cool, dark interior of the shop. Thorn entered close behind them, and the door closed with a tinkling of a bell.

Being a well stocked mercantile, the interior was fairly large, boasting a well stocked front room of knickknacks, treats, snacks, and other impulse purchase items, as well as a generous supply of sample merchandise. Seating ran along a wall, and a half dozen men and women seemingly of various walks of life stood or sat around, some played casual games of chance or gossiped, while others browsed the shelves. Jesse estimated that no less than half worked for Manticore.

As the pair scanned the room, a voice boomed out from behind the counter. "What's a couple o' thievin' ragamuffins like you wantin' in my shop?"

Jesse spun around to see who was speaking, while Thorn kept her gaze in her current direction, watching for someone to possibly use the distraction against them. A towering Bugbear, hairy and menacing, leaned over the counter squinting at them. Jesse flashed a smile and sauntered up to the counter.

"Hey there! I need me a good eighty four feet of solid hemp rope," Jesse said casually, "and let's say, three vials of antivenom." Jesse stared at the proprietor gauging his response. Eight-four was a code for a request of information. Antivenom was code for peaceful parlay. All street slang to tell the guy that he was familiar with the Bright Guild.

"Eighty four feet? That's an awful lot. What'cha purpose?"

"On the nose, eight four exactly" grinned Jesse. "Mainly tying up travel gear. Center out knots, you know. They take a lot of rope." Request confirmed. Need info on Highston.

The shopkeeper scratched his chin, looked over the room, fixing his gaze on Thorn for a moment. "Hemp's no good for center knots. Chaffes and tears. Ya either want another rope, or change your knots"

Jesse frowned. The agent was openly admitting that Highston was keeping information from Essenbeck. A broker shouldn't be revealing that.

"While you ponder, let me tell you what. I'm out of antivenom at the moment," he said, grabbing up a scrap of paper and a sliver of charcoal. He scribbled something on the paper, then slid it to Jesse as he said, "Try this address. They will probably have what you need."

Jesse looked down at the paper. He looked back up and said, "This exact address? You're positive?"

"Or go without," the man said unconcernedly. "No fleas off my back neither way."

"Alright. I'll try here. Thanks." Jesse half turned from the counter, moving toward the door without quite giving the man his back. He half bumped into Thorn to let her know they were done, and they both headed out.

Once outside and a ways down the street, he passed her the note, which read, *"Back round o the store. Ditch tha greenskin."*

"Seriously?" she screamed out. "That racist, pox-munching, Fat-headed, acorn-brained rock-humper is a fucking 'greenskin' himself!"

"Yeah, I get it. Stupid as hell, I guess," said Jesse.

"Do we really need this though? Seriously? I mean come on, if this is how they run their contact points, how put together can the guild really be? They better not ever get me in charge, that's all I'm saying."

"Set 'em straight, would you, girl?"

"Fuck yeah! First, make sure there's a quality head in charge of each city, answering to me at the head so I can make sure all of Manticore is one family. For fuck's sake, they are all under the same name. They act like the same guild."

"Makes sense, I suppose," muttered Jesse, only half paying attention.

"Make 'em all share details. Why fight each other for info? For fuck's sake, we could probably go back there and sell info on the fighting in Highston and Grendel's death for serious coin," Thorn said. "Assuming we could walk out of there alive after, of course."

"Of course."

"We could also probably sell our new buddy to them as well," she said, looking at him sideways.

"Could work. I mean, what?!" said Jesse, looking down at Thorn in confusion.

Thorn chuckled. "Trying to see if you were actually listening. What has you so distracted?"

"If they aren't getting info, what does the broker want with me?"

"What?"

"He told me they're isolating, but if I coded for info, I shouldn't need to step back. And not alone. Something's not right. Let's get the fuck out of here."

"Okay, sure."

They began the journey back to the tavern where they'd found a room. Jesse forced them to make a few stops and buy the dry goods they had actually come for. His paranoia caused him to scan the crowds every time they entered or exited a shop. He couldn't shake the bad feeling. Then he spotted the tail. Three little Street Rats. They were swapping off alleys, only one following at a time, the others paralleling and taking the cross streets. They were good, but Jesse was better.

"I'm pretty sure we are being followed," said Jesse. "Let's duck back into Beckoning territory. They won't follow us there."

 wondered if something could have happened if Highston hadn't fallen under attack and forced them to flee. Jesse had to admit that Symon was a big reason for his shift in mindset.

He gazed down at Thorn. "Would that be so bad? Can we not change? Are Street Rats all we are good for?"

"Fuck that!" Thorn yelled, stopping in the street. "What in the Thirteen Hells is wrong with being a Street Rat?"

"Maybe nothing," replied Jesse. "Maybe everything."

"You think he's better than us?!" she continued. "What? Because he's never been hungry? Because he doesn't steal? Because he had a house and family?

3

The Past that Haunts

Symon sat in silence staring at the fire while stoking the coals. He sat shaking off the remnants of another nightmare. Sleep would come slow tonight, it would be fitful, and rest would be minimal. Different versions of the same dream every night since they abandoned Highston. Visions of his father's shop burning to the ground. Glimpses of his dad blasted away by Investurant magic. The smell of death, destruction, and decay still tingled in his nose. Long past, but ingrained in his memory.

The worst part was Jesse.

He had watched Jesse die. Not once, but twice. His dreams had forced him to relive those visions hundreds of times. Jesse's lifeless eyes staring at him. Terrible feelings of helplessness and guilt gripped him every time he closed his eyes.

Thorn had been tasked with making dinner. She was chopping the vegetables while Symon worked to get the temperature of the fire correct. With his experience, this at least was one task he knew he could do correctly. Those tasks were fewer and farther between nowadays. He tried very hard to keep it together. Everyone kept looking to Symon for answers, but he was still reeling from the loss of everything in his life. Jesse seemed to be taking it in stride and was naturally more adept at keeping information coming in from the towns.

"Move over!" she said, hanging the pot on the tripod over the coals. "It'll be ready soon."

Symon looked up from his reflections. "I cannot tell you how lost I would be without you and Jesse."

"You better be thanking us, lunk. Dragging us away from the city. Traipsing around the 'Khorr like assholes! We're not some fool Hunters!"

"I know, Thorn," Symon said, a growl forming in his chest at yet another complication. If they got stopped by a patrol and mistaken for adventurers but could not produce Hunter Guild credentials they would be detained. Detainment that could result in their past catching up with them. A past that was the result of Symon's father defying Grendel and the new Nobles. "I feel horrible for everything that I have brought into your lives."

"You should, you grot-thumping meat shield! We should take you to the border, drop you off and go back home. In fact, that's what we'll do!"

"I would not blame you. But you cannot return to Highston. Not until the Investurants withdraw."

"Fuck the Shadows!" Thorn barked. "What do they matter? Grendel was the problem, and he's dead."

"Did Jesse not tell you? The assassination attempt was not Grendel. It was the Master. She sent her forces to kill him. Grendel and Manticore just allowed it to happen."

"I know that you dolt!" Thorn sneered. "I was there when Grendel told Jesse everything. But we can hide from Manticore. We can hide from the Shadows."

"I am not sure why the Investurants want us dead. But until then, I cannot think we are safer alone than we are together."

"We can take care of ourselves."

"I do not doubt that," Symon said. "However, both times that the Investurants attacked Jesse, it was the same assassin. It seems... personal."

"Benezia's tit!" she yelled. "When will that arrogant little piss-ant get it out of his fluff-filled brain that he's not protecting me by keeping shit secret!"

Symon hung his head and stoked the coals again, channeling the wind to keep them a deep red. Jesse had assured him that things were fine, but Symon still felt guilt over the apparent divide he had caused between Thorn and the young Isnashi thief. Their lives had been much simpler before Symon's interference.

Thorn sat on her haunches and whistled. It was a lot. "Well, I still don't know why we are running over the countryside heading to the evil empire! We should find a city that we know, and hide. Eventually this will all blow over."

"I know, Thorn. But I have to trust that my father's words were true. That we will find answers in his... homeland."

"You believe that?"

"I am not sure I have another option." Symon's thoughts turned to his fears. He worried that if he did not find more out about his Gift he would become a monster.

"Your dad was a Necromancer. Of course he's going to tell you to run into the darkness!"

"I know. But..."

"Can you picture him in the original war?! Unbelievable!" Thorn shook her head. "He's got to be a bit scary right? You think he raised undead armies? Is he undead himself? Is he a vampire?"

Symon shifted uncomfortably, Thorn's words gave voice to Symon's concerns. Everything he had known about Kyrn had been a lie. "No, nothing like that. He has always been kind. I cannot... He's not... I would not believe that he has evil in him."

She smiled back at him. "I'm just fucking with you. Relax."

The Ennedi stirred the soup and thought hard. He knew that he wanted to explain everything to Thorn, but the words were coming out wrong. He needed them, not for their skills, not because of guilt, but because they completed him. They made him more.

"Thorn, I need you guys. You are part of me now. You are *rieve*." The last word was spoken in Ennedi, and it had a slight rumble in Symon's chest. A purring befitting the large feline that he was.

"That's nice," she said, absently gathering bowls. Then she turned to Symon, a look of confusion on her face. "I'm what?!"

"My friend," said the Gargoyle, "May I inquire after something personal?"

"Um, sure," answered Jesse. "I suppose so. What's that?"

Argyle had joined Jesse in scouring the local undergrowth for additional firewood and kindling to last them through the night. The setting sun mixed with the trees moving in the evening breeze caused a beautiful effect in the forest cover, with deep pools of twilight darkness interspersed with bright patches of fading sunlight. Jesse turned to Argyle, gauging him. There was a look of hesitance and discomfort. It was strange to see the Genbu express emotions in his face. Jesse gave him more attention.

"What's on your mind?" the young thief prompted.

"I am concerned about my place in this company. I have done ill by you in the past, and I fear that clouds my ability to be useful. I would deem it appropriate to limit the trust you can truly lay on my shoulders. Limits that could be hindering for some."

"What?"

"While I was serving the will of Grendel, the will of Manticore, I still hold myself responsible for the daily struggles that we imposed upon you. I often did my best to intervene, to alleviate as much of the unnecessary detriments laid upon you. But it required a crafty disposition that was challenging to hide from watchful eyes. Many times, pain you received came from orders penned by my hand."

"I guess?" replied Jesse. "But, like you said, you've tried to help me. And I don't mean getting out of Highston. You tried several times to warn me off Grendel. You tried to keep me from getting in too deep with Manticore. And when Grendel tried to kill me, you tried to warn me there, also."

"These are true, but there is still guilt and blame to be laid at my door."

"Past is past, right? But you haven't asked a question yet. Quit stalling. What did you want to know?" inquired Jesse.

"Many years ago, you attempted a trial to join Manticore, with Xerian as your sponsor. If you recall, I oversaw your trial. You failed, and I have always been curious as to why? I have borne witness to your skills since then, and you had the capability. Was it deliberate?"

Jesse thought for a moment as he gathered a few more fallen branches before answering. "I wasn't ready. And honestly, I don't think at that time I knew enough to care if I tried," he said. "Should I have tried harder? Maybe. It certainly would have saved me a beating. But really, I didn't have it, mentally or physically. I was just a kid."

"Thank you for your candor, my friend," said Argyle, throwing a larger piece of wood to his shoulders. "But are you not still, as you say, just a kid?"

"Hey! I'm pretty grown up now, thank you! I'm eighteen now, and adult enough by the law and my own race."

Argyle laughed, a deep resonating chuckle. "My friend," he said, "I meant no insult, but you are still quite young, both by society and your people."

"Well, society hasn't ever cared about me before, why start now?" Jesse quipped.

As they progressed in their task, Jesse watched Argyle as he worked towards another question. The Gargoyle developed a more somber tone, and asked, "What was your situation with Xerian, if it is not too inconsiderate to inquire?"

"Xerian?" Jesse's shoulders tensed and there was a pause in his step. He attempted to cover his reaction, however, and his voice was steady as he responded, "What did you want to know? And out of curiosity, what did everyone else know?"

Argyle courteously ignored the signs of discomfort and said, "All that was known by most was that Xerian was your protector and patron. It was also known that you were lovers." He paused a moment, then added, "It was not as widely known that he was violent with you, or how controlling he was. Although considering his reputation as a brute for Manticore, few would have been surprised.

"It was even discussed after your failure if he should retain his rank in the Bright Guild," Argyle continued. "First Sasha's failure. Then yours. It brought his training techniques into question. If it wasn't for your considerable talents, even in the face of failure, we may have never seen your growth in the eyes of the Guild. It was folly to place the success of your deeds on Xerian's shoulders."

"Xerian taught me how to be a Street Rat," said Jesse. "I was alone most of my first summer. He gave me food, shelter, and company. He taught me to hide my wings so I could blend into crowds better. He even helped me build a harness for them."

"Valuable skills and traits that he provided you, sure," said Argyle. "But they came with costs, correct? He had a more depraved side, did he not?"

"Yeah, all that other stuff was true, too." Jesse sighed before continuing, "When he wanted to, he could be really mean. He always said it was for my own good, to remind me to improve. But honestly, I think I've always known that beneath everything else he was a bully. Still, I do believe though, that there was a part of him that loved me. I mean, I have to believe that, right?"

"Why is that, Jesse?"

"I know when we first started having sex I wasn't near ready. That was just the meanest way he could think of to punish me. And it worked! Fuck, that used to hurt so bad. But it continued, even after it wasn't a punishment and I found out I liked it. I think he liked it, too. I don't think it was just him getting off either, not always. I think..."

Jesse's features softened, as he remembered some of the better times. "Xerian did have a gentle side. It was just harder to find." He smiled sadly and said, "But Argyle, he really made it worth digging for. He could be playful and romantic when he wanted to be. I know he was fond of me, maybe even loved me."

"Was he capable of love?"

"I don't know. I think so. I think everyone is capable of love, even if they have never been shown how to express it. I think he may have loved me. I know I loved him."

"Loved?"

"Alright, damn it. Love! I still love him. It's fucked up, but I miss him. What kind of monster would I be, not to still love someone I've been with for half my life?"

"My young friend, you are anything but a monster."

"Rieve is an Ennedi term," Symon started. "It is hard to put into the common tongue, but it is close to clan, or pack, or family."

Thorn stared back at him, trying to figure out what he was vying for. She had dealt with naive, sheltered idiots before. But Symon was far more earnest than most. "Why? Why are we so important?"

"My father and I have lived in Highston my whole life. Felinoids are normally tribal. It is in our nature to bond. Being Tellervo, I believe that is what drove Mistress Daysleeper to run an inn. To keep herself surrounded by others.

"We desire packs, but packs are hard to build in civilization. I tried to build one with Reginald, but it was hard with Geran and Olivar always picking away at him. Even Lara was difficult to find a connection with. Just when I felt like it was truly happening, Olivar ruined that, too.

"I've always been isolated. Apprentices that came through our shop were always temporary. I struggled to fit in with my peers. I have always felt empty. Like there was something missing. That has changed."

Thorn looked at Symon with new eyes. Like Jesse, she always looked at him like he had everything. But they had one thing his coin couldn't buy. Something he always wanted but had never found on his own. Someone to watch his back.

"Something about Jesse made it easy," Symon said. "I have dropped my guard with him. Shown him the truth about my feelings. We are more than friends. He resonates within me. He is *rieve.* With him, comes you. Gruff though you may be, I know that you would do anything to help Jesse. I need his help. I need your help."

"But why do we have to go to Vargarden?"

The big smith rubbed his temples and said, "If they helped the Federation in the first war, they may help again."

Thorn frowned. He wasn't lying, but Symon was holding something back.

"But what if they don't want to help? Let the Shadow and the Khor tear each other apart! We should just go back to Essenbecck. We can hide there, and survive like we always have."

"We have to ask. If they can put the Shadow out, then everyone can return to Highston."

"I don't care about everyone. Just us. You're not thinking of going back to Highston. Why are you so stuck on going to the City of the Dead? Aren't you a bit scared?"

"Thorn," Symon said, his eyes wide. "I am terrified."

"Well then—"

"I am terrified that I am becoming something horrific," Symon said, cutting her off. She saw genuine fear in his eyes. "I am scared to go. But I am more scared not to. Something is happening to me. I need answers, and the only place they exist is Vargarden."

Thorn sat back. Symon's words were undeniable. He'd go with or without them, but he was right, if he went alone it would be dangerous.

Symon shrugged. "Maybe my father left me something to start with. I can rebuild."

"Well, that's great for you! What in the Hells should Jesse and I be doing while you fix your damned life!"

"We will be building OUR lives. I told Jesse before that we could start a shop together. I did not lie."

Thorn looked Symon in the eyes. Again, the sincerity hit her like a hammer. He was genuinely looking to make Jesse part of his life. And unlike Grendel or Xerian, he wouldn't want Jesse to pay the price for it. But she had concerns of her own that needed to be dealt with.

"I do not know what you want, Thorn," Symon continued, giving voice to her unspoken words. "But whatever it is, we can find a way. I know that it must be hard for you in the Federation. Hisse Goblins have an uncivil reputation that I am sure is difficult for you to overcome. It is unfair. Ennedi are carnivores like yourself, but we are deemed peaceful."

"People can lick Mordin's ballsack for all I care!" Thorn spat. Khorric minds didn't see her as a carnivore. They saw a cannibal.

"I know, Thorn. I know." Symon purred. "Perhaps Vargarden will be different. Perhaps they are not as dark as the Federation makes them be?"

"I still don't like this. We should just go back."

"I know, Thorn. But please come with me. I will not let you down. I will not fail you."

"Because I am *rieve*?"

Symon nodded. "Yes, because you are *rieve*. And for that, I shall always be there for you. Whenever, wherever. You have my loyalty, Thorn. And to my last breath, I shall treat your life as greater than my own. *Sacrificar, el brav quaendis undollo.*"

"What does that mean?"

"'A good man knows sacrifice.' My father always said it to me at night. I will protect you as he protected me."

"You're a weird man, Symon," Thorn said. "Anyone ever tell you that?"

Symon smiled at Thorn. "Yes, I suppose that I may be."

"You're weird, but you're not bad." Thorn punched him in the arm. "But if you hurt Jesse, I'll gut you like a fish."

"Your turn, bitch," said Jesse teasingly. "What's with you and Grendel? How did you end up in Highston, and in Manticore?"

"Have you heard of the Genbu?" asked Argyle.

"Other than you, no."

"It is not surprising. Genbu are merely an offshoot of the Draconic race of Gargoyles, and Gargoyles are rare in these lands. Genbu have no wings, and are therefore considered lesser, weaker, and more servile. In many regions, my people are bred to be a servant class to societies of 'proper' Gargoyles. We are also larger than many, and so often act as brutes or beasts of burden, despite our intelligence.

"Because of this, I was brought to the Khorric Federation as a slave. My owner at the time was arrogant, and foolish. He did not know the laws of this

Federation however, and once within their lands, I found myself accidentally freed. The Khorric Federation holds no regard for slavery, at all, and any slaves brought within their borders are automatically freed, never to be returned, their prior owners never to be bargained with."

"Damn," said Jesse. "I forgot other places still had that shit. Fucking slavery, really?"

"Indeed. But even with my new found freedom, I then found myself faced with a problem. The Federation could not bear to perceive me as a slave, but also did not accept me, nor provide accommodations for one such as I. My race has a reputation at least as negative as our young Goblin friend, viewed as the most brutal of all the Draconic lineages. Plus, I had no coin, few skills, and no prospects within Khorric boundaries. I worked what odd jobs I could find, often living out of doors or in stables due to my size.

"Grendel found me at some point many years ago. He demeaned me for my weaknesses. Ensured that I was reminded of how low I sat within the structure of this vaunted Federation. He made it clear that I had few options, and that only he could give me a life that would be more. However, it always came with a cost." Argyle said, ruefully. "Not dissimilar in many respects to yourself and your lover."

"Damn."

Argyle paused, pain visible in his features, as he said, "There have been many cruelties I have been forced to endure, and even more that I have been expected to dole out. I eventually accepted this as a punishment I must bear for a tolerable life." He looked in Jesse's direction, not really making eye contact, and added, "I fear that you, my friend, are one who might understand that sentiment."

"Yeah," sighed Jesse. "I've been thinking a lot about Xerian these last weeks since we left. Its fucked up that I kind of miss him. Yeah, he was hard on me." Jesse paused, chuckled, then corrected himself. "No, he flat out beat me. But yeah, I get you. For years he was all I had, all I knew. The bruises and the shame were kind of the rent you paid, right?"

"Shame is probably the best word for you and I, my young friend. We did what must be done. Bore what must be borne. But never was it our proper selves. Never did either of us allow it to become *us.*"

"You trying to tell me we are stronger for what we went through?"

Argyle grinned as he looked over at his companion and said, "Never would I utter such hollow words."

"Good," snapped Jesse. "Save those empty platitudes for the priests and do-gooders. We aren't *brave* for having put up with that shit, and we aren't *stronger* for having survived! It happened, we experienced it, we moved on. Maybe we learned from it, maybe we didn't. But no lesson learned or skill gained was worth the price paid!"

"And on the contrary side," Argyle added, "those who did not survive were not weaker for having come out of their situation diminished. They did not 'lose their fight' or anything of the kind. The success or failure lies on the perpetrator, not the victim."

"Exactly," cried Jesse. "You get it! Glad somebody does. Symon means well. I'm sure the priests mean well also. But damn, don't give empty speeches if you don't know what you are talking about, right?"

"At least they care enough to help," replied Argyle calmly. "It is not your friend's words that are truly important. It is enough that he cares to give words at all." He made sure he had Jesse's attention and added, "He cares, my young friend. If his words seem empty to you, teach him the words that would aid you. Remember that he listens. He worries. His words matter not, when they are offered in genuine concern."

"Yeah, I get it. You are too wise for your own good, Argyle."

"Something else to remember, if you find yourself despondent of his 'empty words'."

"Yeah? What's that?"

"Be of cheer for your friend. The fact that he does not understand your situation shows that he has had the fortune of not experiencing your troubles, to his gain. And yet, he cares enough to attempt to imagine your woes alongside you."

"True," said Jesse. "I guess that is a bright side."

Jesse gathered a few additional handfuls of kindling, thinking of Argyle's words. Escape from servitude was a brutal process. The challenge to escape the physical bonds was hard enough, the breaking of the mental ones may be altogether impossible. Even here, Jesse felt a pull. "Argyle?" he asked.

The Genbu looked up, eyes still somber and contemplative. "Yes, young one?"

"Did you ever think of going back?"

Argyle smiled back. It was a sad, but somewhat satisfied, smile. "Back home to my kin? Or back to Manticore? Either way, the answer is 'yes.' But that is why it is important for us to accompany young Master Cylkas to Vargarden. The distance will do us both some good. Vargarden will be just as important to us as it is him. You will see."

4

Inside the Shadow

Emaly flinched as the vase smashed against the wall and rained porcelain bits onto the floor. The Master of Shadows, the *Ombramaes,* stalked the room, radiating anger. She was a beautiful woman, appearing to just be entering her middle years. Her bright blue skin glistened as it was struck by moonlight streaming through the window. Her eyes, however, held a light of rage all their own.

"Damn all the Gods!" the Master screamed. "We almost HAD them! Right there in Highston, they were in our hands and we lost them."

Emaly sighed in disappointment. The constant struggle between the importance of their mission versus personal vendettas. A struggle fueled by notions of prophecy and interwoven plots. "Calm, my love," Emaly said. laying on the plush sofa against the other wall. "Remember, we came home to help you calm. Let this go until we return to Sainan."

"We should be there now!" the Master said. "Not here wasting time."

"The pain you feel on that plane is not good for you. You need rest."

"Here or there, the pain is always there, Emaly. I don't belong to either realm!"

Emaly elegantly rose from the sofa to wrap her arms around the *Ombramaes*. The Master was an embodiment of power for the Mumvurii people. A living Avatar of divine power that channeled the will of the *Sangebula*, the Blooded. The woman beneath that Avatar was Emaly's wife. "I'm so sorry, my love. But, at least you belong with us. With me."

A slow, small smile appeared. Just a brief glimpse of the sweet girl Emaly had fallen in love with. "Yes, my pet, I do." The two stood, locked in their embrace. Emaly pulled the Master close, holding their heads upon their shoulders for a few moments. "It will all work out, my love," she whispered.

"Bah!" she snarled, the fire re-ignited in her eyes. The Master pulled away and resumed her pacing. "How do you know this? You only rely on the words of a Witch!"

"I rely on the winds of fate," Emaly said. Authority had crept into her voice. While the *Ombramaes* was the voice of her people, Emaly Le'Arial was a power unto herself. She was the High Sorceress, leader of the Eye of Arcanus, and one of the most renowned spellcasters in the *Sangebula*. "I have gathered three choruses since the beginning of this campaign to guide us. The Thief was always foreseen, just as we were told."

"I know. 'The Father holds the power to rebuke the Shadow. The Son is the way to the Father. The Thief is the key to the Son.' I've heard the words a hundred times."

"'A Thief shall rise to guide the heart of the Son.'" Emaly corrected. "You are blending Grendel's prophecy with ours."

"You told me they ARE the same prophecy, Emaly!"

"I believed they were," Emaly replied. "But now, I'm not so sure. The last chorus was unable to pattern out the timelines as they did before. There is a power at play that I don't fully understand."

"Grendel!' Rhon spat. "Impudent, *Lei'Fein* trash!"

Rhon stood in the doorway. Years of battle training had made him innately stealthy, but it was her distraction that had caused her to miss his entrance. Her lover, Rhon, was a regal Mumvurii Noble. He leaned against the frame of the door, dark hair, cobalt skin, and leather armor glistening in the candle light. His eyes held a fatigue that was not uncommon these days. Stress was taking its toll on them, and they had barely begun this fight.

Emaly pinched the bridge of her nose. "Let's not talk of him. What news do you have, love?"

"They have passed Essenbeck, and are on route to the Deepland Woods."

"Why are they not handled yet?!" the Master asked. "That damned boy could unravel everything."

"Which one?" Rhon said. "The Thief you sent me to kill? Or the son of Kyrn?"

The Master gave him a hard stare. "Both, either, take your pick. They both need to die."

"I am trying, Master," Rhon said. "I am doing everything I can to track them down. I will enjoy killing them each, personally."

"I need this done, Rhon."

Emaly shook her head. "I still don't understand why." This was the side of her lovers that she didn't readily accept. Their bloodlust in this war had amplified quickly. Without her reasoning, their actions strayed to ruthlessness. "Our concern of the Thief is duly noted, but the Blacksmith?"

"Kyrn betrayed me!" the Master screamed. "All of this!" she cried, waving her arms and a grand gesture. "All of this is his fault! Had he not interfered in the last war, we would have our shard, the Betrayers Stone! Not scraping around the Federation trying to find it!

"And the Son... The son is a betrayal! I warned that man that if he ever had another child, I would kill him and his spawn. His very existence is a slap to my face!"

Rhon began to say something, but Emaly shushed him. The *Ombramaes* was caught again in the delicate balance between mortal and avatar. Personal and professional. The madness and pain of her people flowed through her body, and Emaly had experienced what would happen if the wrong words were said. Rhon reached over and squeezed Emaly's hand as they waited.

The Master stood staring out the window, her back straight and fists clenched. Wind gathered in the room, causing the curtains to billow. Shards of porcelain and dust began to form concentric circles around the feet of the *Ombramaes* as the vibrations grew. Emaly had seen her channel the rage of the Mumvurii people before. It was a coping mechanism that the Master leaned on to numb the eternal pain she was in.

"The Thief," the Ombramaes said at last. Her voice echoed slightly, a discordant whisper of the Avatar tinging her words. "The Thief is a danger. I was warned by powerful forces, forces you have confirmed High Sorceress, that he could influence Vargarden. We don't need outside forces derailing us as they did last time. We cannot fail to retrieve the Stone again.

"Destiny, fate, the Gods themselves, or whatever you deem responsible, are pulling us towards victory this time. I can feel it in my bones. To have access to the Thief through our chosen agent, to find the Nemuku... in Highston of all places. To find his son! All entangled together. How can it not be a sign of providence? The Blood calls, and it wants satiated. It wants those boys dead."

Emaly dared to whisper, "But our agents—"

"Not our agents. Khorric agents, Nobles and Manticore thugs, barely to be trusted," the Master rebuked. "Feel free to play out your little contingencies, Sorceress. But I want the Son of Kyrn in my grasp."

"And his little Thief friend," Rhon snarled.

"Satiate the blood, General." The Master waved to the landscape before them. "We must restore our homeland."

Emaly stared at the familiar features which dotted the landscape. So much of it was similar to Sainan, but so much of it was alien. The dark night sky held a purple tint, as the moon shone down brightly. Shadows cast across gray grass and deep red dirt pathways. While this location in Sainan would be in Highston directly, here on Mumvuri, the Shadow Realm, their realm, it was barely more than a small village. This small inn was the largest building for miles in any direction.

"We run short on time, my Master," Rhon said. "My scouts tell me that once the boys cross the boundary into Vargarden they'll be unable to follow."

"Keep throwing scouts at them until you stop them!" the Master said. "Those damned Necromancers are able to defend against our magic. They will complicate things drastically."

"I'm trying, Master," Rhon said.

"Try harder."

Rhon bristled with anger, so Emaly stepped up and put her hand on his shoulder. "Let's focus on what we have done. We've at least taken control of Highston. We've helped these new Nobles seize the Federation. That was the goal, right?"

"Yes." The Master turned towards them. "That much we have done."

"And there is much still to do," Emaly said. "Grendel's plans were to take this realm from the inside. Now that we have control, we leverage this position to uncover the Betrayer's Stone."

"You still think recovering the Betrayer's Stone is enough?" Rhon asked. "After all the damage the Federation has done?"

Emaly nodded. "Yes, I do. The Federation Magi have mistakenly thought they could replicate our magic using copies of the Stone. To power their abominations, they keep trapping souls in imperfect prisons. Souls that turn feral and escape. But they don't go to the Material Realm, they come here. They attack our people. If we can recover the Stone, then it will all stop."

"Or we could just wipe them all out!" Rhon said. "Destroy everyone in that forsaken land."

"The General is right. We should destroy all the Federal leaders. The Academy, the Councils, and everyone else. Break them all!" The Master clenched her fist. "They had their chance to change. They refused."

Shaking her head once again, Emaly ignored the rage-fueled words of her lovers. "You can't let your hate take over, loves. This land is not unsalvageable. They can't all be bad."

"I have watched them! From this war to the last, over forty years, and they have learned nothing! The rich and powerful take more and more. They feast on the less fortunate, and the poor just take it. They don't know any better.

"Generations keep getting turned out, and the Academy educates them on how to best serve their dutiful masters. And if they are deemed useless enough, the Magi can always harvest their soul to power their damned contraptions! It's disgusting."

"I agree," Emaly said. "But to kill everyone? That's extreme."

"It's the best way to break the cycle. Start over. Take the Federation down, brick by brick."

"Besides," Rhon jumped in. "We know they're useless and unable to be controlled. That fool Grendel proved that for us."

"Have you recovered him yet?" the Master asked.

"No, Master," Rhon said. "His body was lost in the battle against Kyrn. He died, his failure complete. We haven't been able to sort through the wreckage to recover him. With us taking over his estates, we should have access to his secrets. I don't have any reason to dedicate someone to it. If we find the body, so be it. If not, let him rot."

"Losing him means building new ties with both of his networks," Emaly said. "We will need both Manticore and the New Nobles."

"A misguided attempt," the Master said. "The 'Khorr is beyond saving."

"It is not our concern, my love," Emaly said. "If the New Nobles wish to reshape this Federation, then let them. All we need is their admission into the Vaults. And we need Manticore's resources to stay informed."

"It disgusts me that the *Sangebula* allowed the Investurants to hold for so long, waiting for this political ploy. They should have been marshaling their forces for a strike."

"*Ombramaes,*" Emaly said formally. This was one of the few times she had to speak to the position, not the person. "Without your guidance, the *Sangebula* faltered. They had no control over the Blood, and there was not a clear avatar. The families focused on trying to reform the Church so they could lead the people.

"The Investurants were not content with sitting idle," Emaly continued. "They wanted to continue what you started. Assisting in this insurrection was the most viable opportunity. It was a chaotic time. We were glad to see your return. Now we are once again united."

"Their failure is nearly unforgivable. The Investurants are military, which never has patience. But the *Sangebula,* being Noble, should be better."

"Yes, Master," Emaly said. "However, now that we are united, we must act wisely. The *Sangebula* shall focus on our goal. We shall recover the Stone and hopefully shut the gate between Mumvuri and the Federation once and for all. The Investurants shall hold these lands while we do so. Once we leave, if the Federation is as corrupt as you say, they can destroy themselves. We need not aid in that."

The *Ombramaes* flourished her hand dismissively. A gesture as close to acceptance as Emaly could expect while she was in this state. "What about reports of this 'Ghost' that I am hearing of?" the Master asked.

Now it was Rhon's turn to explode in a rage.

"That loathsome fucking terrorist!" he screamed, kicking over a small table. "I have no idea who he is, or what he is! He eludes my scouts with ease and strikes much the same. The only evidence of encounters are the dead squads he leaves in his wake."

"How is this possible?"

"I have no idea! We believe he is Shadow Walking, using our own powers against us. Wherever and whenever a scouting party gets too isolated, they are struck down. We've only got one confirmed sighting. A lone survivor of one of the attacks."

"Could it be one of us? A traitor?" Emaly asked. "Considering his abilities?"

"It's possible," Rhon confirmed. "He clearly knows our strategies. He targets our advanced forces, disrupting the flow of information. He systematically cuts off our supply routes. Every order I give, every move I make, he seems to be ahead of. If he's not one of us, he's getting information from somewhere. I am watching all of our field generals carefully, hoping to find the source of any leaks. But, wherever he is getting his intel from, this 'Ghost' uses it with expert precision."

"Damn him to the Abyss," the Master growled. "If he's not dealt with, he'll destroy morale. I must have the Investurant forces at full strength, General. Find this 'Ghost', and tear him apart."

"Yes, Master."

"Rhon, my love," Emaly said. "You cannot be committed to finding the boys, retrieving the Stone, and destroying this Ghost. You're pulling yourself too thin."

"I know my business, my love."

Rhon was angry, and she feared he would not listen to reason any more this night. Her eyes turned to the *Ombramaes* who looked much the same. She needed cooler tempers and clearer minds to discuss strategy. Noting the late hour, Emaly started to turn down the lights. "Let's get some rest. We can discuss all of this in the morning."

Rhon looked at the Master and back at Emaly. Their marriage arrangements were complex, even by Mumvurii standards, but tonight was Rhon's evening. She grasped his hand and walked towards the door, but he stopped her.

"It's your night, my love."

"Yes, Emaly, but let her take it. I've got things to do, and she needs you more than I."

"Okay, I'll sleep with her tonight. But promise me tomorrow. If that works."

"Of course, my love. That will work just fine."

He kissed Emaly one last time. "Be well, my sweet. I'll see you tomorrow." She watched as he gathered his things and headed out the door. This war had just begun.

5

Road's End

"Well, she ain't much, but she's something," Jesse said, and Symon shrugged.

After nearly a month since Essebeck, the edge of the forest came into view. As promised, there was a sizable village located at the end of the road. From all appearances, the village was a lumbering community, but they were also able to see a sizable inn, a decent market, and a few supply shops of notable size. It seemed the community served as a final vestige of civilization before leaving the Khorric Federation. It was aptly named, Road's End.

As Symon walked into the doors of the "Last Hearth," the Ophisi innkeeper glanced up. Even though Argyle had stayed behind, the group was still out of place. The common room of the inn appeared to be all locals, primarily the lizard-like Ophisi, Ukko Dwarves, and Taniwha Dragonfolk. Symon felt a pang of guilt for Argyle. His size and shape made him an outsider wherever they went. He had promised to meet them on the road near the wood's edge in the morning. Symon had promised to bring him a suitable meal.

The innkeeper was quick to work out an inexpensive payment for meals and room fare. Dinner was both filling and relaxing, and both Jesse and Symon were able to strike up conversations which garnered information about their path through the forest, enough that they felt more confident with their road ahead. Many of the merchants had advised them the roads were open to trade. A handful of Vargarden merchants had even been here, but they had returned home mere days ago.

Symon found himself wondering what mischief his old companions would have gotten into here. Reginald and Tomas would likely be discussing the economical impact of the lumber industry within Eithren and how it paled in comparison to the agricultural impact. Meanwhile, Olivar would be berating the food, the quality of the inn, and disparaging the locals for their attire and lack of refinement. As for Geran, Geran would be there licking the heels of Olivar's boots. It seemed a lifetime ago.

"Symon?" Jesse asked.

"Huh?" the Ennedi replied, shaking his head.

"Where in the Veil was your head at?" Thorn asked. "We've been talking to you."

"I apologize. What was it that you asked?"

"We asked," Thorn said, "do you think that woman is staring at us?"

Symon glanced around the inn and locked eyes with a fearsome looking Ophissi. She, Symon believed her to be female, based on the shape of the ridges on her head, appeared to be a scout of some type. This was based on her wilderness gear, sensible leathers, and a custom cloak designed for her six-limbed body. She had several knives and trap-packs strapped to the backpack leaning against her table. She smiled back to Symon and began to rise from her table.

Jesse placed his face in his palm and muttered, "Well, she is now."

"You damned lunk."

The Ophissi glided across the room on her four lower limbs. She grasped the edge of the table with her arms, and the middle limbs rose from the floor, switching in that odd grace that her race was known for, from legs to arms. The second set of arms spun an open chair around, and she mounted it backwards. A slow smile crept across her face. "Greetings, travelers. You are new here."

"Indeed, madam," Symon replied, even as Thorn muttered under her breath.

"No insults intended, but you don't look like you do this often. Where are you headed?"

Symon hesitated, but said, "Var—"

"Oh, we're just getting in some sights," Jesse interrupted.

The grin on the Ophissi's face widened. "Not much to see here."

"We noticed." Jesse smiled back.

"Well, aside from the Road of the Dead."

Symon swallowed the lump that had formed in his throat. He had fumbled and revealed their intentions, putting them at risk.

"Yeah," Jesse continued. "That's the big one. How is it?"

"The Road of the Dead?"

"Yeah, is it as spooky as they say?"

The Ophissi laughed. "Spooky? Perhaps. Dangerous? Incredibly." She steepled the long clawed fingers of her front-most hands. "At least, for the unprepared."

"Ooh," Thorn giggled. She leaned up next to Jesse, and Symon sensed a familiarity. It was as if Thorn had been waiting for Jesse's cue. Her eyes alight with mock fascination, she asked, "What types of danger?

"The trek is wild," the scout said. "The roads here are clear, easy to follow. But as the Road of the Dead enters the forest, it changes. Often, it is not the same as it was before. Travelers enter at all times, but no one sees each other in the woods. Only your path. A hard path.

"It is why," she continued, "nearly all who travel the Road are professionals. Caravans, seasoned merchants, and official emissaries. Not children, like yourselves."

"That's a bit uncalled for," Jesse smirked.

"Uncalled for or not, it is true. Plus, besides the danger of the woods themselves, you face the dangers of the uninvited. Wandering into the woods, you could stumble across a great many unpleasant creatures. And if you make it through? Does anyone in the Land of the Dead expect you? Or are you just going to stumble around there?"

Symon glanced at Jesse and Thorn who were watching the Ophissi closely.

An air of cautious tension was building steadily. Dealings with untrusted strangers was something Symon had failed at many times. He wanted to answer, but kept silent.

"Well, that's why I'm here," the scout said, at last. "To help. You see, these dangers are why persons such as I specialize in travel. I can guide you through the Deepland Woods. See you safely there, and introduce you to their culture before I drop you off. Safe and sound."

"For a price?" Symon asked.

She grinned at him, a genuine look of amusement, while Jesse and Thorn shook their heads in disbelief. "Of course, for a price."

"We do not have much coin. What we do have is barely enough to sustain us. I fear we could not afford such a guide."

The Ophissi glanced at Symon's sword, his father's sword, and her eyes narrowed. "You expect me to believe that?"

"It is true," Symon said. "We are simply refugees fleeing from the conflict in Highston."

"Hmph," the Ophissi muttered. A look of disappointment was visible on her face, but her eyes took in the meager stew and bread the three were sharing. Her eyes softened and she shrugged. "Well, I suppose I've seen stranger. Good luck to you. Safe travels."

"My thanks, my lady," Symon replied.

The scout stood up and crossed the room back to her table. She sat quietly and tipped the rim of her glass towards them in a salute. Symon returned his attention to his companions who were staring at him with unreadable expressions.

He dropped his gaze, his ears wilted and shoulders sagged, expecting a berating. Once again, he had failed them. Jesse could likely tease him for weeks about such a miscue. "I am sorry."

Jesse reached out and placed his hand on Symon's. The Ennedi looked up into Jesse's eyes. "Hey man, it's okay. We just have to be careful."

"I know, I know."

"But she seemed okay," Jesse continued. "So, no harm."

"I still apologize."

"Ah, suck it up, fuzzy," Thorn said. "We got your back."

Symon stared back at his two friends. The earnestness in which they looked back at him was heartwarming. "I expected more of a rebuke."

"Ah, we'll razz the piss out of you later!" Thorn laughed.

"But only when you are ready to laugh back," Jesse said. "We've all been through some shit."

"I thank you," Symon said. "I shall try and do better."

"I know you will," Jesse winked. "Besides, only donkey-dick-sucking losers would try and make you feel worse than you do."

Olivar's face entered Symon's mind. Endless torment about the smallest infractions. The more Symon thought about his former life, the more he appreciated Jesse and his new one. He turned his hand, grasping Jesse's and squeezed it. "Thank you, again."

The three picked over the rest of their meal in relative quiet. A few travelers came and went, but no one else approached them. After a bit, Jesse gazed at Symon again. "Not to be an ass, but what's the deal with that thing?"

Symon followed Jesse's eyes and reached up to stroke his father's sword. The slight vibration in the handle greeted his fingers as a voice entered his mind, as it always did. >*Ka'ski shan'diar 'el staciatos.*<

"I assume your dad made it," Jesse said.

Hiding his reaction to the mental intrusion, Symon pulled the handle, exposing a few inches of blade so that the maker's mark could be seen. "He did."

"It's a nice fucking sword." Thorn said. "It'd fetch a pretty price."

Symon tensed. Even if it was not for the enchantment, he could not sell his father's sword. It was the last memory he had of him. "Well—"

"I'm fucking with you," she said, smiling. "*Rieve* thing?"

"An heirloom."

"*Rieve* thing. Gotcha."

Jesse looked back and forth between the two and suddenly Thorn began to cackle. "See, it's not fun when you get left out!" She punched Jesse in the arm. "The two of you pull that shit all the time. Half completed conversations about 'Old man Zen,' or 'Magic principle blah-blah.' It's annoying!"

"So, you spent hours on the road just waiting to cozy up to Symon and throw it in my face?" Jesse asked, a crooked, cock-eyed grin forming on his face.

Thorn stood on her chair and put her fists on her hips, grinning from ear to ear. "Sounds like me."

"Bitch!" Jesse laughed.

Symon tossed back his mane and laughed heartily. Road travel had been challenging. He was still reeling from the loss of his father, and his livelihood. But for once, he felt hope. A glimpse at a new life.

"We should retire," Symon said. "Still a long way to go." He smiled and pushed a small key with a soap packet across the table. Jesse and Thorn's eyes danced as they realized what it was. "I did have a bit extra. I shall let you fight over who gets the first go."

The three friends shared the single room, and while there was some light teasing about the single bed and how it should be occupied, Symon was insistent in giving his friends the comfort. He was happy to allow the two smaller thieves to share the bed, especially once the innkeeper was able to scare up another mattress to throw on the floor. None of them said it out loud, but the bath and the bedding were welcome after nearly a month on the road.

Symon rolled over, enjoying his first good night for a long time, and slept a dreamless, peaceful sleep.

6

Wraiths

 Emaly and Rhon stepped out of the portal with a small squad of Investurant soldiers fanning out around them. She had been investigating Wraith attacks since she had taken her position as High Sorceress. Since they started the invasion on Highston, she was actively tracking them. She had hoped that by attacking the heart of the Federation, they would finally be able to cut off the source, but they had not been able to locate the Betrayer's Stone. Perhaps, she theorized, following the Wraiths to their origin points would reveal its location.

Emaly's braid swung in the same rhythm as her staff, ticking off her steps between her noble-blooded tall ears. She was attempting, and failing, to steady herself. A desperate howl bemoaned the tragedy of the situation as the wind swept across the wreckage and pulled at her cloak. She came to a stop next to Rhon and her eyes tightened as she took in the landscape. Her grip tightened around her staff, causing her knuckles to creak. The scouting reports had described the Wraith damage that devastated this small village, but it hadn't prepared her for the sight before their eyes.

Before them stood a village of ghosts. Homes and buildings stood solidly, but the small town held no life. Spiritual echoes of the villagers, their livestock, and the plants and crops hung in the air motionless, starkly contrasting the cloth, dust and debris that swirled in the wind. Emaly counted, in her head, nearly four dozen dispatched villagers in the streets. There would be over triple that within the family homes. Over two hundred Mumvurii lost because of the incompetence of Sainan magi and their imperfect attempts to replicate Shadow magic.

The resultant Wraiths were savage, untethered souls that roamed Mumvuri searching to devour the bodies of Mumvurii victims, both Investurant and civilian. The monsters were not capable of corporeal form. They passed through solid objects and structures, and left them undamaged, but any material that possessed life was consumed. They roamed through the countryside, feeding on the innocent and leaving the spiritual remains suspended where their vessels once were.

"This, Emaly. This is why I hate them," Rhon growled. The accented syllables of the Mumvurii language expressed Rhon's rage. He stood gazing at the horizon, scanning for threats. The evening sun cast shadows that rolled over his armor, triggering the enchantments that shifted the edges of his silhouette. He pointed to his squad and gave a signal, dispersing them into the village in search of survivors.

"Rhon, my love, we cannot allow ourselves to become the thing we hate. We must measure our responses," Emaly said.

"Measures be damned. I'll burn their world to the ground!"

"If you have joined my mission, you shall obey my commands," she said. Emaly and Rhon were of similar families in the *Sangebula,* and their regal appearance separated them from the rest of the squad as they took their positions at the outskirts. Their castes separated them. Rhon came from a long line of Investurant Nobility. Regal commanders who stretched back hundreds of years. Generations of command.

Emaly Le'Arial was born a Sorceress. She had risen through the ranks and gained popularity among the Blood. While her heritage provided her the proper ties, she had fought for her position within the *Sangebula.* A fight which culminated in her appointment as High Sorceress and wife to the *Ombramaes.* Many held jealousy against her, but not Rhon. His hot-headed arrogance and bold independence had attracted her, as much as it hindered her now.

"Yes, Sorceress," he snarled.

Emaly watched as Rhon joined his squad. She couldn't help but fear that she was losing a greater part of him each day. That savage warrior spirit in him claimed more and more of him as the war pressed on. While they won battles against the Federation, he lost battles to the darkness within himself. She still loved him, though, darkness and all. She couldn't help but admit that his boldness and zeal had won the day more times than she cared to count. For all his flaws, he was a powerful warrior, a formidable leader, and a great lover.

She adjusted her robes and reached to find her belt pouch. She brought out a battered journal and uncapped a small pen to take down notes. She noted the date, the count of houses, and estimated the number of lives lost. She made special note of the discrepancies between the souls, as some of them were locked in a state of rapture, while others were frozen during their futile attempts at fleeing. Even after all this time, they still held such a limited understanding of the Wraiths, and she collected as much information as possible.

Once her summary was finished, she strode down the hillside. Gathering her strength, her resolve hardened becoming the woman she would need to be to complete her mission. Freeing souls from the state that they were in was an onerous task, grueling and thankless, but it was her primary objective. She served these people and her final duty was to release them. She couldn't bear to see them in this state and being so close was torturous. But, the thought of leaving them in a hellish nightmare was unforgivable.

Guards and assistant Sorceresses shadowed her as she went from soul to soul, casting the necessary spells to release the spirits into the Void. This was one of the largest villages that she had done this in, and she feared that she may run out of Arcanum before she could get to everyone. Maybe, if it was safe enough, Rhon would agree to staying camp overnight and allow her a second day to set this village to rest.

The sun was settling on the horizon, bathing the world in red as she had freed her sixty-eighth victim, when suddenly, the scouts raised an alarm. Her guards edged her to the center of the squad and formed a phalanx around her. Within seconds, the squad, including Rhon, were in a tightly executed defensive formation.

"*What is it?*" Emaly asked.

"*Wraith!*" one soldier responded, pointing at the large, looming, approaching shape. The squads' eyes locked on to it as it crept across the meadow. It was a large smoky blob absorbing and distorting the light, pulling the shadows with it. The edges of the grass below it were decaying instantly as it crept nearer and nearer.

Emaly watched as it shifted its form and for a brief instant became one of the dragons that she grew up listening about in the fables her mother read to her. Its tail and wings swept back as its head swayed side to side in a hypnotizing motion. Two of the guards in front dropped their weapons and began walking towards the Wraith in mindless abandon and three others turned on their heels to flee.

"*Cessandra,*" one of the enthralled guards said. It broke the spell for Emaly.

The Wraiths' unnatural existence in this realm was creating a disturbance in perception and the minds of the Mumvurii. Minds which were desperately trying to compensate for such a void. The Wraith was becoming a nightmare for some, a desperate desire for others.

"*It's mesmerizing us! Form up!*" she called out. She quickly cast an Illusion Protection spell and hung it over the group, allowing them to overcome the disruption caused by the monster.

As fast as she was, Emaly failed to save two entranced guards. The Wraith flooded over them, and she watched as it consumed their bodies. At the mere touch of the Wraith, their bodies disintegrated into a thick dust, breaking away and swirling up into the Wraith. For a moment, the debris attempted to shape around the Wraith, to give it a form of its own. Then the cloud of pieces broke down and melted into a formless smoke, deepening the darkness within the monster. A bone-shaking howl was released from the Wraith as it continued on towards the squad.

"*Emaly, can you banish it?*" Rhon asked.

She shook her head. The banishment spell would be similar to the spell she had been using to release the souls of the villagers. She would target the soul and attempt to guide it into the Void. The spell was taxing enough when releasing tortured souls that desired to move on. To release a Wraith, she would be forcing it against its will. Wraiths were embodiments of wrath and hatred. Their lust to consume kept them anchored to Mumvuri to feed their hunger. She had banished Wraiths before, but a Wraith this well-fed would be beyond her capabilities in such an exhausted state.

"*Retreat!*" Rhon commanded.

Emaly hated it, but it was the right call. She wouldn't be able to conjure the spell in enough time to save any of their squad. While she and Rhon were Blooded and could go ethereal to protect them from the Wraith's touch, the rest of the squad were low-born, and didn't possess enough control of their physical bodies to manifest such power. It would be too great a loss for such a pyrrhic victory.

Rhon, Emaly, and several other squad leaders opened portals to Sainan and fled to the safety of the Material Realm, leaving the Wraith behind. Emaly took deep breaths, staving off the effects of an adrenaline-fueled flight. Where a village had formed in Mumvuri, here in Sainan it was a small plantation. A manor house sat to the south, illuminated by lanterns, watching over the fields. Rhon's face twisted in rage. He pointed to the horizon with his sword, directly at the house, and snarled. "*Investigate.*"

Rhon's squad dashed to the house without hesitation. They swarmed it, breaching the interior within moments. Emaly would have preferred to not do this in front of the rest of her squadrons, but Rhon was bordering on insubordination. She gathered herself and spoke in a commanding, formal tone. "*The Ombramaes has not authorized civilian targets, Rhon.*"

"*She has headed my council in the past. She will do so again.*"

"*Who has command here, General?*"

Rhon smiled at her, a devious light in his eye. "*When it was an investigation mission within our home borders, I deferred to you. Now that blood has been shed and we've returned to the Theatre of War, you are under my purview.*"

Emaly's eyes tightened with anger. It was always challenging to determine the chain of command with two leaders of the *Sangebula*. Normally they divided duties based on mission parameters and feelings, but lately she had been clashing with both her husband and her wife. She could challenge him, but it would cause more division and strife within her people.

A flat cold tone entered her voice. "*There is not a tactical gain for this attack, we will stand down,*" she said.

"*We will secure a campsite and gather for the morning. The Wraith will not escape us, and my orders will be obeyed.*" Rhon reached out and grasped her hand. "*Once we deal with the Wraith, we can camp for a few nights, and give you time to release the remains of the village. Absolve their souls and put them to rest.*"

Emaly smiled at Rhon. There was that tender heart that she knew was deep down. It was a sad smile, because she was lost between the two people she loved and their ambition to make the Federation pay for the terror that they wrought on Mumvuri. A balance of love and hate that she always felt was on a tipping point and would drag her into the darkness after them.

Within moments, a scout returned. Emaly kept her eyes locked on the house as the warrior delivered his report. She watched as the Investurants dragged three people from the house and maneuvered a large orb-shaped metallic creature through the cellar doors.

"*General, we found one of the Old Nobles hiding within the residence as well as this Embros,*" the scout said, beaming with pride. The squad leader brought the Noble before Rhon and dropped him to his knees with a violent kick.

"*Squad, we harbor no quarter for our enemies. Strike the house, kill everyone inside.*" The Investurant warriors did not hesitate. "*As for you...*" Rhon said to the Noble. With blinding speed, Rhon drew his kukri and sliced the man's throat so deeply as to nearly sever his head. "*Destroy the abomination.*"

Emaly sighed and resolved herself to the attack. Walking with Rhon, hearing the screams of the family inside as the Investurants claimed their prize, she drove out the noise and focused on the good they would do tomorrow. She tried to convince herself that it would be worth it in the end.

7

Monsters of the Present

The trio set out with ease upon waking. No one impeded their morning, breakfast at the inn was passable, and Symon had even been able to secure a last bit of supplies with Jesse's negotiating assistance. Perhaps only an hour of daylight was burned before the three were out on the road and headed to the forest.

Though the pavers were no longer present beyond the village boundary, the road here was well cleared and easy to follow.

Argyle had agreed to meet them a short way down the road, closer to the cover of the forest. Symon kept his eyes focused all about them for the first half hour of their trek, but no sign of their companion was seen. Thus far the "woods" were nothing but cultivated trees planted in straight lines and free from undergrowth. The laborers of the village had tamed the edges of the Deeplands, but the scout had reminded them that the Road of the Dead would become unruly in due time.

Beyond the tree farms, Symon saw wild thickets of trees and individual groves that dotted the landscape. On the horizon, loomed the darkness of the "true" Deepland Woods. The smith had envisioned a straight edged border that would separate the civilized lands from the wilderness. He had been wrong. It was a gradual and slow change in the landscape that enveloped them slowly and ominously.

His fur quivered in anticipation and his ears twitched back and forth listening for threats or dangers.

The undergrowth crept in on both sides, the tree canopy met overhead in most places, and the ground became uneven and rough. Even so, the path was fairly wide and easy enough to follow. A rustle in the underbrush caught his attention, and Symon's hand went to the hilt of his sword. He saw that Jesse and Thorn's had as well, so he did not feel unjustified in his abundance of caution. Argyle stepped out with a smile on his face. For an eight foot mound of stone, Symon had to admire the Gargoyles stealthiness.

"Grot-thumping asshole!" Thorn muttered.

Jesse laughed. "Hey, Argyle."

"Did you encounter any troubles?" inquired the Genbu.

"Nope," Jesse replied. "The closest we had was a guide that was annoyed we didn't have the coin to hire her."

"How annoyed?" Argyle asked. There was a touch of anxiety and concern in his voice and Symon tried to take the smell in. Argyle was hard for him to read, so the Ennedi took special note of his tone. "Are they likely to be offended in such a manner as to cause issue? Is this something for us to be aware of?"

"No, relax! What could she do? It's not as if we are sticking around."

Argyle frowned. "The plan was to avoid all entanglements. To remain unnoticed. Anger is memorable. She could come after us. Or she could make a point of recalling your descriptions and passage to others. Especially if someone asks after you. If this causes—"

"She was disappointed, not angered," interjected Symon. "She merely saw easy coin that did not pan out."

"If you are certain," said Argyle.

"I am. And it was my fault, not Jesse's."

"Apologies," Argyle said. His shoulders relaxed, and his chest heaved as a large breath escaped him. That stillness he had took over, and Symon felt relief as well. "I mean not to assign blame, just worry that our plans become complicated. I sacrificed comfort in order to make our group less memorable. I merely fret it was in vain."

"Maybe you are just panicking from spending a night alone in this creepy ass forest," teased Thorn, slapping him on the hindquarter.

"Mayhaps. But am I truly the only one concerned that we may be followed?"

"We are all thinking it," said Jesse. "But seriously, who is after us, and knows where we are? Grendel's dead, Highston is more than two months behind us, and we haven't seen Investurants since before Essenbeck."

"Even still, a cautious worrier often becomes an OLD cautious worrier," intoned Argyle.

"Yeah, with ulcers!" joked Jesse.

Symon pondered the exchange. Highston was a long way behind them, but not to an experienced traveler. They had lost time in those first few weeks trying to find their way and being careful to avoid notice. He was not sure that they had fully escaped the wrath of the Investurants, or Manticore, or anyone else that may have interest in them. "Argyle is right, Jesse. There is nothing wrong with an abundance of caution."

The companions pushed hard that first day, and made good time. Due to the overhead cover, the evening light faded more quickly than might have been expected. With trepidation and after some debate, they decided that a fire would be more beneficial than dangerous. While the days were warm enough, it was still early spring, and the temperature was still dropping at night.

Argyle located a moderate clearing where they were less likely to have difficulty with flammable undergrowth. The day had been tiring, and they bedded down gratefully, setting a rotating watch. Symon had spent the hours of his watch startling at the prowling, active sounds of the oppressive woods. While no significant events intruded, his sleep was fitful and restless once more.

The following morning was much the same as the day before. The road stretched out before them, the canopy began to thicken, and the space between trees became narrower as the trunks broadened. The Ennedi's bones vibrated with an unfamiliar exuberance of life. They were getting ever closer to the heart of the Deeplands. The unmappable barrier between the Khorric Federation and the lands beyond.

"Hey Thorn, girl," Symon overheard Jesse say. The thief had quietly walked a bit faster for a moment to gain a place at her side. Symon sniffed the air and a note of urgency and nervousness tainted the soft smell of down he had become accustomed to in Jesse. "I'm pretty sure I'm seeing something."

"You mean the guys following us?"

Symon fought the urge to turn his head about. Jesse did not want to tip the pursuers off, yet. Symon kept his eyes locked in front of him.

"The fuck you saw them, bitch," Jesse exclaimed, still trying to keep his voice down. "How long ago?"

"A few hours now."

"Well why didn't you say something, if you saw them?"

"Can we do anything about it right now?" she asked. "Do we even know they are a problem?"

"We don't get to all make that decision together? What about Symon and Argyle?"

Symon took the opportunity to close the distance. "Anything I should be concerned about?"

"Give us about ten steps," Jesse said. He and Thorn shared a look, then stopped walking. Symon kept on for the requested distance, and then stopped as well. It took Argyle a moment longer to realize he was leaving the group behind, and to also come to a halt.

Symon turned back to watch. A Hobgoblin and a Gigante, a nine foot tall offshoot of the Humans, hiked up the road some hundred yards behind them. Even from a glance, Symon could tell they were not merchants or scouts on an expedition. They were hunting.

Thorn's eyes looked in every direction except back towards the pursuers. The pair approaching did not appear to be attempting stealth, but were well armed and imposing. Symon checked the clearance and looseness of his blade in its sheath as they eyed the approaching strangers. Jesse gave him a quick hand gesture, so Symon held his ground, occasionally scanning the remaining forest to ensure that nobody else was around.

"Greetings and well hailed," called out the Hobgoblin as they came into speaking range. She had a wicked looking sword hanging from her belt, with nasty looking hooked barbs running down the back edge of the blade, and what appeared to be a long barreled Skyfallen Blaster strapped to her back. The male Gigante at her side was using a massive bladed polearm as walking staff and scowled at the group standing in their way.

"Hello, friends," said Jesse as he stepped forward, smiling. "As you say, well hailed. I hope we are not in your way? We are happy to step aside, if so."

"No, not in our way, per say," said the Hobgoblin. Her eyes scanned the Symon and his friends cautiously. "You do, however, seem woefully under-armed to be traveling through such an area. No Blasters, no bows, no ranged defense at all that we can see. Are you sure you are trying to make your way safely through this road?"

"We're safe enough," said Jesse, dropping the smile but keeping his voice light. "No issues yet."

"Jes?" called out Thorn. "We might have something over here." Symon glanced back to see where she was focused and saw an Amarok. The five foot tall humanoid Wolf stepped through the trees, dark gray fur covered with a cloak of a similar color. His hands held a pair of Blasters trained on Symon and Argyle.

"I'd say you just ran into an 'issue'," smirked the Hobgoblin. To the Amarok she called out, "Fizael, we good?"

Blasters never wavering, the Wolf-like man cycled his aim through the group, one by one. He had a perfect distance for coverage, and a clean shot to each. He called back, "We have the bounties covered, Miss, yes we do."

"So, boy, still convinced you safe enough?" the Gigante's voice rumbled.

"Yeah, I'd reckon he's safe enough," came a voice from the other side of the road.

"What's with all the fucking Skyfallen tech?" muttered Thorn.

Symon's head whipped around, and his eyes danced from the Amarok, to the Gigante, to the Hobgoblin, and now a newcomer. Leaning against a tree, completely casual, was a pure white Tellervo. The short humanoid feline wore an ankle length black coat over a white leather jacket and pants, the edges of which were hooked behind a pair of holstered Blasters.

Symon's body shook with adrenaline. He had been calculating their odds since the three hunters had appeared. Argyle could handle the Gigante size to size, and Symon believed that Jesse and he could tackle the Hobgoblin leader. The Amarok, as well as the advantage of Skyfallen weaponry, had made it a stalemate. Symon sniffed the air, with an attempt at casual calm, and the Tellervo's nostrils flared as well. To Symon, there was a memory within the white cat's smell, something that triggered safety. The big smith smiled at the new man, and he smiled back.

Still leaning against the tree, the Tellervo said. "No reason for it to get dangerous, right?"

"Cocky son of a bitch, aren't you?" the Hobgoblin called in his direction. "Weapons still in their holsters and you want to warn US off? There's a bounty, and we intend to claim it. We are well within Hunters' rights to do so."

"A bounty? Well, now."

"On two of them."

The Tellervo's ears perked up, as the four companions looked among one another. "Oh, which ones?"

"The two we kill first," the Hobgoblin sneered. Calling out, "Fizael, drop the targets!"

Symon spun towards the Amarok, his hand reaching for his blade. He was stopped by the sickening sound of a cracking skull. Where Fizael once stood, now loomed a larger, very familiar, Arktos. He rested the gnarled staff on his shoulder, as the Amarok slumped to the ground. "Only thing he's dropping is his weapons." Hasukawa said, that deep voice carrying through the woods.

"Fizael!" the Hobgoblin cried.

The massive white bear knelt down and checked the pulse of the Amarok. "He will live. Assuming this road does not become a bloodbath."

"Suppose that's up to you two," drawled the Tellervo. He had drawn one single pistol and gestured toward the Hobgoblin and Gigante.

"I see that our quarry is better protected than we were informed," the woman said, her hands raised in an unthreatening gesture. "So let's just write this off as a failed attempt and we shall take our companion and be on our way." The Gigante's lip flared in frustration, but he did nothing to contradict her.

The two hunters slowly started towards their fallen associate. They lifted him to his feet, and the Amarok slowly regained consciousness, but could not keep his footing. The blow had not been as severe as Symon believed, but it would still take time for the wolf-like man to heal.

"Before you go," Jesse called out. All eyes turned to him. "What's this bounty?"

The Hobgoblin snarled at him. "Fuck you!"

The hum of a Blaster holding a charge resonated and reverberated around them. The Tellervo held his pistol trained on the woman. "Oh, now we're all curious."

She looked frustrated for a moment, but then shrugged nonchalantly. "A Bright Guild Hit."

"Oh, you can do better than that."

"Manticore."

"There it is," Jesse said. He nodded slightly as if confirming something he'd been thinking. While the Hobgoblin was cold, metallic even, the Gigante was radiating a sour smell, like spoiled apples. They were hiding something, and the nine-foot tall behemoth was nervous. "Which Guildhall?"

"Essenbeck," she said. "Apparently you arranged a rendezvous and then skipped out."

"So, little Goblin girl here and me?" Jesse asked.

"Yes.

The scent intensified, and Symon growled. Jesse, however, merely smirked. Quickly he dropped his smile and said, "Thank you." He turned to the others, and added, "I'm good with letting them go if you guys are."

The giant Arktos glared at the pair of bounty hunters. He asked, "We won't be meeting you again, correct?"

The woman smiled wickedly and said, "Don't worry."

"Wait," called out Thorn. "Before you go..."

"Thirteen Hells! Are you serious right now?" the Hobgoblin cursed.

"If you are legal bounty hunters, what Hunter's Guild are you with?"

"Who said we were legal?" smirked the woman over her shoulder as they began walking back toward the Khorric Federation.

"A lot of bullshit to go through for an illegal bounty," Thorn said "Where'd you get the names?"

"Right you are, little Thorn. But that information is something you would need to fight for. Is it worth it to you, just for that answer?"

"Get the fuck out of here, then!"

Symon watched the two bounty hunters wander down the road. Jesse and Thorn grouped up with Argyle, their eyes trained on the bright white compatriots. An uneasy tension still hung in the air.

"All of that was over a poorly handled meeting in Essenbeck?" asked Symon, astounded. His nose twitched again, remembering the Gigante's scent. "Surely, you do not believe that?"

Jesse and Thorn looked at one another, paused a beat, and then broke out in laughter.

"What?" asked Symon.

"I believe they are astonished that you caught onto the ruse," Argyle said. "My friend, there is not a chance that a missed meeting with strangers led to a bounty worth chasing outside the city of Essenbeck, much less with a purse worth attracting a team of three Hunters with enough clout to brandish Skyfallen weaponry.

"If they were truly working a bounty for Essenbeck Manticore, legal or otherwise," Argyle continued. "They would not have been so careless with their information. Thus, either someone from Manticore, or an affiliate of Manticore, or some other third party from Highston set the bounty. But it did not originate from Essenbeck."

"Even more likely," Jesse added, now calmed from his laughter, "they didn't even tell us the right targets."

"I believe you are correct," Symon said. "So if you expected them to lie, why bother asking?"

"Two reasons," explained Jesse. "Well, a bunch of reasons. First, it covers our tracks a bit, since we gave them the impression that we swallowed the lie. Second, the confirmation that we're wanted throughout the 'Khorr, not just

Essenbeck. And...” Jesse smiled at Thorn, “we at least found out they’ve been tracking us from at least then, since they know we passed through there. Oh, and that they spoke with the Manticore contact there, since they knew of the missed meeting.”

“In other words,” said Thorn, grinning, “Jesse was fucking with ‘em.”

“Oh, don’t forget that they know our names, not just our descriptions!” Jesse continued. “She called Thorn by name. Oh, and no mention of the Ophissi at Road’s End!”

“Enough,” Argyle said. “We get it.”

“Well now that all of that is out of the way,” Hasukawa said to Symon, “shall we make introductions?”

Symon smiled and pointed towards his friends. “Hello Master Hasukawa, this is Thorn, Argyle, you met Jesse, although he is in a much healthier state than last time.” He turned to the group. “Guys, this is Hasukawa, the man who helped me save Jesse’s life.”

“Oh, shit,” Thorn whispered.

“You have our gratitude,” Argyle said.

“Uh, thanks!” Symon saw Jesse shift uncomfortably. “I’ll try and stop tempting death.”

“Of course, young one,” Hasukawa replied. “It is troubling times.” He motioned over the gunslinger that had assisted them, who came over and sat on Hasukawa’s knee. “This is my husband and hunting partner, Kiko.”

“Pleased to meet you all,” Kiko said.

“Your timing is...” Symon hesitated, trying to find the right words. “Convenient. How does that keep happening to line up? Were the two of you coming from the Federation? Were you following us?”

“We are actually headed the other way. We are returning from Vargarden at the moment,” stated Hasukawa.

“And you just happened to meet us on the road, at the same time those hunters did? Bullshit,” said Thorn, laughing.

Kiko chuckled as well, as he bumped shoulders with Hasukawa and said, “Oh, I like her. Can we keep the scalawag?” Then to the rest of the group, Kiko added, "No, we were off seeing the Witch about something, and she strongly implied that if we came to this spot, at this time, we would be glad of it. And so we are!"

Symon's attention piqued. He had read many rumors and legends regarding the Witch in Deepland Woods as he studied the War of Night. Stories that added new layers of horror to the barrier between the Khorric Federation and Land of the Dead. "You know of the Deepland Witch?" he asked. "She is real?"

"She is real indeed," Hasukawa said solemnly. "A force not to be taken lightly."

"What is she like?"

"Knowing of the Deepland Witch and experiencing her are two distinctly different things." Hasukawa said. "Conversations for another time to be sure. For now, we are here to help you, and then be on our way."

Kiko piped up excitedly, "Oh please, Papabear. Show them?" He nuzzled into Hasukawa's neck fur, teasingly muttering, "Pretty please? He is so much fun!"

The four companions looked at one another in confusion as Hasukawa chuckled, then kissed Kiko on the forehead and pulled out a whistle made of a small bone. He inhaled sharply, his massive chest expanding, and then blew into the whistle. It produced a hollow sound, but quiet, no more than blowing through a hollow tube. Then seconds later, a multi-pitched fluted melody could be heard distantly in the trees. The music started softly, but grew in intensity and volume, passed over them as if a wave, and fluttered off into the deeper forest.

"It isn't much," Hasukawa said. "But it should suffice to guide you safely on the rest of your journey."

"Excellent!" squealed the smaller Tellervo. The lazy drawling accent could still be detected, but Kiko's obvious excitement hid the indifference to his earlier tone. "Ya'll get to meet your new best friend. Might take him an hour or more to find you. But he has been summoned, so he will come."

"Who will come?" asked Jesse, grinning at Kiko's antics.

"Masuulka," answered Hasukawa. "The spirit guardian of the Deepland Witch, and the guide of those woods. Stay to the road and he'll overlook you."

"And why, pray tell, is he 'so much fun'?" asked Argyle.

"Because he is a prankster!" laughed Kiko.

8

An Unghastly Welcome

Symon stood on the crest of a small ridge, sun on his face, overlooking the valley before them. Rolling hills of cultivated fields stretched out for miles ahead in all directions. Waves of green wheat grass, grass that would turn golden in a few months, undulated in the wind that blew gently by. Neatly trimmed, triple rows of orchard trees, banks of tightly wound grapevines, and compacted and well-maintained roads bordered each acre of farmland. Separating them into little fields all evenly divided. All-in-all, it was breathtaking.

Jesse let a low whistle escape behind Symon's ear. "Not what we were expecting, right?"

"No," Symon replied. "Not at all."

After the terrors the group had had in the forest, it was a refreshing change. The land did not resemble the dark and depressive stories about Vargarden that permeated the Federation history classes. It was a vibrant, rich, and well organized terrain, laid out as far as their eyes could see. Symon could spy a small village sitting on the opposite edge of the valley, and beyond that the tips of building tops that marked the city of Vargarden. It would take them a day or two, he estimated, to make the city proper and begin their quest. The long arduous journey was not over yet.

"What did you expect?" Argyle asked, irritation creeping into his voice. The Genbu had been lost in thought, staring blankly across the horizon with his head tilted to the side. Symon wondered if the group's lack of travel experience had started to wear on Argyle's patience.

Jesse smirked. "I don't know. From the stories and what you said, I expected it to be... well..."

"Not to mention the creepy forest we just traversed," Symon said.

"We expected it to look like dead shit," Thorn said. "You know, gray fields, dusty, crags and shit. And clouds. Lots of clouds!"

"Fair enough," Argyle nodded. His tone was softer now, more understanding, and Symon smiled. The Genbu turned to Symon and said, "Where should we start?"

"I am not sure, Master Argyle. All my father gave me was 'Return to my homeland. You have much about your heritage you need to know. Train your gift, and make me proud!' Those were his only words. Now, we are on our own."

"He spoke nothing of his past?"

"No," Symon replied, a soft growl passing his lips. "He told me that he was not originally from the Federation. A refugee.

"But he hid his past from everybody, including me!" Symon's mane was rising from his neck. "He lied. Lied about who he was. Shining Court! He lied about who we were. Our name is not Cylkas. He changed even that when we arrived in Highston."

"Your name's not Cylkas?" Jesse asked.

"No," Symon said. "Cylkas was our 'Federation' name. Our true name is Cyl'Karrick."

"An ancient name form," Argyle said. "Similar to the names of those in the early days of the Federation. The Kal'Khorric lineage became the original family that formed the Khorric Federation. Over the history of the region, the powers that be shortened names to drop the familial links and state merely the root of the bloodline.

"Names like 'Kal'Khorric' or 'Cyl'Khorric' simply became 'Khorric,'" Argyle continued. "The shortened versions became fashionable, and then became the standard. It is rare to see lineages holding that pattern in these days."

"Like A'Dynell?" Jesse asked. Symon understood his friends were giving him time to regain his calm. Changing the subject away from the trauma.

Argyle smiled. "Yes, indeed. Master Zenesul most likely reclaimed that heritage, even twisting it with an Alvan variant, as a thumb to the Federation."

"Crazed old man."

"How do you know this?" Symon asked Argyle, cautiously. "None of this is covered in the histories."

"Not common history," Argyle replied. "It is documented in the Noble Annals and other such manuscripts. Grendel used to force me to listen to his proposals for the nobility courts in the Federation. He would describe these historical idiosyncrasies to give context to his plans and make sure he was prepared for all angles. The Alvan members appreciated those petitioners who respected the heritage, and Grendel played that game well."

"Well, shit," Jesse said. "Good thing he was a manipulative bitch. At least he left us lessons that we can use."

"I suppose that is accurate," the big Gargoyle agreed.

"Ah, the dishonest figure in YOUR life," Symon said looking at Jesse.

The winged boy came over and wrapped an arm around Symon's waist. "It is what it is."

Argyle paused for a moment, allowing the moment to pass. He continued, "Then I believe we should make our way to the city. That would be the best place to start. With your father being part of their army, I would say his records are most likely to be found there."

"That makes sense," Symon said.

Jesse tensed beside him and the thief and Thorn shared a look. Thorn made a motion for Jesse to continue. "Yeah, about your dad, Symon," Jesse said, hesitantly. "We've been thinking about it, and we're not sure that it adds up good."

"I agree."

"What do you know, Symon?" Argyle asked.

"Nothing. Well, next to nothing," Symon said. "That is the problem. My father abandoned his country. Was it by choice? Was it forced exile? What trouble did he leave in his wake?"

"You have been in the Federation for two decades," Argyle said. "Surely any immediate danger has passed."

"What is twenty years to the undead? Do we know?"

"Well, that's kind of our point," Jesse said. "The war was nearly fifty years ago, right?"

Argyle cocked his head and Symon waved his friend on.

"If your dad was in the war, then he would have been at least our age. So that would make him in his mid-sixties or seventies?"

"To be honest," Argyle said. "If he was a field general like the man in Symon's stories, Rakar, claimed his father to be, his service would have been longer than a young man could have accomplished. I would insist that he is nearly eighty or ninety."

Jesse exchanged another uncomfortable look with Thorn. "So, yeah, he didn't look that old. But, you know, I don't know how old... Or I mean, when someone like you..."

"Oh, for fuck's sake," Thorn said. "How old do you cats live?"

"Ah, that is an interesting thought," Argyle said. "We have not discussed the lifespan of the Ennedi."

Symon chuckled. It was an impolite question to ask in society. Highston elite very rarely discuss mortality in open conversation. "I guess we do not talk about it much. Federal studies go over racial lifespans in our classes, but we do not dwell on it. It was something that Lara and I discussed, because she was part Alvan and was going to live longer than I would. It affected our plans for the future. But I just never think about it with others."

"And for those of us who didn't get your fancy schools, how long would that be?" Jesse asked.

"Most Ennedi live to be around eighty years old. A few historical marks of some living to a century, but eighty is the standard." Symon thought about it, realizing his father was certainly beyond those years. "Our coat also grays just as most races' hair does. Streaks of gray or silver can show our age."

"Well, then, your dad either looks REAL good for his age, or he may be into some dark magic," Jesse said dryly.

Thorn shrugged. "Could your father be THE Father?!"

"No!" Symon said.

"No, he would not be," Argyle said. "Symon said his father and the agent from Vargarden spoke about the Father as a person. Someone other than themselves, who was responsible for Vargarden. It would not be Symon's father. But he could still be dabbling in immortality."

"Rakar also called my father 'Nemuku,'" Symon said. "A name I could not place that night, but now can remember from the history books. He was not just a general…" Symon let out an exasperated sigh. "He was the lead general of the War of Night. His name was on the charter of the Battle of Enfeld. Tens of thousands of deaths lay at his feet. He was the most ruthless and efficient destroyer that Vargarden had.

"I just…"Symon shook his head and looked at his feet. His father's secrets constantly plagued him, leaving him trying to answer questions that he had no knowledge of. He feared that while Vargarden may provide him answers, they may not be answers he wanted. "I have nothing. And I am scared. I spent my entire life looking up to a man who may not have ever existed. Who knows what I will find about him there? My father hid so much. I am sorry guys, I just do not know what we can expect here."

"It's okay, Symon," Jesse said, stretching to wrap his arm back around the smith's shoulders. "We'll go in, get what we need, then we head back to the Federation. We can hide in the big cities until this shit blows over."

"Yes! That's what I'm talking about!" Thorn said excitedly.

"Yes, thank you. Once we get there, you all can go back. Once I figure out what to do about my Gift, I will hopefully one day join you. But until the Shadow fades, we may not have many choices. I am sorry for my part in all this."

"Grendel's the one to blame for all this," Jesse said. "He's the one who brought the Shadows in. I don't know why they want me dead, but they tried to kill me before they tried to kill you." He laughed nervously and punched Symon in the arm. "If it weren't for him, we'd still be sitting at a desk with old man Zen barking about how I botched the last form."

Symon squeezed Jesse's shoulder, returning him to a side hug. "Yes, I suppose we have that. But we will get you cleared and home where you wish to be."

He scanned the valley again, trying to pick out the best path. "Should we avoid the villages, or stick to the roads?"

"I would say we should go to the villages," Argyle answered. "The people may provide insight that could prepare us for the city."

"Yeah, plus, our rations are running low, and both Thorn and Argyle need some dried meat," Jesse said.

"Okay, we should head to the closest one then. Once we have what we need there, we can proceed to the city."

"Sounds like a plan," Jesse said. "Let's head out then."

Jesse kept his eyes scanning the horizon as they headed down the hillside of the ridge. The road wound back and forth to keep the slope manageable while affording them a wonderful view of the village and surrounding areas ahead. As they got closer, the villagers, who had been dots in the distance, became clearer shapes. It was a small village, with only a few dozen inhabitants, and the population was entirely Gnomish.

It was a sedate and tranquil village, but still had an aura of life. The small houses around the town were well maintained and there was a modest inn just off the main road. Nestled next to the inn was a small general goods store. The travelers saw livestock, so with the hopes of a good stew and fresh jerky in front of them, they livened their steps and entered the village. Little eyes watched them as they traveled the streets towards the inn, wary but not threatening. The Gnomish residents would wave hesitantly, and smile as Symon waved back. Jesse kept a smile on his face hoping that a friendly demeanor would hasten them to a comfortable stay.

As the group looked around the street, they could see occasional skeletons sitting outside the homes of the villagers. There were bright banners and colored streamers hanging in windows that accented the macabre decorations. Jesse shifted his vision into the Arcane spectrum and found that the skeletons were infused with spells. The low level of Arcanum present all around them formed an eerie atmosphere that the young thief struggled to shake.

Out in front of the store, its proprietor swept the small porch. Her gaze fell on the four companions as she wove in and out of a half dozen small skeletons sitting in tiny chairs. Adorning each skeleton were floral wreaths and leather thongs beaded with scrimshaw amulets carved with runes. The runes shone like points of starlight in the Arcane spectrum. Jesse's skin crawled with anxiety as the aura of Necromancy fell over them.

The shopkeeper was an ancient little gnome who stood barely three feet tall. Her tiny bun bobbed steadily as she whisked away the day's dirt and dust. A smile broke her weathered face as she looked up towards the travelers. Jesse flinched as the woman held her broom out and the closest skeleton stood. Grasping the broom, the undead entity resumed sweeping wordlessly where the woman had left off. "Welcome, strangers," she said in a cheerful and high voice. "How can I help you?"

He exchanged a worried look with Symon who nodded uncomfortably. A quick glance confirmed the location of Argyle and Thorn, just in case the situation turned dangerous. Mustering his courage, Jesse stepped forward and flashed that innocent sideways smile he had perfected over the years. "Hello, ma'am. We're in need of some supplies. This looks like a really nice store. Do you think you might be able to help us out?"

"Of course, dearie," the old Gnome said, still smiling. Her voice was pleasant, yet Jesse scanned her for any deception. "Would you also like a place to stay for the night?"

Jesse shrugged and gave Symon a questioning look. The Ennedi stepped forward and replied, "We are on our way to the city. We would welcome a brief rest from our long journey, madam. But we must decline. We have little coin. And that we have is Federation issued. I hope it will suffice for trade goods?"

Jesse paused. He hadn't considered that Vargarden might not honor Khorric coins. Thorn gave him a slight smile and the boy shook his head in return. Giving her permission to steal would only draw unwanted attention, unless he had time to gauge a distraction. His eyes returned to the Gnomish woman.

"Are you folks from the Federation? Are you emissaries?"

"Something like that," Jesse said.

The shopkeeper's smile broadened and Jesse stepped back hesitantly. "Well, then, let us get you settled into the inn, and I'll take down a list of what you need, and we can negotiate a fair price." She turned and made a small gesture that caused two of the skeletons to rise. "Follow my kin to the inn and see my husband, he'll get you roomed, and a fresh dinner."

"Madam," Symon said. "I appreciate your hospitality, but we cannot afford lodging, I assure you. Supplies are all we require."

"Posh!" she retorted. Her gaze turned to the horizon where the sun was already dipping towards sunset. "It is too late in the day for you to make much way toward the city. Plus, I can only imagine how tired you are, if you braved the Woods." The Gnome motioned the skeletons forward. "We can work something out, I'm sure."

"We could not impose like that," Symon said.

"No, no. No imposition," the Gnome grinned. "If you are headed to the city, we can petition the patrons of your visit to cover the costs."

Jesse and Thorn looked at each other making sure that they had caught those words correctly. "We can use credit? Not to question you, but we are strangers. How would that work?"

That broad grin deepened and the little innkeeper laughed. "Ah, you Federation travelers. You always get confused. We have a system. Whatever travel costs you've accrued here, will be covered by your patron, no worries about that."

"What if we don't have a patron?" Jesse asked.

"Oh, dear," the lady said. "I'd heard, but didn't think I'd see anything. Refugees?"

"Something like that."

"Oh, well, then..." she said, tapping her finger on her chin. "Then, you'd be covered by the municipal funds. 'Tis charity, but won't harm none." She gazed at Jesse and Thorn, then a hard look at Symon. "I know it might not feel 'heroic' but you may just need to set aside pride and let us help you. Plus, you boys look to be searching for something, and I don't mind helping out a stranger from time to time."

Thorn was shaking her head subtly. Jesse understood. In Highston, there were no handouts. Everything had strings attached. Strings that put you in the clutches of a Bright Guild or corrupt Church officials. Everything came with a price. But there was nothing to argue with. She was right. The day was late, travel would be hard, and the four obviously needed a rest.

"That is mighty generous of you, dear lady," Argyle said, relieving Jesse of the responsibility. "I fear that your rooms, cozy as they may be, could be limiting to someone of my size."

"Oh," she chuckled. "You're right. Quite a large fellow you are. Would you be too proud to sleep in a stable? I could bring out extra cushions and make it quite cozy."

Symon shrugged at Jesse, who looked at Thorn blankly. "I guess, we'd be foolish to turn it down," Jesse said with a nod of thanks.

"Well, that's settled," she said, clapping her hands together. "Yes, we can set you up. But let's get you squared, and tomorrow we can send you off to the city. Just hand those packs to my kin, and we'll handle the rest. Call me Jessie."

Thorn snickered. Jesse punched her in the arm and the woman gave him a questioning glance. "I'm also Jesse."

"Oh, dear," Jessie laughed. "Coincidences abound. Well, then call me 'Miss Jessie' to avoid confusion. Although, handsome as you are, I'm sure folk can figure out the difference."

Jesse laughed. He couldn't escape the feeling of dread that Vargarden had over them. The town felt like a painting. Pleasant enough, but just not 'real' enough. Years on the streets gave his anxiousness a sharpened edge. But honestly, he wanted to like her. She was nice.

The skeletons took the travel packs from the travelers and trudged into the inn. Symon slid over next to Jesse and whispered. "What do we think? Is this for real?"

"Either she is exactly who she is pretending to be..." Jesse smirked. "Or our bones will be ground into bread by morning.”

“No,” Symon replied, nodding to the skeletons. “Cannot believe she would waste our bones as food.”

“Good point.” An uncomfortable knot formed in Jesse’s gut. He walked inside the inn, ignoring the sense of unease that twisted him.

9

Vargarden

The companions had spent the night being treated to all the hospitality that Miss Jessie had described. The meal had been excellent, with generous amounts of meat for both Argyle and Thorn. The innkeeper had even packed a small amount for the day's travel to the city. Their exit had been unexpectedly grand. Flowers and skeletons lined the street as the gnomes gave a small honor parade to the guests who honored their small community. One of the gnomes had even offered to carry them on his wagon for a few miles, speeding their travel significantly.

Symon's eyes wandered the landscape with a blend of curiosity and concern. He was not the only one. Jesse and Thorn both had an acrid scent undercutting their usual aroma. A scent of heightened anxiety and nervousness that belied their paranoia. Argyle was, as usual, a stoic dead spot in Symon's perception.

By mid-day, the four travelers had reached the outskirts of the city of Vargarden. The air was still crisp and cool. The sky was still blue and sunny. The fields around them, however, had changed dramatically.

Flanking the road were rows of simple stone markers, polished stark white, evenly spaced with precise care. Hundreds of rows, each incredibly long, stretching out for as far as Symon could see. Grave markers.

The earth between the markers remained freshly turned, grass only appearing at the markers themselves, giving the graveyard the feel of recently cultivated farmland. For nearly half a mile, Symon and the group walked through the cemetery that surrounded Vargarden, taking in the solemn statement it made. Symon could not even remember the last graveyard he had seen in Highston. The Federation focused on life, not loss, and Symon had little experience with death until recently. Here, tens of thousands of bodies must lay beneath that land. Vargarden did not hide their dead.

"This is more what I expected," Jesse said at Symon's ear.

"Indeed. It feels..." Symon stammered. "It feels..."

"Like we're waiting for the headsman to swing?"

"Yes."

Jesse reached up and stroked his shoulder. "What do you want to do?"

"Not much of a choice. We press forward."

The four travelers crossed the threshold into the lower city and could still hardly believe the sights. Vargarden was easily as massive as Highston, and yet the streets were still very tightly laid out. Some roadways were barely larger than the carts that passed, passing for what would be an alley at home, causing the city to feel claustrophobic. The cramped nature made travel slow, and careful, especially with someone the size of Argyle.

While there were shops, carts, and people everywhere, it was surprisingly clean. The city was vibrant and full of energy. And it was... old.

Highston was founded shortly after the Devastation and had seen six hundred years of existence. Vargarden was much, much older. Symon examined the buildings they passed carefully, watching layers of history unfold before his eyes. Buildings that themselves were older than Highston. Intricate carvings of fearsome beasts formed arched buttresses interspaced with tiered towers and fluted rooftops. Ceramic and stone blended into a beautiful mosaic of architecture that felt more timeless than the simplistic angular buildings within the Khorric capital. Vargarden people took pride in their city and that was reflected in the care and condition of each and every aspect of the place they called home.

As they approached the gates to the inner city, the walls loomed high above them. The walls were intimidating, nearly forty feet tall, and the ramparts were decorated with stone faces and vine work. On the wall, they could see patrols of skeletons in gleaming armor and bows on their backs. The patrols were much more tightly packed than similar patrols in Highston, and these guards were fully focused on their task.

Standing at the gates were two Ukko Dwarves in plain robes of greens and blues. They loosely organized the line to enter the inner city so the two attendants, Symon would hesitate to call them "guards", could easily interact with everyone as needed. It appeared that many of the visitors were well recognized and the attendants were friendly. Still, their eyes scanned the crowd as people passed through the gates, occasionally stopping someone to request some form of documentation as an official visitor.

Symon and his companions continued to approach, getting ever closer to the gate. He spied several niches in the wall, each containing a skeleton standing motionless. His ears and tail twitched and the fur on his back stood taller. The macabre fear of being watched by hundreds of undead eyes weighed on his sensibilities, and Symon had trouble peeling his gaze away from the skeletal guards. "Ho! You there!" One of the attendants pointed to Symon. "State your business, please."

"Hello, good sir," Symon said. "We are here seeking refuge."

"Vargarden isn't known for taking in refugees, young one," he replied. "What brings you to us?"

"Sir, we have fled the Federation due to the invasion. The Investurant armies have returned and much has been lost."

"Aye," both men nodded. "Reports of civil war were received months ago. We're sorry to hear that."

Jesse joined Symon, standing by him for support. The boy thief smiled sadly, "We barely escaped Highston the night of the insurrection. We fled here."

"Long way to travel," the attendant said. His eyes weighed the boys' intentions, looking for any sign of malintent. "But it doesn't explain why you are here. The Federation and Vargarden didn't part on good terms at the end of the War, so you at our doorstep is a bit... suspicious."

"Yes, sir," Symon said. "I can understand that."

The Ukko frowned at Symon. "So, why? Of all the places you could run, why

Vargarden?"

Symon swallowed hard and Jesse reached out to squeeze his hand. "I believe my family is from Vargarden. My father grew up a refugee in Highston from the original war. He studied Necromancy here and was once a soldier. As his last request, he bid me return and seek out training."

"Your sire sent you here for training?"

"Indeed, sir." Symon hesitated, "I am a 'Gifted' Necromancer."

Both attendants looked at each other with surprise. The one who had been leading the conversation stared hard at Symon. "You believe you are a Necromancer?"

"Yes. I discovered my Gift last year. Hiding it from the Federation."

"And who is your sire?" the attendant asked.

"Kyrn Cyl'Karrick, sir."

"Nemuku Cyl'Karrick?" the man asked, his voice full of astonishment. "Your sire is Nemuku Kyrn Cyl'Karrick?"

"Yes, Kyrn Cyl'Karrick is my father. I am Symon Cyl'Karrick."

"Call the magistrate immediately!" the man shouted. There was a mixture in his tone of alarm, relief, and excitement. None of these feelings assuaged Symon's anxiety, however. Without any additional commands, a dozen skeletons stepped out of their niches, green crystals in their chest collecting the light, surrounding the party and drawing attention from the general public. A small boy dressed in the same color robes as the attendants dashed in the direction of the castle.

Symon and Jesse shifted nervously. He saw Thorn's eyes dance around, already plotting an escape path. Even Argyle was taking a defensive posture. Symon took a step forward, waving his group to calm. He would have to trust that they could handle this diplomatically.

"Sir," Symon said. "There is no cause for alarm."

"Silence!" the Ukko snapped. "Nothing further until the magistrate arrives."

A crowd had gathered around to watch the spectacle. Whispers in the crowd became an audible murmur as the name "Cyl'Karrick" was repeated. The other attendant shouted for the crowd to move on and additional undead warriors stepped in to disperse them before it could become a mob. The ring of skeletons detaining Symon and his friends tightened, drawing closer and more imposing.

"Symon," Jesse whispered, "what's happening?"

"I do not know."

"What do we do?"

Symon's head swiveled all around, looking for an option, but found none. His shoulders slumped in defeat. "I do not know." Symon had feared that his father had secrets, but he had no idea that it could have been this bad. He could not allow his friends to pay the price. "Good sir!" he called to the Ukko. "I will submit to whatever you need, but please allow my friends to pass."

The attendant stalked forward, his face stern and unreadable. "I beg of you, sir. Keep quiet until the Magistrate arrives. Anything you say can only cause further complications."

Minutes ticked away excruciatingly slowly, as Symon stood silent until a stout, Gnomish gentleman in dark purple robes finally arrived. Decorum had apparently been discarded due to the urgency of the situation, causing the Gnome to run the entire way here. His face was red and he was breathing heavily. Pushing his way through the crowd, he shouted, "Where is he? Where is he?"

"They are right here, Osi," the gate attendant said. The Ukko stood at a salute and gave a respectful smile. "Detained per the Accords, Section three. Subject has been instructed to provide no additional statements until your arrival, Osi."

"Excellent, Deacon," the man cried. Turning to Symon, he said, "I am Magistrate Jurdanus, and you are the boy claiming to be Kyrn Cyl'Karrick's son?"

Symon stood proud, his tail twitching behind him. "I am the son of Kyrn. I am Symon Cyl'Karrick, known as Symon Cylkas in the Federation."

"Ah, yes," Jurdanus nodded. "Indeed, you bear his likeness."

"You knew my father?"

"I knew of him," the Gnome said. "I was just beginning my tenure when the campaign began."

"What's all this?" Jesse asked, incredulously. Symon attempted to hold him back, but Jesse was unable to hold his concern in check anymore.

"We'll get to that," the Magistrate replied. Again his eyes trained on Symon. "Symon Cyl'Karrick, in the name of the Father, in accordance with the sanctioned laws of Vargarden, have you returned to claim rights to your Sire's household and all responsibilities of House Cyl'Karrick?"

"I do not know..." Symon stammered. He looked at Jesse with worry in his eyes. Jesse shrugged. This sounded like nobility issues and was well beyond either of their understandings. Symon turned to the Magistrate. "What does that mean, sir?"

"You claim to be the rightful heir of Kyrn Cyl'Karrick. Yes or no?"

"Yes, sir. I do."

Jurdanus grinned. It was a smile of satisfaction that did not detract the serious look in the Gnome's gaze. A look of a hunter watching prey take the bait. "Then, it is my responsibility to place you under arrest."

"What?!" Thorn and Jesse exploded. "Why?!"

The attendants shifted defensively, and the ring of skeletal guards raised weapons. Eyes turned to Argyle, his looming bulk filling the space with an ominous threat of violence. Symon would not allow this to come to blows. He placed a hand on Jesse's shoulder and gently pulled him closer. "There has to be a mistake."

Magistrate Jurdanus, it appeared, was also committed to diplomacy and waved the Deacon to rest. The undead legion lowered their arms in response. "There is no mistake, son. Kyrn Cyl'Karrick was the target of several outstanding warrants. By law, these warrants are transferred to the rightful heir of the House Cyl'Karrick. These crimes have loomed over the Black Legion and tarnish the reputation of their legacy.

"Symon Cyk'Karrick, you will bear the charges of Dereliction of Duty, Violations of Necromantic Regulations, and various other crimes of war." The Magistrate smiled broadly again. "It is an honor to be the one to do this today."

"Now wait a damned minute you throg-licking—" Thorn started. Symon placed his hand over her mouth and shook his head.

"I have this," Symon said to her. "So my father WAS a criminal?"

Jurdanus nodded. "He broke several regulations at the end of the War. Dozens of open reports and infractions. We had always hoped that this would one day be able to be put to rest. Until judgment can be rendered, these crimes hang over the heads of all of us. Surely, he would have told you."

"No, sir, he did not. I do not believe my father ever planned to return."

The man's eyes saddened. "That is tragic. But today, you've returned to claim responsibility and close this matter for good. Go with this squad. They shall take you to the High Courts and see to you until judgment can be rendered."

The Deacon who had detained him, gathered three skeletons and approached Symon.

"This is unfair!" Jesse said to the magistrate. "What did Symon ever do? He's never even BEEN here before!"

"I understand your concern for your friend, boy," Jurdanus consoled. "But it is our way. The sins of the Sire pass to that of the generation beyond. Until this is handled, the entire Cyl'Karrick family would be held accountable. Your friend is doing his duty."

"This sucks!" Thorn said. "All this way, and nothing."

"Yeah, what happens to us?" Jesse asked. The thief gestured to Thorn and Argyle. "We came here for HIM! Now, you're taking him! What do we do now?"

The second gate attendant looked at them. "Until a judgment can be made, we would recommend that you go directly to the palace and await Master Cyl'Karrick's appearance in court. A room can be obtained at the inn nearby. A special counsel is already being called. This is a momentous day."

The ominous finality of this sounded horrible. If any of the War of Night tales were accurate, then Symon was being held responsible for more criminal acts than they could count. In the Federation, this would be a death sentence or a life in the Maw. Most likely a public execution on the Phase Dias, where he would be atomized by the Skyfallen device for all to see.

"Which way do we go?" Argyle asked.

The attendant pointed to a large castle with many high towers. "The court will be held in the main chamber at the Palace. Just head in that direction. You will wait outside there until the trail can be completed."

"Outside?" Jesse asked. "Why can't we go in? He needs us!"

"This is a military trial, not open to civilians."

"But this makes no sense! Symon's not in your military..." Jesse started.

Symon could see the gate guard losing patience with Jesse.

"Jesse," Symon said. "I will be alright." The Magistrate and the Deacon nudged Symon towards the palace and began his march. Symon looked over his shoulder and watched as Thorn and Argyle led Jesse towards the gate, still spitting questions at the guards. "Jesse, please. Please, I will be okay!"

The crowd parted before them, and within moments Symon lost his friends in the blur of people behind them. His footsteps grew heavy as he approached his fate.

10

Problems of the Head

Emaly stood at the window gazing over the landscape of Highston. Deep, steady breaths formed a cadence that was punctuated by the cracking and flexing of her knuckles. Counting the buildings, Emaly attempted to calm her mind. Compared to Mumvurii architecture, the city looked like a collection of children's blocks, all assembled in tight and even stacks. Only here towards the center, close to the large Hulls, did the architecture change to have texture and curves. Gone was the softness and organic fluidity of her beloved Mumvurii skylines. The tension she felt was reflected in the harsh angles that surrounded her daily here in this befallen city.

There was no tradition here. Highston had been cobbled together century by century by hands that lacked a central ideal. For seven centuries, spanning multiple regimes, the Khorric people had built with an eye towards trends and popular opinions. The result was a hodgepodge of architectural influences from different places throughout Sainan. Both within the Khorric Federation and beyond. Layers and layers of change and clusters all centered on the Skyfallen wreckage that anchored Highston.

Those Hulls loomed over the city, but in her mind they also loomed over the war. Before the Devastation here in Sainan, the Mumvuri people seemed to be unaffected by the Federation and their tampering. She had been looking in the library for accounts of the event but had found them lacking in objectivity. Something had made the Federation back away from their uneasy peace with Mumvuri and set them on the path that led to the Wraiths. And the Wraiths were what this war was all about.

The Lord's High Council Chambers provided her a grand view over the city, but no grand insight. As filled with rage as she was, Emaly felt that the moniker given to it by Manticore was more aptly appropriate. The Devil's Spire.

"Incompetent... Arrogant... Ignorant... *Lei'faer* trash!" Rhon snarled.

He had been ranting and raving behind her, spouting profanity and curses in a continuous stream of consciousness since the Manticore agent had left. Emaly turned to the table, her attention drawn to the dead stares of three severed heads. A message from Manticore, the eyes of the Amarok, Gigante, and Hobgoblin held a sadness of failure that had been repaid with swift brutality. Manticore's new leader had made a special display to show the consequences of breaking agreements with the Bright Guild.

"I told you not to send them," Emaly said. "Those boys should be on their way to Vargarden. I told you we should be following the prophecy."

"And I told you that you are treading dangerously close to sedition."

"Oh, come off of it, love. I'm not asking you to rebel, I'm asking you to back me up and return to our original plans! A goal you wouldn't fight if you stopped and thought about it for a moment."

"You are asking us to back down!"

"No, I'm asking you to SLOW down!" Emaly huffed. The frustration caused by Rhon's mindlessly brutal agenda had not faded enough to keep the tone from her voice. "Let our original plans take their course before you go stomping about and smashing them!"

"You heard the *Ombrameas*, Emaly! She wants those boys found!"

"And you've spun it into a personal vendetta against Grendel..." Emaly paused. Bringing up Grendel was touchy with Rhon. The crime boss had insinuated his way into the plans of the Mumvurii. His death had caused nothing but confusion as Emaly desperately tried to sort out information she had verified versus hints and rumors from Grendel. In the wake of his death, Rhon had simply vowed that if Grendel was for it, then he must be against it. "Well, against Manticore now."

"They owe me!" Rhon snarled. "If it wasn't for that *Lei'Fien* we would have had everything we needed on the night we took the city!"

"It is still—"

"I will take it out of the hides of each and every member of that cesspool! Starting with Grendel's replacement!"

"Rhon, the more you antagonize Manticore and the New Nobles," Emaly said. "The more they take it out on the innocent people of the Federation."

"There are no innocents in this war."

"We seemed to think they were there at the beginning. When we were just targeting the rich, the powerful, the elite." Emaly thought back to the conversations the three of them had had in bed years ago. "We were supposed to free both our people and theirs. 'Break the yoke of the Federation once and for all!' Do you remember that?"

"War evolves! We knew there would be casualties on both sides. You must get used to it."

"My love, I understand that. When we began this war, the *Sangebula* knew that there would be massive casualties on both sides. But I'm worried that we are going beyond the intention of the battle. That we are no longer weighing the consequences of death."

"I will do whatever is necessary to win!"

"That's what I'm afraid of!"

Rhon growled savagely, the glass in his hand exploding into a shower of sparkling fragments as he clenched his fist. He crossed the room and was nose to nose with Emaly, rage dancing in his eyes. Rhon hadn't ever been an abusive lover, but his bloodline had a history. Before the rise of the *Ombramaes*, his clan had been only male dominant. Non-males or non-warriors were still considered weak in their family. This war had brought his people to the forefront and their influence was being seen in these moments. He was dangerously on edge, and Emaly knew it. He was a fierce warrior, known far and wide as an artist of violence.

"You're too SOFT!" Rhon spat. "You need to stand out of the way and let me do what is needed. If you can't, SHE will! She's the only woman who overcomes your pathetic need to care for others."

"There it is," Emaly breathed, her voice dripping with ice. "This is what I'm talking about, Rhon. You forget yourself. Back down, or I will back you down."

Rhon's eyes tightened and then cleared as he realized what he was about to do. He backed away, shaking his head in shame. "I'm sorry. It's just that I don't understand why you are so attached to these people, Emaly. Would you choose them over ours?"

"It's not only these people I'm concerned about. It's you." She gestured to the landscape beyond the window. "This is not our objective. We are not here to 'win this war.' We came to deliver Highston to Manticore. We've done that.

"Manticore should be focused on finding us the Betrayer's Stone." Emaly put her hand to her face in frustration. "The moment they find it, we are done with them. With all of this. Your obsession with these boys, and the pissing match you have with Manticore, is endangering everything. Our soldiers included."

"Those boys could lead us to disaster."

"Or lead us to our salvation!" Emaly scoffed. "All we know is the 'Thief' is a key. There is no guarantee that holding him is to our benefit."

"Grendel wanted them. They must be important."

"You HATED Grendel! You never trusted him! And now you want to hang the war on him?! His words?!"

"I trust in HER. If SHE believes they're important, they ARE important."

Emaly sighed. "I love her, too. But she's not rational right now."

"There you go again," Rhon said, giving Emaly a withering look. "Sedition."

"It's not sedition to care about her. It's not sedition to question her actions when they endanger herself, us, and the lives of our soldiers."

"She's the *Ombramaes*. The top of the *Sangebula*. She's our leader. We owe her our loyalty, our servitude. And she's your lover and my commander, we owe her our hearts."

Rhon stalked through the room, brushing aside a servant who had begun to collect the larger pieces of glass that lay on the floor from his earlier outburst.

Emaly gave him his moment, allowing the blood rage to settle. She could feel his struggle. The strategist in him battled with the obedient soldier, who waged war with the gentle man who was Emaly's husband. He looked up at her with sadness in his eyes.

"Think about what she is going through, Rhon. She feels the Blood even more than we do. Take all that fear and all the anger that we feel flowing through our people, and imagine what she's feeling."

"She hates the Federation. What they have done to Mumvuri. But more importantly, what they've taken from her personally. That hatred is justified. We must make them pay."

Emaly placed her hand on Rhon's face, stroking away the pain. "That's what I'm trying to tell you, love. She's too invested in this to think clearly." Rhon stiffened under her touch, and Emaly attempted to soothe him. "You both feel the anger of our people and process it differently than I do. I know you want to sate your rage against the Federation, but we've already done that damage. Let these new nobles tear their nation down, brick by brick. We must focus on what's important."

"You've always been too soft, Emaly. I love you, but you aren't built for war."

"Maybe I am not. But I just don't want to see my two greatest loves fall into darkness. The last scouting report confirmed that they escaped through the woods and should be halfway to Vargarden by now. With their city's spectral shields, and those abominations on patrol, pursuing them now would be madness."

"But we must have them!" Rhon shouted. "I almost had them, time and again. I don't understand how they keep escaping my grasp."

"Love, they are beyond us now. I know they are important, but it's time for us to focus on our original goal. The Betrayer's Stone. It has to be here in the Federation. That's the key to eliminating the Wraiths and freeing our people!"

"The prophecy says the Thief is the key."

"It's not a prophecy," Emaly said. "Just like my sisters and I, the Witch would be speaking words from a Divine Chorus. It sees only the possibilities. Right now, my love, there are too many decisions that remain unmade. The Witch may be talented, but she is not infallible. For now, we'll agree that the Stone remains a key."

"And you still think that gambling on the Thief reaching Vargarden is a wise idea?"

"Even Grendel's message was unclear on the Father's role. I'd like to see all the pieces on the board before we make a decision."

"Can you control the Thief? The Son?" Rhon growled. "You seem confident that this plan of yours will work. How can you be so sure?"

"You have your sources, I have mine."

11

A City of Strangers

Argyle stood in front of Jesse, his head cocked to the side in that funny way he often did, and the thief took a long look around the city. The group had walked the inner region for an hour or so, absorbing the sights of the old city. They feared to stray too far from the Palace and miss the announcement of judgment.

The cobblestones below their feet hummed with vibrations of busy feet. Thousands of pedestrians went about their day-to-day lives, unaware of the momentous decision Jesse and his friends awaited, weaving in and out of shops instinctively. They were surrounded by locals who were well acquainted with the rhythm of this city, familiar with the patterns of the street traffic, and passed them with polite smiles or curious glances.

Looming above their heads, a towering clock clicked off another hour and tolled a bell. Every minute seemed to stretch out as Jesse worried about the fate of Symon. No word had been shared from the Palace, and whispers of the arrest were only rarely heard in the streets. The commotion earlier had barely impacted the normal lives of Vargarden and her people. Jesse watched, helplessly, as the city moved on with its day..

His hip stung with pain as Thorn landed a punch and yelled, "Jesse!"

"What?!" he asked, looking down to her, rubbing his hip. "Damn, bitch."

"I called your name three times."

"Sorry. Lost in thought. What did you want?"

"Ugh. I was asking if you remembered last summer. You know before all this chaos happened. Do you remember when you asked me how we got where we were?"

Jesse did remember. The number of changes to their lives in the last nine months was overwhelming. Jesse had known that their simple lives needed to have more, but he would have never asked for this. "Yeah."

"Good, good. So, I was thinking here... Jess, sweetums.... How the fuck did we get here?!" Thorn exploded into a flurry of slaps and punches at Jesse's thigh. Snarls and spittle flew from her mouth as she took out her frustrations on him.

Jesse finally pushed her away. "Damn! What the fuck?"

"I told you, we should have never left the Khorr. It's shit, but it's shit we know."

"Symon needed our help!"

"A fat lot of good that was. 'Oh, hey, hello. Sure, I'll go to the gaol.' What in the Thirteen Hells, Jes?"

Jesse sighed in defeat. There was no arguing that they had gone from one bad situation directly into another. "You're right, Thorn. What do you want me to say?"

"Don't say anything. Let's just go home."

"That may not be the best option—" Argyle started to say.

"And leave Symon?!" Jesse asked incredulously. "You can't be serious!"

"He wanted to come here, let him stay!" Thorn spat.

"Would he leave you?"

"What does that matter?"

"Would... he... leave... you?" Jesse asked, drawing every word out pointedly.

"No, he wouldn't." Thorn admitted.

"So, we can't leave him. We see what the judgement is, and if needed, we figure out how to get him escaped from gaol, and then we go from there."

Argyle began to speak, "Again, that may not be the best—"

"Why? He's not one of us." Thorn rolled on.

"Thorn, I know he's not one of us. That's why we have to do it!" Jesse looked at Thorn, eyes filled with sadness and earnestness. "Think about it. He shouldn't care about us at all. When I took out all our anger about him being rich, he let it slide. When we betrayed him and broke into his house, he forgave us."

Jesse knelt down and looked her directly in the eye. "And, when I nearly died, he healed me. Every time he could have given up on us, he didn't. We owe him!"

Thorn pushed Jesse back and snarled. "We shouldn't owe anybody anything! We should go back out and take care of ourselves, like we always did. What can be given can be taken. Right? If he's holding it over our heads, then fuck him! We only track favors from people with the strength to call them in! We go, leave him in the dust."

"He's not... That's not what I mean... Thorn." Jesse was trying to find the words to explain how he felt. "He's not holding it over us. I am. I NEED to help him."

"He's the reason we're in this mess to begin with! Manticore and the Shadow are after him! Not us!"

"I am unsure that is particularly accurate," Argyle said, his low voice a rumble behind them.

"Shut up, big guy," Thorn said at the same time as Jesse asked, "Go on, Argyle."

Argyle paused for a moment, and then said, "While it is true that Grendel wanted to exploit Master Cylkas, those plans had been laid out for years. It was a coincidence that you formed a bond with young Symon. Grendel decided to take advantage of it. Manticore put you in the eyes of the Shadow."

"So, what?" Thorn said.

"We traveled all this way for a reason," Argyle smiled. "We should at least put forth the effort of devising what it might mean."

Thorn gave Argyle a withering look. "You're not helping, Genbu."

"My apologies. Please continue your argument." Argyle shrugged his massive shoulders. "But you may endeavor to do so without drawing further attention."

Jesse glanced around and saw eyes politely look away. Their little "domestic disturbance" had gathered a small crowd who immediately disbursed when they were noticed. The skeletal guards posted along the walls stood motionless. Unlike Highston, no one was looking to throw them out, they were simply "new and interesting" to the inhabitants of the city.

"All I'm saying is that HE made the choice to come here. He needed it. Not us. Let's just go home and hunker down until this shit blows over."

"You want to hide? Hide!" Jesse yelled. "But, why can't we just hide here?"

"Look around!" the tiny little goblin spun her arms waving at the city surrounding them. "When I heard 'Land of the Dead' I didn't expect that it was like time itself died!"

Jesse's face squinted in confusion. "Huh?"

"I am also curious. What do you mean?" Argyle asked.

"It's like all progress stopped," Thorn continued. "There's only Ukko and Gnomes as far as the eye can see!"

"So?" Jesse asked.

"We are thieves! We make our lives blending into the background. How are we supposed to hide in this? A goblin, an Ishansi, and this hunk of stone. We are supposed to stay unnoticed?! Blend into the background? This background doesn't work for us! At all."

Jesse sighed. While Vargarden sprawled over an immense area and, by Jesse's guess, was actually larger than Highston, it did seem... simpler. Brought to his attention, Jesse did see that Ukko and Gnomes made up the vast majority of the population. While there were a decent amount of humans visible, the other races of Sainan were sparse.

"Well, it's not as mixed as Highston... but neither was Essenbeck. And look, there's a half-orc over there!" Jesse pointed across the plaza to a half-orc man unloading a small cart of lumber.

Thorn reached up and grabbed Jesse's arm, throwing his hand back to his side, her eyes rolling in frustration. "And you could point him right out, because he's the only one! That's my point. We stick out."

Thorn walked the group to the edge of the main square and let them take a moment to gaze across the landscape in detail. After a moment, she said, "And look, do you see there's no Skyfallen tech?"

"And?" he asked.

"And... either everything is backwater developed. Which it clearly isn't. Or they have magic or physical protections in place that we don't know anything about. We'll be starting over from scratch! We know shit about the magic, or laws, or anything here. I mean, Symon got arrested. Symon! What hope do we have?" Thorn's voice was pleading. Jesse could tell for the first time in a great while, she was actually nervous. "Oh, and don't forget... all the FUCKING skeletons! Armed skeletons!"

"Mistress Thorn does make several valid points," Argyle said solemnly.

"See?"

"Her mistake, however, is seeing the only opportunity here in Vargarden being thieves."

"What?!" Thorn and Jesse said together.

Thorn stomped her foot and laughed. "What options do you see, Genbu? You want us to become bakers? Join the church and volunteer at the soup kitchens?"

"No," Argyle said. "But we are refugees. That does afford us some opportunities that would be shameful to discard."

Jesse looked at Argyle, quizzically.

"We could petition the palace. Request an audience with the Father."

"Please?!" Thorn scoffed. "Be serious."

"I am serious," Argyle said, his brow furrowing. "Quite serious." His massive forepaw swept out, mimicking Thorn from earlier. "Look around, as she said, and take it in. The two of you have been squabbling unchecked for some time now. No guards have moved an inch. No 'concerned citizens' have stepped in to admonish you. As the lady said, this is not Highston. This means you are not Street Rats here. Do not limit your expectations to only those which you have experienced."

"So, we just wander into the palace and ask for Symon back?" Jesse asked.

"Not as direct as that, I would assume," Argyle said. "Perhaps we trade information with them. Update them on the status of the Investurant invasion. Offer knowledge of Manticore. Curry favors until we get enough curated to request intervention on Master Cylkas' behalf."

"With the Father?"

"Likely not him. But a representative. Perhaps a member of their ruling class, or a delegate such as one of their Nobles?"

"And it doesn't solve the problem!" Thorn barked. "We don't belong here! Even if we get your boy back, what then? We just shelve our plans because of him? A man who can't EVER know what we do?"

Jesse looked at her flatly. "I know he's a pain in the ass sometimes, but Thorn, he's a good guy. We can figure it out."

"He's too 'good,' Jes! He'll never live our life. Look at the three of us. We're all criminals. Always have been. He's not. He's a liability.

"And, he's made you soft, too!" Thorn continued. "Look at you! We talked about blending in... You're not even hiding your wings anymore!"

Jesse flexed his shoulders and the soft feathers of his wings whisked against his neck. She was right, of course. Xerian would have never allowed him to make such a mistake. Symon made him feel more true to himself. It wasn't the best course of action for a criminal. However, Jesse couldn't just turn his back on the Ennedi.

"He's the reason we got out of Highston. We can teach him how to survive."

"He's got no guile! He can't lie, he isn't subtle, and those big paws of his will never pick pockets."

Jesse countered, "He could be our muscle!"

Thorn stared at Jesse, "If we do it our way, we don't need muscle. We don't get caught."

A low chuckle escaped from Argyle's throat. "Good points, both of you."

Again, Thorn's glare settled on Argyle with disappointment. "Zip it." The gargoyle held his paw up.

"If you are insistent on returning to the criminal life, Miss Thorn," Argyle started, hesitantly, "he could be your legitimate face. His father trained him to operate a successful business in Highston, which is no small feat." Argyle looked at the two thieves with sincerity. "He could start a similar shop wherever we go, and we can use it to start shipping routes, and smuggling operations. With some small effort, you could be the start of a legitimate criminal enterprise."

"Could work," Jesse said. "Where do you want to start? Essenbeck?"

Thorn shook her head. "No, Manticore is running that, and they're racist shits. We'll never get a footing there."

"Ugh," Jesse sneered. "First it's all you can talk about and now it's shit?!"

Thorn shrugged her shoulders and smiled her best devious and toothy grin. "I'm fickle."

Jesse grinned back. "Fine, what about Altazio?"

The goblin turned up her lip in disgust. "Altazio? Pass. Same issues as here, we'd stick out."

The thief ticked off another location in his head. "Okay, how about Esterwich?"

Argyle shook his head at the suggestion. "Those mountains are supposed to contain nomadic gargoyle clans that fled here millennia ago from my homeland. If they take after our ancestors, I would prefer not to return to slavery."

"So, a definite no," Jesse agreed. "No slavery for us."

Thorn's eyes sparked with an idea. "What about Vurgarom or Naryn?"

"River cities?" Jesse asked, surprise laced in his voice.

"Yea," she responded. "Why not? Water means trade and travel. Lots of opportunities for us."

A broad grin split the Genbu's face, "And of course, I would be the muscle."

Thorn spun to Argyle, surprise dancing in her eyes. "What?!"

Jesse smiled slyly and said, "You did say back in Essenbeck that you wanted to run your own Bright Guild." He put his hand on her shoulder. "It could work."

Thorn looked at both of them, looking for a counter argument and finding none. Her shoulders and little pointed green ears wilted in defeat. "Fine, we get the cat. But I still hate this place."

12

Sins of the Sire

Symon had been ushered into a tiny cell and left to wait for the last few hours.
The cramped room was sparse and simply decorated. Only a small table, a
wooden bench, and a tidy cot adorned the chamber. Bare walls muffled the
sounds of conversations of passersby, as two guards stood solemnly flanking the
door. The room did not feel like a prison, but it was certainly a far cry from a
luxurious waiting area for diplomats.

Time stretched out, passing slowly. Uncomfortably.

Symon sat staring at the wall, worrying about Argyle, Jesse, and Thorn. He
was such a fool. He had ignored all the stories, put aside his fears about this dread
realm. He had hoped that perhaps he could convince Vargarden to help the Federation once again. That somehow his father would be remembered positively and
his reputation used as a bargaining chip. Instead, he had walked voluntarily into
the jaws of danger. But worse, he had put his friends on the chopping block with
him.

He had dragged them all this way, hoping to find answers about his father.
Now, all his fears were confirmed. The stories from the War of Night were true.
Vargarden was still holding the War against the Federation. His father was a mon-
ster among monsters. Destruction, terror, and chaos were the only legacy Kyrn

Cyl'Karrick had left here. Now Symon would pay the price for those sins. The fate of his friends was less certain.

He sat for another hour until anxiety overcame him, forcing him to move. Symon paced around the room, small as it was, his tail twitching nervously. The guards watched him closely, but did nothing to interfere. Pacing for nearly ten minutes did nothing to calm his restlessness, and Symon sat back down, trying to calm himself, holding still for another five. This cycle repeated itself two or three times as the wait stretched out, grating his nerves and forcing his mind to run through the same devastating scenarios. Jesse being exiled out of the city and forced to return to Highston. Jessy being thrown into prison with him. The two of them being executed publicly. It was excruciating.

The guards parted, revealing an Ukko dressed in exquisite royal armor. While similarly shaped, the Ukko's breastplate and pauldrons were tinted black and trimmed in gleaming silver. He wore dark green vestments and a rich blue cloak with the hood pulled back. In his hand, he gripped a large halberd that rapped against the floors with authority. While just under four feet tall, he was an intimidating man. His shoulders seemed the same width as his height, and eyes barely visible through the black hair and beard that engulfed his face. The look of a weathered soldier, not a soft city trained guardian.

"You are summoned," the Ukko said simply. His deep voice resonated with command and offered no room for argument.

The Ukko escorted Symon down a long, ominous hallway. The narrow space was barely enough to accommodate Symon and the Ukko side by side, No windows or doors were present in the hall, only stone. This was the hall where someone would have no escape from their fate. A long march towards judgement. The final journey for those who would face their crimes.

"I served with your sire during the war," his escort said. His voice held an edge to it. It was clear that his guard wanted this over, as well. "This day has been long in coming."

They paused at the end of the hall which emptied into a vast main chamber. The entrance was made insignificant by the grandiosity of the features in the rest of the room. At one end, two arched main doors towered over the lushly carpeted walkway. The aisle ran down the center of the room, splitting the chamber evenly and was flanked by rows of benches designed to hold dozens of people. At the end of the carpeted path, a long, sturdy wooden table stood broadside on a raised platform facing the audience, occupied by five stern-looking figures. Before it sat a dais for a speaker to stand on and address the court.

The Ukko nudged Symon into the center of the room and led him towards the dais. A dour-faced Gnome stood atop the dais waiting for Symon to take his place. The five judges watched silently as Symon stepped towards the platform trying to ignore the eerie quiet of the vast courtroom. No beings were set in the benches on either side of the aisle, and only a few guards, a handful of attendants, and a lone clerk, standing next to the dais, were present.

"I had hoped an event like this would have called the Father to attendance," the Ukko soldier muttered under his breath. "Apparently not."

Symon's eyes drifted to an alcove set in the wall above the court table. In the alcove was a large black throne, but it was empty. He did see a smaller chair next to the throne and a shadowed figure shifted in it as the court was called to order. The guard nudged him again, and Symon stepped up onto the stage next to the Gnome.

The tiny man glared up at Symon over the rims of his spectacles. His robes and tight cap spoke of him being an official of some type, and his demeanor hinted at a solemn duty. The Gnome's stare reminded Symon that he was being weighed and measured against a standard he was not familiar with. The Gnome turned to his podium and opened a scroll he had and nodded to the court clerk. The head council at the table looked up to the mysterious being at the side of the throne and received a small nod.

"We call this court to order. Under the watchful eyes of the Crown Prince, in accordance with our duties to the laws and people of Vargarden, and with the authority of the Father himself, we organize this trial to record the charges presented, decisions of this court, and outcomes of such decisions to the ledgers of the Undead Legion." The council member's voice would have been heard clearly in a crowded room, but echoed in the empty space adding to the dread creeping into Symon's mind. "Tratesi Erdo, are you prepared to levy the charges?"

"Yessir," the Gnome said.

"And Symon Cyl'Karrick, you have identified yourself as the rightful Sire-head of the Cyl'Karrick family?"

"Yes... Sir," Symon said.

"Then we shall proceed."

The Gnome flicked his wrist finishing a small spell and his voice was amplified much the same as the Head Councilman's was. He spoke clearly, "Council, the charges presented here today have been maintained by the Undead Legion for seven and forty years. During the war, multiple accounts of Nemuku Kyrn Cyl'Karrick's actions in the theater of war, located within the boundaries of the Khorric Federation, have been documented and recorded.

"The reports were recorded separately and all accounts are in agreement of the events and have been deemed to confirm the actions of Nemuku Cyl'Karrick unquestionably. Since these crimes were committed under the Legion's purview but occurred outside of the boundaries of Vargarden, the charges could not be rendered judgment under a Legion Marshall, but instead must be brought before the High Council and the Father.

"Vargarden laws state that due to the nature of the crimes, that the Cyl'Karrick family must be present to face the accusations. With no representative, the Undead Legion has been provided no opportunity to levy the charges and clear the ledgers of this black mark on our reputation and records."

The members of the High Council stared intently at Symon. He felt the mantle of shame settling over his shoulders. Kyrn had run away without facing his actions. Symon could scarcely believe his father's cowardice.

The Gnome walked up to the clerk's table and unfurled a scroll that was nearly three feet in length. "The complete list of the war crimes and cultural violations committed by Nemuku Cyl'Karrick are listed here in their entirety. The most severe of which was his disregard for the tenants of the Vargarden Priesthood where he ordered the clerics under his command to raise the fallen Federation soldiers and engage them in the Battle of Enfeld.

"The clerics who cast the spells necessary for this event have all been cleared of the crime as their actions were ordered by a superior officer. All charges of these clerics have been formed to this ledger and are ultimately deemed to be the responsibility of Nemuku Cyl'Karrick adding to the need of this trial."

Historical accounts of the Battle of Enfeld flashed in Symon's mind. While the records were sparse, accounts of fallen Federation troops were well documented and had been the fodder of nightmarish tales told for forty years in the Khorric Federation. The Ennedi's ears wilted, and his shoulders slumped as he lowered his head. His father had not only violated the law willingly, but had forced the men and women serving him to violate them as well. The horrors of Enfeld were finally coming home to roost.

"I ask the High Council, under the watchful eyes of the Crown Prince, in accordance of our duties to the laws and people of Vargarden, and with the authority of the Father himself, do you agree that the notary procedures have been satisfied to declare the charges against the Cyl'Karrick family with the rightful witness of their sole representative?"

The council members each reviewed their scrolls in front of them and exchanged glances. "We do," the Head Council said.

"Thank you," the Gnome replied. "And you have reviewed the summary doctrines, identified precedents, and the resultant recommendation of Grand Minister Kufo, Minister of War for the Undead Legion?

"We have," the members of the council replied.

"Excellent." Symon watched the Gnome walk back to the center and step onto the dais next to him. "We've been waiting for this for a very long time," Erdo whispered to Symon. The Ennedi's heart was heavy, holding the guilt of his family and this realm. This would be the moment. This would be the moment the past destroyed the memory of the Cyl'Karrick family once and for all. Tratesi Erdo magically amplified his voice again. "It is with great honor that I ask for the High Council to take the recommendation of the Undead Legion and dismiss all charges."

Symon nearly turned to the Gnome. He couldn't believe it. His mind couldn't process such a sudden change in direction. He had gasped out loud, and the sound had been clear enough to interrupt the court.

"Order," the Head Councillor said. "Order. Tratesi Erdo, we have reviewed your statements and the recommendation of the Undead Legion and accept. The Undead Legion is now free to clear the ledgers of all crimes committed by Nemuku Cyl'Karrick. While against our tenants, all accounts deemed this to be the only available course of action. His violations, while unfortunate, saved hundreds of living Vargarden soldiers, and thousands of Federation civilian lives."

"Thank you, your honors."

"And it is our understanding that with his crimes cleared, that you seek to honor Nemuku Cyl'Karrick with a Crest of Valor within the halls of the Legion?"

"Yes, your honor," Erdo said. "With the crimes on the ledger, we were prevented from nominating him."

The Head Council smiled. "Then I wish you well and hope that your nomination is cleared by the Undead Legion Halls within the year. You have our support and blessing in the vote."

Erdo bowed. "Thank you, Council." He turned to Symon. "Thank you, young man. We have been anxious to clear this matter, it is an ease on all of our hearts to clear your sire's name and give him the honor he has truly deserved."

The Ukko's hand clapped Symon on the back. "Indeed. Your return has everyone relieved. Erdo, it was good to see you."

"Yes, Balkir, you as well."

"And no, I haven't changed my mind. I like the duties of balladry."

"I didn't say anything," the Gnome smiled. "Retirement suits you, but you're still Legion."

"Old bones, old ways."

Erdo walked away, and Balkir smiled up to Symon. "The High Council ordered to take you to the Crown Prince's chambers where he will meet you. You will be under his authority as a royal visitor until your family estate can be prepared for your return."

"The Crown Prince?"

"Yes, Crown Prince Caleb will be eager to meet you. It is our tradition to greet dignitaries with the appropriate respect due to your station."

"What about my friends?" Symon asked.

"We will announce the verdict in the square within the hour," Balkir smiled.

"Once the paperwork has been filed and cleared, we'll gather your companions and they'll join you here in the palace."

"Okay," Symon said. "I guess I shall go to see the Prince."

13

Rushed Royal Entanglements

Jesse hurried after Symon, who pushed their pace a little more than was strictly necessary, as they made their way down a corridor of the palace. Jesse, Argyle, and Thorn had heard the chimes and had rushed to the palace to hear the proclamation of Symon's innocence. Then some large Ukko guard officiously pulled Jesse forward and told him he was wanted inside. Argyle and Thorn had chosen to remain outside, and Jesse had been caught in a whirlwind of activity. Symon's new-found excitement had him bouncing on his feet and was not lost on Jesse, who still had not been told the cause.

"I cannot wait for you to meet him," Symon said. "He seems most capable. I have a feeling we were quite fortunate to have him pick us as an assignment."

"The Crown Prince?" Jesse asked. He smiled at the slight mind-reading that Symon and Jesse had developed over the last year. "Is he that special? I still don't get why a Crown Prince would be assigned to handle a pair of refugees like us." Jesse almost stopped, but he couldn't help muttering, "Regardless of your father."

"What is that supposed to mean?" Symon asked, stopping them in the hall.

"I don't have a problem with him, necessarily," responded Jesse. "But come on! Even you have to be dizzy with all the turns. He's a blacksmith, but he was a general and a necromancer, then he's a criminal, then he's not. Every time you get an answer, it's another question! And he's like a hundred years old."

"No he's not," Symon chuckled a bit at that. "But you are right. However, I do think that is EXACTLY why the Crown Prince has taken an interest in us. I think my family is a curiosity to him."

"So, then maybe we can ask this Prince Caleb," Jesse said dryly. "See what family you still have here. If any."

Jesse had mostly been able to keep the bitterness out of his voice, but there was still a tinge of jealousy he couldn't hide. Symon and Jesse had lost their families. It was a big thing they had in common. If Symon had found family, it would be only a matter of time before Jesse would lose his friend, too. Symon would have everything, Jesse would have nothing. The Ennedi turned to him, and Jesse saw Symon's nostrils flare, taking a deep breath in. Whatever scent Jesse was giving off, Symon was picking it up. Hiding his emotions would be impossible.

"It is not like that, Jesse," Symon said, his eyes softening. "The Prince could just be good for—"

"No, I get it." Jesse said shortly. "It's a big world, you just have to find friends with money and power to help you control it. Same as always, right?"

Jesse knew he was being petty. He didn't want to be. He wasn't even angry at Symon. He was angry with himself, and angry at being angry. The reason they had come to Vargarden was to get answers, and they were right here in front of them, but now Jesse was reacting poorly. His mind told him everything was okay, but his heart was screaming that his life was going to be ruined again. A dark vortex of emotion threatened to open up and swallow him. He hated it. Hated the fear. Hated the anger.

"So, this Prince? What's his deal?" Jesse quipped, that tinge of venom still present.

"To be truthful," Symon said, "I am not quite sure."

"Oh?"

"Yes, his father, the Father, is the emperor. But from what I can see, the Father is the figurehead ruler of Vargarden. The vast majority of daily decisions and rulings come from a Council, not too dissimilar to the Khorric Federation. Also, with the Father being an undead ruler, I am not sure how he bore a child, or if there are any inheritances that would be granted. It is a very intriguing scenario."

"So this guy Caleb," replied Jesse, "is a figurehead guide? And the son of a figurehead leader? With nothing but a figurehead title? Trying to show off for a couple of figurehead visitors?"

"You can be snarky all you want," Symon responded. "At least we are being welcomed, given aid, and our questions answered. As opposed to being lied to, used, attacked, and ran out of our homes."

"Sorry," said Jesse. "I don't know why I'm being so shitty."

"It will be fine," Symon said. His big arm wrapped around Jesse's shoulders, pulling him in. "WE shall be fine. You will see. Focus on the good things. We are here. We are safe. And whatever crimes my father had committed are forgiven. Now we can focus on what is next for us."

Jesse snuggled his head into Symon's shoulder and squeezed him back. "Thank you."

"Besides," continued Symon, "I really want you to meet the Prince. There is just something about him, and I really want to get your opinion."

"What do you mean?"

"He is... different," Symon said. "Somewhat cold and detached. His answers are simply stated, normally not much more than a 'yes' or 'no.' And when he does elaborate, it sounds like he is reading from a history book."

"Alright..." Jesse smirked.

"He is... I am unsure how to say it. He is intelligent. Very intelligent. But he does not have that storyteller quality that Master Zenesul had. It is more of a dry, lecturing manner that makes you feel like you are supposed to already know what he is telling you."

"So why are you excited for me to meet him, then?" Jesse asked wryly. "He sounds like a dick."

"I am drawn to him," Symon admitted. "Even though I do not understand it. Even with those reasons not to be. Something about him feels... right."

The echo of Jesse's envy rang through him like a bell once again. "Oh. Great."

Symon frowned, as he tried to choose the right words to convey his meaning. "I don't know. I felt like I needed to be there with him. Like I belonged there." He paused as they crossed an open courtyard, then continued. "I felt like you always picture it told in heroic stories. The stories about fate and destiny."

Jesse could see the confusion and frustration on Symon's face. They had never really discussed Symon's feelings or attractions. Jesse had always assumed he was attracted to women based on his broken relationship with Lara, but maybe there was more to it.

"I just," the Ennedi said, waving his hand in a rolling motion as if to guide the ideas from his mouth. "I just want your opinion. I want to know if it is just me, or whether there really is something about him." Then as if stating his true concern or expressing an idea that had just occurred to him, he added. "Or whether he was using magic on me."

"Wow, okay," replied Jesse. "So, he's got you twisted. One minute, you are so impressed by this guy, so in awe, that it's all fate and destiny. The next, it might all be spooky evil magic being used against you?!"

"No," Symon grumbled. "It is not like that. It was more like a connection. I just want to see if you feel it, too."

Jesse frowned back at Symon. He was trying hard to tamp down the jealousy he felt at the moment. "Alright," Jesse said, relenting. "No prejudging. You know that I can get along with anyone when the situation calls for it."

They walked the rest of the way in silence as they made the twists and turns through the palace grounds. By this point, they were in a far removed wing of the building. Here the walls were made with a warm, polished stone, interspaced with brass plates holding something like sconces for torches. But instead of a torch, each housed fist-sized amber stones that gave off a gentle Arcane glow. This light would have discolored the polished white marble tiles of the floor, were it not for the glass skylights placed every fifty feet or so. Sunlight gleamed off the walls and floor of the hall causing the dark oak doors down both sides to stand out in sharp contrast.

Jesse wearily eyed every inch of the hallway, looking for the telltale signs of defensive wards, secret exits, and other probable defenses. Symon had memorized the path to the royal apartments, but Jesse was surprised they had been left unescorted. However, there was nowhere for them to go. The dark oak doors were shut tightly, sealing them into the chosen path. Jesse believed that if they caused any trouble, a response would be only moments away.

The final turn of the corridor brought them before a whole new set of doors. Unlike the dark stained oak of the rest, this double set of doors were a warm honey-colored wood. The grand entrance to the Royal chambers of the Prince. The wood was marred, however, in flowing Arcane scripts burned into every inch of every plank making up both of the ten-foot doors.

As they approached, two skeleton warriors stepped out of narrow alcoves to each side of the doors. Jesse cursed under his breath, still not used to the macabre guard that Vargarden was using. But even after only a short time here, three things stood out as unusual to Jesse about these skeletons. First, neither skeleton was adorned with any decorations, ribbons, or clothing aside from their shortswords they carried in scabbards strapped to each femur. Second, unlike other sets of skeletons they had seen, both of these skeletons had control crystals set in their rib cages, rather than just one of the group. And finally, the crystals themselves were a deep blue, rather than the emerald green they had seen on all of the other skeletons so far.

Jesse followed Symon's lead and stopped at the motion of the guards. While the two skeletons did not advance, neither did they assume the stiff pose of attention that the two boys had become cautiously accustomed to. The two felt more 'natural' than other animations they had seen, casually standing by the doors like guardsmen in Highston would. After a mere moment, a young, high voice emanated in the space before them, a familiar ethereal echo permeated its speech.

"Greetings, Symon. You have returned quickly. It is good to have you back in my company."

Jesse noticed a visible relaxation in his friend's shoulders as the Ennedi replied. "Greetings, again, your highness."

Jesse wasn't sure what it meant. The voice unnerved Jesse more than a little. While a pleasant-natured tone, there seemed to be little emotion behind that voice. It also was soft and rather high in pitch, very childlike in sound. It was not what Jesse expected, at odds with the description Symon had given of a man at least their own age.

"Please, gentlemen," continued Caleb's voice. "Join me for refreshments."

As the voice faded, the two guards stepped to the sides as the doors were opened from within.

"Are you sure you've got the right person?" asked Jesse in a whisper. "He seems a lot chattier than the 'yes or no' kind of person you said he was."

If Symon answered, Jesse missed it. He was distracted by the detailing of the main doors themselves. The arcane script was minute and intricate. It was also very delicate work, burned into the wood in such a way to work within the grain of the wood, seemingly never crossing the darker wood grain lines. And though he might be imagining it as his viewing angle changed, the patterns of the script seemed to shift and flow. It was layers of Arcane forms built in breathtaking arrays. Strengthening forms, Protective forms, and dozens of others that Jesse could recognize easily, but would take hours to devise the purpose of their combinations. Jesse looked to Symon to see if he had also noticed, but realized that Symon only had eyes for their host.

The Prince approached them from a set of doors to the right. The entire chamber was built to promote such a grand entrance. The chamber was done primarily in creams and off-white colors, working from the white tiles that had made up the floor of the hallways, to many thick cream-colored rugs. Several lounge sofas formed a circle around a wide, low, circular table in the center of the room.

The table and legs of the sofas were all made in the same soft honey-colored wood of the doors, although thankfully lacking the arcane carvings. Spots of color were splashed across the room in the form of throw pillows and wide runner cloths draping the sofas, as well as cloth mats and napkins laid out around the table. All various shades of blue, ranging from pale, powder blues to bright, primary blues to deep navy blues.

All of this tied together visually to introduce the master of the room.

The Prince had the vibrant blue skin of an Investurant, a dark blue the color of deep ocean, or smoky cobalt. He was perhaps Symon's height, but was all limbs, thin and gangly like a colt. The Crown Prince looked quite at home in this kingdom of death, his fine cut clothing making him appear so skeletally thin that Jesse wanted to joke if he had functioning organs or muscles. Long black hair flowed down his back, straight and shiny, meshing well with the black and brilliant blue robes he wore, a few shades brighter than his skin. Unlike most of the Investurants they had seen in Highston though, the Prince's ears were prominently pointed. Of all the ones they had encountered, only Rhon had had ears so tall.

"I trust the day finds you well?" Prince Caleb asked. "I am happy to help you with whatever you may need, and to provide whatever you may require."

The scene was already discomforting to the senses. Hearing the echo of the Prince's voice coming from the skeletons behind them as well as from the man ahead of them was unbalancing. Memories of Rhon's attack swam through Jesse's mind. His fingers reached instinctively to his belt where his knife would have been, had it not been taken when they entered the palace.

Jesse looked over at Symon and whispered, "Um, is there something you forgot to mention?"

"Hush," reprimanded Symon quietly.

"You hush!" Jesse snapped.

"Don't worry," Prince Caleb said. "I'm not Mumvurii."

"Jesse!" Symon growled. The smith raised his voice to speak to their host. "Good afternoon, your highness. We appreciate you seeing us on such short notice. We hope it has not been too soon?"

"Flowery language much?" muttered Jesse under his breath. If Symon heard him, he gave no sign.

"We are not in court," muttered the Prince, wringing his hands together and not making eye contact. "Call me Caleb."

"Your highness... Caleb," Symon said, stepping forward to address the Prince. "I would like to introduce you to my friend and compatriot, Jesse."

The Prince nodded his head slightly in Jesse's direction, but his attention stayed clearly on the older Ennedi. "I congratulate you, again, sir, on clearing the family name of Cyl'Karrick. Long has the anxiety of the Cyl'Karrick issue been discussed in the halls of the Legion. It must be a satisfaction to have resolved it."

Jesse recognized immediately what Symon had said earlier. Everything that the Prince said had a quality of being recited. The words were right, even if they were overly courtly for Jesse's taste, but the feeling was wrong. It was eerie.

"Does your friend here likewise have such a distinguished family name?" Caleb continued.

"I apologize but he—"

"Olben," interjected Jesse quickly. "My family name is Olben."

For the first time he looked up to really look at his visitors, and Jesse got his first clear look at the young man's eyes. They were a deep, crystalline-looking olive green, much darker than the emerald color typically seen in most green-eyed individuals. They were all the more striking for their uniqueness. The look, no matter how brief, showed a flash of intelligence and power, before flicking away. Jesse couldn't determine if it was a look of shyness or guilt, the Prince's hesitation however was noticeable.

"I see," said the Prince quietly. "Does that name have bearing within the Khorric Federation? Or from the Ishanshi people? I have only known a few Isnashi myself, so I don't recognize it."

Jesse and Symon looked at each other, unsure of how to proceed or answer. However, the Prince seemed to not wait for one. He glanced toward Jesse, again, almost making eye contact, but slid his gaze back to his hands. Caleb turned away and gestured vaguely toward the couches. "Would you care for refreshments?"

Symon ushered Jesse to one of the couches and sat beside him. The Prince took the couch on the end nearest to Symon, folding his lanky frame into a position that seemed like it would be uncomfortable, but phased him not at all. His attention seemed to stay on Symon, no matter how distracted that attention was.

Jesse took the opportunity to slip his vision into the Arcane spectrum, searching for any tendrils of magical influence over himself or his companion. The room had a number of energy sources his sticky fingers wanted to explore, but there was nothing that seemed to be providing the type of influence Symon had expressed concern over. Jesse couldn't deny that Caleb did have an unexplainable familiarity and allure.

"We appreciate the level of hospitality we have been shown thus far, your high... I mean, Caleb," said Symon.

"Yes, of course," Caleb said, as he toyed distractedly with the hem of the throw pillow under his arm.

"You have an awe inspiring home here. Are all of these your quarters, alone?"

"Yes."

Jesse was starting to see what Symon had meant. Getting any kind of conversation going was hard when it was so one sided. The silence between the visitors reached an awkward point, and Jesse finally asked, "So, what's our choices?"

As Jesse looked around the room, trying to find a topic of conversation, a tall, thin, four armed skeleton approached carrying a pair of trays. One held three goblets and a pair of pitchers, the other a collection of small bowls and saucers. The skeletal servant offered a selection of food and drinks, with a living grace similar to the guards. Jesse's brow furrowed as his Arcane sight was unable to discern a connection between the crown Prince and the skeleton's control gems. It was curious, and he vowed to find an opportunity to ask about it.

As Caleb inventoried the snack trays, Jesse came to realize the magic functioned as an extension of their host. For as Caleb would mention an item, the control gem would flare slightly and the skeleton would gesture to the appropriate dish. There was no delay between the automaton hearing the spoken name and it lifting the dish. It was not awaiting command words, nor gestures given by Caleb, it simply reacted. It was unnerving, and yet fascinating to realize the level of control being so casually presented.

"Is it hard controlling your skeletons like this?"

"No," Caleb said. "The difficulty was in crafting the control gems in the required ways, as to promote the required connections. Once established, control is quite intuitive." Without warning Prince Caleb unfolded his legs and tossed his plate on the arm of the couch. The undead servant caught the small plate unasked before it could fall to the floor. Keeping his goblet in hand, their host walked a few feet away to a tall bookcase.

As he browsed the titles, Symon and Jesse looked at one another in confusion. Symon then spoke in a stronger voice. "We appreciate the audience with you, Caleb. It is nice to make an acquaintance such as yourself in this strange land."

"Of course," Caleb said. "The differences between Vargarden and the Khorric Federation are quite numerous."

"Well, we thank you for your time and help."

"I am capable of providing any assistance requested, my new friends. What can I do for you this afternoon?"

"Well," began Symon, "we were wondering about my family here. As you pointed out, my father's name is apparently well known here. So I wanted to see what bits of information I might be able to find."

"What information could you need?," replied the Prince.

"Any would be appreciated," Symon said. "I know nothing but the lies he told in the Federation. His history here in Vargarden is a mystery to me."

"What information could I have that you do not already have access to?"

"That is it, your highness. I have nothing. I do not even know where to begin."

"I'm confused," Caleb said, his attention still on the books, his back to them. "Did you not say you were claiming your family legacy?"

"I am, yes," said Symon. "Was that not the matter cleared up today in the courts?"

"Not the crimes," said Caleb, turning back to face them. "I meant, are you not here to claim your family lands and house?"

There was a pregnant pause, a lengthened silence, before Jesse blurted out, "The fuck?!"

14

An Unfamiliar Familiarity

Symon tried to split attention between seeing the city, listening to Jesse, and trying to pay proper attention to Prince Caleb on the journey. Marching across the city surrounded by a troop of skeletons that the Prince had called a "Welengam", they were destined for the ancestral home of the Cyl'Karrick family. Jesse and Symon had tried making conversation with Caleb as they walked across the city, but had little luck. The Prince's nobility separated him from the group, but not in the arrogant way that Olivar had held himself. It was more of a lack of understanding of what to talk about. They awkwardly discussed the weather, and Caleb tried to point out interesting features found in the city, but the conversation was clipped and sparse. Sometimes even strained.

The procession was drawing looks from everyone as they passed, but it was no more than innocent curiosity. Argyle and Thorn had joined them, and the uncommon sight of their forms appeared to draw more attention than the undead escort. Symon could scarcely believe how at ease the commoners were around the skeletal guard. All combined, it brought a discomfort to the trip, but none of them knew how to address it.

Caleb slowly walked them down the stone path toward Kyrn's manor. It was not the sight that Symon expected to see. Rather than a rundown home, left dormant for nearly four decades, the grounds were vibrant and well kept. The estate itself was eerily familiar. It appeared that Kyrn had built their home in Highston with this home in mind. The walls, the yard, were all laid out simply and stately. The major difference that Symon could see was the addition of a mausoleum off to the east of the main house.

"It looks... well cared for," Symon said.

"Yes," the Prince replied.

"More so than I expected."

"No more than routine maintenance."

"So, this is expected?" Symon asked. He glanced at Jesse and saw the recognition he was looking for. In Highston, the home would have been reclaimed by either the city or vagrants within weeks of being abandoned.

"Oh, yes," Prince Caleb said, finally recognizing Symon's confusion. "Your family home has been looked after for the last few decades by the Yurolinto family. Strykecaptain Yurolinto served your father in the war, and they were friends. He and his kin have looked after it for this time."

"This is normal?" Jesse asked. "How much does Symon owe them?"

"Nothing."

"Nothing?" Symon asked.

"Of course not," Caleb said. "The deeds are quite specific."

"What if my family had never come back?"

"There are inheritance deeds," the Prince calmly explained. "The Yurolinto family were instructed to care for the house. If a proper claimant to the Cyl'Karrick line did not return, the Yurolinto's could choose to inherit the house or release the property to another family. Traditionally we allow for two generations of caretakers to expire before executing property transfer clauses within the Will of the dead."

Jesse and Symon exchanged a look of awe. The formality, longevity, and integrity of this culture were a stark contrast to the fast paced lifestyle of the Khorric Federation. They planned generations ahead rather than years. The people of Vargarden lived at a much slower pace and on their own time.

One of the priests, referred to as "Deacons" here, that escorted them waved a hand, and sent a skeleton ahead to knock on the door. The door swung open, revealing a small foyer beyond and a young lady standing in the center of the entryway waiting for the group. "Welcome home, m'Lord," she said.

The convoy separated, a dozen skeletal warriors flanking the pathway, leaving Prince Caleb, two priests, Symon, and his friends standing on their own in front of the estate. "Don't let it get to your head or anything!" Jesse whispered with a snicker. Symon elbowed Jesse, but swallowed hard at the over-formality they were being subjected to.

"Osi," the priest who had commanded the skeleton said.

"I can take 'em from here, Malden."

"Yes, Osi," the priest saluted.

Prince Caleb nodded, and simply said, "I shall leave you to it."

The Prince turned on his heel and strode down the pathway, the priests and Welgeid following in his wake. Symon stared agog as he tried in vain to wrap his mind around the details of the situation. "Uh... Thank you," he muttered.

"Do 'ya wanna come in?" the lady asked. "I c'n show 'ya 'round."

Symon turned to the door, his senses alive, taking in the sight of his home and the woman in charge of handling the exchange. Looking her over, he saw she was quite striking. Athletically built, slightly taller than Jesse, she wore a green silk dress with floral brocade anchored by dark black hair and black boots with tall heels. Dozens of bangles, made of several precious metals and stones, adorned her wrists and arms, highlighting the pale, slightly nutty brown color of her skin as well as the defined muscles. She was a mysterious blend of femininity and power that Symon had not often seen in his social circles.

A glance to Jesse revealed that his friend was hesitant, too. The winged Isnashi looked back and forth between the estate and the royal procession as it left. "Jesse, can you join me? I do not think I can do this alone."

"Yeah," Jesse said, patting Symon's arm and looking up at him. "I got your back."

"It appears the architecture is not sufficient to support my bulk," Argyle said, examining the front door. "Being too big, I shall walk the grounds."

Jesse nodded. "Good call."

Symon smiled and turned his eyes to their goblin companion. "Thorn?"

"Oh, like I'm missing this?!" she said. "You can bury your nose in Orlam's taint if you think you can keep me out!"

"Well, then," Symon said. He directed his gaze to the woman in green. "I thank you for your attention. We would appreciate a moment to adjust to everything."

"Aye," she said. "Take 'ya time." Her voice had a small lilt to it. A familiar cadence his ears recognized, but his mind could not place. He knew he should be able to, but the whole experience was a confusing mash up of new and old sensations.

Symon, Jesse, and Thorn entered the foyer, and their eyes scanned the room quickly. To the right was the dining room which would turn to the kitchen. On the left, the small hallway would lead them to the offices, bedrooms, and other such chambers. The highlight, however, was the wall behind the woman and the carved plaque that hung on it.

"Wow," Jesse said. "This place is really just like your old home."

"Sorry?" Symon asked, glancing at him

Jesse gave him a wry smile. "At least we won't have to figure out where things are."

The blacksmith sighed and nudged his friend with an elbow. Jesse and Thorn had been tasked with breaking into Symon and his father's home in Highston to collect information. Consummate professionals, the two thieves likely knew the layout as well as Symon himself did. It was a rough spot in their friendship that they could laugh at now, but it had not always been so. Symon smirked, his tiny fang peeking out, "I keep forgetting that you were paid to break into our place."

"Like Hells you do!"

"Job's a job," Thorn said. "Move on."

"Yes, Thorn." Symon said smiling. He examined the carving carefully. Where the Highston plaque had been simple, just a few leaves and acorns of Kyrn, Aida, Symon, and Taryk, there was so much more displayed on the one here in Vargarden. Dozens of names stretched out over all of the branches. Each engraved on leaves, dark or vibrant, the tree stretched the length of the wall and top to bottom. It was breathtaking. Symon's fingers reached towards it.

"Careful, now," the woman said. "The new work is still settin'."

"What is it?" Jesse asked.

"It is a heritage tree," she said. Symon and Jesse turned to her.

"Yes, it is," Symon said, turning to her. Closer up, Symon could see that while she was mostly human, the black in her hair was a dye, covering a wave of bright green hair, which likely spoke of a Nymph blooded heritage. She smelled like fresh moss, sandalwood, and leather. "I am sorry," Symon said, voice dry. "Our manners are horrible. Forgive us for not introducing ourselves."

"No need," she said. "I know who 'ya are. C'n no deny 'ya sire's legacy."

Like lightning, the voice connected with Symon's past. The tilt and accent of the man his father had met in the shop before the invasion. She had the same slightly hawkish nose that her father did.

"You must be related to Rakar," he said, absent of decorum.

"Aye. I am his daughter, Moria."

"Apologies, again, my lady, that was rude." Symon smiled. "Thank you for taking care of my family home. It is lovely."

"Of course," Moria said. "My sire and yours were very close. T'was our pleasure."

"So, the heritage tree," Jesse interrupted. "What can you tell us?"

"Symon, 'tis your tree," Moria began.

"I am sorry," Symon looked down. "My father never told me about our family. I would not know where to begin."

"Oh," she said. "Well, then I'll try." She gracefully went to the plaque and pointed her finger at Symon's leaf. "The root here is the current leader of the family. My sire sent for the mason as soon as he returned from seeing yours. 'Tis still new work, but should be finishin' soon.

"From here..." Moria continued, raising her finger to the slate of Kyrn's leaf and the coppery brass of Aida's. "And then from here you c'n connect to the rest of the family. The acorns here are the descendants of that line. Your brother Taryk is here, under your sire and mother."

Symon stared at the names he knew. Taryk, Aida, Kyrn, and himself. They were the only part of the tree that was familiar. He smiled as he examined it. The little cluster was flawless, without the little chip by Taryk's name as the one in Highston had had.

Her hand slid up the tree to the branches above. "Here you c'n follow the names of the family b'fore. Aunts, uncles, grandparents, and everyone. Each of these leaves are someone in 'ya family. And if you look closely, you can see little acorns nestled in these clusters. Those are cousins and such."

"And what do the colors mean?," Thorn asked.

Moria smiled, "A'ya, sure. The bare stone leaves are those who are here in life. Those who have passed on... They are the brightly colored ones. Deeper 'ya go into the tree, the brighter it is! It's a celebration of the past.

"Your tree goes back," she paused counting. "Three generations. 'Course, it'd be larger, but your sire was an only child and his long life made it a bit shallow."

"Shallow, right..." Symon murmured. He stared in wonder at the upper branches. Moria was apologizing for a smaller tree, but Symon could barely take in the fact he had family, let alone the size of it. Names stretched back, with little dates carved in line. Those dates were something new as well, different from the Highston version. The date, '437 ST' was carved under his father's name. He tapped it, "What does this date mean?"

"Tha' year 'ya sire was born," she said simply.

"Shit!" Jesse exclaimed. "That means your father is over two-hundred and fifty years old!"

"Told you so!" Thorn exclaimed. "Thrice damned necromancers!"

"Yes, Nemuku Cyl'Karric was quite adept at Healing. He had learned much about extendin' his life and had quite the career."

Symon and Jesse turned to Moria astonished.

"Not anything like tha Father," she continued. "Tha's different magic altogether. But impressive n'n'tha'less."

A solemn silence sat between them. Symon simply did not have words to express his thoughts. "So, all this is Symon's family?" Thorn said, thankfully filling the void. "All back over three or four hundred years?"

"Aye," Moria agreed. "Look, right here, this is the leaf of Maiya Kal'Khorric.

She'd have been the first of your Ennedi bloodline here in Vargarden in 316 ST."

Jesse, Symon, and Thorn stopped, slack-jawed. "Kal'Khorric?" they all asked at the same time.

"Ayup, my sire told me about her," Moria said. "When Elanna Khorric came to Father back 'round then, she asked that one of her cousins be given a place in a good family here. Something about settlin' the noble bloodline. Maiya Kal'Khorric was that cousin."

"So, Symon is blood-related to the Empress Elanna Khorric?" Jesse asked.

"Yep," Moria nodded.

"Un-fucking-believable!" Thorn muttered.

"I can show you the tomes," Moria said. "Let 'ya learn about your family."

"That would be great," Symon said. "I have a lot to learn."

As Moria turned to escort them, Thorn tapped the leaf with Aida's name. Just like Highston, it had a skull shape. "Why are some of them shaped this way?" she asked.

"Those are family whose bones are lost," Moria said, tone heavy. "When a family member dies and their bodies cannot be claimed for the crypt, they're marked like this."

"Do you know what happened to my mother and brother?" Symon asked.

"No. Other than their passin', I don't. My sire and I hadn't known you even existed, sorry. He sent home orders from Highston and asked for this all to be carved, but I hadn't the chance to speak with him."

It appeared that Kyrn had left a lot of secrets in his wake. This was just one more. Symon stepped back from the heritage tree. So much of his past was now here in front of him. He needed to breathe and let it all soak in. "We shall have to request one for my father," Symon said quietly. "He died as we escaped Highston."

"Oh," Moria said. "Sorry. Didn't know. I'll see it done."

"Can you show us the rest of the house, please?" Symon asked.

"O'course. Come on," Moria said. "Lots to see."

The group made their way through the manor. Again, it was very much laid out like the Highston house. Small dining area, small sitting area, a modest kitchen, it was all accommodated for. But it wasn't all the same. As they approached the back, the manor changed significantly from Symon's humble house in Highston. The bedchamber hall was large enough to be considered a "wing." Two stories, the halls ran long and there were half a dozen or more more bedrooms, and a small study where his father's office would have been.

When Symon believed they had discovered everything, instead they found the biggest addition to the manor. A library.

Shelved from wall to wall, a desk in the center facing away from a hearth and fireplace, the entire space was filled with tomes and manuscripts. Books and scrolls filled each shelf. Symon could see topics from many disciplines. War, magic, and history, there were books everywhere. As Moria had hinted, there was even an entire section devoted to Symon's family history.

"Zenesul would love this place," Jesse whispered.

"It is incredible," Symon said. "Absolutely incredible."

"Whelp," Moria called out from the doorway, "if y're good, I'm gonna pack up m'things and go back to my parents' house."

"Pack up?" Symon asked. "Have you been staying here?"

"Aye, moved in shortly after receivin' my commission in the Legion. T'was easiest."

Symon was suddenly struck by the realization that he was forcing a woman out of a home she had grown to care for. A house she had called home. Guilt wracked him as he looked to his friends for guidance. Jesse and Thorn seemed oblivious to the implications and were wandering the tomes.

"Please, my lady," he said. "Do not go. I would not care to be responsible for such an inconvenience. You may stay here. Perhaps you could teach me more about Vargarden, until we can decide what to do with the estate."

"No. 'Tis your house," Moria said. "I knew t'was always possibly a short stay. 'Sides, we wouldn't want anyone to talk. Two unmarried folk, of an age, stayin' together all alone."

"We would not be alone," Symon said. "Argyle, Jesse and Thorn will be staying here as well."

"We are?" they asked.

"Of course, you are," Symon stated. "We will have plenty of room and days ahead of us."

Moria looked at the group. Symon watched her weigh the options. "Okay, I'll stay for a few days. Just 'til you get your feet under 'ya. Plus, it'll make my assignment easier."

"Assignment?"

"Aye," she smiled. "Received orders this morning. Y'all are under the survey of my squad. We're to be your escorts while 'ya are under Royal Review."

Jesse, Thorn, and Symon exchanged glances. That had certainly caught their attention. "Oh..." Jesse said. "Great."

15

The Ombramaes

>*Feed. Strengthen.*<

The woman known as the *Ombramaes* wandered the streets of Invuri, the capital city of the Mumvurii people, soaking in the fear, anguish, and rage of her people. The flood of power numbed her to the pain her body constantly felt. Eased the strain of existing in two planes of existence at all times. Drowned out the voices that existed in her mind driving her every step. She opened her essence and embraced her role as leader, immersing herself in the responsibility she had to the Investurants, the Sangebula, and the common folk of Mumvuri. She lost her sense of self as she took on the mantle of the Master of Shadows, the *Ombramaes.*

Eons ago, the Mumvurii and a powerful necromancer had come together and breached the barrier between the material plane and the realm of shadows. The Goddess Amarant, called by this event, formed an everlasting channel to her divinity for both the Mumvuri and Sainan realms. A channel that was meant to solidify the bond between the realms and solidify the pact of peace and prosperity.

To protect this channel, Amarant bestowed her gifts upon an Avatar, a beacon to guide this power through the world. In the material realm, the necromancer became a single body of power, an eternal being with the power of a God.

The Mumvurii distributed this power among their leaders, becoming the *Sangebula,* the blood of power. Each family kept their bloodline strong, and bred carefully to maintain those powers and blessings provided by the *Sangebula.* Together, they guided each and every step of the Mumvurii with an eye on greatness and prosperity. At the top sat a divine vessel, chosen of the blood, the Master of Shadows.

Her family, even with the latest corruption, still had the strongest bloodline, purest to the original lineage. As long as there was a female heir, the title and gift would pass to her. It was a heritage she wore with pride. The *Ombramaes* believed that this leadership and blood rule bestowed by her people at Amarant's blessing meant that they had been favored with more wisdom and insight.

>*Free us. Avenge us.*<

The Mumvurii had chosen her. The Blood had chosen her. She represented them. She was their Goddess, made flesh. And she would prove their superiority over the realm of Sainan and her people. Particularly those of the Khorric Federation.

They had been granted only a glimpse of what the power of Amarant was capable of and they had corrupted it. The first campaign had shown them what the power of the Blood could do. The *Sangebula* proposed a truce. The Mumvurii and the people of Sainan could reclaim their agreement. The pact could be maintained, if the Federation promised to quell their vanity, to cease their abominable deeds. A bargain had been struck. The Khorric people had lied again.

She promised the Sangebula that the new campaign would be more effective. More brutal. She would hold no mercy for those who had betrayed them. Her eyes had been set on Highston since the beginning. Knowing that this was the heart of their betrayal.

She would find the Betrayer's Stone and return it to Mumvuri where it could be destroyed. She could strike at the heart of the Federation and end this relentless suffering that they caused. And then, she would turn the Investurants loose. They would exert their rage across the Federation and destroy it. Take it down brick by brick and expose those in power for the selfish mongers that they were. The *Ombrameas* would have her vengeance.

>Destroy them. Make them suffer.<

She hated this accursed land. Even her allies were useless. Grendel, serving as her advisor, had begged that she seek the Witch in the Woods. The Crime Boss had insisted that a renowned oracle would be able to discern the location of the Stone. Instead, the Ombramaes had received only cryptic answers. The Son would destroy the bond, if the Son wasn't destroyed before. The Son was the key to many things. Absolutely useless.

The *Sangebula* didn't believe so.

The so-called prophecy aligned with one Grendel had received. The Father, the Thief, and the Son were the keys to destroying the existing Federation. Grendel would rise to the top of a new regime, and would end the suffering of the Mumvurii people.

Allied, they had set on Highston, focusing their search there. Grendel had even located the Thief, using him as a tool of his own devices. She didn't care. The Thief was for Grendel and the Federation. She had ordered his death as easy as she had put on her boots in the morning. She grew impatient with Grendel and Manticore's machinations. Her rage grew and grew by the day. All she needed was the Stone.

She ordered the attack on Highston. Determined to find the Stone in the halls of the Elysium, she waged an assault on the Nobles, the Magi, and anyone else who might have the secrets. If the curse of Sainan hadn't disrupted her plans that night, they would already be home and investigating the Son. But Grendel had interfered. The Thief had lived. And then... Kyrn Cyl'Karrick.

>Cheater! Stealer! Hypocrite!<

Through all the damned realms, she hated no one more than she hated him. He had stolen her birthright. All the work the Investurants had done in the first campaign, he had ruined. It was under his agreement that the Khorric Federation be allowed to walk away. The treaty they broke. It was his fault. Without his intervention, none of this would have happened.

Now, Grendel and Kyrn were dead, but their legacies continued to pester her. The Thief and the Son of Kyrn had fled to Vargarden. The prophecies were in play. She understood none of it and it angered her. Rage filled her and the voices in her head continued to swirl. The pain threatened to unravel her once again.

She continued her walk of the city. Every street that she turned down, her subjects turned and offered their supplication. Heads bowed, hands outstretched with their palms up, they whispered her name. *Ombramaes.*

The power of Amarant filled her, and she disappeared again into the adulation. It overtook the agony, overcame the fear, swallowed the rage, and allowed her to once again hope. Hope that the war would end, and that she would see the liberation of her people from the nightmare of the Wraiths. She would also free the innocent people of the Khorric lands, what few there were, from the slavery that their masters yoked them with, even though they couldn't see it themselves.

"*Your highness?*" a meek voice called behind her.

She turned, her gaze fierce and power dancing in her eyes. A messenger dropped to her knees and held a missive in her outstretched hands.

"*Rise,*" the Ombramaes commanded.

"*Ombramaes, General Rhon has found a window of opportunity in the defenses surrounding Vargarden. He awaits your approval to move against the Prince as we speak. He says the Son is within our grasp.*"

At the sound of Rhon's name, she came back to reality. He and Emaly were nearly the only remaining links to her true self. The woman under the crown of *Ombramaes.* She took in the words and did the calculations. Rhon was bold, but it could work. If they could get in, find the Son themselves, they could make an attempt to tip the scales...

"*Yes!*" the Ombramaes said. "*Good news at last. How many troops does he request?*"

"*None, your highness. He's planning a solo mission. An assassination.*"

The Ombramaes smiled. It would be like Rhon to take matters into his own hands. Rhon didn't intend to tip the scales. He intended to upend the entire table. She knew why Emaly loved him so. He was the most confident man she had ever worked with. This would be a great stride forward in the war.

>*Break him. Tear it all down.*<

"*Approved,*" she said.

16

Daughters and Sons

Jesse and Thorn sat watching Symon as he stretched out, working through his sword forms. They had been in Vargarden for just under a week and Jesse was still trying to wrap his head around the changes. Symon, for his part, had seemed numb as well. They had decided to take a morning and "go back to routines," sparring like they had at Zenesul's house so many times before.

After a rigorous morning, Jesse was decidedly taking a break, while the big Ennedi chose to keep pushing on. Thorn was nibbling on some jerky and Argyle was lounging in the corner taking in the shade. They could have been back in Highston.

It was later in the afternoon, and though the air was crisp, Symon had stripped down to his shirt and was running through a particularly challenging kata. He moved with a grace that Jesse still smiled at. Big and powerful, but elegant. Jesse still admired his physique with a sense of something akin to longing.

The Ennedi paused in mid form, his ears locked backwards and his nostrils flaring.

"Mind if I join?" Moria asked from the doorway that led from the house to the courtyard. Symon was arrested mid action as all eyes, including him and his watchers, snapped to her.

Gone was the delicate dress and bangles that they had come to know her by. Instead, she was dressed in leathers, layered in blacks and browns. Her cloak was intentionally ragged and would serve to blur her silhouette in the wilderness. Her hair was tied back in a severe tail and her eyes were darkened with coal as well as her lips painted black. She carried herself with a professional air and an edge of danger.

"Well, I'll say it," Thorn said as the moment stretched to an uncomfortable silence "Damn the Gods, girl, you scary!"

Moria smiled at Thorn, her white teeth flashing behind those black lips. "Thank 'ya."

"Anytime."

"Of course, you can join," Symon said, stepping forward and clearing his throat. "We would be honored to train with a Palace Guard."

"Nay," Moria said. "Tha' guard is all retired Legion, Priests, or Welgeid. I'm still active."

Thorn whistled. "Fierce."

"Aye, trained under my sire. I got my commission nearly a decade ago and since then have gotten my own squad. Same unit that my sire served in."

"So you are a scout?" Symon asked. "I believe that is what I heard my father say to yours. Why would you be assigned to us if you are not in the Palace Guard?"

"My unit is special. We're scouts, interrogators, assassins... whatever else is required," she said, her voice deadly serious. "We identify and 'liminate threats." Jesse felt a chill run up his arms. He held no doubt she could take on anyone if needed.

She smiled again, and her voice regained that bright lilt it normally had. "So, 'ya look to be 'versed in the old forms? Tha's good."

"Yes, my father provided me with some instruction, and then the Federation provided swordsmanship classes that I attended."

"And is it usual for 'ya to do your trainin' without armor?" She looked at Thorn. "She's the only one of 'ya that seems to be wearing her gear."

Jesse pulled his shirt back to reveal his leathers underneath.

"Devious," Moria said, smiling. "You'd fit well in my unit."

"Oh, I'm not military material." Jesse snickered.

"Yeah, I s'pose not." Moria turned to Symon. "So it's only you who chooses to train this way?"

"I am not sure that it is a choice," Symon said sheepishly. "This is what I have always done."

"So 'ya never train in your armor? How do 'ya adjust your training to battle?"

"There is nothing to adjust. I do not have armor."

"What?!" Moria asked. Her voice was filled with shock. "You've been runnin' from Vesters this entire time, fightin' out of Highston, and 'ya got no armor?"

"No."

She turned to Jesse and Thorn. "And y'all knew about this?"

Jesse put his hands up in surrender. "We just ran after him. Not on us."

Moria shook her head in disbelief. "Unbelievable. No wonder the Feds need our help. Sendin' troops out half-trained and ill-equipped."

"Well, now," Symon said. "I am not a Federation troop. I was training to be a smith like my father. I never joined the Federation military or Academy formally."

"Well, I still w'ld expect 'ya to have some protection."

"I did not intend to fight. It all happened very fast."

Moria smiled at Symon, and Jesse watched his posture relax a tad. She said, "Well, we'll address that. Ya' fancy coat won't protect you forever."

"Indeed," Symon said. Jesse could see the pink tint in Symon's ears. He was embarrassed. Jesse could understand. Running around like a hero of the folk tales and expecting that he would be protected by good fortune. That's not how the world worked.

"I'm sorry," Moria said. "Forgive me. Ya' didn't get raised in the life like I did. Shouldn't be hard on ya'."

Symon smiled. "No, you are correct. I should be thinking of these things. I appreciate it."

"Well, we'll work on it," she said. "But for now, let's see what ya've learned." Moria walked down the rack of weapons, brushing her fingers over the handles. She came to the training version of a bladed staff. She picked it up, gave it a spin, and nodded. "This will do."

Thorn leaned to Jesse. "Even odds, he's on his ass in three."

Jesse took a moment to evaluate Moria. She had broad shoulders and a deep "v" shape that flared to an hourglass at her hips. She carried herself with a casual grace that spoke to extensive training. Jesse had an instinct for fighters to avoid, and Moria was setting it off. "I ain't taking that," Jesse said. "She could destroy us all, I bet."

Symon walked to the center of the courtyard and took his classic stance. His size and tight frame had proven itself as a great defense, so he settled in as he always did. Jesse waited to see how she would approach.

Moria spun the staff from one hand to the other as she walked into the make-shift ring. "Ya' ready?"

Symon nodded. And then Moria exploded into action. She planted the butt of the staff into the dirt propelling her into a flying kick. Symon absorbed the kick in the shoulder, and as she landed her staff swished back and forth, pulling his blade up high. She then dropped to her knee, delivering a sweeping kick that took his feet out from under him. She sprung back up, and rested the blade of the staff at his neck.

"Yield," she said down to him.

Thorn rolled over in laughter. "Gods be damned, I told you!"

Jesse was trying not to laugh, knowing that Symon would be flustered. But the irony of this being so similar to their first spar was not lost on Jesse. Symon underestimated his opponent. Then he paid the price.

Symon looked up at Moria, his eyes filled with awe. "You are amazing," the young Ennedi whispered.

"I took advantage," she said smiling. "You're not set up for someone like me." She reached down and pulled Symon to his feet. "Old bones, old ways."

"That is something my father said."

"It's an old Legion sayin'. My sire says it all the time, too." She looked over at Thorn and Jesse. "Anyone else wanna go?"

"Hells no," Jesse laughed. "I'll watch the rematch though!"

"So, what's next?" Symon asked.

"Well, let's get an actual spar in. See what 'ya got when I don't just jump 'ya. Then, we'll talk 'bout expanding your skills. If 'ya are anythin' like the stories 'bout 'ya sire... 'Ya could be quite the fighter when we're done."

"Sure," Symon said, hesitantly.

"Then, I'd like to have 'ya come to dinner tonight with my family."

"Dinner?"

"Aye, my sire has returned, and he's anxious to meet 'ya." Moria smiled at Thorn, Argyle, and Jesse. "All of y'all."

"Oh," Symon stammered.

Jesse watched him carefully. There was something more than just nerves there. Jesse still couldn't pin down his friend's intentions. His reaction to both Caleb and Moria had confused him further. Eventually, Jesse would have to figure it out.

Symon finally said, "Yes. That sounds delightful."

Symon was disturbed from his focus by a knock at the door. Dinner with Rakar, Moria, and the rest of the family had made Symon even more anxious to dig into his own family's past. He had been studying his father's books since he had returned from their home. This library was an extensive look into who the man, Kyrn, had been.

"Come in," Symon called out. Tentatively, the door opened, and Rakar peeked inside the study. The lanky man was cloaked in dark attire, leathers and a travel cloak. He slipped around the door, just barely opening it, and closed it quickly behind him. This was a man who was used to being unseen and kept to the shadows.

"Good 'eve, M'Lord," Rakar said. "I give you blessings for this night." The man stood motionless, slightly bowed head, waiting for Symon to reply in tradition.

The silence stretched out uncomfortably until Symon huffed. His shoulders tensed and a small growl escaped his throat. This was yet another example of how lost Symon felt in this city. He had been given a home and access to information, but no direction. There were no set expectations for him. Nothing to tell him what to do. His entire life, Symon had been guided by hands prodding him to his potential. Here, he was on his own. He took a deep breath, relaxed, and took the situation head on.

"Rakar," Symon said. "My apologies, I am still learning customs here."

"No 'pologies needed, M'Lord." Rakar raised his head and shifted uncomfortably. "In fact, 'tis why I came to see 'ya."

Rakar was looking at Symon with a sense of loss. It was clear that there was more about his intentions this night than a simple call.

"Please, sit," Symon waved to a chair. He pulled out a pair of glasses and a bottle of brandy.

Not moving, Rakar just stared at Symon. "'Tis something, young sir. Ya' remind me so much o' him."

Symon faltered. His emotions were torn, and that sensation threatened to break him. He spent most of his time looking at his father's things and trying to keep a distance between the memory of the man in these halls, and the father that he had known and loved in Highston. But it was just a crutch to escape thinking of the loss he truly felt. Symon had lost his father twice. Once, when the truth of him had been revealed. And once again, when his life was taken by the *Ombramaes*. To have someone connect the past and present was too difficult for him to handle.

His fingers reached unconsciously to his father's sword that laid against the desk next to him. The strange vibration comforted him. He still did not know why. The sword awakened beneath his fingertips and that voice resonated in his head.

>Ka'ski shan'diar 'el staciatos.<

"Sorry, m'Lord," Rakar said. "I d'dn't mean to cause 'ya grief."

"No, I am still attempting to come to terms with all of this. It is not your fault."

Rakar unbuckled his sword belt and laid his weapons on the corner of the desk. Twin shortswords, slender blades with broad curved tips. He folded his cloak neatly over them and sat down. He nodded to Symon. "Aye, I thought our ways c'ld be a bit much for 'ya. All our efforts to preserve life and mem'ry. Y'all in the Feds, take great pains to forget your pasts."

"We do not," Symon said, voice stern.

"No 'fense, m'Lord. It's not your aim, but it is what happens." Rakar actively avoided eye contact. "But 'tis not my place to say."

Symon glanced at his father's study. It was a refuge of his heritage. He had records of his grandparents and great-grandparents. Symon stood and took a tome from his shelf. "What do you mean?" Symon asked. "I have seen books like this back home."

"Aye, the recordings are the same," Rakar agreed. He pointed out to the mausoleum. "But tha' is our way. I've heard 'ya haven't communed with 'ya kin, yet."

Symon's feline eyes cut through the dark and could see the skeletons of his grandparents on their stone dais. They were sitting, bones clean and well decorated, watching and waiting. There was a reverence to them that Symon could not ignore, but had yet to explore. His eyes lingered and his shoulders relaxed as he began to understand Rakar's intentions.

"Even when you and your sire were gone Fed side, I w'ld come and keep the crypts in order. Knew you'd be back some time."

"Was it odd that my father appointed the Yurolindos as caretakers?" Symon asked. "Is there so little of my living family?" His words felt awkward. While the Cyl'Karrick name seemed small in the eyes of the great families that he'd seen since arriving in Vargarden, it was still more family than he'd ever known.

"Nay, your lot is well to do here. Goes back generations. One more now, I s'pose. There's 'nough of 'ya to hold the house. But, I was just closer to 'ya sire than most. S'pose he felt more comfortable with one he served with."

"So, you served with my father in the Legion?"

"Aye, 'ya sire and I go back a bit. He was already Nemuku when I was but a rookie."

"Can you tell me about him?" Symon asked.

"What'cha want to know?"

"Was he always just pretending?" Symon asked, tears welling up in his eyes. "Was the 'good man' just an act? Why was he such a monster?"

"Boy. Don't say that 'bout my Nemuku. He w'rn't a monster at all."

Symon held up one of his father's journals. "This says otherwise! All these deaths. All these atrocities!"

Rakar gave Symon a flat stare. A soldier's stare. "Aye, he did 'em. But he did 'em because they needed doin. Tha's why Father sent him."

"What do you mean?" Symon pleaded. "How could he forgive himself for what he did?"

"I believe he n'er did." Rakar paused. "Let me tell you 'bout the man I knew."

Rakar took a sip of the brandy and thought for a moment. "When I was a rook, he was already in service for over a hundred years. Your sire was smart. Whip-smart. N'er knew someone with so much knowledge on war. But he read ever'thing and forgot little.

"When I began, I was a coward. Shook on the field," Rakar said. His eyes held a touch of shame, but it was distant. "Couldn't take the crowds, I s'pose. But instead of loosin' me, m'Lord pulled me up to scoutin'. Let me run on my own. I took to it quick. Half the time, I didn't know why I was lookin' or what I was lookin' for, but he always seemed 'ta.

"The war was happenin' in the Fed while I was trainin', but when we got called..." Rakar smiled with pride. "Nemuku pulled my Legion card and brought the unit with him. T'was during those years that I learned 'tha most about 'ya sire. Made friends with him."

Symon refilled both glasses. Rakar was lost in his story, so Symon did not dare interrupt him.

"T'was a greatness about him," Rakar continued. "But it came at a price. He couldn't be friendly to many people. He was always prepared to lose. It took him to darkness. He said he needed to look at numbers, not folks, so he could make the best decision."

Symon said, "'*The ledger lines of your men will balance your ambition against the reality of conquest. Waste them in reserve, and your goals will fall short of their ultimate measures.*' "

"Aye!" Rakar said. "Tha's it exactly! You sire said that all the time."

"In his own words, he said that was the belief of monsters."

Rakar nodded sadly. "Aye' I think tha's where he grew to believe. I knew many good men, but not a lot of great men. Kyrn was a great man, who grew to be a good one."

"But how?" Symon asked. "What happened?"

"You, I'm guessin'. You and the family."

Symon flinched. Rakar had said the words with such sincerity and finality that it left little doubt to his true feelings. Nemuku Cyl'Karrick, one of the greatest generals in Legion History, had turned it all in for a mundane life. "But how did he absolve himself of all..." Symon waved the journal in the air, "this? I still do not understand how everyone can look at what he did and not still see the monster."

"Mayhaps b'cause 'ya are readin' the words he wrote? 'Ya are seein' that he felt the guilt, and he saw himself as 'tha monster, too," Rakar said. "Mayhaps, it's because, like him, you only see the damage caused," Rakar said. "Trust that 'ya sire saved more lives than he hurt. And that no one else could have won what he did. The Fed's owe him a lot, and from what I see, all they gave was blame. All 'ya life, y've heard 'bout the 'Big Bad Nemuku' and the evils of Vargarden."

"Yes, even the Federation instructors tell horror stories about Vargarden's part in the War of Night," Symon said.

"Disgusting, is what it is," Rakar spat, his voice full of fury. "He helped pull them from a war they started, and they threw shit in his face!"

"Prince Caleb said the same thing."

"Aye," Rakar agreed. "Prince Caleb has the right of it. Your sire was a great man. Gave away ev'rythin' to the War. Gave away ev'rythin' for THEM. He deserved better. Someday soon, I hope 'ya can look at those notes and understand why 'ya sire did what he did. Tha' 'ya see he made the only choices he could."

"That is what I am afraid of," Symon muttered.

"M'Lord?"

"Nevermind," Symon said, changing gears. "Do you know how he ended it? Ended the War? Nothing I know of explains that. Even the Prince does not know how the treaty occurred."

"T'was a myst'ry to us all. Even I d'dn't 'til the night...," Rakar paused, struggling against the next words. "Until the night 'ya sire died. When I went to

Highston, your sire penned a letter for me. Explained a lot of the things I d'd'nt know. More than I expected."

"Can you tell me what happened?"

"Aye," Rakar nodded. "I'll tell you a bit, then I'll give you his letter. His own words will be better for you. That's f'sure.

"Tha' last battle, the Shadow had been at Enfeld for a fortnight," Rakar started. "The initial push was rough, let me tell 'ya. The Federation had barricaded themselves tight, and the Vesters were poppin' in and out, day and night attacking whatever they could. Normal defenses d'dn't work with that lot. Fed's were at their wits end.

"So when we arrived, first thing Nemuku did was draft a Grand Welengam from the bones and send them down to make us some space. Shadow folk ain't got much magic that hurts our Welgeid so it was a tactic that had worked well. Except the Vesters were ready this time."

Rakar sipped his brandy and smiled a sinister grin. It was the look of a soldier that respected his opponent, but still despised them. Symon sat on the edge of his seat. He had waited since childhood to hear the truth of Enfeld, and here it was in front of him.

The old man continued, "They d'dn't engage us. They drifted out and tele-ported only to attack the Feds, and kept out of our blocks as best they could. Enfeld was bigger than the other cities, and the Vesters changed fronts o'er and o'er. T'was ugly.

"To tell you true, it was nearly over 'fore it began," Rakar said. "They just kept at it. Thinnin' Fed lines and reinforcing troops from their Shadow plane. So Kyrn told the Legion to Raise. Raise everything."

Symon was versed enough in the Arcane arts to understand that Raise came with its capital "R." Raising undead.

"Now, 'tis against our tenants to Raise the dead without a family's permission. But it was the only way to fill the gaps in the lines. Fed gaps. So, the Deacons did it without question. Knew it was the right. Feds didn't react so well.

"The fighters were scared. The Magi were pissed. But Nemuku weren't lis-tening to anyone, just saved the day. Once the dead units were Raised, they joined the fray and we finally got tha' bit of breathing room."

Symon whistled underneath his breath. After all this time, he was putting the details together. The stories of the siege matched the descriptions that Rakar gave. The Federal records focused more on the savagery of the two opposing forces, and less about the hopelessness that Rakar spoke of, but it made sense to Symon.

"Then the Arcanists linked up and put a soul wall up around the city. The soul wall was able to keep the Vesters from teleporting in."

"I have seen something like that from him."

"Aye, your sire studied Vester magic. He began to understand how to beat them. But their Master was a vicious one, too. Tricks we played only worked once. So here we were stuck in a Fed city, surrounded and protected. They couldn't break us, but we couldn't break them either. We was locked."

"So what did you do?"

"M'Lord took off."

"He what?!"

"Aye, he took off and ran to a source. Thought he could draw information from the Deepland Witch."

Symon shook his head. "The Witch in the Woods? The one from the fables?"

"Yep, same. And when he came back, he was different."

"What did she do to him?"

"Showed him the truth. That's what he said. 'Saw the truth'." Rakar shook his head. "So he went and called parley with the Master. They went in. Spoke for some hours. Then, came out of that tent, and we all went home."

"What happened?"

"They came out, started sending troops home. Vesters left, Legion left. The Feds were left holding the bag, but they went back to normal, too. It was all over, and up until a few months ago, I didn't know why. No one did."

"The Federation Academy said they brokered a deal," Symon said. "That they ended the war."

Rakar laughed out loud. It was an eerie sound, harsh and wicked. "No Fed was in that tent. Just the Master and Nemuku.

"The war ended because the Witch did something tha' took the fight out of both of them."

Symon stared at Rakar. This whole tale was still more legend than facts. It seems that nobody wanted to talk about Enfeld.

"I've got the letter you sire penned at my home. You're not ready for it yet, but when you are you can come find me."

"How will I know when I am ready?"

"There's a secret 'ya ain't found yet. When you find it, you'll know, and then you will be ready."

Rakar stood and quietly gathered his belongings. His belt secured, his cloak tightened, he turned and went to the door.

"Where are you headed, Master Yurolindo?" Symon asked.

"Got some b'ness to handle," Rakar smiled. "Nothin' to worry 'bout. I truly hope you'll learn about your sire. Learn who he was and see the good through the bad. But remember, he loved you. I've got no doubt 'bout that. And when you are ready, I can show you how it is I know."

Symon started to respond, but Rakar was already through the door. The night felt quieter. Symon glanced at the journal and turned back to the mausoleum. He had no idea where to begin, or what to do. Rakar had left him with more questions than answers.

17

The First Indications

Jesse approached the end of the hall with no small trepidation. He had been summoned. By the Prince. While Jesse had been summoned dozens of times by Manticore, this was different. He felt exposed, his skin crawling with each passing glance. No secrets. No hidden alleyways. Just him, walking up to the Crown Prince of Vargarden. In broad daylight.

The thief's eyes glanced back at Moria, who trailed behind him. Her eyes never left him. She was wearing her leathers, armed to the teeth, and as silent as a housecat. She just stalked his trail, watching. He inclined his head towards the door, an unspoken question of whether to proceed. She returned an impatient nod and Jesse turned back to the door.

Taking some time to calm his nerves, he studied the arcane writing flowing through the wooden doorway. And flowing was the best way to describe it.

Jesse had been correct in his initial impression that the script was actually moving. He shifted his vision into the arcane and found that the doors glowed with a very subtle, muted, but substantial power. At first, it appeared to be a protection spell form but Jesse realized it was more mental, perhaps a mood alteration spell. Even that didn't feel right. It was something else. Something very subtle. And it was fascinating. Jesse was so intrigued, he didn't even realize he was stepping forward until the two guards moved to block his path, their control gems glowing a deep sapphire blue.

"Um, I'm here to see Prince Caleb?" he said, looking first at one skeleton and then the other. He really wasn't sure yet how this was supposed to work. Neither of the skeletons moved out of his way, but at least they had not reached for him, or drawn weapons. Jesse was surprised that even in the Arcane spectrum, he could sense nothing from them. By all accounts he could detect, they had no arcane impact about them. He had no idea of how the Arcane forms would be hidden, particularly because of how the other Welgeid appeared, but the Prince's were special. It certainly added to the mystery. His mind raced trying to figure out how this worked. He didn't know if his voice would summon the Prince or if the Prince had to be paying attention to the gems. He had to trust in the Arcana of old and stand his ground.

Without warning, both guards dropped back a step and bent into a bow, one mirroring the other, causing Jesse to jump a bit at the unexpected movement. The ten foot tall doors began to open and the two returned to their respective cubicles in the walls, gesturing as twins for Jesse to enter. He did so, a reluctance slowing his faltering steps.

As he entered the main room, Jesse looked around. He did not see the Prince anywhere in the vast room, and called out, "Hello? I'm not trying to intrude. The guards let me in." A small chuckle caused Jesse to turn to Moria who hid her smile behind her hand. "What?" Jesse asked.

"Nay," she said. "Nothin'. Don't mind me none."

There was no other response from the room. Letting his curiosity get the better of him, Jesse proceeded to the shelves on his left. He wanted to examine many of the magical trinkets he had caught glimpses of on his first visit. Jesse did his best not to touch, but quickly cast a few identification spells on several of the more intriguing items.

It was an impressive collection. Most items were of lower magic, but all were of high quality in their craftsmanship and materials. The ones that caught his eyes, however, offered inlaid spells that were of impressive power. A few he recognized as being very dangerous if you didn't know what you were doing with them. He knew he wouldn't pocket anything here, but if this stuff had been in the house of one of his marks back home, he could have set himself up for a few years with this score.

Jesse turned at the sound of a foot scuff behind him, and found the large four armed servant approaching him. He quickly backed away from the shelves in case his infraction had accidentally drawn its attention. Jesse's hands raised and he was suddenly lost in a flash of memory. For the briefest of moments, it had been Xerian striding toward him, an angry scowl on his face. Jesse caught himself and pushed the fearful memory from his mind.

The young Isnashi's eyes turned towards Moria in embarrassment, but she stood stoic and nonplussed. Her eyes hadn't left him, but she appeared to lack any concern or unusual interest at all. Staring at the servant once again, he found himself wondering if this might be a skeleton of another Lindorm. Jesse didn't know many of the species, other than Xerian, so it would be interesting to find out more.

A cool, clear voice resonated from the crystal in the skeleton's chest. Jesse recognized the higher pitched, childlike tone of the voice, but it sounded slurred or groggy. "I apologize for my delay. I'll be with you shortly. Please ask Reneforte for any refreshments."

Jesse cursed himself silently. He was also confused because even though he had been summoned, it appeared he had woken the Prince up. He looked up at the towering skeleton standing before him. "Reneforte?"

The servant bowed in acknowledgment, surprising Jesse yet again. He had not seen such intelligence or independence from any of the undead he had interacted with thus far. This one seemed somehow intelligent, or at least partly sentient. He would definitely ask about that at some point. Jesse slipped into his arcane vision and once again was unable to detect any Arcane interaction in the automaton.

"Do you have any more of those lemon ice drops from the other day?" he asked, trying to regain some control. "Or some of that red juice from before?"

Reneforte bowed once again and strode off toward the back of the room. Jesse watched him go for a minute, then drifted casually over to the bookcase that the Prince had distracted himself with during their prior visit. Again he did not touch, but browsed the spines. Most were in old black or brown bound leather. Many had titles engraved but none were in a language he could read. Jesse did pick out enough of the symbols to recognize it was the same writing as the Vargarden book Zenesul had shown him once upon a time.

Within moments, Jesse detected movement near himself again, and Reneforte returned, setting a tray on the low round table surrounded by couches. He watched as the servant poured a goblet of the deep red juice, loaded a saucer with a scattering of the confections, and turned wordlessly to stare at him. A moment passed, and the skeleton brought both treats over to hand to Jesse. He accepted both, and out of either reflex or an overabundance of caution said, "Thanks".

As he took a sip of the tart but delicious juice, Reneforte stepped back and made its way to stand at attention behind one of the couches. Realizing awkwardly that he had no spare hand to pick up one of the treats, Jesse followed over and sat down on one of the couches facing the skeleton. He sat his drink down so he could enjoy the iced delight savoring the sweetness. Jesse glanced at Moria, his hand pointing towards the treats. She merely shook her head and continued to stand at the door. Jesse shrugged and his gaze went back to Rennefort. "Can you tell me what these are called? I forget," Jesse asked, holding one of the iced confections up toward Reneforte.

The skeleton merely stood staring blankly. Nothing lit up or activated within either the visual or Arcane spectrum. Jesse smiled at the lack of verbal response.

"Antequines," called a voice from behind Jesse.

The Isnashi spun around in his seat, nearly sending his plate and its contents flying, to see the Prince emerging from a doorway behind him. It was clear he had just awoken, stifling a yawn as he approached. He was dressed in a floor length black skirt, its waist hanging low off his prominent hip bones. He was also shirtless, the brighter blue skin of his ribbed torso flashed in patches beneath long dark blue robes that trailed behind him.

"They're a traditional layered sweet that are often popular with foreign dignitaries," the Prince said. "I do hope you like them."

Jesse quickly sat his plate on the table and stood up to greet his host. He tried to unobtrusively wipe his fingers off on his pants leg and gave a bit of a bow, not knowing what was expected of him. "Of course, sorry. Thank you. Uh, hello."

"Don't do that," said the Prince as he staggered over.

"I'm sorry, highness? What did I do?"

"Bow," the Prince replied, sitting on another of the couches. "It's unnecessary."

The Prince grabbed a robe from one of the hooks on the wall, and pulled it around his shoulders. As before, he folded his body into the seat. The Prince was barely seated before Reneforte was setting another goblet within arms reach, and had moved to stand behind the Prince. Prince Caleb pulled his waist length black hair from behind him and draped it over the back of the couch. Without any apparent bidding, the servant began brushing the tangles out of his bedhead.

Jesse shifted awkwardly, unsure of how to proceed. Moria gave him a nod and motioned for him to take his seat. He settled back on to the couch and stared at the Crown Prince of Vargarden waiting for something, anything, to happen.

"Jesse Olben," said the Prince quietly.

"Just Jesse is fine, your highness-ness."

Prince Caleb stifled a slight giggle but quickly composed himself. "Just Caleb, please, just Jesse."

"Yes sir."

"Caleb," the Prince almost whispered. He wasn't looking at Jesse, but a smile played across his down turned face as he said, "Not 'highness', not 'sir', not 'Prince,' just Caleb."

"I'll try to remember that," Jesse said. He paused a beat, then added a bit quieter, "Caleb."

They sat in silence for a few minutes, picking at the small treats between them. Neither seemed to know who should speak first. Finally the Prince said, "It's uncommon for people to discard their family lineage. Why do you discard yours so easily?"

"Huh? What do you mean?" Jesse stammered. His cheeks flushed as he remembered his manners, and the position of the man in front of him. He amended his response. "I apologize. I don't understand what you are asking.

Discard my lineage?"

"Your family name," replied Caleb. "You declined my use of it. Most visitors prefer to be called 'Master such and such', or 'Sir this and that.' It's unusual to use your 'common' name so soon, is it not?"

"Oh," said Jesse, somewhat embarrassed. "Yeah, about that." He paused, drawing out the words of his sentence, speaking reluctantly. "It's not actually a family name, precisely, exactly, for real."

The Prince cocked his head inquisitively, but did not speak.

After a few minutes of silence, Jesse blurted out, "It was my mother's name, okay? You guys were going on about family and history and I was jealous!"

Caleb picked at the hem of his skirt and said, "I see."

Time stretched out again as the Prince ate another antequine and leaned his head back for Reneforte. After another quiet pause, he asked, "So, you don't want to use the name because you're ashamed of your mother?"

"I loved my mother! Why would I be ashamed of her?"

"So, you do want to use the name?"

"I just don't know what you expect," Jesse said. "No one's ever asked for my 'family lineage' before. I don't know how you pick a name."

Caleb said. "It differs from culture to culture. If you are proud of your mother and you gave her name as your family name, there is honor in that. Some cultures add an honorific from their language. Jesse 'son of' Olben, if you will."

"Oh," Jesse said. "I'm not fancy enough for that."

"Good. Then Jesse Olben, it is good to make your acquaintance."

"Really? That's it?"

"She is your family," Caleb said simply, in his high, quiet voice. "There is honor in having that as your given family name. Here, it shall be so."

Jesse sat in thought for a moment. He didn't know how to feel. He had been alone for so long, with no one caring about his past or history. He had always just been a Street Rat from Bunlo district in Highston. Jesse didn't even know if this was a big change or not. The Prince could be humoring him, but everyone seemed to take Jesse seriously here. He looked up realizing that the Prince had said something else. He chided himself for not paying attention. "I'm sorry, I missed that."

"You 'loved' your mother?" repeated Caleb. "You said you loved your mother, yet you also honor her. She has passed on, yes?"

"Oh," Jesse said. "She died, yeah. When I was eight."

"My condolences," the Prince said. There wasn't any pity or sympathy in his voice, simply the appropriate response for someone's loss. Jesse barely remembered his mother. He didn't even know what they did with her when she died. "So, you were raised by your sire?"

"My sire? Oh, no. I didn't have a dad."

"How did that happen? Arcane conception? Divine intervention?"

Jesse stared at Caleb's eyes, watching them alight with hundreds of possibilities. His words had been taken literally. A small smirk formed on the young Isnashi's face and he giggled slightly. "No, sorry. I mean, I'm sure there's a man out there who made me happen... but I wouldn't call him a 'dad.' Mom was a whore, so who knows what customer may have knocked me into her."

"I see." The disappointment in the Prince's eyes was clear. A false mystery. "A... 'whore' you say? Not a term I've come across in my research."

Jesse couldn't help it any longer. He laughed. A full laugh filled the room. Caleb stared flatly back at Jesse not seeing the humor. Jesse finally continued, "You know, a whore? A streetwalker, a bed wench, a conker, a coin lass." Seeing a lack of comprehension still, he added, "A prostitute? No? Nothing?"

Jesse blushed slightly, having to explain it. To speak so directly about his own mother. "She worked in a brothel. She had sex with men for money."

Caleb put his finger on his lips, a gesture eerily similar to Symon when he would try to recall something from his memory. "A harlot," Caleb said. "I do believe Willum the Bard has a fable about one."

"Oh, sure."

"I see," Caleb smiled. There wasn't any judgement, just a man learning. "So if she passed on and you had no father, who cared for you?"

Now would come the judgement. Or worse, the pity. "I did," Jesse answered defiantly. "I found what I needed, and I made my own way. Always have."

Jesse watched Caleb's reaction. It was as flat and expressionless as it had been. "That's a feat, Jesse Olben. Some day, you must walk me through the details of your childhood. An ancestor-less development would likely result in an independent personality. I'd be interested in hearing more." The Prince stretched his arms wide and yawned deeply. "So please, what may I do for you this afternoon?"

"Oh damn," said Jesse. He realized they hadn't even gotten to the summons. "I'm sorry I woke you up." Then realizing what he just said, he put his hand over his mouth. "Shit. I cussed in front of a Prince! Damn, I did it again!"

Prince Caleb chuckled at the unfortunate outburst, as did Moria. The three exchanged looks of confusion and embarrassment. Jesse was sure this was supposed to be a formal occasion, but it had gotten off track. He leaned into the discomfort trying to lighten the mood.

"Ha, gotcha!" said Jesse, smirking at the Prince. "You laughed, so I win!"

Caleb's eyes raised in surprise. Jesse grinned like an idiot at him, relishing his opportunity to meet those olive eyes. He wasn't feeling some mystical draw like Symon did, but Prince Caleb was certainly cute. And there were so many mysteries about him that also made for a powerful draw. Whether the man knew what he was doing or not, his robes were flashing just enough chest to really tease the young thief. But right now he was totally distracted by Caleb's eyes. He was heartbroken when the Prince dropped his gaze back to his lap. But he saw the Prince kept a small smile on his lips as he raised his goblet to meet them.

"Oh yeah," Jesse stammered, pulling his gaze from the Prince's pale, smiling lips. "The reason, yeah. Um, Symon said something about requesting access to the, uh, the Vault of, uh, Xaradia, Xanrida, or something like that? Moria was telling him that there would be records there he should read, but that we needed your access? Your summons said there was an answer?"

"The Vaults of Xarania," answered Prince Caleb. "Yes, Master Cyl'Karrick's petition was approved. I will provide an escort myself."

"Sweet," said Jesse. He watched as the Prince rearranged his robes, flashing more of his chest. "So... what do we do?"

"It will take a few days to arrange."

"Oh, sweet," Jesse said. Confusion once again crept through his mind. This seemed like an unneeded visit for something so simple. He repeated, "So, what do WE do?"

"Ah, well, let me finish getting dressed, and you and I shall discuss the Khorric Federation, if you would?"

"Sure," Jesse shrugged. "I'm still sorry for disturbing you."

"Your arrival was quicker than anticipated."

"Oh."

"Traditionally, you would have sent a messenger to accept my invitation. Then I would send a messenger to propose times."

Jesse's cheeks flushed again.

"But I find it refreshing," the Prince said. "It was a nice surprise. So, let me get myself ready, and you can tell me how Guilds work."

"Guilds?" Jesse asked.

"I know they are the cornerstone of commerce in the Federation, but the licensing structure seems cumbersome. I'm hoping you'll be able to explain it." Caleb waved off the servant Reneforte and got to his feet. "Give me a few minutes and I shall be ready to accompany you."

"Uh, sure." Jesse watched Caleb disappear around the doorframe. He was nothing like Xerian, or Symon for that matter, but there was something about the man. Jesse had no desire to talk about the Federation, but he'd talk about anything just to stay with Caleb a bit longer.

18

Phantoms

The candle burned low, and Symon's eyes were heavy. It had been a long day. He had spent a decent amount of it with an Arcanist known for Healing. She had reviewed the structure of her spells. They made sense, but like his studies with Master Zenesul, they had felt cumbersome. Since then, he had been exploring his father's library and the hour had grown late.

On the desk was a physiological manuscript from five centuries ago. It focused on the impact of the races introduced when the Devastation had occurred. Symon had at first been fascinated by learning about the Coleope, Gauch, and Ogres, but the writing was dry and he had lost interest in the text. Instead, he was idly examining charts and diagrams of the anatomy of Skyfallen races, which was beyond his understanding.

Symon scanned the shelves of his father's library, his library now, as his frustration grew by the passing moment. While so much information was collected here, none of it seemed to help.

He had family charters and war journals, even the medical journals that his father seemed to favor, but nothing gave him insight into "who" his father was. So much of this house felt familiar, and Symon found himself often instinctively finding items or places within the walls as if he were still back in Highston. Most of it spoke to the disciplined and curious mind that Symon had known Kyrn to have, but not to why he was that way.

Symon wondered most about the reason Kyrn joined the military. It was perhaps that gap of information that conflicted him so greatly about his feelings regarding Kyrn. All his life, his father was there for him. He was a kind, practical, and sometimes stern man who had taught Symon about life. Lessons about taking pride in your craft, dedication, and servitude. Whether those were personal qualities, or imbued to him by the Legion, Symon was unsure. The truth must be somewhere in these words, but he had no idea where to find it.

Symon growled and slapped the desk in frustration. A small gasp of surprise followed by footsteps in the hallway caught his attention. His nostrils flared, and filled with the scent of Moria. Rushing to the door and glancing down the hall, he saw Moria hurrying towards the room she had been staying in. "Moria?"

"Apologies, m'Lord," she said. "Saw your light on. D'dn't mean to disturb 'ya."

"No, my apologies. I did not know that you were still awake." That wasn't exactly true. Since they had arrived at the Cyl'Karrick estate, Symon had been keeping an eye out for when Moria was around the house. She had left earlier today, and he had not known that she would come back this evening.

Moria squinted at him and gave him a small frown. Symon felt like she was weighing him and his words carefully. A little sigh betrayed the stress of her day as she said, "Aye, it was a late eve."

"I hope everything is well."

"As it can be, s'pose."

Symon could see that Moria was dealing with something, but was uncomfortable pressing her for details. Like Prince Caleb, Moria fascinated him. He was concerned with saying the wrong thing, of scaring her away, so he often found himself failing to find the right words. Instead, he just stood there in the hallway and stared.

As the situation became uncomfortable, he finally relented. "Do you want to talk?"

"Uh, sure," she replied. A small smile formed on her lips. "If I'm not burdenin' 'ya."

"Of course not, madam," Symon waved her into the library. "To tell the truth, I could use the distraction. Before my frustration gets the better of me yet again." He smiled sheepishly and allowed her to take a chair. He grabbed a few glasses, poured some brandy, and offered her a drink. Symon leaned in to hand her the glass and breathed deeply. She smelled like springtime. A light floral fragrance, like roses, layered over the nutty, wood-like smell that the Nymph-blooded had. It was intoxicating.

She shivered slightly, having just come in from the chill evening. Symon stoked up the fire, placing another log and letting the heat and light pour into the room. He turned to Moria and smiled. "It is a cool night."

"Aye, so 'tis," she said, offering him a smile back. "Summer's still tryin' to claim her nights from spring's harsh grasp."

"And your attire is much more suited for the warmth of the sun, than the light of the moon."

Moria's eyebrow raised slightly and Symon kicked himself mentally as the words left his mouth. She was gorgeous, a floral dress that was cut at the knees and bounced when she walked. It was a perfect lavender color that complimented her nut-toned skin and the natural green highlights of her dyed black hair. He had simply meant that it was probably cool, but now he had realized that he could have insulted her.

She chuckled and said, "Aye, 'tis a spring cut for sure. Sh'ld've taken my cloak with me, but d'dn't intend to be so late."

"Of course, of course," Symon stammered. He paused trying to figure out a path of conversation which would allow him to recover his dignity. He slowly raised his glass to his lips to sip while he thought.

She smiled at him and then said, "I was out, ending my courtship. 'Twas a harder conversation than I expected."

Symon sat coughing on his drink. The simplicity of her statement and the flatness of her tone, as well as her timing, made him sure she was prodding him for a reaction. Of course, he had expected that she had been courting. She had some fae blood for sure that youthened her appearance, but with her experience in the Legion he put her in her late twenties to early thirties. She was a beautiful woman with an excellent family. He had convinced himself that she would be beyond his measure to court, himself.

Recovering his composure, Symon said, "I am sorry."

"No disrespect," she said, cocking her head at him again. "You are a horrid liar."

Symon flinched. His ears flushed with pink as his skin heatened from embarrassment. "I am truly..."

"No, no," she waved. "Don't take it personal. I've just been trained to see when folk are holding back."

"Yeah, I mean... No, I am not withholding."

"Are 'ya jealous of him?"

Symon frowned. She had put him in a spot where his feelings were at war with his manners. He stilled his mind and pushed the thoughts of vying for her affection at bay. "How can I be jealous? I do not know him. I barely know you. It would not be appropriate."

Her laugh was almost musical. She looked at Symon. "Aye, that's it. That's the truth right there."

Symon frowned at her. "I do not know what you are talking about."

"Okay, okay. I'll let it go. For now."

"So you ended your courtship?" Symon asked, desperately trying to change the topic.

"Aye, he weren't happy with our situation. He's never understood my duties as the caretaker here. And now that you've come back, he's grown vocal about it."

"I am sorry. I did not mean to come between the two of you."

That small weighing glance returned to her eyes. She smiled. "'Ya do mean that, that's good." She waved her hand to dismiss his concerns. "But 'tis'n't your fault."

"Surely with my being back for the family name, you could relent your duties here."

"Aye, I could. That's what he said, as well. But I don't want to," she said. "For one, I wouldn't change who I am for a man for any reason. He will accept me for all, or not. For second, I have grown fond of the Cyl'Karrick family and feel that I can help you, as my sire helped yours."

"Oh, of course," Symon said. Her independence inspired him. While he struggled to find out who he was, she was self assured and committed to her identity. She was strong, both physically and mentally, and that ember of attraction flared to life in him once again.

"So, it ended, and that'll be that," she smiled

"Yes, and you will be welcome here for as long as you like."

Moria pulled a small blanket from the back of the chair and wrapped it around her shoulders. The two stared into the fire letting the silence stretch and the warmth of the room settle in. Symon filled his glass and swirled the brandy while he thought.

Finally, he asked, "Was he a soldier, or a noble?" Again, Symon gave himself a mental shake. Something about her made all the intelligent questions he could ask escape him, leaving him a driveling fool.

"Neither, he was a gardener," she chuckled.

"A gardener?" Symon said with genuine surprise. In Highston, a mere civil worker would have little chance of courting a woman of Moria's status.

"Yes, he performs garden care for the city," she said simply. "He has done some beautiful work around the public gardens and parks. "

"Oh, well, that is interesting." Symon struggled to wrap his head around the social structure in Vargarden. It was why he tried to convince himself that he was unworthy of a courtship here. In Highston, he and his father had difficulty maintaining their social rank because of the nature of Kyrn's profession in the eyes of the nobility. There was a clear separation of those who worked with their hands versus those who managed the money for those professions. It was refreshing to see that perhaps it was not as much of a burden here, yet also inconvenient because it meant that Symon would have to blame something else on his inability to pursue a relationship.

Lost again, Symon had no idea what to do. Healing magic called him, but was deemed as extremely dangerous by those he had consulted with. His skills as a blacksmith would allow him to start a small shop, but he feared letting down the

Cyl'Karrick name in Vargarden. He considered joining the Legion, yet was terrified that he would become a monster like his father.

Jesse and Thorn wanted to go home. Jesse had been becoming more and more irritable with each passing day. But to go home, they had to address the war. For some reason, everyone had wanted Jesse dead, and until they sent home the Investurants, it would be too dangerous for them to return.

Symon was no soldier. Nor was he a politician. He was just a simple man trying to do the right thing. Prince Caleb had told him a special council session had already been called to discuss Vargarden's responsibilities. However, the council still remembered the War of Night, and the Federation's turn on their allies was not easily forgiven. Maybe, just maybe, Symon could convince Jesse to stay and they could start a life here. Maybe he and Jesse could figure it out together.

Symon raised his eyes and found Moria staring at him. "Well, in the small moments that I have been here in Vargarden, I can say that it is his loss. You are a wonderful woman, Moria. And it would truly bless any man to have you in his life."

Though she tried to hide it, Moria blushed furiously. Her scent rose and filled his mind yet again. She was genuinely surprised. "Nay, ye'r too much."

"Apologies, my lady. That was too forward."

"Nay," she said, "just unexpected. And undeserved." A small tinge of shame crept into her scent as she stood. "Give me a moment." Moria walked out of the library and the door closed behind her. Symon wondered if he had pushed the situation too far. Flirting was unnatural to him. His previous courtships had all been initiated by a friend or by the women themselves. Even when he had courted Lara, his conversations were better than this. Symon was normally confident, sure of his words, easy to engage. Here, everyone left him tongue-tied more often than not.

A few moments later, she returned holding a small packet of books. They were leatherbound and old, though they looked well maintained. The spines were well oiled and had not cracked. She smiled and her eyes ducked slowly to the floor as she sat them on the desk. "I should've given these to ya, soon as you arrived. But I wanted to spend a few more days with 'em."

"What are they?" he asked.

"Your sire's journals."

"Oh." Symon stared at the stack in awe. This would be centuries of notes left in his father's hand. His words, living through those books. Kyrn's thoughts about himself, not a research topic. This was what he needed. His mind lost in possibility, Symon muttered, "Thank you."

"Aye." Her eyes rose slowly to meet his again. "Not much of a blessin', am I? Selfish and all."

Symon sat forward in his chair and gently took one of them into his hand. The leather was smooth and soft, worn by years of use. He opened it and examined the page, his heart soaring with hope and inspiration. There in this journal was the same neat handwriting he had grown used to seeing. His father's tidy script filled page after page.

"Do 'ya know?" Moria asked, filling the silence. "'Ya sound like I imagin'd he would. The way 'ya speak, 'ya words remind me of him."

"Many people have told me that I take after him," Symon said, absently.

"'Tis true, from what I see. But I ne'r met him, just the books."

Symon's mind raced. While another key to the puzzle, there was still a mystery to be solved. The memory of Kyrn Cylkas, business man in Highston versus Neumuku Cyl'Karric, the terrifying nightmare of the Legion. Timidly, he looked to Moria, who had made her way to the door. "Moria?"

She turned to him, that smile still on her face and a sadness reflected in her eyes. He held her gaze for a moment and then choked out a small, "Thank you." His eyes locked once again on the journals, and even though he knew the answer due to the age of the books. He had to ask, "Does he mention my mother?"

That heartache was the source of Moria's reflected melancholy. Symon's loss of family. She shook her head gently. "Nay, I'm sorry."

"I figured so."

"From what my sire and I can figure, Nemuku didn't meet her until after the campaign. All these are leading up to the start."

"Well, it is late, and we should retire." He held the book in his hand. "Thank you, again."

"Aye," Moria said. "'Tis much to do in the next coming days. We need our rest."

"Good night, Moria."

"G'Night, Symon."

Moria walked out and headed down the hall towards her chambers, and Symon began to spread the coals and dampen the fire. He looked one last time at the stack of journals. A long night awaited him.

Hasukawa stepped out from behind the corner of the building. The shadowed figure before him stood motionless, the heavy rain sliding down his cloak. The hilt of a bastard sword protruded from the cloak off his left shoulder and the hilts of two curved short swords peeked out just over his hips. His hood was pulled up obscuring his face, but this did not matter. The Arktos knew who this man was, and even having once called him friend, Hasukawa was still nervous.

The figure spoke out in Mumvuri, his voice quiet and hoarse, but with a natural cadence that fit the harshness of the language. His words were barely discernible over the sound of the rain. "*If you are here, Hasukawa, then so is Kiko. End the game and bring him out of hiding.*"

Hasukawa grinned and raised his staff, jabbing the tip upward twice, then lowering it. At his signal, Kiko stepped out from the other end of the alley, huddling under a wide brimmed hat and trenchcoat pulled tight. "If my husband is meeting with one who has taken *Masina*, the Path of the Ghost, I am going to be watching his back."

The Ghost ignored those words, eyes locked to face the Hasukawa. The Arktos gave his husband a small sign to back down. The warrior before him was more than determined, he was dangerous. Road's End suddenly felt very isolated.

"*You know why we're here?*" the Ghost asked.

"*No, but I can guess,*" replied Hasukawa, also in Mumvurii.

"*I am hunting members of the Sangebula. I need assistance.*"

"That was my guess."

"You know the method of Quinnar, the Spirit Strike?"

"Yes," said Hasukawa, *"I know this technique. Sadly I cannot teach it to you."*

A pause hung in the air as the Ghost tensed. A slight growl escaped his throat and he asked, *"Cannot, or will not?"* Behind him, Hasukawa felt Kiko tense as well, his hands moving to the blasters on his hips.

"In matters of honor, is there a difference?" Hasukawa asked.

"I must have this knowledge," said the Ghost. *"It is the only thing that matters. I must hunt those who can shift to the immaterial, to destroy them. It is beyond honor at this point."*

"I understand." Violating the honor of his sect was something Hasukawa couldn't take lightly. The technique was simple, but it was ancient even by Vargarden's standards and never to be known outside members of the Order. In life, the Ghost would have known the gravity of the request, but *Masina* meant he didn't care. Once *Masina* was sworn, the results of the pact was all that mattered. Anything that happened in the time between was forgotten. The ends didn't just justify the means, they defined them.

For the first time, the Ghost shifted his footing, barely a movement, and Kiko drew his blasters. Hasukawa, however, remained calm and unmoving.

"You will not help?" growled the Ghost.

"You are dead," said Hasukawa, *"so you no longer have honor. I, however, must maintain mine."*

"I am dead, so there is no dishonor in teaching me."

"An interesting point," said Hasukawa. Then, switching languages, he called out to Kiko with a grin, "He says that since he is dead, there is no dishonor in teaching him."

"Is it a point you can sell?" asked Kiko. "Personally, this is one Ghost I would rather not die from."

"You have made your point," Hasukawa said to the Ghost. *"I don't like it, but you are correct in your need of Quinnar. I will teach you."*

The Ghost began to slowly draw his swords. Hasukawa laughed and said, "Don't bother. I'm not teaching you here in this raggedy town, and I am not teaching you in this miserable rain. Come with us. We shall find someplace we can be comfortable. You may be dead, but you can still catch cold!"

19

Bodies and Bones

Jesse had sprinted down to the Fruja Gate, the unofficial entry into the Raio Ward, to join Prince Caleb and his escort. While it was a mere fifteen minute walk from the gate to the Cyl'Karrick estate, Jesse was determined to squeeze in some extra time with the Prince. As they walked, Jesse continued to turn on the charm, working perhaps a little harder than he might normally to keep the Prince engaged. Unfortunately, the results had been mixed, and Jesse was beginning to doubt if the ploy had been worth the effort.

Finally, he decided that if his normal charms wouldn't work, perhaps a more unconventional approach would. "If I may ask, your Princeliness," he said, snark infusing his tone.

Caleb paused mid step, and his head turned to Jesse in mild shock. "Princeliness? Seriously?"

Jesse laughed, pleased with himself. "No, I'm teasing you, your high Prince holiness Caleb." Caleb once again stared at Jesse, making rare eye contact. Those green eyes made Jesse smile. He made a mental note, and decided he would make this into a game, to see how often he could get the Prince to force eye contact. Those eyes were all the more intriguing for how rare the opportunity to see them was.

"I just wanted your full attention," Jesse smiled. "I did have an actual question though."

Caleb nodded, encouraging him to continue. His royal guard, twenty Welgeid, two Deacons, and a half-dozen of Caleb's own Welgeid and Reneforte, all began moving down the street again.

"Your guards and Reneforte," he began. "They are connected to you somehow, but I can't detect any arcane connection. You aren't using command words or active spells, yet they act at your will."

Prince Caleb looked up in surprise. "You can detect the arcane? Most curious."

"Yeah, it's a trick that Old Man Zen taught us. Technically, it's a spell form drawn by our eyes and fed with a little Divination essence, but Zen just told us it was a technique of relaxing our eyes."

"Fascinating," Caleb said, his lilted voice amused.

"Yeah," Jesse said. "So, how come they don't show in the arcane sight?"

"The Welgeid are raised through an Arcane bond to the Father," Caleb explained. "Each Deacon has the ability to tap into a nexus of Arcanum and shape the spell to animate the bodies of our ancestors, traditionally in groups of ten to twenty at a time. They are not sentient, so to speak, but can obey direct commands and are proficient in the fighting capabilities they had in life. I've done research to determine how limited the proficiency is, and how it is imbued into the bones, rather than the muscles, but have yet to come up with a full hypothesis to investigate.

"The unfortunately misnomered 'control' gems," Caleb continued, "are a basic construction of Messaging spells that allow the creator of the gem to express their desires and needs telepathically to a recipient who wields the gem. They are a bit of an Arcane relic, nearly lost to time, because most sentient beings can be communicated with directly using much simpler forms of Message spells. The first Arcanist in Vargarden creatively applied the gems nearly..." Caleb paused as he searched his memory and Jesse just stared agog.

"...nearly two thousand years ago. It was quite revolutionary in the structure of our Legion forces and the Palace guard. Without the need for a Commander within speaking distance of the Welgeid, the armies became more expansive and living Legion Personnel became more flexible within the realms of their assignments allowing for more responsive troop formations.

"To put it in terms of Federation structural magic, it is a hybrid approach of what many would consider Divine magic, but utilizing a more Arcane connection. They've referred to us as warlocks in your literature, although it is a widely distasteful term."

Jesse shook his head. He didn't believe he had heard Caleb string that many words together at once. It was almost more than he'd ever spoken in a single sitting. Caleb looked back, his eyes sparkling in the sun, a small smile on his face. Jesse returned the smile and laughed.

"You didn't explain why I can't see your connection to the gems. I can see all theirs." He gestured at the Deacons.

"Sorry, that's a secret I learned from The Father."

"The Father is like your king, right? But not really, because there is a council?"

"I suppose," said Caleb.

Jesse didn't want to get sidetracked in politics. He was afraid he would lose Caleb to those short stunted sentences again. He shifted the topic back to magic. "So this special technique is also why yours are so much more full of life than all the others we have seen here in Vargarden?"

"Yes," Caleb smiled. "And no. While my gems are constructed differently than the Deacons, both to hide the connection to me and to allow for more subtextual communication, the secret to my Raisings is a more nuanced approach that relies on some of my own Arcanum and structural binding spells.

"Most constructs, you see," he continued, "are little more than objects, vessels to be commanded by the holy priests of Vargarden. Mine are rare, in that they are Soulbound to me. Soulbinding is something that is done in many rituals throughout Vargarden culture, but our tenets don't clearly outline their practice in Raisings. So, because I took some liberties, they are Raised connected only to me. Not the Father. They are more like extensions of myself, of my subconscious."

"That's amazing!"

"How long have you been studying magic?" Caleb asked.

"A bit, why?"

"Most Elysium Magi I have encountered are significantly older than you. Yet, they don't express nearly the grasp on the finite details you seem to. Plus, they are often hesitant to discuss Necromancy."

"Well, you can blame Zen for that," Jesse laughed. "He really beat the 'Ask questions to learn, ask more questions to teach' mentality into my head."

"A fascinating mentor," Caleb smiled. "But you discredit your own intellect. If you don't mind, can I ask about your training?"

Jesse was amazed at the turn in attitude in speaking with the Prince. The more they discussed Jesse's Arcane training, spells he knew, and tricks he had mastered, the more the Prince opened up. He became animated, he maintained eye contact, and spoke fluently and authoritatively. The walk across the city was over far too quickly for them both.

"I will be saddened to leave your presence, Jesse Olben," said Prince Caleb as they arrived at the threshold of the Cyl'Karrick grounds.

"Why does it have to end?" asked Jesse teasingly.

He had spent the last few minutes of their walk finding excuses to touch the sleeves of the Prince's robe, or his shoulder. Light, innocent touches that could be taken to mean nothing, or could be viewed as invitations to more. They had not gone unnoticed by Prince Caleb, but he had given no response as of yet, whether of enjoyment or offense.

"Sadly we must part," the Prince replied. "Moria has prior approval for escorted visits to the Vaults, and Symon Cyl'Karrick will easily be given the same due to his sire's station and history."

Prince Caleb turned his full attention to Jesse. Jesse could see him forcing himself to look up and maintain eye contact as he said, "With no insult or diminishing of your own person or worth, there is no such familial excuse I can currently give to gain you access. Or that of your other companions." His gaze dropped, and Jesse could see his shoulders slump. "I do wish it were otherwise, but perhaps it is also for the best. This situation brings me into utter conflict."

Whether petulantly, confusedly, or perhaps merely rudely, Jesse gave a "hmmph" of disappointment, pushed the front door open without invitation, and made his way inside, leaving the Prince to stand alone on the porch.

"He's such a bitch," grumbled Jesse.

Moria and Symon had left with the Prince, off to explore their lofty Vaults of Xarania, where apparently worthless commoners were not welcome. Argyle was off exploring some new part of the capital. Only Thorn was here, and she was sitting on the bed next to him.

The house boasted half a dozen bedrooms, but the two were comfortable together, and had chosen to continue sharing. Jesse teetered on so many conflicting feelings. He wanted privacy, but needed Thorn there by his side. He wanted his own room, but didn't want to be greedy and put undue stress on Symon's household. He felt trapped and alone, yet was surrounded by people who let him come and go as he pleased. It made little sense.

"Come on," said Thorn. "He's nobility. What would you expect? When have we ever found a Noble worth a damn?"

"Symon seemed alright," Jesse countered. Then he added under his breath, "Or at least I thought he did."

"The blacksmith WAS only a rich boy, not a Noble. So he was only half worthless. Now..." she got a devious little grin on her face. "What's this about 'he did'? What's the cat done to piss you off?"

"Nothing," sulked Jesse. "I was just kind of hoping, is all."

"I thought you were over him?" inquired Thorn, her ears raised in interest. "Are you still gushing over his big, strong muscles?"

Jesse looked over at his friend in surprise. "No! We talked about that. It was just a bit of a crush. That's been months and months, Thorn."

"You sure? I seem to recall a certain little Isnashi who kept staring at a certain muscular chest and pointed out the outline of a certain something that could be seen in a certain someone's trousers."

"Shut up," squealed Jesse, cheeks flushed with embarrassment. "I wasn't that bad!"

"Sweetie, you were practically drooling at times. And when I asked if you were already getting in his pants, you just answered, 'not yet'!"

"Alright! Symon's hot. There, you happy?! I said it."

"But have you told him?"

"No," Jesse said. "There's no point now. Did you see the way he looked at him? It's like I disappeared."

"Jes, grow up and grow a pair," chuckled Thorn.

"All that 'connection' is Vorlak shit," Jesse grumbled. "What about me? I could connect."

"Then jump in there! Tell Symon how you feel before it's too late."

"I told you, Thorn. Symon was just a tease, a crush. He's a good friend, but nothing more. It's not about him."

"So what's your problem? Why is he suddenly a bitch?" Thorn stopped, a look of surprise coming to her face. Her ears raised tall, and her sharp, needle-like teeth flashed in a grin that became a laugh.

"Ha! Symon isn't THE bitch, is he?" She leaned over, shoving her best friend's shoulder playfully. "It's the Prince, isn't it? You've got a new fantasy to keep Miss Rosy Palm company at night?"

"Damn, bitch! Shut up," squealed Jesse even louder, shoving her back. "It's not like that."

"Um, you just said it is!"

"No, I didn't... I mean..." Jesse flopped onto the bed. "I don't know what the fuck I mean."

"Why not? He is cute, for a blue guy."

"No, I'm not thinking of him like that. He's not my type. He's scrawny. I like big burly guys. Like Symon or Xe—" Jesse cut off before he said that name. Thorn frowned at him. "Besides, it wouldn't work. He's... I don't know, above that or something."

"Thirteen Hells," said Thorn, her ears folding back in wonder. "I never thought I'd see this day again."

"What?" What do you mean?"

"I've seen this look on your face before, sweetie. With Erin!"

"Erin?" said Jesse, completely confused. "What about him? What do you mean?"

"Jes, honey bumpkin, I've been hoping to see this again. The Prince is no crush. You're falling in love."

"What? No! Fuck that! The hell you say that for?"

"Fine," she said. "Don't admit it."

"I barely even know him! You don't just fall in love instantly with someone!"

Thorn crossed her arms, playful yet defiant. "You'll see. Soon enough you'll admit it to yourself."

"That's shit and so are you," said Jesse petulantly. "But even if I was, it wouldn't end any better than Erin."

"Fuck you, Jes! One day you are going to learn that your friends are right, and you are worth a damn! Fuck off that he's a Prince. You've got just as much a chance as anyone else."

"That's not it, girl. My worth don't matter here. This is divine fate, destiny intervening, will of the fucking Gods and all that."

"What's that mean?"

"I wasn't lying! Symon and his holy highness-ness have some kind of a mystical, born to be, connection. I've checked. It's not magic, not Arcane. But watch them the next time they are in a room together. They won't be able to take their eyes off each other." Jesse punched his hands into the mattress. "It's hard enough to get Prince Caleb to give anyone the time of day, that I see, but he gets in a room with Symon... It's different. Nobody else seems to exist. It's not just him. Symon half slaps me down to stop me interrupting. He barely knows I'm there."

"Damn," muttered Thorn. "What kind of thrice damned luck were the two of us born into?"

"I don't know, but it fucking sucks, Thorn." Jesse's voice faltered. "If I go after Caleb and I win, I lose Symon. If I go after Caleb and fail, I could get us all kicked out of Vargarden. And then I lose Symon. If I go after Symon, it's the same odds. They all point to me being alone."

Thorn looked up mischievously. "Want me to kill him?"

"Him? Which him?"

"Either? Both? Do we care?" Thorn gave a toothy grin, obviously trying to tease Jesse back into a better mood. "Which would make things easier?"

"No," Jesse said, grinning back. The smile didn't last, however. "No, we will do what we always do with those that don't do us harm. We'll wish them well, move on to bigger and better, and then come back to rob them blind!" He ended this with a triumphant cry and a cackling laugh.

Thorn laughed with him, then after they worked through their silliness, she said, "Good. You and I are wasting away here. The beast obviously needed to get away from Manticore. The blacksmith found his dear daddy's house, so he's set. But you and me? What's for us here? We don't know the people or the layout. We don't know the laws. What can we steal here? Where can we fence it? We can't just keep waiting for the axe to fall."

"I know," said Jesse in reply. "People like you and me, we know how this all works, when people like Symon never learn. Yeah, we got a house here, we get full bellies twice a day. But we aren't earning it. We both know, if it's given, it can be taken away."

"Truth, sweetie."

"One faltered step, one argument," Jesse paused, swallowed, and added, "one jealous boyfriend, and we could find ourselves on unknown streets, or worse, a dungeon. You said it. Symon wasn't a Noble in Highston, but here? Here he might be."

"Shit, you're right." Thon shook her head. "Then why push him away like you always do? It's like you're begging for it."

Jesse flinched as an image of Xerian flashed through his thoughts. "I don't know, Thorn."

"I mean, if you're gonna cut and run, then just go. Don't rile him up. His father... Wait, here they keep saying 'sire'. He was only the head of their entire army, and probably like the fifth oldest person in this creepy ass kingdom. Hell, he practically has a mansion here. Some fucking blacksmith."

"Lord Cyl'Karrick, we should call him," answered Jesse.

"So we stay for the wedding, let them get started on their butt babies, and then we two bolt? Go home?"

"Yeah, but Highston is a bad idea," said Jesse. "We are known there, the Investurants could still be there, and who knows what the situation on the streets might be. But there are plenty of other options. We were just in Essenbeck, but then, Erin was going to take me to Karlslund. Or hell, we could go as far as Vogfaldur and learn Dorne. It's all still in the Khorr, which we know. And we know how to avoid Manticore agents. Or maybe since we don't have affiliation anyways, why not another Bright Guild like Beckoning?"

Thorn chuckled and subtly shook her head.

"What, girl? Spit it out."

"Nothing"

"No, what?"

"You swear by the Court Primaris that you aren't in love, and then in one breath, you mention Erin, his home city, his born language, and his Bright Guild. Boy, you're screwed."

20

The Vaults of Xarania

Symon followed Caleb and Moria down the streets of Vargarden, winding their way to the Legion stronghold. The small entourage of aides, skeleton guards, and some of Moria's men made the travel go smoothly, as the citizens of Vargarden cleared pathways in the streets with respect. The aides and soldiers exchanged smiles and greetings with the civilians as they passed, and there was a calmness about the occasion which spoke of leadership familiar with their people.

Symon still marvelled at the city. The architecture had varied little as they traveled, speaking volumes to the age of the city. As they passed from ward to ward, though, he was able to pick up subtle differences in their distinct feeling and aesthetic. Families who had lived in these wards for generations had left their imprint through banners and decor, occasionally borrowing subtle changes from outside influence. Tradition infused with cultural heritage gave each ward a personality and the people within were much the same.

One of the aides had been a constant narration of points of interest and historical insight. Caleb would interrupt now and again to expand on information from time to time, but was otherwise quiet and reserved. Symon watched the interplay between Caleb and Moria and tried to assess their familiarity with each other.

From what he could tell, Caleb and Moria had run into each other occasionally, but they were not overly acquainted. The arrival of Symon and his friends had changed that, and they expected to see more of each other in the upcoming months as Moria or her team escorted Symon or Jesse through the palace. Watching the two of them interact reminded him of how strange the situation had become. His mind swam with thoughts of Caleb, Moria, and Jesse, and how he was forming new bonds with each, as he discovered what each meant to him, and how differently each fit in his life.

The differences, but also the similarities, meant Symon was never sure how to react. From the moment he had met Caleb he had felt a pull toward him. The Prince filled a void in Symon that he had never realized existed. It was as if Caleb had been a part of him his whole life, but had just now become "real." A spiritual connection that was drawn between them. Symon had checked, like Master Zenesul would have advised him to, and saw no Arcane connections or spell forms, but it felt magical.

Moria was more visceral. Because of her knowledge of the Cyl'Karrick family, she seemed at ease around Symon. He, however, felt like a bumbling fool, the oblivious foreigner. Their conversations were casual, comfortable even, once they began, and they had a lot of interests in common. Unlike the aristocrats back in Highston, she was more practical and connected to the views of common people. A woman holding the elegance of the elite society, while living in a working class mentality. She reminded him of Jesse in some ways.

And Jesse was troubling Symon deeply.

There was a rift forming between him and his friend. Symon could feel Jesse looking at him for answers, Yet, the more they uncovered here in Vargarden, the more Jesse pulled away. Symon desperately wanted to give back to the young Isnashi to repay him for everything he had done. Symon loved Jesse very much and wanted only to take care of him and protect the young man. The blacksmith had looked to reach out and talk it over with Jesse, but every time he tried, something had interfered.

"So, what do you think, Master Cyl'Karrick?" the aide asked.

Shaken from his thoughts, Symon replied, "About?"

The aide gave him a hard glance. It was clear that Symon had missed something.

"My apologies, sir," Symon said. "I was lost in a thought regarding a personal affair. I missed your topic. I beg your forgiveness."

"I was asking you about how you feel about your first foray into the Vaults of Xarania."

Symon hesitated for a moment. A small part of him still deferred to authority and did not want to ask questions that could make people uncomfortable. But that part had been challenged by Jesse and Master Zenesul. The Vaults seemed like a dark secret. One he would have expected in Highston.

"To be honest, I am apprehensive," Symon said. "Can either of you tell me more about what I should expect in the Vaults? Why is it so secretive? Why could Jesse not join us?"

"No offense was intend'd," Moria said. "It's dif'cult to describe to outsiders. Not that ya'r an 'outsider.' Well, 'ya kinda are not bein' raised here. Well... 'ya know?"

"Yes, Lady Yurolinto is correct," Caleb said. He reached over and placed his hand on Symon's arm. "However, you seem to be a very intelligent and capable man. So maybe together, we can help you understand."

"To understand the Vaults, I s'pose you should know more about death conscripts," Moria continued. "As 'ya can tell, we handle death a bit dif'rent than the Khorric do."

Symon nodded. "Yes, you do."

"So, when someone passes on here in Vargarden," Caleb said, "the family executes the death conscripts and inheritance deeds to the will of the deceased. It is how the Yurolindo family came to oversee your estate. The wishes of the dead. Their property rights, distribution of wealth, and their position in the afterlife. It is all part of the conscripts.

"Everyone has the choice of how they wish to serve their family or the nation after their passing." Caleb paused. Symon watched the young Prince as he thought through the words. It was rare for the young man to expand on a topic, so Symon did not wish to press. "Some want to lead their family by residing on their grounds, others offer their bodies to general service, and others conscript their bodies to the Legion for service in defense of our lands."

Caleb turned Symon's shoulders so that he was looking down a side street. His hand raised and pointed at a tiered tower with fanning roofs that were draped in gold and green banners emblazoned with the symbol of Vargarden. "For those serving their families or their communities, the District Priests will provide the family with magical services to raise or speak with their loved ones in accordance with the conscription testament."

Moria smiled and added, "Aye, and we would lay them to rest in the fam's cemetery, or the district, as needed."

"Indeed, that is correct." Caleb said. "If you look closely, you can see most families have enough space for one to two generations at their home. As the family ages, we will move the older generations to the district crypts as the family needs."

"So what is in the Vault?" Symon asked again.

"We're gettin' there," Moria said.

"Those who file conscription with the Legion are handled differently," Caleb explained. "For their first term of service, or about a century, they are interred at the Black Yards. Did you see them as you entered the city?"

Symon remembered the rows of grave markers, stretched out beyond the city. "I saw some cemeteries, yes."

"Those are the Black Yards. The bones of soldiers ready to Raise at a moment's notice when called to the defense of Vargarden."

"Aye, those are the front lines," Moria said, pride on her face. "We inspect the bones annually, or after a service call, for damages and condition. If they pass the inspection, they are laid back to rest, if not we move them to their final restin' and end their service."

"Otherwise," Caleb said, "if they pass through their first term, they are moved to the Palace as guards of honor. You have seen them in our halls."

Symon nodded.

"There's lots of paths of service," Moria said. "We c'n walk 'ya through them at a later time. But this all keeps the service of Vargarden stable and keeps us from having all of our undead out and about. T'would be a great deal o' bones in the streets if we didn't have a limitation of service, you understand?"

"Of course," Symon said, but his thoughts were struggling to keep up. Hundreds, if not thousands, of undead servants throughout the centuries were all circulating through the ranks of Vargarden. An organized, methodical, and painstakingly rigid catalog of service. It was overwhelming.

"Which brings us to the Vaults," Caleb said. "The Vaults are for those ancestors who are beyond their terms of service, have contributed greatly to the welfare of Vargarden, and are honored eternally for it."

"Oh," Symon said. Somehow he had expected more. "So, why the secrecy?"

"Respect, privacy, and in some cases, security."

There was the term that Symon was waiting for. Highston had been notorious for rewriting the history and narrative to control information to the common people. Governments seemed to think it was dangerous for people to know the truth.

Caleb seemed undeterred, and continued, "There are three layers of the Vaults. The Public Access layer, the Privileged Access layer, and the Private Access layer.

"Residents of the Vaults who held common positions and terms of service are interred at the public access level," Caleb said. "Anyone is welcome to visit these Vaults provided they have a family member within and wish to pay tribute. There is also an annual recognition ceremony where we open the Vaults to all to pay homage to our guardians. I attempted to get a special access pass for your companions to the Public Access layer, but it was not approved at this time."

Symon stared hard at Caleb, searching for signs of frustration. Olivar would have been livid if his requests had been denied, and would expect Symon to share in that anger. Caleb instead looked serene and contemplative.

The Prince said, quietly, "I do apologize that it was unable to be honored."

Symon and Caleb exchanged looks, each unsure of how to proceed. Slowly, the group continued to progress towards the grounds of the Vault in silence.

"Tha' Priv'leged layer," Moria said, breaking the silence, "is for those who held protected positions in life such as Strykeleaders, Captains, Generals, and such. Members of their families may visit, and a Legion detail must escort 'em during the visit."

"So, it's just military secrets?"

"Not secrets. Just officers were under watch of the Legion. And gov'ment officials, as well," Moria said. "Basically, any who would have been protected by us in life. It's an honor thing."

"That makes sense," Symon nodded. "And it does not seem unreasonable."

"We think so," Moria added.

"The Private Vault is reserved for those under the Legion's protection, still," Caleb added. "This is where great leaders, high-level nobility, and protected citizens are laid to rest. Once you have claimed your family's heritage in full, which we will do today, you will gain access to the first two levels. Unless you join the service of the Legion, you will only have approved access to the Private Vaults."

"Do I have family in the Private Vaults?"

Caleb nodded, "Yes, you do."

"So I would not be able to see my family? Without you?"

"It is unfortunate, but true."

Symon pondered the implications for a moment, but it was almost too much for him. Vargarden definitely treated their dead differently than the Khorric Federation, but it also was complicated by the fact that Necromancers could speak to the dead directly. These protocols were not to protect the people, but to respect the dead. It would take him a long time to adjust to the laws and customs, but he was curious.

"And then, there's the library," Moria said after the silence had drawn out.

"Yes! The library!" Caleb grabbed Symon's hand and pulled him down the street again. He pressed the pace, leading Symon by the hand as they walked. Finally, they reached the grounds of the Legion Stronghold, and before them was a towering building with fanned eaves at each level. Ornate pillars of stone, with arcane and divine glyphs carved into each, stood imposing their presence over the group as they entered the grounds. Symon was reminded of the Highston Academy and his thoughts swirled yet again.

"The Vault is this way," the Prince said. Caleb pointed to a small archway that stretched over a tunneled entrance leading to a set of gilded stone doors. As the outer doors to the vaults swung open, Symon's fur rippled, as a blast of cool air rushed past him. The air in the Vaults smelled pure and clean, a sanitized scent different from what he immediately considered the "outside world."

"Welcome to the Vaults of Xarania," Caleb announced.

Symon strode through the enormous room and glanced around. Stone dividers, with dozens of doors carved into them, formed aisles throughout the chamber. Flowers littered the walkways and lamps illuminated names of the families represented in the tombs. The number of bodies in this room was beyond Symon's comprehension, but there were numbers and letters carved into the ends of each aisle which led him to believe someone knew the exact number.

Moria took Symon's hand and walked towards a door located to the rightmost corner. Caleb grabbed Symon's other hand. "Come this way, we'll go directly to the third layer and then I'll show you the library."

Symon followed the two of them. His attention was split, as he felt that familiar tug towards Caleb, yet his fascination with Moria took his eyes. He struggled to accommodate both of them, and his social skills were being tested to their limits. He desperately wished Jesse had joined them on this trip.

They continued down the Vault and approached the next door. This had two elite living guards dressed in ceremonial armor flanking it. They stood silently and saluted the Prince as he approached and then opened the doors allowing the group to reach it in stride. Caleb, Moria, and Symon walked through as the aides and attendants stopped and waited outside.

"No skeletons..." Symon started. "I mean, there are no Welgeid here?"

"Nay, the Vault enchantments interfere with Raisin', so we only staff with Living Legion," Moria responded.

"I have something to show you," Caleb said excitedly, still pulling Symon along. The back of the anteroom held three large stone daisies and chairs atop them. In the center chair sat a skeletal figure draped in golden robes, floral necklaces, and beaded thongs of leather and gems. The figure was regal, and Symon could see the Ennedi features present in the bones of the face. The caretakers had carved her name into the base of the throne, illuminated by the lanterns to each side, "Maiya Kal'Khorric".

Caleb and Moria had stepped back respectfully to allow Symon to connect to his ancestor. The young man dropped to his knees and waves of emotion and events of the last few months washed over him. His shoulders shook slightly as he started to cry. They allowed him a few moments, and then both stepped up to place their hands on his neck. Symon's hands reached up and held theirs in his, appreciating the comfort of these fast friends.

Symon stood up and wiped his eyes with his arm. Smiling at both of them, he took a breath and said, "Apologies. I did not anticipate that this would be so moving."

"Aye," Moria said.

Caleb nodded.

"This is beautiful. Thank you."

"We honor those who came before, and your family is important to Vargarden," Caleb said. "I am happy that you are here."

"Yes, I can see that."

Moria took Symon's arm. "Now that Prince Caleb got his gift for you in, it is time to show you mine." They walked towards another niche in the stone mausoleum and Symon could see large wooden doors carved with vine work and writing. The guards opened the doors and beyond Symon could see a library beyond.

"The reason we are here, with Caleb, is to officially add your sire's name to the Legion's registry of the dead. He will be marked unclaimed, but then you can take over his estates. Also, we will pick up the markings of his last enlistment collection. Now that his dereliction is absolved, we can retire his service to term and add up what he's owed. What *you* are owed."

"What I am owed?" Symon asked.

"Yes, your sires' gold reserves have taken care of the estate quite well," Caleb said. "Lady Yuralinto has done quite well at management and you have a sizable amount left. However, with the resolution of his service, his retirement wages must be calculated and distributed."

"What?"

"Aye," Moria smiled. "With this, you should be well to do. I'm not sure what legacy you wish to leave. But, 'ya should have options. At your age, you could follow your sires' steps in the military?"

"I am no warrior." Symon shook his head. The thought of the Brownie decaying in his hand filled his mind. He would not make a career in killing. He could not.

"Ya's family also has a history of artisans," Moria said. "Craftsmen are well respected here."

"Yes, my father was a smith in Highston."

"Nemuku Cyl'Karrick ran a forge?" Moria asked, voice incredulous.

Symon nodded, smiling, "One of the finest in the district."

"Intriguing," Caleb said. "You also are a Gifted Necromancer?"

"Yes. It seems I have many options. But only after we free the Federation from the Investurants and Manticore."

Caleb's face went flat. A look of disappointment and frustration, mixed with concern. He said. "The war, of course, is important. I would just assume it would be handled by others. You said yourself that the Legion is not in your future."

Symon frowned. Caleb was right, but he did not understand that it was all his fault. His and Jesse's. The war between Grendel and Highston came through his home. He had to find a way to right it. Instead he said, "Thank you, Prince Caleb. It is nice to have a place here. The Khorric Federation has been my home for my whole life. It may not be perfect, and I may be more welcome here, but I have to take care of that first. Then I can focus on making my way in Vargarden."

"We c'n understand," Moria said. "Can't we, m'Lord?"

Caleb looked at her, then looked back to Symon, but that flat look did not waver. "Of course."

"So what do we do, now?" Symon asked.

Moria waved him to the back of the library where a few Legion members, all Gnomes, had gathered. They wore the robes of notaries, and their little hands were smudged with ink. "They are here to take down the details, and we start the process of your estate. This may take some time."

Symon walked to the table hesitantly. The head of the Notaries looked up and grinned. "Master Cyl'Karrick, it is wonderful to meet you. I knew your sire for a few years, he was a good man."

"Thank you."

"Let's begin."

The afternoon passed as they filled out document after document, but it filled Symon with a sense of stability, with Caleb at his side. The young Prince guided him deftly, helping him make decisions that would lend a better legacy for any family he might start here in Vargarden.

21

Heart of Stone

A week had passed since the Vaults. Jesse walked in the back gardens of the Cyl'Karrick grounds, trying to enjoy the well-tended greenery, but really trying to avoid his friends. He was preening his wings and allowing the spring coat to come in and replace the winter's colors. For the first time in a while, they had color. The tips and trailing edges were coming in a soft rose pink.

Jesse turned and saw Argyle sitting, as always, stone still, with his head cocked to the side and a slight smile on his face. "You want something?" Jesse asked.

"Just admiring your wings and the way they accentuate your effeminate manner," Argyle replied.

"Effeminate?" Jesse's tone took a sharp edge. His sexuality was never an issue in Highston or it would appear here in Vargarden, but he wasn't sure of Argyle's implications.

"No insult intended. The color is quite striking with your hair. They suit you. I just have never seen them beyond the dull grey they always are. They are noteworthy, and give you a certain 'flounce' that I have not seen in you. You seem different.

"If only, you were not wasting it on this melancholy each and every day." Argyle growled.

Jesse, startled, looked up in surprise. "Excuse me?"

"We shall call an end to the pacing, moping, and introspection for the morning, shall we?" said Argyle. "You shall accompany me today. The others have already been informed."

"I'm not moping," Jesse grumbled. He thought for a moment, shrugged, and got up from where he had been sitting. He jogged over to Argyle, who abruptly turned and began leading them from the estate. "So does this mean I get to see where you go every day?"

"Did you not know where I have been visiting?"

"No. Nobody knows."

"That is surely not the case," Argyle said, nodding towards one of Moria's scouts. "I would be highly disconcerted if it manifested that the Prince was not receiving regular briefings on our routines."

"Oh, well maybe HIM." Jesse didn't bother hiding the mild venom he felt from his voice.

"Why such disdain for our host?"

"Host? No, nothing."

"Come now. Have I, in the past, betrayed a confidence you have placed in me? Please allow me to hear of your thoughts, that I may offer my own."

The two quickly left the interior of the city, passing through the ancient walled gates, and began to enter the city exterior. The streets became narrower, the crowds around them fuller, the buildings more densely packed. Jesse had no idea where they were or where they were headed, but then, he was barely paying attention.

"It's fine you want to help," Jesse said. "I'm just being silly. It's stupid, childish even."

"My friend, I told you a month ago that you were yet young. Childish issues are your forte. However, I do not believe that your present concerns are so base. I implore you to tell me."

"I'm just tired of being dumped on, is all."

"Oh? What Skyfallen Clade has the fates thrown across your path this day?"

"It really is nothing," said Jesse. "I think I like someone, they don't like me, end of story."

"Ah," said Argyle. "I see now the source of your dismay. But why do you believe such feelings to be childish?"

"I don't know," mumbled Jesse. "It just feels like jealousy is so... petty."

"My dear boy, matters of the heart are neither insignificant nor juvenile. They impact those both young and old and have been the cause of many curses, from rivalries, to murder, to the fall of nations. Do not deny your thoughts as petty, unless you admit them to be mere flights of fancy."

"Yeah, but I don't really know him," said Jesse. "Maybe it is a flight of fancy?!"

"Well, then, let us discern the reason for your infatuation. Are you enticed to be in his presence?"

"Uh, obviously."

"What draws you to him? Is it his looks? His station? His companions?"

"I don't know," faltered Jesse, at a loss as to how to answer. "I have no idea about his companions. I get the impression that he doesn't have many. His station? It's high, but that's more of a turnoff. You know I fucking hate Nobles."

"So he is nobility, and he is solitary. I see. Pray, continue."

"That's it."

"Come now," Argyle smiled and continued. "Does he reflect in your mind that of a past lover? Is he a person you would traditionally be attracted to?"

"Um, well no, I've only been with Xerian and Erin. He's not like either of them." Jesse glanced at Argyle and decided to be completely honest. "Neither is he like Symon, who I also had a crush on. He's just different."

"So, you are drawn to him, and not a ghost of your past. He does not adhere to your traditional standard of attraction, and yet you are drawn to him. He has flaws that you acknowledge, yet do not dissuade you from your thoughts of romance. This is pleasing. And, my young lad, it does not appear that it is a flight of fancy."

"Thorn thinks I'm a lovesick shorgath, but I think she's nuts."

"Describe him for me."

"Oh come on," said Jesse, playfully shoving Argyle on the shoulder. It was like pushing against a stone wall and had no impact on the giant creature. "Don't pretend you don't know I'm talking about Prince Caleb."

"You dishonor me," Argyle laughed. "It was most certain that you were talking about the Prince as your paramour. I ask that you not describe to me what I would see if I were to look upon his visage. I ask that you not even tell me what your own eyes see. Instead, tell me what your soul sees when you gaze upon Prince Caleb."

"What?!" asked the young Isnashi.

Argyle stopped, moving them both to the side of the cobblestones out of the way of passersby. "Close your eyes," he said. When Jesse just looked at him in frustration, Argyle repeated more forcefully, "Close them."

Jesse huffed out in annoyance but did as he was told.

"Good, now picture the Prince."

"Oh come on," Jesse snapped, opening his eyes and looking back at Argyle. "This is stupid."

Argyle gave a long, disappointing look, then turned away. "I can see that my opinion is not welcomed."

"Really?" said Jesse, trying to give a grin. "I thought I was the only one babyish enough to sulk." When Argyle did not return the banter, Jesse blew out another sigh and closed his eyes tight, adding, "Fine. Alright, I'm picturing him. Now what?"

"Concentrate. Tell me what you see," came Argyle's deep voice from much closer than Jesse was expecting. He was startled, but quickly settled back into the sight he was trying to reimagine. The Gargoyle's words held power and rolled through Jesse's head as his view of the imagined Prince sharpened and intensified.

"I see blue," he said softly. "Lots of blue. Deeper than a clear sky, but not stormy. More like a poorly clouded sapphire."

"Go on."

"He's there. In the blue. Flowing darkness around him. Darker blues, black, flowing but gently. More like a breeze through a dark forest than a thunderstorm." A pause, then, "Surrounding that is a field of tan and white, acting as a frame but also a fence."

"Why is it a fence?" came Argyle's whispered voice.

Jesse was entranced at this point. No other world existed except his friend's deep, quiet voice, and the flowing images in his mind's eye. The words drew out of him without conscious thought. "The Prince doesn't have anyone. He is bordered on all sides by aides and teachers, but they're not connected to him. His Father has the warmth of a grave. All of his confidants are as cold as books. He has literally made his own friends."

"Tell me more."

"He is so... different," replied the teenager. "He moves with grace, as a branch swaying in the wind. It's a grace I've rarely seen outside of dancers on display. He's delicate, slender, but not weak, not sickly. In fact, he has never been ill."

Jesse saw a shield within the blue. An aura around Caleb that spoke to something that had troubled him. "I've always wanted a protector. Someone who I can belong to. I've been drawn to men who are strong, tall, muscular. The Prince is tall, but none of the rest. It bothered me. But now I see he has strength without those traits. He is a protector in his heart.

"His chest is a cage, confining a tremendous heart. His stomach holds the perfect curves. His hips are sharper than your claws. The fingers of his hands, more delicate than the dorsal feathers of my wings. His, well," Jesse's ears turned red, "there are areas yet to be explored. His nobility is in his bearing, not his attitude. He's... regal."

Once more the deep voice whispered in Jesse's ear, "And do you love this man?"

Confusion swept away the amorous look from the boy's face as he answered, "I don't know. I want to, but he loves another. No, that is wrong. He feels he belongs to another. And I don't know him well enough for love. The lust is there. The desire, the infatuation." Quietly, barely a whisper, Jesse added, "I want to love him, but I don't. Not yet."

"You have done well, child," said Argyle in a stronger voice. "You may open your eyes."

As Jesse opened his eyes, his mind became shocked as his senses were flooded with the sights, sounds, and smells of the busy street. His skin tingled, that danger alert triggered, as he realized how much he had been missing for the last several minutes. Jesse stepped away from Argyle, nearly stumbling, and cried, "What the fuck was that?"

"My apologies for any unexpectedness or discomfort. I merely wished to aid you in exploring the truth of your situation."

Jesse lost all decorum in the sheer overwhelming nature of the situation. "What was that shit I said?" he yelled. "How did I know that shit?"

"Again, my apologies. Perhaps I should have asked first. I provided you a touch of Divination to assist you in gaining what you needed to learn. The results can be unpredictable in their assistance, but at no point did you lose control of your faculties, and all that you uttered was true, even if it was unknown to you before you spoke it."

"So all that about him having no friends and being all alone? That's—."

"All truth," interjected Argyle. "Come, let us continue."

"So that also means," Jesse sighed, his eyes lifting slightly. "If all that is true, I mean. He's not already in love?"

"From what you were shown, he does believe himself to belong to another. A betrothal perhaps?"

"Gods I wish!" Jesse laughed. It was a sarcastic, mirthless laugh expressing his hopelessness. "Not that easy. He has a connection of some type with Symon. It's not a spell. Not Arcana... Maybe Divine?"

"I have noticed that the Prince does tend to favor his attention to our Ennedi friend when in his company," said Argyle.

"Yeah," said Jesse with a defeated sigh.

"Almost as much attention as each of them attach to a certain Isnashi we both know."

"Now you're stringing me up!" teased Jesse.

"On the contrary, sir," Argyle responded. "It is more subtly presented, but it is most assuredly there."

"Well, fuck that!" Jesse laughed. "Thorn's told me about the love triangles she reads in those little books she borrows from Mistress Daysleeper! They're vorlak shit! I'm not doing that."

"We shall certainly find out," Argyle laughed.

Jesse bathed in the sunlight as the two companions continued on. His step was noticeably lighter, and Argyle had helped. Soon they arrived at a city park, cut out from the crowded streets and packed buildings surrounding them. Lush grasses spread throughout the clearings, dotted with freshly blooming springtime flowers. Small copses of great trees stood interspersed through the park, providing shade and breaking up the space into more private sections.

"Wow!" Jesse said. "This place is beautiful. Is this where you go all the time?"

"It is one of them, yes."

Jesse took in the district and realized they weren't in a glamourous area. It looked more like his home in Bunlo district. "The houses here. They're not rich. This isn't their noble district is it?"

"It is not," said Argyle. "In the Khorric Federation, such openness is lavished only on the wealthy. Vargarden apparently makes more of an effort to share the natural bounty with all classes."

Cynical, Jesse huffed. "Maybe this is just an older part of the city, and the buildings fell to the poor with age, leaving them the park by accident?"

"Nay, this is by design," responded Argyle. "We have seen many areas of the city, if you pay attention, where buildings and whole blocks have been repaired or even razed and rebuilt. This city is not so static as it may appear, and this land could easily have been developed. It appears that the people of this kingdom are unbelievably cared for.

"The parks, the cemeteries, temples, and libraries are all here for the use of even the poorest citizen," Argyle continued. "With food and shelters given for those who need additional assistance. All under Vargarden are afforded the attention of their neighbors."

By this point, they had reached a fairly unoccupied corner and Argyle stopped and turned. "You may join me here in the open sky, or avail yourself of the shade provided in those trees. But I would ask that you stay in my company for a time, and debate your options with your heart's troubles."

Argyle grinned, then added, "Or it may transpire that you are too uncomely to woo said object of your desire!"

"Wait a minute," squealed Jesse. "Did you just fucking call me ugly?"

When Argyle began chuckling, Jesse jumped on his back, digging his hands into the rough scaly skin. He dug into his sides, trying to find a breach in the rock-like hide, endeavoring to find a ticklish spot. The Genbu's chuckle became a full laugh, shaking his huge frame and jostling Jesse nearly off his back. Argyle's laughter subsided as Jesse heard a high-pitched squeal of laughter and something hit him from the left. He turned in surprise to find a Svartal child having bumped him during his attempt to climb Argyle's back. Another sound of delight was heard a few dozen yards away, and Jesse turned to see a Skink child running their way.

Realizing he was about to lose his status as king of the hill, Jesse quickly climbed down and stepped back. Within perhaps fifteen minutes, a dozen children of various ages were climbing all around the monstrous Gargoyle, having the time of their lives as he peacefully lay there, basking in the sun and attention. Jesse jumped as, with no warning, Argyle raised his head and issued a tremendous roar. The children scattered and squealed in delight. This was obviously part of the routine, for while the children momentarily scattered a few yards, they all were laughing and running right back to climb him again.

When the chaos subsided, Jesse asked, "Argyle, do you really think I have a shot?"

"My friend, that is truly for you to determine." Argyle flopped down on his belly, for all the world like a rathhound, sighed contentedly, and said "You may bind yourself out due to some mysterious fate, perhaps Arcane or Divine, or you may fight the fates, and take what is yours. Who can say whether you may succeed? You may find the fates too powerful to overcome. Or you may discover yourself to be the key to a destiny far greater than you have known."

22

Jumping at Shadows

Argyle's words had run through Jesse's mind for days. Finally, the young Ishanshi took Argyle's message to heart and began looking for opportunities to meet with Prince Caleb. Jesse started looking for opportunities in conversation that the Prince might be needed for something, or that a message might need to be sent. When these opportunities presented themselves, Jesse used them to full advantage. Every moment with Caleb was filled with intention.

As awkward as it had started, the two became more friendly as they went. Surprisingly friendly. A touch on the arm. A joke or shocking statement that forced eye contact. And of course, the sneakiest of ways in, discussions on spells and Arcana. As the Prince's emotional walls dropped, an abrupt shift in Caleb was noticeable. Jesse found Caleb almost always touching him in some way. A soothing and familiar touch. To keep it going, Jesse spent days wracking his brain to remember details and lessons from Zenesul. He even braved bugging Symon to try and remember the more boring history and theory lessons they had sat through and Jesse had ignored.

However, what turned out to work best also turned out to be the most fun. Jesse began showing Prince Caleb what spells he knew, and particularly, what shortcuts and tricks he had learned. Jesse was saved from feeling like he was showing off and bragging by the Prince's rapt attention. The Prince even complimented Jesse on ways he had found to cut down on Federation casting times. Tips and tricks, points and counterpoints, they spent days diving into the more detailed nuances of casting.

The young Isnashi had almost acclimated to the presence of skeletal warriors hidden in the recesses of the palace. Only select areas, such as the palace gardens were free of them. Today, as they walked through these gardens, Jesse was explaining how he was able to meditate in the mornings and commit a certain number of spells to memory for instantaneous casting later in the day.

"Is this not a standard practice?" asked Prince Caleb.

"Hardly," laughed Jesse. "Elysium Magi can do it from their tomes, but Zenesul is the only other person I've seen do it from memory. But, he's so crazily unconventional for someone living in the Khorr, I don't think much of it."

"The core?"

"Sorry, Highness. K-H-O-R-R. The 'Khorr' as in the Khorric Federation. It's kind of a nickname on the streets."

"So, Master Olben," the Prince said. "If you can refer to the 'Khorr' then, I beg you will please refer to me as Caleb, as I requested."

Jesse looked up in surprise and no small amount of embarrassment. "I'm sorry!" he said. "I forgot again."

"I like it when you blush," said the Prince quietly.

"Well then, I'll have to blush more often," Jesse teased. "Keep saying cute things, and I'll be sure to make it a habit."

As Jesse predicted, the quip led to the Prince giving another bout of eye contact. And, like all good things in Jesse's life, it did not last nearly long enough. However, the young Isnashi did notice that the Prince still had a bit of a smile on his lips as he asked, "What is your Arcane Influence?"

"My Arcane influence?" asked Jesse. "Like why I do Arcana?"

"No, your Arcane Influence," Caleb replied. "The focus of your Academy."

"Oh, I'm not in the Academy."

"I thought the Federation referred to all structured Arcana in terms of

Academies or 'Schools'?"

"Right, but Zen hates that."

"Oh, I see," Caleb said. His voice was sharp and clipped. Jesse could see he was losing the thread of the conversation and Caleb was struggling.

"But," Jesse said, hopefully, "I met Master Zen through my... old boss. I learned Arcana as a method of survival and expanding the skills needed for my job."

Caleb returned that soft smile. "I was actually asking after your Native Essence. Your Arcane Influence for a more crude vernacular," said Prince Caleb. "Although I would also be quite interested in hearing more about your motives for learning the Arcane, as well."

"Oh, like my Sphere?"

"Yes!" Caleb's eyes lit up. "You are aware of Spheres?"

"Oh, yeah," said Jesse. "Zen calls them Spheres. He was REALLY excited about Symon being a Necromancer. But all the spell forms he taught us rely on me knowing the Aether and Brace forms. Why is there all these different ways to refer to the different branches of Arcana?"

This time it was the Prince's turn to look up in surprise. "You were taught Aether and Braces? Not Academy Formulaic Structures?"

"Oh, sorry," Jesse playfully smacked himself in the forehead. "Yeah, you literally just said Arcane Influence. Uh, I don't know. Are you sure you want to talk spellcraft with a dunce like me?"

"Dunce?" The Prince frowned as Jesse grinned widely. "Ah," he said. "Another jest."

"Yeah." Jesse tucked some hair behind his ear and watched the Prince. Caleb knelt down to inspect a small greenish-yellow flower. After inspecting its leaves, the Prince drew a small arcane symbol in the air, whispered a word, and energy flashed into the plant, causing it to fill out and brighten.

Still staring at the plant, Prince Caleb said, "Can you show me your Sphere?"

"Oh, yeah! I can try a spell. Don't know if it's my Sphere or not." Jesse squatted down and tapped the same plant the Prince had just invigorated, drew out his own arcane symbol above it, and said, "*Farroos!*" The upper leaves began shedding light, quite visible in the late evening's twilight. Jesse looked up at the Prince, grinning and gesturing at the plant.

"Yes, Light," breathed Prince Caleb. "Your influence is Light."

"Really?"

"Yes, I saw when you touched the Veil."

"What?!" asked Jesse, incredulously. "You can actually see the Veil?"

"My apologies," said the Prince. "I misspoke. As Meister Bartolomae would say, 'Proper speech may breed contempt, yet soft speech breeds misunderstanding.' No, I merely meant I was able to notice your Arcane Influence at the moment you released your spell. Your natural affinity is reflected in your Aether and it's why you would naturally reach for that type of spell when asked to show your Arcanum."

"Soft speech, huh?"

"Which breeds misunderstanding, correct," said Prince Caleb. Then quieter, he said, "Though I would prefer to explain myself a hundred times than to give you cause for contempt."

"So, the way we talk to each other does matter?"

"Yes."

"I'm sorry," said Jesse, real concern in his voice and body language. "I know my rough Street Rat speech isn't what you're used to, and I'm real sorry if it makes you feel like you need to change yourself."

"I'm not changing because I need to," Caleb said. "But because I desire to. I've been told that my words can often make others seem uncomfortable. I would hate to make you feel that."

Jesse smiled, tension draining from his shoulders. "I've been practicing since I met Symon a year ago, working to clean up how I talk. But I like the way you talk. I hope you don't change for me."

"Shall we agree to learn each other's manners and do our best to accommodate?"

Jesse smirked. "You mean, let's just talk to each other how we talk?"

"Agreed."

There was a pause between them, tension grew, new but just as thick, as each stared at each other, debating whether to push the topic further. Birds sang around them, their voices ringing throughout the surrounding trees, as well as the sounds of various people moving along the edges of the garden. Finally Jesse decided to relieve the Prince of having to say anything further by changing the subject.

"Anyway, yeah," said Jesse, "I guess my Sphere is Light. The spells that come easiest to me are illumination, shielding, and movement spells."

"So, Light, Force, and Transposition..." Caleb murmured. "Interesting. In that case I have a few spells that may be of some interest to you. One would be quite of use if you ever come into contact with those who use Necromancy for evil. Of course, it might come into more immediate use for you against those of Mumvuri."

"Mum- what?"

"The Investurant's home plane. What you call the Shadow Realm," replied Prince Caleb. "Anyway, Sunburst is quite a powerful spell that creates instant daylight. It is a more powerful, more broad version of what you just cast, with a higher concentration of energy."

"Sounds amazing," Jesse said. The Isnashi allowed his vision to slip into the Arcane spectrum so that he could watch the steps of the Prince's casting. The Prince, for his part, slowed down his gestures to make it easier to follow.

"As you can see, the core foundation of the spell is actually the same as what you used," the Prince explained, his fingers drawing a pair of inter-laying circles in the air. Each form sat, one inside the other, connecting portions by sharing glyphs between the two. Caleb's hands split apart and each form followed as he showed them in the air. "But this part is new. Do you see?"

"I kind of see what you are doing," said Jesse. His eyes struggled to follow the speed in which Caleb was drafting, as well as the perspective of being on the wrong side of the spell. "But it is reversed from this side. Do you have this written down somewhere? Somewhere we could study it together?"

Caleb smiled, slyly. "Here, try this." The Prince released his form, allowing the arcane image to break apart and dissolve into the air. Then to Jesse's amazement, he watched as Prince Caleb began redrawing the same form again, this time as a mirror image, corrected to Jesse's point of view. The level of comprehension of the forms Caleb was displaying was insane to Jesse. It was mastery on a level of confidence unseen in the Federation. Messing up a single glyph or line could spell disaster and yet the Prince drafted it as steadily as before.

The young Isnashi realized the Prince was showing off. It was an attempt to impress him. Which it had. Jesse chuckled and took his opportunity. "You're cute! Crazy, but cute! It's impressive that you are bold enough to try to draw the spell backwards, but I still can't properly see the hand movements from that side."

Jesse ducked under Caleb's arms and snuggled backwards into his body. Jesse's wings tucked beneath the Prince's armpits and rested gently behind his torso. Caleb let the spell go, dissolving it once again into the Aethos with no effect. Jesse could smell something on Prince Caleb, not quite floral, but not medicinal. A sweet, somewhat spicy, smell of dried herbs and petals. It could be a soap, a lotion, perhaps a faint perfume, but something very pleasant was there and it was intoxicating.

Beneath that, another smell, something he was beginning to identify as the Prince's own aroma. Symon had introduced Jesse to the power of scent. The Ennedi could use it to determine moods, intention, and much more. Jesse wasn't as proficient. And suddenly Jesse became very aware that he didn't know how well he smelled. He became very self conscious but fought the urge to pull away. "Draw it normal," he whispered.

Caleb drafted the form for a third time, and Jesse focused intently. He desired to return the Prince's earlier showcase. To impress Caleb as much as the Prince had impressed him. Now that he was in Caleb's arms, it made sense. The foundation of the spell was familiar to Jesse, it only required a few extra strokes to gather more Arcanum. It would be at the top of Jesse's capacity, but not beyond it.

The young man smiled, stepping away from the Prince. "Let me see if I got it." Within seconds, Jesse had the form structure intact. He cheated by using his recalled spells in the morning, snapping a brace form into being instantly. His fingers traced the needed additions and began to fill the spell with his Arcanum. The Prince's delicate blue fingers brushed Jesse's hands pausing the spell.

"How long have you been studying Arcana?"

"I don't know," Jesse frowned. "Three, maybe four years... I think."

"You are merely a boy. You don't particularly look old enough to be proficient."

"Hey!" exclaimed Jesse. He gave the Prince a sour look. "I'm plenty old enough. I'm eighteen! Remember, I've been taking care of myself for a long time. I haven't been a 'boy' in some time."

Caleb looked back at Jesse flatly. "My apologies. No offense was intended," said the Prince. "I merely meant that the Federal Elysium doesn't begin training Magi until they are your age. By bypassing them, you are unique in your age. Let alone your progress." He reached toward Jesse's drawing. The Prince stepped forward into Jesse's space, touching shoulders again. "You did invert these two areas, however." He pointed first at one line, then at a glyph near to it.

Jesse smiled. "It would still connect and fill properly. Call it a flair."

Caleb grinned. "It's an arrogant approach."

"But I have it!" Jesse said with childish glee. "What is the command word?"

The Prince looked over at Jesse, doubt in his eyes. "You have it? You are certain?"

"Test me, bitch!"

Prince Caleb's eyes widened in utter surprise. Blood rushed into Jesse's face and he raised both hands to cover his shame. His gaze flitted around the courtyard, looking from side to side, half expecting to see guards rushing to accost him for his offense.

"Orlam's balls!" Jesse said, mentally kicking himself as more coarse language escaped his lips unbidden. "Fuck! I'm so sorry! It slipped out, I swear!"

"Did you—" gasped Prince Caleb. Caleb's words were lost in a torrent of laughter. Not a stately, refined chuckle. A full belly powered, maniacal laughter. Jesse looked at the Prince in confusion trying to come to grips with his shock. The Prince started again. "Did you—" laughter reclaimed the words as Caleb again lost his composure.

The Prince's laughter became infectious, causing Jesse to join the Prince in the hysteria.

"Did you just call me..." the Prince struggled through laughs. "a 'bitch'?"

"I'm really sorry," Jesse said with a smile. "Too long hanging out with Thorn. I forget myself sometimes."

Jesse's peripheral vision obscured as a dark blur appeared from nowhere, cutting their mirth to pieces. A burst of Arcane energy rang against the sound of a blade, protecting the Prince from a stabbing attack. The force knocked Caleb flying into a line of shrubs. Jesse instinctively grasped the hilt of his sword, attempting to draw it from his hip. It was in vain, however, as the pommel had been tied to the sheath as were all weapons within the palace not carried by guards.

Jesse cursed and drew a short blade instead, hardly a weapon intended for damaging an opponent, but more of a utility or cooking knife. He reached across his abdomen with his right hand, blindly hacking at the leather straps binding his sword. With his left hand he began casting a defensive spell, not for himself, but in an attempt to give the Prince some form of protection. Jesse could see a small amount of blood trickling down Prince Caleb's hand, and hoped like mad that any injury wasn't serious.

'Rhon... Rhon... Rhon...' the word forced itself into Jesse's mind unbidden. Over and over, just as it had in the streets of the Ricon district in Highston. Sure enough, the dark blur came again, this time from the other direction. Jesse's Shield spell blocked the blade, ringing out into the courtyard. The Isnashi's eyes darted back and forth trying to track the shadowy form. New laughter, this one cold and calculating replaced the earlier sounds. "Yes, my pets... fear me."

"Shit!" cried out Jesse. As loud as he could, he began screaming, "Investurants! Attackers in the gardens! Help the Prince!"

In horror, Jesse watched as the familiar form of Rhon, the Investurant assassin, materialized before him. The Isnashi tensed, but terror gripped him when Rhon focused not on Jesse, but Caleb. A sinister smile formed on that blue face as he turned to face the Prince.

Jesse sacrificed a moment to look down at his progress and saw that he only had one of three straps cut through. Remembering their last meeting and Rhon's ability to phase weapons past his own, Jesse abandoned the attempt to cut free his sword and concentrated on building a second Shield.

It was completed just in time, for as he spoke the command word, Jesse sensed another attack. Acting on instinct, Jesse dove to the ground on his side, flipping the arcane disk in front of the Prince once again. Nothing struck the barrier, which fell uselessly to the ground, bouncing against a bush, but the fading light was blotted out for a moment as the insubstantial black form of the Assassin passed through the space Jesse had just occupied.

Caleb rolled away from the attack, his toe catching the discarded Arcane shield and flipping it into his hand. Blood drops flicked into the air as his other hand began another spell form. Rhon snarled, his hand forming a spell of his own. The tension of the cold showdown washed over the battlefield, as a battle of speed and Arcane talent began.

The inquisitive part of Jesse's mind paused, curious as to which of them would finish first. Then the horrible realization of failure struck Jesse. This was not a game. Jesse was wasting his time. The Isnashi reached toward the unfinished spell. The form, still held in his mind, materialized in front of him. He gathered his Arcanum and poured it into the brace form. Sweat dripped from his brow as his energy quickly drained. The taxing spell took shape in his hands. But fear stopped him. He realized that he knew the pattern, but their lesson had been interrupted. He had no idea how to finish the spell.

"Caleb!"

"The command word is *Ferrelius!*" cried out the Prince.

The assassin turned instinctively to see what was going on behind him. Jesse completed the last push of Arcanum and called out, "*Ferrelius!*"

Rhon shrieked as he was bathed in an intense blast of directed light, bright as the noonday sun. The Investurant dove to the side in self preservation, but even still was hit by a blast of arcane energy emanating from Prince Caleb's outstretched palm. The blast burned away a part of the Investurant's cloak, striking him, shredding the shadowy cloth into mist to be carried away in the breeze.

Snarling, Rhon whipped his arm forward, sending one of his Kukri spinning unerringly at Prince Caleb. Jesse cried out a warning, even as the Prince casually, almost lazily, flipped Jesse's recovered barrier spell into the path of the flying sword. The Prince's eyes tightened as the dagger that had been sent directly behind the Kukri, slid past the barrier which had already dropped too low to impede the smaller blade, disappearing into the Prince's cerulean robes.

Cries of alarm cascaded into the courtyard as, from multiple directions, came a veritable wave of skeleton guards rushing and bounding in their direction. Rhon blasted shadowy energy at the Welgeid, but the spell splashed harmlessly off their bones, not slowing them at all. Black robed priests spilled into the courtyard from many of the arches as well.

Rhon, crying out in frustration, dove toward the Prince. Caleb made a sudden flick of his wrist and disappeared in a flash of light, reappearing a dozen feet from Jesse. Rhon corrected in flight, and phased forward, tucking into a roll and grabbing up his Kukri. With a practiced cast, a portal opened behind the assassin as he regained his feet. "This is NOT OVER!" Rhon screamed. The assassin threw himself into the portal which disappeared immediately.

Jesse's breath was suffocated as an avalanche of bones and steel crashed over him, burying him. He could see glimpses of Vargarden Deacons and guards between the gaps in the cage of skeletal warriors pinning him to the ground. It was several agonizing minutes of Jesse listening to the confusion and panic of multiple voices before he finally heard Prince Caleb's voice amongst the others.

"Where is he?" Caleb called out.

"Your majesty, we're still locking down the perimeter."

"No, not the attacker. Where is Jesse? Where is he? Is he injured? Is he still here?"

"In here," Jesse shouted, trying to make himself heard.

"Get us out of here," the Prince said.

Moments later, the skeletons pinning Jesse down began to lift themselves off and he was allowed to extricate himself. As he found his freedom, Jesse saw Caleb pulling himself to his feet from within another pile. The two dusted themselves off, looking around at the chaos.

"Whether for good or ill, the guards are programmed to look to my safety above all else," Caleb said. "Apparently, they see you as an honored guest and they moved on my vicinity. That is why you were gated as I was."

"It's all good, Pri—,"

Prince Caleb's knees buckled and he tipped forward. Jesse, quickly as he could, took the Prince's weight and helped him to a nearby bench. "He's injured!"

Jesse peeled back the Prince's left sleeve. They both winced as a nasty looking slash was revealed. Jesse smiled realizing that despite their skin tones, underneath the meat and blood were the same red as his own. "It will be okay, Caleb." There was a pale, milky secretion along the edges of the cut, which almost seemed to be bubbling slightly. Pointing it out with the tip of his knife, he asked, "Is this something from you, or is it from the blade?"

"It would appear to be poison," a gruff voice sounded from over Jesse's shoulder. One of the black robed priests was inspecting the injury. "And I might suggest," he added, "that you put the knife away when in the presence of so many guards."

The Deacon looked over the wound and hissed. The skin around the wound was dry, cracked, and necrotic. It was spreading fast. Jesse leaned forward. "Can you help?"

"Of course," the man in black grumbled. "It's not poison, it's cursed spellcraft. Vile 'Vesters!" The priest's eyes glowed green, pulling energy from someplace, not the Veil that Jesse could see. The man whispered a small prayer in a language the Ishanshi couldn't make out. The wound lit from within, puss and ooze pushed its way from inside, and then a small black mist hissed out. A vague skull shaped green insignia formed and dissipated the dark spell. Within a moment later, the Prince's wound was totally healed.

"By the Gods!" Jesse wondered.

"By the Father," the Priest corrected. "My Prince, the knife wound is closed and the curse counteracted. We need to get you to safety."

Prince Caleb reached out and touched his fingers to the priest's forehead and said, "Thank you for your assistance and sacrifice." He allowed the two to help him to his feet, and said, "I will allow Reneforte to see to anything else."

"Guards!" The priest shouted. "Get reports on my desk. Immediately! And see the Prince to his quarters. Master Olben, you're with me!"

Caleb turned to Jesse. "I showed you that sunlight spell mere minutes ago, and your first casting was in a combat situation."

The young man grinned. "I told you I had it," he said, and then seeing that

Prince Caleb was looking at him, he grinned and mouthed, "Bitch."

"I'll see you soon!" Prince Caleb said. "You, my friend, are a formidable opponent. I am fortunate to have you as an ally."

Jesse allowed himself to be led away, but gave a mocking bow as he departed. "Anything for my Prince."

23

Monsters of the Past

"To explain the Shadow, we must first understand the nature of the world, Arcana, and how our kingdoms are connected," Caleb started. "We shall begin at the epoch of creation, with the ancient beings that created the essence that would become our reality."

"Oh, the Gods..." Jesse said, a snide tone under his words. "Great."

Symon settled in on the Prince's smaller sofa. He glanced at Jesse who was tense and worried. The Ennedi's nostrils filled with an acrid, pungent aroma of possessiveness and jealousy that reminded him of Olivar. Jesse had been on edge since the attack, but Symon was not sure that was the reason. An unease was growing between the two friends. Symon hated it.

"Jesse," Symon chided. "Let Caleb speak."

"Yeah, of course. Let's dig into Divine plans and connections. If it can mess with my life, then let's see how that seems to be wrecking everyone else's."

Symon started to respond, but Caleb's eyes stared blankly back, waiting on his cue to proceed. Symon would have to uncover Jesse's issues at a later time. Nodding to the Prince, he asked, "The Gods?"

"No," Caleb shook his head. "Not the Gods. Creation. All of this, I believe, was created by beings far older than the Gods, and more powerful."

"That is blasphemy!" Symon said. "The Gods are infallible."

"So your Federation would have you believe," Caleb said. "The priests there have carefully crafted a system of hierarchy, dependency, and dogmatic connections within the governing structure of the Khorric Federation. All of it depends on your understanding of THEIR understanding of the Gods. However, it doesn't account for Gods across the Realm and the cultures that are devout to them."

Symon started to object, but could not. Another Federation lie was destroyed by simple observation and logical thought. Another control had been broken. Symon reached out his hand and touched Caleb's. That acrid tang from Jesse flared. Symon shook his head and smiled. "Thank you, my Lord."

"Evidence points to ancient beings that created the very essence of our existence, and they were responsible for the creation of the Gods themselves. Few texts speak of these Ancient beings, but I believe them to be very important. It is even believed that it's possible that a skirmish between a few of them may have been the cause of the Devastation. However, that's a topic for another time.

"To understand our history with the Shadow," Caleb continued. "We must discuss our connection through Arcana. The concept of Arcane Influence and Essence. Symon, how much do you understand about your Gift?"

"Zenesul explained some of the Gift to me. But he was hesitant to explain my Gift, due to its nature. I was only aware it was Necromancy shortly before the fall of Highston. And was forbidden to speak much about it."

"A wise approach in the Khorric Education system. I take it that you were given the same premise explanations of Spheres that Jesse received from Master Zenesul?"

"Yes," Symon agreed. "Spheres, Brace and Aether forms, Structured Arcana versus Gifted. I still have a lot to learn, but I feel like I have a good start. Will you be able to explain why Necromancy is so dangerous?"

"It's not Necromancy that is dangerous," Caleb said, dispassionate. "It's not even about danger. It's about control. The Federation maintains a grip on Arcana through structured spells. With their structure comes hierarchy and politics. With that hierarchy, they control who has power. And over the years, the structure of the Academy has been able to keep certain Arcane Spheres unexplored.

"Gifted Magi often go untrained, which is dangerous," Caleb continued. "Without discipline, the Gift could escape the control of its wielder. Casting using one's Gift is often tied to emotion or instinct. It doesn't imply the balance or limitations found within Structured Arcana. It's dangerous to ignore."

Symon thought of the nightmares and the detritus of bones he awoke to on the road. He had been tapping into his Necromancy unaware. It had terrified him.

"Even beyond that, your Gift would have been problematic within the Khorric Academy. The Empress forbade teaching Necromancy to guard her secrets, and the rule of her forbiddance stuck," Caleb stated. "There were a lot of secrets that would have been a threat to her rule, so she began isolating them quickly. With over two hundred years to work through this, it was easy enough to build a government structure that protected her."

Symon nodded intently. Everything Caleb said rang true to how Symon had learned the Federation controlled information. The young smith leaned forward in his chair, but Jesse kicked back, haughty. "Yeah. Great. We all love Arcana, but what does this have to do with the War. And their attack here?"

"Jesse," Symon said sharply. The smith could hear a clicking sound under Caleb's breath. There was a scent of irritation and confusion beneath the air of control that the Prince was showing. Symon nodded. "I apologize, your Highness. Please continue, we shall endeavor to hold our interruptions."

"Jesse, it's a fair question," Caleb replied. "Arcana is what binds the Mumvurii and the denizens of Vargarden. Our connection through Essence. All of creation started with Essence. There are simple or pure Essence such as Fire, Light, or Force. But even those are slightly altered by our existence in the Material plane and are not viewed in their "true" form. This muddled apparition of Essence is more evident in other simple forms such as Earth or Water, you see, where the Material existence of this element is essential to its impact in our world.

"These Essences are known to many cultures by many names. Spheres, Schools, Nodes, whatever they are called, they are the key. A Sphere is our focus into the ethereal or Arcane energy. And our Arcanum is bridging that energy into the Material realm to act in accordance to our will.

"Necromancy is a complex Influence. Complex Influences, unlike their

Simple counterparts, touch or contain multiple ethereal threads from related Essences. Because we are Material beings progressing through Time," Caleb said in a voice where you could hear the capitalization of those words. "Our Necromancy has a strong connection with Death, Life, and Body. Our ability to manipulate the tendrils between a living being and its body gives us power. When we Raise the dead and Animate them, it's because we give them an echo of the Life Essence that ran through them. This connection to life is present in all mortal beings and we can manipulate it at our will.

"Some of the most powerful Necromancers could bring those on the brink of death, or even beyond, back to life by restoring them to their body."

Symon remembered the first night Jesse was attacked. The strange Arktos that appeared and helped Symon bring Jesse back from the brink of death. A chill ran down his spine, thinking of how close that he had been to losing his friend.

"And that's where our connection to the Soul sphere lies," Caleb said. "A simple brush on this Sphere is connected through the other three, and this blends into what we know as Necromancy. But we can only touch Soul through our Material connections, through the rest of the Spheres involved in Necromancy. This is, I believe, a limitation of our existence in the Material plane.

"The Investurants, however, approach it differently. The Soul Sphere is where the Shadow magic has an Arcane resonance with Necromancy. It works the same on both Material and Shadow, but it's not limited by the rules of Material. It's like we are pulling on the same thread, but from different segments and for different reasons. The similarities, and differences, that the Investurants present are what make them formidable opponents to us."

Caleb took a breath and Symon glanced at Jesse. Jesse started to prompt Caleb, but Symon shook his head. He had learned that the Prince had a very specific way of approaching topics and that any interruption might be devastating to the narrative.

"Their detachment to their Material Essence allows many of the Investurants to shift between planes," Caleb said. "This gives them a significant advantage in tactical movement. Within the history of Vargarden and Mumvuri, we once had an agreement to share this travel with partnerships between our peoples.

"The Realm of Mumvuri is similar to the Material realm, but there are fundamental deviations. These deviations are present in all aspects of their culture. Their connection to the Arcane Essences, the layout of their home world, and blood of their Nobility. First, let us talk about the similarities. If you were to travel to that Plane, you would discover several familiar locations. The Sexsor Mountains, the Moaning Expanse, and the Yyaleskin Jungle would all be present, although named differently. The shape of the land and these features are echoed in the realm of Mumvuri.

"Cities and cultural centers, however, are located in different places, although mostly close to where you would expect them, being resource centers for life. Wildlife and terrain features stretched out in locations as they are here. You will also discover the marks of major landscape events such as earthquakes and floods that are similar to those reflected in our history.

"While the order and location of these things are similar to our realm, it is hard to predict or map in historical terms as the rules of Time and Being are different from ours. Before the Devastation, the Arcanists of Vargarden had an alliance with the Mumvurii people." Caleb pointed at a map of Vargarden hanging on the wall. He smiled, "Our alliance allowed us limited access to Mumvuri and you could enter a portal, travel across their lands, and reappear here in Sainan leagues away.

"After the Devastation, we formed an alliance with the Khorric Federation. It was intended to be an extension between all three kingdoms, but the Federation didn't see the value of Mumvuri the way we did.

"Skyfallen Gateways had made the Mumvuri travel options obsolete in Khorric eyes. There was little incentive for them to join. The Father did strike an accord with Empress Elanna, and that lasted until her passing. I believe it was at this point the conflict truly began. And while the resultant War was severely harmful, ultimately I believe the conflict pointed out that the Shadow and Material people were never intended to exist in the same realm."

Jesse looked at Caleb, "Wait. I thought you just said we're connected?! And that we have an echo something with the Shadow. Why can't we exist together?"

"It is an issue of similarity, yet incompatibility," Caleb said. "Many sources lead scholars to believe that the Ancients created Sainan and Mumvuri as different versions of the same creation. Almost like they were experiments competing towards a goal they devised. A goal we as mortals could know nothing about, nor comprehend. We have the same Essences. Essences such as Earth, Fire, Time, and others. Just in different amounts or combinations. Our major differences are present in Body, Life, and Soul. It's our implementations of Soul that damages us both."

"Shit!" said Jesse.

"Indeed," Symon chimed in. "Is this the cause of the war?"

"A bit," confirmed Caleb. "But let's not get ahead of ourselves, we'll get there in a moment. I want to go back to Soul. Soul makes up a great deal of Shadow magic. And it's why Necromancers and Shadow mages have an uneasy relationship."

"Uneasy?! We're at WAR!" Jesse shouted.

"Jesse," Symon said. "Let the Prince explain at his own pace."

Jesse huffed, rolling his eyes, and slumped back in his seat. "Fine. Whatever you two want."

"Returning to the Shadow, let us talk about the differences between them and us," Caleb continued. "The Investurants, as well as other inhabitants of Mumvuri, don't have the same connection to the organic material that Body is made of. Instead of their Souls being connected to their Body, like us, they connect their Body to their Soul. And the highest Nobility among them can phase their Body into a state between existences."

"They can turn into Shadow," Jesse said. "I've seen that."

"Correct," Caleb nodded.

"It is this state that connects their Shadow Sphere to the Soul Sphere in a way that our Necromancy cannot. Where we manipulate the Life and Death Spheres to pull souls back, they have the ability to connect directly with the Soul Spheres. And there is great power in this ability.

"When the original War of Night broke out, the Federation was not prepared for what the Shadow was capable of. Transitioning between the Material and Shadow realms, their warriors were able to scout the land without facing their enemies and then portal back directly behind enemy lines and strike from ambush.

"Then they used Arcana unlike any known here." Caleb said. He gave a wistful smile, betraying his passion for unique Arcana. "Spells like Coldfire and Wraithblades, which can ignore walls and armor, but burn and cut flesh. The Federation had no protection against this. These spells disrupt the very Soul from the Body. They are as effective and deadly as any spells we know but are undefendable by almost anyone. Except, of course, for Necromancers.

"When the Federation brought Vargarden into the war, the playing field leveled. Our Welgeid, our undead troops, have no souls, thus making them impervious to Shadow magic. And the most powerful Necromancers have learned to guard our souls by shielding our Life paths and the connection to our bodies. There are even a few of us, like your Sire, Symon, that have rebuilt their Soul and Life connections making their Soul a battery for Life. It's one of the secrets to extended longevity that only the rare and most non-conformist of Necromancers have pursued."

"Like the Father? Your Father?" asked Jesse.

"No, different from that. It is for another reason. The side effect is an Extension of life, not immortality," Caleb answered. "It provides Necromantic healers a more powerful trade for the Law of Equivalence when structuring their spells. Life for Life does not Heal, but it merely spreads the damage out. When Healing major wounds, trading Life takes a longer toll on the caster."

Symon thought about the two times he had healed the nearly dead. Both had drained him for days afterwards. The Priestess here in Vargarden had confirmed that he had shaved a bit of his Life off, making it unrepairable. Caleb had the gist of it. Too much Healing would shorten the life of a Necromantic Healer, unless they found a loophole in the Law.

"So my father was the monster I believed him to be?" said Symon. "A brutal mind. A nearly immortal mind. A war machine."

"He was Nemuku," Caleb said.

Symon flinched. "I have heard the stories."

"No, you haven't. You've heard the Federation's tales. They are not the same." There was a look of pride in Caleb's eyes. "I have studied Nemuku Cyl'Karrick's tactics. Trust me when I say, there was no one more capable of winning that war. And while many lives were lost, they were lost only when necessary. And when the war was at its critical point, only our Nemuku had the strength to make the impossible calls.

"Vargarden is steeped in tradition. Our laws, our values, and the Legion's doctrines are all based on a foundational need for tradition and heritage. Only someone who was willing to sacrifice it all was able to make the call required. A call that brought the war to a standstill. The one you were on trial for when you first arrived."

Symon shifted in his seat, the weight of the words burdening him. It still did not make him more comfortable with what he had learned of his father. The man had been willing to destroy everything for victory. Even himself.

"The only thing I've never been able to determine is how he negotiated the end of the war. The two fronts were dead-locked. Neither leader wanted to expend resources in a contest that would gain them nothing. So the Master of the Investurants and our Nemuku met in secret. Suddenly, both forces withdrew. The Legion returned to Vargarden with the treaties and spoils of war, but without the Nemuku. It was thought that he may be lost to us forever. But then you came home."

Grief swelled inside him and wrestled with the rage. Tears welled in his eyes, and Symon forced them back. Caleb's hand reached across the desk and rested on the back of his own. A small sad smile on that cerulean face. Jesse glanced at Symon, sorrow also in his eyes, but the moment they flickered down to Caleb's hand the acrid scent of jealousy flared once again.

"I should have asked you already, but how old are you?" Jesse asked. "Were you here when the Legion returned?"

"No," Caleb laughed. His laugh was a bit cold and distant, like someone who knew what laughter was supposed to sound like, but had little practice. "I am merely a student of history and magic. I have dedicated my life to uncovering mysteries of magic and to do that, I must learn all I can. It helps that I'm the Crown Prince and have been able to travel the world with the Father's envoys. I have gathered information from all known corners of this Realm."

"So, what do you want from us?" Jesse asked. "What could we give you? That you don't already have, I mean."

Caleb gazed directly at Symon. Caleb opened his desk drawer and removed a long, narrow, intricately carved, black box. Sitting the box on the desk between them, the Prince opened the box and exposed the contents. A glimmering, slender, purple crystal on one side, and a wicked looking, ornate dagger on the other. The Prince's shoulders arched forward and his eyes intensified. "Did Nemuku Cyl'Karrick ever tell you about the Shadow Shard?"

"No," Symon said, eyes downcast. "He never spoke about his life before Highston. He never told me about any of this. I am sorry."

"Damns," Caleb cursed. "I was hoping to get some light on how he got it back for us."

"What is it?" asked Jesse.

"No one knows for sure," Caleb replied. "It was once a gift between Mumvuri and Vargarden. But now, I think this is the reason that the Investurants keep returning to attack the Federation. It was under Khorric control before the war. From what I've been able to study of it, it contains very powerful Shadow Arcanum."

The two boys exchanged glances again. Again, feeling the importance of this conversation, and what it could mean to this new war.

"I explained earlier about the differences between our world and the Shadow world," Caleb said. "I believe that it is important to understand that we may not be able to exist in the same plane of existence naturally. I think this Shard is the reason why it's even possible... at all."

Symon looked over the dagger and was fascinated. It wasn't a design he was familiar with. Barbed edges, a nearly non-existent quillion, and a metal he had never seen before. His hand reached towards the blade instinctively, and then he looked up. Caleb nodded and he picked up the blade.

The blade felt... wrong. It almost vibrated in his hand, and he could feel what he could only describe as a separation between it and his hand. The blade was fighting his contact. A slow burn started in his fingers. It wasn't exactly painful, but it was certainly uncomfortable. "*Ka'ski shan'diar 'el staciatos,*" a voice said in Symon's head. It was a different voice, but Symon's thoughts immediately raced to his father's sword.

"Shit," Jesse shouted, dropping the crystal on the desk as Symon let the dagger go. "What the Hells is that?!"

"Did you hear a voice, too?" Symon asked.

"Hear what?" Jesse shook his head. "No, I didn't hear anything, it's just touching that crystal was fu–" he hesitated. "Messed up."

"The dagger is the same," Symon said to Jesse. "It is like they do not want to be here."

"Exactly," Caleb said. "As if they exist against us. This is why I think the Shadow and Material aren't supposed to work together."

"So, if the Shadow don't want to be here. And we don't want them here. And the only reason they can be here is this Shard..." Jesse mused. "Why aren't you just giving it back to them?"

"It's a conversation that has been held," Caleb said. "First, we're not sure what the Shard is. The 'Key Theory' is only one of many. Some of the council feel there is a danger to the unknown and are hesitant to return it. The Father seems to be personally attached to the acquisition of the Shard and has recused himself from the decision. In time, I believe the council will agree to return it."

"And until then..." Jesse huffed. "Innocents can just die."

"Jesse!" Symon chided.

"Come on!" Jesse said. "You know it's true. Nobody cares that poor people will suffer. Just sit in the ivory towers and play your games of King's Tower, right?!"

Caleb frowned. "He's not wrong. I think many on the council forget that there are real ramifications to the decisions they ponder. Our traditions are not expedient."

"So no one knows what the Shard is capable of," Symon said, trying to pacify Jesse. "Nor do we know how dangerous it is. Therefore, it is unclear if we are handing a weapon to the enemy."

"Basically," Caleb said. "Even after these many centuries, we know little about the Mumvurii people. Nor their magic. Take this weapon for example.

With Shadow magic being able to manipulate the Soul, some of the most powerful Mumvurii Magi have learned to bond souls to objects. This dagger," Caleb gestured. "is a Soulbound dagger. While the motives to create such a weapon are still unclear, the power contained in this dagger is immense. I theorize that the Soul contained inside has seen countless generations, and would likely share that knowledge with its wielder. And I also believe that if a Shadow mage held it, they could draft arcane energy from the blade expanding their abilities to cast. It's a weapon unlike anything I've ever seen."

Jesse pointed to the crystal, "So we don't know what this is or why the Shadow wants it?"

"Correct."

"But because this," Jesse pointed to the dagger, "is a weapon. Then the Shard could be, too."

"Correct," Caleb said. "And it is unclear what the Khorric Federation has done with the Shard while in its possession."

"What do you mean?" Symon asked.

"This is all theory, you understand," Caleb started. "I theorize that because of our Material separation, no mortal mage has ever been documented with Shadow Arcana abilities. Necromancy is the closest we've seen. However, this crystal could allow a mage to tap into that Essence. Primal connection to the Shadow Sphere.

"Luckily, the Shard's magic has a lingering effect. So, this next part is not conjecture, it's able to be proven. I can make out some of the spell forms that were laid over it. The Federation has been tapping into Souls and binding them to replicas of this Shard. Creating Soulbound batteries to power... something."

"What?!" both boys asked at the same time.

"Yes, I think that the Federation is trying to bind Souls," Caleb stated. "But I don't think that it is as simple as it sounds. This dagger is eloquent. It's a creative Arcana. This dagger is a masterwork of magic, and its use, while subtle, is an endless repository of power. The Federation is not that artistic.

"Now, we return to theory. I believe the Federation has always envied Vargarden's armies. I believe they want automatons. But since the public would be squeamish about the dead, they were trying to hide it by placing Souls into these batteries and animate them. I can also see the sacrificial rune etched into the previous spell forms. I think they were attempting to synthesize the crystal and capture Souls."

"No," Symon shook his head. The Khorric Academies had fallen quite far in his eyes over the last year, but he could not believe they would stoop to this level of betrayal. "No, there are boundaries that even the Elysium Magi could not cross."

"Symon," Jesse whispered. "I think Caleb is right. I think the Feds have lied about what the Embros are."

"You don't think..." Symon's eyes went wide as he made the connection. He had seen them in the Federal Academy, the huge machines with their glowing crystal cores. The Elysium had said they were Skyfallen, but if those crystal cores were Shadow Shard replicas, there were hundreds if not thousands of sacrifices to account for.

"Embros?" Caleb asked.

"Yeah, the Embros," Jesse said. "Giant automated defense mechanisms that protect property. Only the rich and powerful have them, and they are unstoppable."

Caleb's brow furrowed. "This is not good. I was hoping that they hadn't succeeded before the Shadow Shard was removed from their possession."

"They've been importing 'new' Embros models all the time," Jesse said. "Maybe they're still making them."

"Incompetent morons," Caleb hissed. "If they are replicating replicas, creating Shard copies from Shard copies, there could be flaws. Flaws beyond what even I could predict. I must convene with the Council immediately."

24

The Gift of Freedom

Jesse stood on the manicured grass of the Cyl'Karric gardens, his hands clasped behind his back, eyes downcast, lost in a riot of colorful flowers, his wings swinging open and closed gently, in time to some internal rhythm. The days of chaos had not set well with him, and being cooped up at the Manor had not helped. Surrounded by people, he felt isolated and alone.

"I was told I would find you here," Prince Caleb said, stepping out into the garden path.

Jesse did not look up at hearing himself addressed, but the tensing of his shoulders alerted that the Prince had been heard. Jesse was still struggling to control his disinterested attitude. He knew that it would throw off Caleb's intended conversation, but his emotions were swirling.

"How's your Council sessions been going?" Jesse said at last. Jesse was still looking away, refusing to break first. "To what do I owe the pleasure?"

"They've been fine, thank you," said the Prince awkwardly. The Prince's hand reached out to grip Jesse's shoulder. "As I expected they would go. I was somewhat surprised to find that you did not attempt to visit me these past few days."

"It was implied that fewer visitors to the palace would be preferred for the time being," said Jesse. He turned to face Prince Caleb, his face cold and difficult to read. "Plus I was given the impression that I was not wanted around for the moment." The Prince winced at his words. "Something about needing more time."

"That was unfair," said Prince Caleb. "The time I requested was to sort out the information we've gotten as well as the ramifications of the attack. Although it is clear that, despite my arm, you are the wounded one."

"I've done what you asked, Caleb. What do you want from me? You told me to wait, be patient." Jesse paced the courtyard. "But while I give you time to explore whatever you are going through, you invite Symon to the palace. Now you are upset that I did what you asked? Now you say I'm unfair?"

"This may be a first," said the Prince. When Jesse looked at him in frustration and confusion, he elaborated. "You just called me Caleb without being prompted."

"By the Saint's tit!" yelled Jesse. "Every time we talk you practically beg me to call you Caleb. Now I do, and you don't like it?"

"No, I truly appreciate it. You finally see me as a person and not a title."

"I've always seen you as a person," said Jesse. "Even when I was scared of the title." He paused, then asked, "So if you are here, talking to me, does this mean you are through exploring your divine insta-love with Symon?"

"You are being unfair again," the Prince said flatly.

"True," said Jesse. "But right now I'm in the mood to be a snarky, petulant child. Love it or leave it, oh high highness-ness."

"I didn't spend any time with Symon."

"Really?!" Jesse snarked.

"Correct," Caleb said. "He was a guest of Minister Kufo to provide a report on Nemuku's return of the Shard. He said the same thing that he did in my chambers. No more, no less."

"But nobody thought to invite me?" Jesse said.

"There was nothing to invite you to. The interview was less than a quarter of an hour."

"He was gone all day!"

Jesse watched as the Prince heard those words. The Prince was confused. And then it all hit Jesse. He hadn't even considered the paperwork that Symon would have had to do. A sly smile appeared on Jesse's face. So, it hadn't been as romantic as Jesse feared it had been.

"So, you really didn't see Symon?"

"No," Caleb said. "Just Administrators and Diplomats."

"All in a day, right?" Jesse smirked. "Your Highness?"

Prince Caleb returned the grin. "Now you are teasing me. Keep it up and I will withhold my present to you. And here I was, intending to reward you for your patience."

"A present?" asked Jesse, that teasing smirk remaining across his face. "You must want something from me, oh Princely Prince-ness."

The Prince crossed his arms and attempted to imitate a pouting attitude. Caleb had no skill at the deception however, and both were soon giggling at his act.

"So, CALEB," Jesse made a point of stressing the name as he approached the Prince. "What is this present? Now you have me curious."

"What else would I give you, Jesse, but Arcana," said Caleb. "Well, that and freedom."

"Freedom?"

"Symon and I did have some conversations before. He was rather forthright about one of your rather unique hobbies." Jesse was curious, but also wary. Symon had no place exposing Jesse's past, especially to the Prince. Seeing the look on Jesse's face, Caleb moved beside him, shoulder to shoulder. "Watch closely," he said, beginning a new spell form in the air.

Jesse's eyes focused and he watched with rapt interest, as Caleb completed the circle, whispered, *"Hervestoll."* The Prince disappeared in a minor flash of light and a slight 'click' sound.

The young thief's eyes darted around the courtyard in confusion, trying to determine what had happened. Finally, he spotted Caleb standing several dozen feet away, a broad smile on his face. Jesse quickly recalled how the Prince had used this in the fight against Rhon. Jesse was delighted and awed that he was being shown the spell. Just as quickly, Caleb cast it again, disappearing and reappearing right next to Jesse.

"What do you think?" Caleb asked.

"Nice," Jesse said. That fear of being given something only to have it taken back gripped Jesse's stomach. He asked, "You really want to teach me this spell?"

"I really do. My gift to you."

"It is an incredible spell," said Jesse, "But you seem to be making it a bigger deal. I feel like I'm missing something."

The Prince's brow furrowed in frustration. Jesse flinched, thinking of the ways he probably just offended Caleb.

"Don't get me wrong, I'm impressed. I just think I'm not seeing it from your point-of-view."

Caleb took hold of Jesse's arm, linking elbows with him. "I told you," Caleb said, "Symon informed me of one of your interests. It is that which I am thinking of. Are you prepared for your first Translocation?"

Jesse swallowed hard. "Sure."

Caleb reached out and brushed Jesse's feathers. Caleb leaned in and kissed him on the cheek, his breath warm in Jesse's ear. "Stretch your wings, and fly. *Hervestoll.*"

Jesse's world flipped over and his vision went black. A moment later and all of his senses came back full force and Jesse floated weightlessly only briefly, before the wind began to rush past him. Then in a mix of awe and elation he realized that he was falling, several hundred feet from the ground.

Jesse joyously spread his wings wide, catching the afternoon wind, reveling in the familiar tug to his shoulders as his wings took his weight. He looked around over the spread of the capital city before him. The principal cathedral to his right, the government buildings ahead, the palace to his left. The warm afternoon air was full of updrafts, and Jesse took advantage of them to swoop from side to side, rising and falling, as the currents allowed. The last opportunity, Jesse realized, had been that night with Symon, the night that Rhon attacked him in the Ricon district. He took full advantage of the opportunity, stretching out the flying session for as long as possible before realizing how exhausted his muscles were, pointing his way back toward the Cyl'Karrick gardens, and allowing himself to drift ever downward.

As details on the ground came into focus, he was able to see that Caleb had lain down in the grass to watch Jesse in flight. He was now clambering to his feet as Jesse approached. Jesse's strength waned so he ended his flight and swooped down. He landed a bit harder than intended, dropping to one knee in sheer exhaustion, his wings drooping in a shell around his form. Caleb moved quickly to his side.

"What is it?" asked Caleb. "What's wrong?"

"Nothing at all." Jesse looked up, a contented smile on his face. "Just haven't done that in a while, and you sent me half the world up into the sky." He stood, rolling his shoulders and flexing his wings, in an effort to stretch both. He then reached out and grasped the Prince in a hug. "Thank you, Caleb. You probably don't know what this means to me."

"I had an idea."

Jesse's stomach dropped. Even this moment between the Prince and himself had Symon's thumb on it. "Yeah, yeah. Symon and all that," said Jesse, his voice falling. He led Caleb over to a bench so they could sit. "So what's going on with you two, then?"

"I do not know," Caleb said. "He is different from anyone I've ever met. Whenever we are together, he is certainly interested in paying me attention. Yet, he also speaks fondly of Lady Moria at times. I can ask more directly, at the cost of possibly giving offense."

"So what does that mean?" asked Jesse. "Do you want to be with him?"

"I've never had the luxury of thinking of just a relationship," Caleb said sadly. "It's always been a political choice."

As the sun set in Vargarden, Jesse's anxiety had finally gotten the best of him. He had to get out of the house. The silence was driving him crazy. Symon was driving him crazy. Not knowing how to handle Caleb was driving him crazy.. There was no corner of the yard he hadn't seen. He had to go.

A few minutes of searching led him to find Thorn in the upper floors of the Cyl'Karrick home. Home to a few bedrooms, much of this area had been closed off and was being used for storage for unneeded furniture. It appeared that Moria had kept it tidy. After four decades, as impossible as it seemed to Jesse, there was little dust to be seen. Just stacks of well crafted items.

"What are you doing up here?" Jesse asked when he finally found her.

"Just helping Symon with some inventorying of the the house," she smiled mischievously. "Apparently nobody has been up here for years."

"Does Symon know you're helping him?" Jesse grinned back. "Let me guess, you're doing some appraising while you are at it?"

"Gotta keep the old skills up, you know."

Jesse began wandering aimlessly around the room, lifting a sheet here, peeking in a chest there. His attention couldn't settle on anything. Thorn noticed his listlessness, and stopped what she was doing to watch him. She waited patiently for Jesse to say something. The young thief knew she wouldn't press, it was on him. She was depending on him to say something. It didn't take long.

"I'm sick of waiting," Jesse finally snapped.

"Waiting? Do tell."

"On the Prince. On knowing anything about what is going on. On figuring out our next step."

"Of when it will all end?" Thorn asked, hesitantly.

"Want to get out of the house? I kind of need to not be in the same place as Symon right now."

"What's with the two of you?"

"I'm not sure," Jesse said. "But... I just need space."

"Sure. It's hours after sunset, but I know of a few areas still open."

"Of course you do," Jesse said.

"You're not the only one who's uncomfortable, Jes."

"I'm sorry." Jesse looked at his friend and saw her sad smile. "I appreciate it. But, I was thinking of something more..." Jesse paused, giving his best friend and partner a knowing look and a mischievous grin, "traditional. For us, at least."

"Oh, I like that." Thorn hopped to her feet. "Let's go."

Twenty minutes later the pair was perched atop a tiered tower structure, likely a church or temple of some kind by their reckoning, with flared rooftops and intricate sculptures. They looked down at the streets and buildings of the capital city, a hundred or more feet below them, letting the peace of the city wash over them. It was quieter than Highston. But big cities never officially sleep.

"This does feel almost like home," said Thorn. "It's been a while since we have run the rooftops together. Their buildings are funny though. I'm not used to their roofing techniques." She squatted down and ran her clawed fingers over the glossy slate tiles. "They are so much slicker than I'm used to. I keep thinking I'm going to lose my footing."

"I feel like we've both lost our footing," said Jesse quietly.

Thorn sat down next to Jesse, joining him in dangling their feet over the edge, swinging them lazily and enjoying the night air. She wrapped her arm around his waist and snuggled into his shoulder. Jesse's mind swam with conflicting thoughts. All of the changes and chaos had shaken him. Fear battled excitement. He was overwhelmed by the potential of great things, but the terror that it wasn't real. Deep down, all he wanted was to go back to a simpler life.

He muttered, "I have the absolute dumbest thing on my mind, Thorn."

Thorn remained silent, attentive but patient. She cocked her head slightly in his direction, however, and her ears showed she was paying attention.

"I miss Xerian," Jesse said quietly.

Thorn snapped her head around.

"He was an absolute shithead, I know that," Jesse said. "Every time you warned me away from him, you were right. But I knew where I stood with him. I miss snuggling in bed with him, listening to the rain. I miss cooking side by side while we listened to the couple next door arguing. And as fucked up as it is to say, I miss him hitting me."

Rage flared in her eyes and she started to sputter.

Jesse continued, "At least when he hit me he was paying attention to me."

"Want me to smack you on the back of the head so you will know I'm paying attention?"

"I'm being serious, Thorn. Yeah, it's screwed up, but like I say, I knew the ins and outs. I knew how to draw him out of a bad mood. And even though Xerian was rough, he really did have his good side. He could be really sweet when he wanted to."

Thorn scoffed, but otherwise kept her opinions to herself.

"This is so fucked up," Jesse yelled out angrily. "I've tried everything I can think of! But I don't know how to fucking flirt! I can get him to smile, I honestly think he's interested, but I have no idea how to get him to admit it." Jesse hung his head, both in frustration and defeat.

"This is about the Prince?" Thorn asked. "You still haven't done anything?"

"I've never had to pursue someone," he said. "And yeah, it's really about Caleb."

"Oh, 'Caleb' now, is it?" Thorn smirked.

Jesse chuckled slightly. "Hey, he bitches every time I call him anything else. I'm trying here."

"So, Xerian kind of grew into whatever the fuck that was, and Erin picked you up at a party. You've always been the prey, never the hunter. So basically, you brought me out here to teach you how to date?"

"I don't know about that. That doesn't seem to be your strong suit."

Thorn rolled to the side, using her momentum to put everything she had into punching him in the jaw. Jesse nearly fell off the edge of the roof. His vision blurred and his head spun from the impact.

By the time he could regain his senses, Thorn was forty or more feet down the side of the tower. Jesse threw himself off the side of the tower. He let himself free fall for a few seconds, then unfurled his wings to slow his descent, gliding in circles around the tower until he found a space to cut her off.

"What the fuck?!" he shouted.

"You are an absolute asshole," Thorn said. "You know that, right?"

"I'm sorry. Yes, I'm an asshole." Jesse's face betrayed his confusion.

"And do you know WHY you are an asshole?"

Jesse backed up. It was very clear, from her voice to her face to her posture, that Thorn was pissed and itching for a fight. She wasn't playing around. He had crossed a line and he wasn't sure where.

"Thorn," Jesse said. His voice pleaded and his hands opened up. "I'm really sorry. I thought I was playing around. We always rib each other."

"I thought we were fucking friends. I thought we looked out for each other."

"What the Hells? What did I do, other than apparently tease you in exactly the wrong way?"

"You dragged me out of Highston!" she shouted. "You took me away from my life, from my home! From everything I knew!"

"Girl, we can always go back. The city will be waiting for us. I highly doubt either of us had any property that can't be replaced tenfold here."

Thorn screamed in rage. She turned her back to Jesse and began to make for the edge and descend to the next rooftop.

"Thorn? Seriously, what am I missing here?" Jesse searched her face, trying to read behind the anger, and only now realized she was crying. "What's going on? What am I missing?"

She dropped to her knees. "You really are so fucking selfish sometimes," she said quietly, almost to herself. Then she looked up at Jesse and said, "You took me away from Highston. You took me away from Akosa."

"Who?"

"We've done so much together, and it never occurred to you that I might be seeing someone?" She shook her head and chuckled, a mirthless, chilling laugh.

Jesse was absolutely stunned. Thorn may as well have slugged him again, for all that his brain seemed to be comprehending what she was saying. "Seeing someone?"

"Jes, sweety, oh selfish bitch of a best friend, I've been seeing Akosa for more than six months. What did you think I was doing whenever you were off somewhere? Did you think I was sitting at the Tackle waiting for you to do a job with me?" Thorn's anger seemed to have played itself out. "Akosa is a fish merchant down in the Haraab district. He co-owns a market stall with a business partner."

Jesse hung his head. He really was an asshole. His best friend in the world, and it never occurred to him to think of what she might be leaving behind. Then something occurred to him. "Why did you never say anything to me? I tell you everything."

"Why did you never ask?"

He thought for a minute, then said, "That's fair. I'm an asshole. What can I do to get you to forgive me?"

Thorn grinned sadly and said, "Get me back home?"

The next day, Jesse decided. Decided to claim his new life. Decided to stand up for himself. Decided to not let the fear win.

He headed out to the palace with the intention to lay everything out and be direct with Prince Caleb. He was definitely going to tell him how he felt. At least, he was pretty sure he was going to let him know he was interested. Or at least give a strong indication. At least drop a few well meaning hints. His anxiety flared again, and at this point he would do good merely to get up the nerve to broach the subject out loud.

'Who am I fooling,' Jesse thought as he made his way into the halls of the residential wing. *'I'll be lucky if I'm not tongue-tied by the time I see him.'*

The young Isnashi approached the Prince's door, announced himself, and was immediately shown in. Prince Caleb was reclined on one of the couches reading a book. Reneforte stood behind him, brushing his hair. As Jesse entered the room, the servant set down the brush, gestured to an adjacent couch, and walked toward the back wall. Mustering his courage, Jesse took a chance and sat on the same couch as Prince Caleb. The Prince looked a bit surprised, but withdrew his feet and curled them under himself to make room.

"I always mean to..." Jesse started. Chiding himself, he delayed the subject. "I always mean to ask you. What's the deal with the script on your door? I mean it's gorgeous, of course, but there is obviously a purpose. I can't detect what it is actually doing."

"Oh," the Prince chuckled softly, setting down his book. "I was at a point where privacy started to mean more to me than it had. I had done a lot of research and my Arcane studies were going well. So, I planned out a protective ward. One that would deny entrance to any I did not give specific permission for entry."

Reneforte approached then, offering Jesse a goblet of juice and a small plate of antequines. "Thanks, Ren," Jesse said, quickly.

"My grand project failed, of course," said the Prince. "It took months for me to realize it, though. My tutors played along, pretending it had worked. It became kind of a running joke among them. They felt it was appropriate to placate me because I was a child. I was eleven."

Jesse smiled at that, trying to picture the Prince as a child and imagining how cute he probably was. His mind also flashed back to himself at that age, recalling many of his own earlier attempts at new skills. Imagining someone else fumbling around with something beyond their skill but being unwilling to accept it made him smile.

"Naturally, I had them all replaced," Caleb said, shaking Jesse from his daydream. "However, we came to realize there was AN effect occurring."

"Oh, wow!" Jesse said. "Yeah, That would make sense. 'Intent has nothing to do with Arcanum. Results are based on the reality of patterns, not the wishes of the caster.'"

"An interesting way to phrase it, but superficially true, I suppose."

"It was something Zenesul used to say."

"Ah," said Prince Caleb. "In this case, however, the unintended effect was social, not Arcane." Jesse cocked his head in curiosity, as the Prince elaborated. "Palace officials and visitors, people who knew nothing of the Arcane or the nature of what had been done to the door, became more deferential and respectful once they entered my apartments. It seemed that just the presence of the script, inert and powerless though it is, still attracted curiosity and inspired unease. It promised power, and people assumed defenses had been put in place. Only those who knew entered, the rest turned away. So in the end, it accidentally served its intended function."

"Nice," laughed Jesse.

"I know you didn't come here to ask about my door," Caleb said. "What can I do for you?"

"Who says I didn't come here just for that reason?" Jesse asked teasingly.

"Oh? Taking a page from my book?" asked the Prince, trying to hide a smile behind his goblet. "Making up pretense and excuses to visit me?"

"Perhaps I am," said Jesse more softly. Approaching the subject, his embarrassment began to flush his cheeks and ears. An uncontrolled giggle threatened to escape him if he didn't hurry. In a rush of recklessness, Jesse decided to just go for it.

"I'm coming here because I like you, Caleb. I want you to know I like you, and I think you like me," he blurted out.

"Oh," responded the Prince.

Nearly speaking faster than his tongue could keep up with, Jesse continued, "I know I'm a nothing Street Rat and you are a Prince, but I don't know if that is a barrier or really even matters here. You've said it might, but I don't know what you meant. So, I just have to lay it all on the line and say it out loud.

"I've never asked anyone out and even if I did I don't know how you guys do it here in Vargarden. Maybe I'm doing this right or maybe I'm stabbing myself in the thigh. All I know is I can't keep it to myself any longer. Would you like to 'court' me? Or let me 'court' you? Or whatever it is."

The Prince stared at Jesse as all of this was said, in such surprise that Reneforte froze as well, brush in hand. Then after a moment, the Prince looked down at his lap, giving a quiet, "Oh."

They sat in silence for several minutes. Finally Jesse spoke up, after it seemed clear to him that Prince Caleb was not going to. "Did I just make a mistake?" asked Jesse. "Did I just fuck up?"

His heart sank into his stomach as the Prince looked away. Almost as a way to give the impression of a lack of witnesses, thereby trying to save Jesse more grief, Reneforte turned and walked away, brush still held in hand. Jesse wanted to cry in frustration and embarrassment, but summoned every ounce of training at hiding his reactions and barely managed to keep a neutral face.

"Tell me I didn't misread the situation," Jesse pleaded, when the Prince still did not speak. "Is there some situation here I don't know about? Are you betrothed? Is it my lack of social station? What can I do?"

"It's not you," Caleb said, finally. "You are not reading the situation incorrectly. It's just more complicated than I would like it to be." The Prince quieted for a moment. "However, my hands may be tied, metaphysically speaking. And until I resolve that, I cannot in good conscience pursue anything with you."

'Fuck Symon and fuck this link' thought Jesse. "You mean Symon? For the Shining Court, what is this link?" His anger and frustration bled through into his words. "I know it's not Arcane in nature. I haven't seen anything actually connecting you two. You are advanced enough that if it were, you would have worked out its nature by now. Right?"

"While I appreciate your confidence in my capabilities, I do not profess to hold all knowledge. You are correct. It's not Arcane. It is also not Divine, that I can determine. I've requested a quorum of Deacons and Arcanists to study Master Cyl'Karrick and me to determine what it may be. What the Gods or possibly the Ancients have deemed necessary."

"Are you telling me to back off? That I have no chance?"

"I am saying that as much as I enjoy what time we've spent together, I am not sure if we can go forward until we know more," the Prince said, still not looking at his guest. "We need to explore this bond. This connection between Master Cyl'Karrick and myself. To figure out what it means."

Jesse remained on the couch, his teeth clenched. Confused and dejected, he chided himself for exposing his feelings.

Prince Caleb added, "My wish would be that I deny this bond or find it to be superfluous. That I could be with you."

Caleb rose from the couch and walked into his bedroom, leaving Jesse to feel small and dirty in the large lavish room. The Prince's words rang in his ears. It wasn't Jesse's fault. It was this bond. It was Symon.

25

Problems of the Heart

"Do you ever plan on leaving this library?" asked Jesse. "Or are you staying until you've read every book?"

Symon looked up from his desk and the tome in front of him. He had been so engrossed that he had not even realized Jesse had entered the library. He stretched and popped his neck, realizing how long he had been reading.

"Jesse," Symon said. "It is good to see you. I think getting out of this room would be a grand idea. I am actually happy for the break. Would you care to join me for a snack?"

"How 'bout a sparring first?" Jesse asked. "Work up a good appetite."

Symon was mildly surprised. There was an odd scent coming from his friend. It was similar to the acrid jealous one he had perceived in Caleb's chambers, but mixed with a ferrous scent of determination. "Well that is curious. You can easily be convinced to join a sparring session, but I do not ever recall you actually requesting one."

"New days," Jesse said.

Symon marked the page he had been reading and set down the journal. "Certainly. I am sure I could use the exercise."

Ten minutes later and the two were squared up. Each had their practice swords at the ready. The group had been in Vargarden long enough that Moria had commissioned wooden practice weapons in the style of their daily carry blades. "Three touches?" asked Symon, as he rolled his shoulders and stretched his arms.

"Sure," replied Jesse, his face scrunched in concentration. Symon attempted to read his friend's mood. The scent was growing stronger and Symon was surprised to see what appeared to be anger.

"Is everything okay—" Symon started to ask.

Jesse exploded into motion at him. Unlike his normal style, these were hammering blows. Jesse was putting his full weight into each of them. Betraying his size, the strikes hammered over and over into Symon's defense.

The Ennedi was able to counter, using his traditional, steady, centered style. But the speed the smaller boy was putting into his attacks meant Symon was using all his concentration to keep up with where the next blow would strike. It also meant, however, that as close as the flurry was coming to overwhelming Symon, he could see that Jesse was going to quickly wear himself out.

"*Essevoy*," shouted Jesse, using his off hand to throw a pile of webbing in Symon's face. It was a dirty trick that Symon had not expected. One they had agreed not to do to each other anymore. Something was bothering Jesse. This wasn't a spar. It was a fight.

"Jesse—!" Symon tried to say, before Jesse worked past his defenses, punching his side with the point of his practice blade, and hammering the edge into his arm and shoulder. "Ow! Damn! Yield, hold! Jesse, stop!"

Three more blows landed and Symon winced, fighting not to hold his side. As they stopped, Symon caught his breath, wiping the thick, sticky cobwebs from his face. Then he saw Jesse, doubled over trying to catch his breath as well, but still snarling in fury.

"Jesse, what is going on?" Symon let his concern fill his voice. "What did I do?"

"You're an asshole," Jesse yelled. "A fucking asshole!"

Symon cocked his head in confusion. "What?"

"You bastard," Jesse spat. "You always talk about how you don't take from us little folk, But here you are, being handed everything, and instead of leaving something for the rest of us…" Jesse screamed. "You are taking everything from us! From me!"

Symon pleaded, "Jesse, calm down. Tell me what is going on. What am I taking?"

"You have a mansion now," Jesse swept his hands gesturing to the grounds. "From what I hear, a fortune sitting in a merchant's coffers. You're getting a family! New relatives. New history. Even a whole new country that you belong to!"

"All of which I share with you," Symon said, carefully. "I consider them yours, too."

"Except you won't share where it's important!"

"What do you mean?"

"Caleb!" Jesse yelled in frustration. "You're sitting on the fence between him and Moria. Are you stringing her along as badly as you are the Prince?"

Symon's eyes darted around the courtyard hoping they were alone. His mind tried desperately to catch up with the younger man's accusations. "Jesse, I have no idea what you are talking about. How does the Prince factor into this?"

"This 'connection' you have with him. Divine fate. Love at first sight and all that!"

"Divine what?"

"Have you seen yourself whenever Caleb is in the same room? You can't keep your eyes off each other. You can't keep your HANDS off each other. At least with Moria you are a bit more subtle. Even if you fawn over her just as much."

The tips of Symon's ears turned red, as he once again scanned the courtyard. Blissfully alone, he sighed. "Wait, Jesse, what are you trying to say?"

"Are you really this clueless?" groaned Jesse. "Symon, even if you are in love with both, Vargarden tradition won't let you date both. You are going to have to choose."

Symon knew that to be untrue. Several houses were built on plural marriage families, but it didn't seem appropriate to bring that up with Jesse at this time. Instead, Symon focused on the implications of his friend's words. Jesse believed Symon to be in love with the Prince. He was jealous. "Choose? Jesse, are you saying that I am in love with the Prince?"

"Yes, you..." Jesse paused, censoring himself, "You... You..." he sputtered. "Aaargh!" he finally screamed. "Choose! By the Thirteen Hells, choose! You are driving Caleb crazy, and you are making me feel like shit for liking my best friend's boyfriend."

Symon laughed in relief. Jesse's anger renewed and Symon realized it was a mistake to make light of his friend's feelings. Quickly he curbed his reaction and held his hands up in supplication against Jesse's raised sword. "Whoa, whoa, I'm sorry!"

"Jesse," Symon began. "I apologize if there has been any confusion. I apologize if I hurt you, or Prince Caleb in any way. It was never my intention. There is no choice to make."

"You can't have them both!"

"Nor should I," Symon said. He walked up to his friend, lowering his voice in case any prying eyes were outside of his perception. "I have no feelings for Caleb."

"What?" asked Jesse, freezing in confusion. "But Caleb—"

"I am not romantically interested in Caleb, Jesse."

"But your connection?"

"Whatever this connection is," Symon said. "I feel no amorous inclination toward the Prince. Do you think he feels any for me? Have you talked to him about your feelings?"

"Yes," Jesse replied. He lowered his sword, looking away in embarrassment. "He doesn't know what to feel about you. I wouldn't blame him. I mean, you already know you're hot, right?"

"I would choose not to comment on that." Symon said, grinning.

A minute passed, then another, neither sure how to proceed. Finally Jesse said, "I'm sorry if I hurt you."

"It matters not," Symon rubbed his bicep where Jesse had hit him the hardest. "Whatever pain I am feeling, it appears you have been feeling worse." He chuckled. "You did manage to lay into me quite thoroughly. Was that web spell planned, or was it a rash decision?"

Jesse looked ashamed. "I planned the ambush. I'm sorry." Despite the regret, Symon could detect a temptation for the thief to give in to his playful impulses. "I was pissed, and really wanted to take you down a few pegs."

"You always do," Symon chuckled. "I apologize if I gave you cause to be upset with me, I truly had no idea that anyone thought much about my romantic intentions. I often forget that you are inclined to male companionship and would factor my actions into your relationships."

"You dolt!"

"I know," Symon smiled. "But truly, I have never had affections toward the Prince. He is a nice guy, but I have yet to find myself romantically inclined toward any man."

"Even me?" Jesse said jokingly.

"No," Symon's nose wrinkled disapprovingly. "You are my little brother!"

"I'll try not to be insulted by that," Jesse replied. "But I get it. I crushed on you at first, but it's always been more brotherly."

Jesse hugged Symon tightly, and Symon returned it. The aroma of friendship, warm and sunny, almost lemon-like, filled his nostrils as the tension drained from both of them.

"So you really don't mind if I try to do something with Caleb?" Jesse asked.

"The very fact that you are becoming comfortable using his name rather than his title tells me that you should. If you feel that he is inclined."

"How can you notice what name I call him, and yet be so oblivious to Caleb's attention towards you?"

"I honestly do not know."

"But yes," Jesse said. "I think he is interested. He was just afraid."

"I apologize," Symon said. "If he is afraid to tell me, perhaps I should clear the air myself. Make my intentions known."

"It would help. If not me, it would help Caleb. He's confused."

"This connection is troublesome, but I shall handle it," Symon said. "Quickly." Symon motioned Jesse over to a group of chairs set around a small patio table. Once seated, Symon said, "I have a question for you. It was not purely your feelings towards the Prince that inspired your fury. Please look me in the eye and tell me, is there a problem you and I need to discuss about the house and our conditions here?"

Jesse tried to look away, but Symon reached out and took Jesse's hand in his.

"There was more said in your anger. You mentioned this house, and money. Please. We are friends. Brothers. Please, tell me all of it."

"It's low of me," said Jesse quietly. "I'm not proud of it."

"Pride has nothing to do with this. Tell me what you are feeling."

"It's just, you have everything. You had a great house and a thriving business you were set to inherit. When the war took that away, we were equal. Now you've moved up to a mansion. Back in Highston, you had friends who were Nobles. Here, for all intents and purposes you are one."

"I would hardly say I'm a Noble."

"Seriously?" Jesse quipped. "You are going to argue with me on this?"

Symon hesitated and Jesse lost himself into another fit of anger.

"Seriously?! In what way are you NOT a Noble, Master Cyl'Karrick? Your family lands? The family money? A family name and being the son of one of the most famous military generals this kingdom has ever produced, to hear Caleb and Moria tell it. You have servants in your house, for fuck's sake!"

Symon stammered. "I don't have servants!"

"The Hells you don't," countered Jesse. "I don't care that you cook your own meals. Have you not seen the housekeeper coming in once a week on Moria's instructions to clean and change the linens? Or the pair of gardeners that are here twice a week to tend the grounds?"

"Wait, what?" Symon was flummoxed. He changed his own bedclothes, and cooked his own meals. He also tidied up after himself in the library. But he had not considered the rest of the house. Of everyone else's chores. Nor where the supplies came from. His obliviousness showed once again.

Jesse laughed. "You really never leave your library, do you, LORD Cyl'Karrick?"

"I apologize. You are correct that I did not realize."

Jesse patted his shoulder. "I'm sorry, too. It's not your fault. And I'm sorry I screamed at you."

"You made a point, though. What is your concern?"

"I guess I'm just jealous," admitted Jesse. "You've shared, yes. But that hurts almost as much. Everything I have here comes from you. If there is one thing I have learned from life on the streets, anything given can be withheld. There is no work for me, so I can't contribute. I'm a sponge here. A mooch. I have nothing of my own, either to support myself or to offer you in return."

"I had no idea," said Symon. "I want to say that of course you owe me nothing, and that I would never deny you a place here. But I am beginning to realize that would demean the point you are making." Symon could see that Jesse appreciated him not dismissing his feelings on this.

"I feel bad about it," said Jesse. "Like I'm being ungrateful for your hospitality here."

"No, it is a valid feeling," said Symon. "You have fought all your life for everything you had." Symon remembered Jesse's 'friend' back in Highston. "Even when someone else supported you, you paid heavily for what you were given."

Jesse's eyes softened and Symon could see the pain from those days. "Exactly." Jesse paused and continued. "I've only ever known the underworld. I've only ever lived there. All my skills are from there."

Jesse stood up and paced before the tables. "But I don't want to go back. Even if there are those kinds of guilds here, they are not going to talk to someone who hangs out with the Crown Prince and lives in the Cyl'Karrick Estate. Nor would the Prince hang out with criminals. So, I can't exactly go back to living that way. Earning just enough of my own money for meals or to get my own rooms. I'm stuck."

"I am guessing that Thorn feels the same way?" asked Symon.

"Worse," said Jesse. "She misses the thief's life terribly."

Symon nodded. His life had transferred to this new world, but theirs... Theirs had been shattered. He again had not thought of the pain of transitioning and loss from their point of view.

"And also, she left behind a man she was seeing."

Symon coughed. "Intriguing!"

"Yeah, I just found out myself," said Jesse. "We'll talk about it later. But, I promised her if we could figure out a chance, we would try to get her back to Highston, even if I can't go."

"Do you want to go?"

"Sort of," Jesse admitted. "But not really. As much as I don't know what to do now..." Jesse shrugged. "I don't really want to be a criminal anymore."

"If she left, it would be a big change," Symon smiled sadly. "You would miss her terribly, I am sure."

"She has been my cohort for years, yeah. But she's miserable here."

"I do not see an immediate solution to Thorn's predicament." Symon paused, thinking, before he finally said, "But I do have some suggestions for yours. We did once consider opening a Forge together. That is still an offer. But in the meanwhile, you could check in with the Ward's Deacon. She has been most helpful in finding me tasks to perform."

"Wait?" Jesse said. "You're... working?"

"Indeed," Symon smiled. "Contrary to belief, I DO actually escape my chambers from time to time. I have been apprenticing under a Healer here. I am attempting to plan a full service 'repair' shop. A place where I can mend both bodies and properties. With charitable options for those who cannot afford more. A balance of a profitable shop, but give back where I can. Let my family money do good for more than just myself."

"You're a big, soft ball of surprises, you know that?"

"But still a bit dull-witted." Symon stood, and held Jesse's hand. He pulled Jesse into a hug. "Forgive me for being so blind to my surroundings?"

Jesse's muffled voice echoed in Symon's chest. "Of course. And I'm sorry I attacked you."

Symon chuckled, a purring laugh which shook them both. "Of course I do. But please, next time tell your troubles to my ears and not to my ribs!"

26

New Lessons, Old Lessons

It was nearly two weeks before Jesse was able to get in to see Prince Caleb again.

It seemed that the Prince was bogged down in meetings and council business. Jesse assumed that it had to do with the attack, or decisions about the Khorric Federation, or the Shard they had discussed. But even though Jesse had sent a few requests to inquire about meeting the crown Prince, he had received back only a single message, delivered with a package.

> *Master Olben.*
>
> *I regret that my time has not been my own as of late. I have received your request for a meeting, and intend to arrange such at the earliest opportunity allowed. In the meantime, I beg of you to continue your studies, as well as your training. I believe you may find the enclosed items to be of interest.*

The package contained a selection of four books. One was a treatise describing the philosophy of Vargarden, espousing The Father's views on Necromancy, the type of community he had worked to build, and the religious structure of the temples in Vargarden. It was curious due to the timing of his meetings with Deacon Baktu, the healer Symon had recommended. It was, however, a fairly quick read, but left Jesse wondering how much of it was inflated propaganda. Still, Jesse had an idea that the others might find it interesting.

The second book felt more like a personal inclusion, which made Jesse smile. It was a student manual written by the Sorcerers of Asoterra, focusing exclusively on the sphere of Light, and its ideal spell groupings. Little notes hand-written into the margins helped focus his attention to tricks and quirks that would make casting easier for Jesse.

The third book was the real treasure.

It was a journal written in Prince Caleb's own hand. It was rambling, eclectic, and disjointed, but seemed to be a collection of Caleb's thoughts on all manner of subjects, from history, to magic, to the worship of The Father, to political views on neighboring regions. Jesse spent days absorbed in the journal. In his more intro-spective moments, Jesse could admit to himself half the book he would have found boring, if it wasn't specifically Caleb's thoughts.

The fourth journal was also in Caleb's hand, but was merely a copy he had made of a treatise on Vargarden military tactics involving the Undead legion. Jesse had found himself skimming it only lightly since Caleb didn't write it, only copied it. He could see its true value was for Symon, as the original was written by Nemuku Kyrn Cyl'Karrick, so he wondered why Caleb had sent it to him.

As there was no mention as to whether the books were a loan or a gift, Jesse had spent his time reading as much as he could. Two weeks of relative peace until Moria had shown up.

"Jesse," said Thorn, poking her head into their bedroom door. "Get your ass downstairs."

Jesse looked up from his book, only half registering what she said. "Huh? What's going on?"

"Moria is here. She's looking for you."

"Me? What does she want me for? I'm sure you mean Symon, right?"

"Yes, I'm the dumbass who completely misunderstood her saying, 'Get Jesse' and should have known she really meant Symon."

"What would she want ME for?"

"No idea," said Thorn. "You would have to ask the sexy badass soldier she brought with her."

Jesse's feathers stood up a bit straighter, his instincts chaffed. An armed escort didn't traditionally equate to good news. Jesse said, trepidation in his voice, "Okay. I suppose you have my interest."

"Then maybe get your ass downstairs and see what's up, maybe?"

Jesse stashed his book and left with Thorn. Together they entered the practice courtyard and found Moria and Symon speaking. He punched his tiny Goblin friend in the arm and laughed. "See, I told you she was looking for him!"

"Jesse!" Symon called out. As he turned, he revealed a slight man standing with him and Moria. The man was about Moria's height and slender like her father. Dressed in Legion gear, his black leather glistened in the sunlight. But the feature which immediately grabbed Jesse's attention were the man's wings.

Large, feathered wings, starting at a deep tan at their Crest, blending to a soft cream as they moved down, until moving to an off white along their lower edge trailed from the man's back. They were larger and healthier than Jesse's own, which had been neglected most of his life. Armed with a fairly long short sword and an offhand dirk, the man was clearly a soldier.

"There 'ya are," said Moria. "Jesse, this is Paulson, Third Sergeant of the Eleventh Support Company."

Jesse stepped forward and extended a hand in greeting. Paulson moved to meet him halfway, grasping wrists in a warrior's greeting. Symon stepped to the side, motioning for Thorn to join him over on the viewing benches.

"I know 'tis rare for me to call on 'ya, but..." Moria stepped up to address Jesse. "Believe it or not, Jesse, I'm here on official orders."

"The Crown Prince," interjected Paulson, "has arranged for me to provide you combat training."

"Wait, are you going to teach me how to actually fly?"

Paulson stared at Jesse and walked around him, examining his wings. "As it was explained to me," said Paulson, "you can glide, but have not yet been able to fly? Is this correct?"

"Yeah," said Jesse cautiously.

"I sadly would be able to do little to assist with that. If you did not build your shoulder muscles from an early age, there is unfortunately not much chance of catching them up now. I am sorry."

"So what are you planning then?" Asked Jesse, disappointment etched on his face.

"Just because you cannot fly, doesn't mean your wings aren't being underused, my boy. They are good for more than just flying."

"Aye," Moria said. "Paulson here'll show 'ya some rather unique and specific techniques to use those wings." She smiled. "And put some meat on them bones."

Jesse spent the next hour with Paulson showing him how to use his wings to help maneuver in unusual ways. They worked on using the wings' assistance to jump back or sideways over larger distances, which Jesse had experience with, but also on how to use them for visual distractions in dueling.

Jesse was given strengthening exercises, with practice instructions and routines. But it had not ended there.

Paulson began visiting daily for an hour of personal instruction. Sometimes Jesse would duel with Moria. Other days, Paulson would bring in another Legion member when Paulson wanted Jesse to have experience fighting against a particular type of opponent or weapon style. On his most recent visit, Paulson handed Jesse a staff with a kind of a weighted hook on the end. It looked odd in wooden form, and Jesse was confused until Paulson pulled out its real counterpart.

"This is a qinglong," said Paulson. "It is a much lighter, shorter weapon compared to most pole arms. More in line with a spear, but with the slicing blade of a halberd. It is a popular weapon of Isnashi, due to the extra maneuverability and reach. I want you to start working with it, and see if it is a weapon you might consider.

"With your size and the maneuverability your wings can provide, I would like to see what you might be able to do with the extra reach provided by a light halberd," Paulson said.

The weapon he was holding was a wooden pole banded with four thin steel strips running its length. It was perhaps six feet long, and was topped with a smaller, narrower version of the traditional axe and spear head combination of a military halberd.

"I'm not exactly looking to fight in the military," Jesse answered dryly.

"Never said you were, my boy. But the Prince said to train you, and begging your pardon, but if you are going to accompany my Prince, I'd rather you have options."

"Are you trying to say it's too dangerous for me to be around the Prince?"

"It is what it is," said Paulson. "You're an outsider fleeing a war. I've no idea what troubles you might carry with you. It's my understanding that you've already been involved in an attack."

Jesse pulled a scowl, but Paulson responded, "Pull all the faces you want, but I will see my Prince safe."

So Jesse practiced. It seemed like every time he wanted to slack off, there was Moria asking him when he had last practiced. Between the exercises, the sparring, and the new books, Jesse had quickly gone from bored to overwhelmed.

Jesse watched Symon as he put the bowls out for the day's first meal.

"Moria not around this evening?" asked Thorn.

"No. With her extra assignment from the palace," said Symon, pointedly frowning at Jesse, "she is looking for more time with her family at the moment."

Jesse stared back at Symon and laughed. "If you want me to apologize, not gonna happen. If I can't see my crush, you can't see yours."

"It is not like that."

"Of course, it's not." Jesse looked away and took a drink, satisfied when he saw Symon grin in his periphery.

"Well, I suppose we both get what we want tomorrow," said Symon. "We have all been invited up to the palace. It seems that the Prince would like us all to join him for the afternoon and to be his guests at a dinner."

Thorn scowled. "Why does everyone assume I want anything to do with that place?"

"Come on, girl." Jesse put his arm around his friend and said, "Free food and likely some entertainment."

"It would also appear," said Symon, "that the purpose of both the afternoon and the dinner is that they have received an emissary from Highston. We are being invited to hear what they might have to say."

"Wait!" Jesse said. "Are you serious?"

"Indeed."

"Oh, we have to see that."

"Fine, I'll go," groused Thorn. "But I don't have to like it." Jesse laughed and squeezed her shoulder.

Moria arrived later to join them for their noonday meal, explaining that for everyone's convenience, she had been assigned as their escort for their visit to the palace. She was more serious than usual, and Jesse wrote it off as her official duties. He still had difficulty reading her. She was far more alert than most of the guards he had duped in Highston. But it was weird seeing her as a person, too.

"Under the current order," she said, "all visitors t'the palace are required to have military escort at all times."

"What if we split up?" asked Thorn.

"Don't split up," deadpanned Moria.

Jesse hid his grin behind a chunk of bread he was holding and said, "There goes our quality time, Symon!"

"Hush, you," chuckled Moria. "I'll just'n have you buried under another Welgeid like what h'ppen'd in the gardens. 'Alone time'."

"Or I'll sit on him for you," added Argyle.

"That'd work!" she laughed.

Jesse rolled his eyes at the Genbu. Argyle had been pretty quiet since they'd arrived in Vargarden. Unlike Thorn, he wasn't unhappy with the change, but he was more reserved in his approach. Spending most days at the parks, Argyle would sometimes talk with Jesse about the gardens. Jesse had spent hours describing the flowers and trails he had walked in the palace grounds. To Jesse, it seemed that Argyle was much like himself. Done with the criminal life and looking for peace.

At the gates of the Cyl'Karrick grounds, they were met by a rather intimidating escort of a dozen Welgeid, two priests, and four soldiers, including Paulson. Jesse liked the fellow Isnashi, but still found him rather serious and intimidating. He had found the soldier did not have an appreciation for jokes when sparring. Jesse smiled at the warrior, but his attempt was met with a flat, appraising stare.

The walk to the palace was uneventful, and within an hour they were being shown into a room very similar to the one in which Symon's trial had been held. A Gnome and an Ennedi sat in one of the middle rows talking together in hushed voices. Near the back of the room, a raised alcove above the large court table housed a large black throne. Next to the throne sat a smaller throne-like chair, in which sat Prince Caleb, bathed in shadow. As the party entered the chamber, the Prince stood and gave a small wave of greeting. He used a set of narrow, hidden stairs to descend to the main dais, then walked down to join them.

"It is good to see all of you," Prince Caleb said. "I apologize that my time has been monopolized of late."

Symon stepped forward, nodding in greeting. "We understand quite well how busy the recent events must have made you. I hope you have been well?"

"Well enough, thank you." Jesse saw Prince Caleb glance briefly between Symon and himself. His eyes held a mysterious look, as if trying to gauge how things stood between the two and himself. "My earlier injuries were nothing compared to the mundane duties that have occupied me so greatly."

"I am glad to hear you are well," said Symon. "Considering the locale, is it appropriate to call you 'Caleb', or would 'Prince' be more appropriate here?"

"This is not a formal tribunal," the Prince replied. "As long as you are not officially addressing me on Vargarden business, Caleb is perfectly acceptable."

"Well in that case, CALEB," said Symon, stressing the name, "Per our last conversation, I believe Jesse has a few things that he would like to discuss with you alone, when it is convenient."

Jesse slapped Symon in the back and whispered, "Bitch. When did you go see Caleb?"

"A few days ago. One of my few sojourns away from my library," Symon whispered back, a deep chuckle in his voice.

"A heads up would have been appreciated," Jesse responded, chuckling as well. He squeezed Symon's arm in appreciation then he addressed Caleb. "Only when it is convenient, your lordly highness-ness." Jesse said, as he added a grin and a wink.

"If I may," said Argyle, "I am curious. This is a personal meeting, why we were called to chambers here, rather than joining you in private. Has it to do with the current state of security?"

"No," said Caleb. "Merely a matter of convenience. There is a Khorric Federation representative preparing to address the council in the main chambers next door. I thought you might want to hear what the 'official' reports are, as well as see one of the representatives."

Jesse's danger sense flared up. They were potentially fugitives. His voice found courage and he spoke up, saying, "Aren't you worried more about the representative seeing us? Could it be someone who knows one of us? Wants us arrested?"

"There were conversations between Khorric and Vargarden law officials discussing the amnesty granted to you by our lands. For now, it is agreed that you are safe within our borders. If you return to Highston, it may be different. From what I understand, of the two speaking dignitaries, that is not a concern," said Caleb. "You will see. Have faith that Vargarden knows what it is doing."

A priest approached Caleb and whispered in his ear. Caleb nodded and the woman walked into the alcove where the Prince had been seated. The escorts directed Jesse, Thorn, Symon, and Argyle to join the Prince in the private booth. Men and women were beginning to trickle into the main chamber room in small groups, some taking prominent seats, others finding seating in the side benches.

"Please, my friends, make yourselves comfortable here," Caleb said, gesturing to the chairs. The seating looked comfortable. There was even a lounge, which was described as being for Argyle, if he would like to be comfortable as well. The soldiers and priests were seated with them as well, while the attending Welgeid arranged themselves in a semicircle standing behind the group.

"Jesse," said the Prince, "Would you please join me above?"

Jesse looked up at the dais, as did most of their group. They could see that the priest Caleb had spoken with had just finished setting a stool next to Caleb's chair, and was descending the steps to join them.

"Is it really okay for me to be up there?" asked Jesse, uncertainly.

"I am inviting you," said Caleb with a smile. "That makes it okay." He looked around at the soldiers and guards, then added, "You may want to leave your sword belt with Lady Moria, however, just to lessen any tension."

Jesse did as suggested, then joined Caleb up above. He could see Thorn shaking her head and snickering as he climbed the tiny steps and took his assigned seat. He and Caleb had barely been seated when the room was called to order.

From a side door walked five figures, who took the seats at the court table just below Caleb and Jesse. The man in the center chair remained standing as the others sat around him. A hush fell on the room as they sorted themselves, then the man in the center, an Ukko Dwarf in thick, dark robes, turned and looked up. Caleb gave a nod and the man turned to address the crowd.

27

Harbinger

Symon watched with a smile as Jesse took his seat with the Prince. Now that the air had been cleared, he hoped for the best.

His eyes turned to the Ukko who addressed the gathered crowd. With sharp eyes, Symon could recognize the signs of a small casting. Whatever Arcana the Ukko had done, it amplified his voice, allowing it to carry across the room, adding gravitas to the already impressive acoustics.

"Members of the Council and honored guests, we have gathered you to welcome our emissary from the Khorric Federation. He has traveled long to see us, and it is our duty to hear his words. He joins us here in our hall, and I cede the floor to him."

The side doors of the chamber opened, silhouetting a robed man as he strode into the aisleway. Every flame in the lanterns throughout flared a bit brighter as the dark-skinned man, dressed in red robes, mounted the dias. Symon's breath caught as the Magi pulled back his hood exposing his long white hair, swept back and cut even across his back in a pristine plated style. His stark white goatee had been trimmed to a neat point, contrasting his dark brown skin, and his gaze had grown hard with the recent battles. The wizard's presence had changed so much that Symon could barely recognize him. But he did recognize him.

Zenesul A'Dynell, his former master, had come to Vargarden.

The Ukko copied the Spell form used earlier and placed it on Zenesul. With a nod, the officiant said, "The floor is yours, Master A'Dynell."

"Thank you, Magistrate," the old man replied. Turning to the audience, he began, "Illustrious members of the Council of Vargarden, I am honored to be here. The Khorric Federation has officially requested that I present myself to you as an emissary. They believe I am here to serve the New Nobles and to pave the pathway for their official representatives who shall follow me. And while that order was my official duty, it is not why I am here."

Symon leaned in, his attention rapt, solely focused on his old mentor. His mind soaked up every word, committing this moment to memory. Symon knew that Zenesul would never serve the Elysium or the Federal Academy, let alone the Lord's High Council, blindly. Zenesul's goal would always be to better the situation of the Federation's people, regardless of what the leadership had deemed appropriate. Symon shifted uncomfortably, waiting for Zenesul's next words.

"The Khorric Federation is now under the regime of the so-called 'New Nobles.' They claim to have liberated our Federation from stagnation and out-dated policy. I am here to ask you to not believe their lies." Murmurs rumbled through the chamber.

"They will tell you that the old leadership was incompetent. That they were greedy. That they cared only for the good of themselves, and not the common people. Those words are true." Zenesul stood tall behind his podium. "What they won't tell you, is they are the same. That today, Nobles from the old blood are hidden within their manors, cowardly hiding from the wrath of the new leadership. That the people who work for those Nobles are being tortured, starved, and imprisoned for the crimes of their masters. They will not tell you that they have imposed curfews throughout the major cities. That they limit the number of people in open areas to prevent insurrection.

"They will show you part of the story. They shall not reveal the whole truth." Zenesul took a deep breath and gripped the podium with his hands. "The truth, the whole truth, is that the New Nobles are merely a front for a corrupt, fascist movement under the influence of the Bright Guilds of Highston."

Shock rippled over Symon's flesh. His fur stood on end. Symon could scarcely believe the bluntness of Zenesul's words. He was committing treason in front of everyone.

"Their reach is nothing more than a power grab. There is a resistance within Highston. A resistance that opposes this new power. A resistance that I have led for many months now.

"I am Magi Zenesul A'Dynell," his mentor said, "Master of the Eighth Shura, Terra Arcana. I do not come to you as a supplicant, but as a herald. Vargarden cannot stand by as the Khorric Federation is taken by corruption. A corruption apparent in the choice of allies. The Investurants have overstayed their welcome in the Federation. When will they turn their eyes to you?"

Symon turned to Argyle, who had cocked his head to the side as he watched the speech intensely. Thorn stepped up next to the railing before Symon, and whispered. "Well, this just got a hell of a lot more interesting."

"Symon stated that you have things that you wish to discuss with me?" Caleb said in a low voice. "I can assure you, we will not be overheard from here."

Jesse turned to the Prince from looking down on the crowd. "Shouldn't we be listening to what is being said?"

"I have already spoken with Master A'Dynell. Everything he is saying are things that you've already informed me of. While it is of importance to the Council, I'm unsure of how it will be received. But that is a conversation for the Council and myself later."

"But he's committing treason! And that's, that's—"

"Yes, Jesse," Caleb nodded. "We know him as the Harbinger, Hero of Tollerheim."

"That's Zenesul."

"Yes, that was quite a surprise when I talked with him earlier." Caleb smiled.

"When he asked about you, I deduced that this was your mentor. I understand him to have been out of favor with the Elysium since the end of the war. I did not know he had taken students."

"Only bratty Street Rats and Necromantic blacksmiths, apparently," giggled Jesse.

"Intriguing nonetheless. It does explain much about your style."

"Rebellious?"

Caleb gestured to the impassioned speech of resistance below. "It would seem so."

"And he asked of me?"

"He did," said Caleb. "You and your friends will be given every opportunity to meet with him as well, to reconnect." Jesse laid his hand on Caleb's arm and smiled in thanks. The Prince smiled back and continued, "But as I originally inquired, what did you wish to discuss with me?"

"Oh, that," muttered Jesse. His blood thumped in his ears as his heart began to race. His desire was so close, but he was struggling to find his words. "Are you sure this is the time?"

"All time is important," Caleb replied. "We've had so little of it lately."

"So I talked to Symon," Jesse started. "About you. Well about him and you, and that bond or connection or whatever you guys have going on."

Jesse glanced down at Symon, just as the young Ennedi was looking up in their direction as well. At the unexpected eye contact, Jesse waved, and Symon smiled back.

"So, he is interested in exploring what the connection means. He feels it's important. But, he has 'never had amorous intentions toward a guy', or something like that."

"Yes, he advised me that he was disinclined to have a romantic relationship with me." Caleb smiled. "He was quite tactful about it."

"He always is," Jesse laughed. "But get this! I think he's tits over tail feather for Moria!"

"Oh! He left that particular detail out of his speech."

"Right? I don't think either of them know it yet."

"So, he is disinterested with me and desires to allow us both to resume the romantic pursuits of our hearts, free of the burdens of any political or Divine interventions."

"Yeah, but you say it even prettier than he did," Jesse said, giggling quietly.

"Pretty or not, what does that mean for you?"

"For me?" asked Jesse, pulling his hand back from Caleb's arm. He could feel his face flush as his ears turned nearly as pink as the primary feathers of his wings. "Well, I, um—"

"I don't mean to put you on the spot," said Caleb. "But I am not always great at social cues. We've had talks that may have implied your intentions, but it would help me greatly if you just said it plainly."

Here it was. Jesse's opportunity to either grab what he wanted or flame out. There were no more excuses. Nothing standing in his way. If he failed to act, it would be on him alone.

"Fuck it," whispered Jesse, more to himself than to anyone else. Then, looking into Caleb's eyes, he said in a slightly louder whisper, "I like you, alright? Happy? There, I said it."

Jesse's face redoubled in rosiness, color passing into a pale red and creeping up his cheekbones to his forehead. He watched Caleb intently waiting for a response. Slowly, the Prince smiled and reached out, grasping Jesse's hand and returning it to his arm, leaving his own hand atop Jesse's. "I like you as well, Master Olben." He grinned. "I said it as well. Happy?"

Zenesul spoke for nearly a half hour, giving an impassioned speech about the truth of the Investurant occupation. The outlook he painted was bleak for Highston. Symon's eyes welled with tears as he heard of the brutal tactics employed by the Investurants and the newly formed militias of the New Nobles. People imprisoned for the smallest infractions. Personal liberties stripped away from the poor yet again. Layer by layer, his old master exposed a frightening portrait of tyranny.

While the Resistance was preparing to rally troops and throw back the regime, he feared they would need sanctuaries for the eventual refugees. They had sent emissaries for aid to Dorne, and the lands beyond the Gate, for supplies and relief efforts. But the message delivered by the Khorric Federation had already been heard, and help was slow to respond.

Zenesul's speech began to ramp up in passion as he came to his closing remarks. "The New Nobles have enslaved the people, and have paid off the Elysium and the Federal Academy. Because of the ignorance of these organizations and their insistence on controlling the narrative, the Khorric people will suffer. The official emissaries will ask for you to stay any military support. They will request a treaty of aid and complacency.

"I remember your service in the previous campaign. I was honored to fight by the side of your Deacons and Arcanists. I shall remember the Necromancers and the efforts, the sacrifices, made by your troops to defeat our enemy and provide the Khorric people with freedom from the Shadow. I know what the Investurants truly mean to Vargarden. And what they should have meant to the people of the Khorric Federation."

Zenesul paused one last time, taking in the room before him. "The wants of our flawed leadership are in distinct conflict with the needs of our people. If the Khorric Federation will not ask for you to intercede in the war, I have no such hesitation. I cannot imply a formal request. I will be labeled a heretic or worse when my words here today are known, but the Shadow will fall over this land and will not stop at the borders of Khorric. Whatever they seek, they shall find it eventually. Unless you help stop them."

The crowd buzzed as politicians whispered their concerns. The palace had already been attacked by the Investurants. Zenesul's words fell on open minds. If there was a reason for Vargarden to fear war, Zenesul had found it. If the plea for innocents would not convince the Council, perhaps the hatred of the Investurants would.

"You realize he's betrayed the Feds... again?" Thorn asked in Symon's ear.

"I do."

"He's just a giant 'fuck off' to the Feds and their politics." Symon looked over to Thorn, her little yellow eyes reflecting the dancing lights in the chamber. "I'm remembering why I liked that guy."

Jesse joined Symon, Thorn, and Argyle as the audience was escorted out in a controlled fashion. The four companions were led to a spacious sitting room filled with plush chairs and colored pillows in a variety of reds and oranges. A platter of fruits and cheese sat atop a dark wood table before a pitcher of mulled wine. A small tray of dried meats cut into different sizes was laid out, meant for their carnivorous members.

The young Isnashi kicked back in the chair and snagged a wedge of cheese. "Did you hear that end part?"

"I heard the entire thing," Symon said. "I could hardly believe what I was hearing."

"Yeah, the old man just does not give a FUCK!" Thorn laughed. "By Orlam's taint, I've never seen someone just outright call the Khorr on their bullshit like he just did. And exposing Manticore? Just..."

"It worried me," Symon said. "The things he said. I know they are true. And I know Zenesul has never pretended to be the biggest fan of the Academy, the Elysium, or even the Federation itself, but I have never heard him outright defy them like he did today. To commit treason."

"I am surprised as well," Argyle nodded his head, "The old man has most definitely flirted with the lines of permissible behavior in the past. His allegiance to Manticore was tenuous, but he was always available when a job was required that involved injury to a compromised Magi or Noble. It would have been most predictable to ally himself with those in the Nobility who had ties to that same bent. I truly expected Manticore to have Master A'Dynell within their grip."

"I don't expect there's anyone who has Zen in a grip," Jesse said. "So, what's next? From the sounds of it, the next lot that will arrive are just the same richy-rich donkey-fuckers we would expect from the Khorr."

"I don't think it matters!" Thorn slapped her knee. "That crazy old man isn't afraid to put his thumb in the ass of the establishment!"

Jesse and Symon gave her withering looks.

"What?! He isn't," Thorn replied. "If I had to guess, he's got something on the Elysium. I think no one wants to push the bastard, because they are afraid of what he's capable of. So they shoved him in the corner for years, until they needed him more than they feared him. Now, he's back out in the light and he's doing whatever the fuck he wants."

"You may be right," Jesse said. He turned to Symon, "You think it's all that 'Harbinger' business?"

Symon's head snapped around in surprise. "What did you say?"

Jesse smiled. It has been common in Highston for Jesse to have information that Symon didn't. His naivety had been a building block of their friendship. Here, it had grown more rare. It felt good to have a brief return to the old days. "Caleb called him the 'Harbinger', 'Hero of Tollerheim' or something like that. Something from the first war."

"My father's journals speak of someone named 'Harbinger'. While they did not serve together, my father described him as a major impact on the war. Father called him a 'Volcano Mage.' Apparently, the Harbinger was a source of devastation against the Investurants in the south. Neither the Legion, nor the Federation seemed to have control of him. Caleb thinks old man Zen is THE Harbinger?"

"Yep."

"Well, that would lend credence to Thorn's theory. A powerful Magi like that would be either a boon or a bane to the Elysium, depending on their political leanings. And Master Zenesul is not the 'sit down and shut up' type."

"No, I am not," a familiar voice said behind him.

Jesse whipped his head around to the door and as Symon stood up and stepped towards the door. "Master Zenesul!" they exclaimed together.

"Boys, it's good to see you!" Jesse saw the old wiry mage's face soften immediately and in an instant become the mentor they had left in Highston. "Symon, you look well. Stronger than the last time I saw you."

Jesse popped over the back of the chair and bounced into Zenesul's arms.

"Zen, you old fool!"

"Jesse, my boy! You look great! You're uncovering your wings now?"

"I am! We've got so much to catch you up on!" Jesse spied Caleb standing in the doorway with Moria at his shoulder. "A LOT to catch you up on."

Symon and Jesse started to blast every detail of their journey from Highston, their time in Vargarden, and the personal changes. Talking over one another, it was an onslaught of information and Jesse's words flowed fast and free. At last Zenesul held his hands up in defeat. "Slowly, you two. There will be plenty of time for everything. And I look forward to catching up."

Jesse smiled at the old man. He was confused by the feelings he had. Zenesul had always been a contact for him. A reliable resource. The elation of seeing him happy and healthy surprised Jesse. Suddenly, Jesse realized how much he had missed Zen's wisdom. How much he had missed the old man himself. He hugged his mentor once again, and the old man ruffled his hair.

"Symon, let's talk about your Gift, if you don't mind. I had fears about it. Have you found what you were looking for here?"

"Yes, Master," Symon said. "It has been a revelation."

Symon began to explain what they had learned from Caleb, Kyrn's journals, the Deacons, and more. It was thorough, exact, and almost verbatim, as Jesse would expect. He smiled and pulled Caleb aside slightly as Zenesul and Symon sat down to talk about it further.

"What you said before, that you like me and I like you. Does that mean you like, *like me*? Like, want to find out if the tail feathers match the wingtips?"

"Excuse me," Caleb commented. "You, my friend, have been spending too much time with that Isnashi officer."

"Hey!" said Jesse, laughing and playfully slapping at Caleb's hand. "I can be funny on my own without that birdbrain!"

"Well," Caleb said, smiling. "I'm unsure of the courting rituals in Khorric culture, but it may be a few encounters before physical intimacy is involved."

"Well yeah," said Jesse, his smile turning slightly from humor to nervousness and his cheeks gaining a pink tint. "I'm just trying to make sure I have the right end of things. I've always liked guys. It appears you do, too. But I'm not..." he pointed at Symon. "I don't look like him, you know?"

"Ah," said the Prince. "So you wish to determine if you are my 'type.' So to speak?"

"Yeah," Jesse said. "I mean, I know you said that you like me... but I mean. How will it work?"

"I am so sorry, Master Olben," Caleb said. "I know that in Highston, Nobility is a major concern and that there are laws and practices that provide your guidance in relationships. Here in Vargarden, it is only the family heritage. If my family and your family agrees, then we are given sanction to court one another."

"And if one of us has no family?"

"For all intents and purposes, you are your own family." Caleb said. "Or possibly a Cyl'Karrick. But either way, it would be up to you or Master Symon. Both of whom I believe are in agreement."

"So?" Jesse asked.

"Yes, Jesse. I am particularly fond of men and the possibility of pursuing a more than platonic relationship with a man. I am not beholden to any political restrictions, nor familial ones." Caleb took Jesse's hand in both of his. Jesse looked up in relief and their eyes met, both of them giving soft smiles. "I am quite interested in one man in particular. May I call on you for dinner? A social evening just you and I, to get more acquainted."

28

The Jesse Job

Symon entered the house and was surprised to find Thorn on his heels.

"What?" She asked.

"It is just unusual for you to follow me."

"Well, Argyle was going to go to that thing in the palace. Jesse is going to be all dough-eyed from his talk with the Prince. And I don't want to explore any more of this stupid city. So, I get... you."

"Well," Symon said. "That is lovely. I was headed to the library. I am hoping Master Zenesul may stop by later this evening."

Thorn chuckled, wryly. "Surprise, surprise."

Symon sat down at his desk and began browsing books on Vargarden history and military campaigns. Thorn was tossing her current book down when Jesse burst into the room.

"The Prince just asked me out!" he cried.

Thorn leaped back, while Symon jumped, nearly falling from his chair.

"Wait! What?!" Thorn said in disbelief.

"You heard me!" Jesse said, face flushed.

"No, you're yanking us! No way!"

"Hey! I know what I heard." Jesse retorted. "He said," Jesse pitched his voice high, and flattened his tone to mimic the Prince. Symon could not help but be reminded of their conversations in the diner regarding the Bright Guilds. Jesse was a performer. "'I would like to call on you for dinner. A social evening just you and I, to get more acquainted.' Those were his exact words."

Symon grinned, pleased for his friend. "That is the formal way to ask someone on a date."

"Thank you, Symon! And..." Jesse said, glancing back at Thorn.

"Well, tweak Sylath's nipple and call it a party!" Thorn said. "That's a big deal."

"You blasphemous Troll!" Jesse smiled. Symon shook his head. Sylath was the Khorric Goddess of Lust. It would be just like Thorn to call on her in such profane terms. Symon watched as Jesse's features melted to a frown. "Shit. It is a big deal. What the Hells do I do?!"

"Easy, friend," Symon said reassuringly. "Thorn and I will help you. When is this event?"

"Tomorrow night!" squealed Jesse.

"The Prince wastes no time," Symon replied.

"Bitch, relax," Thorn said with a toothy grin. "We'll help. Let's start with what you will wear."

"Yeah," Jesse said. Thorn grabbed his hand and led him from the room. Symon followed as they climbed the stairs to their bedroom.

"Let's see what we have to work with," said Symon as they crossed the room and opened the wardrobe.

"I have my black jacket or my red jacket. What do you think?" asked Jesse.

"Red," Thorn said. "It's newer."

Symon frowned. They were travel coats. Daily wear for light duty and wandering the city. They were not dinner coats. "We should see the tailor down the street. Pick you up a new coat. My treat."

"No," Jesse said. "I just bought the red one when we got here to Vargarden. It's fine. I already have more coats than I can wear at once. I don't want too many."

Symon winced briefly, thinking of all the things Jesse had suffered in his life. He had never been able to safely rely on anyone or have a comfortable home.

The instinct to keep his possessions to only what he could carry was showing itself. "Please, let me get you one. There is plenty of room in the closets."

"No, I'm good." Jesse clipped. Symon knew not to push any further.

"So let's at least take the day," Thorn chimed in. She glanced at Symon and nodded understandingly. "We can preen you up, trim your hair, brush your wings. We can clean up your coat and trousers, make sure they are crisp. We can actually make this fun!"

Jesse smiled at his long-time friend. "Thanks, girl. You know that sounds nice." Jesse walked over and glanced into the mirror. He smiled his goofy grin and then paused.

Symon once again watched Jesse's posture change. It was as if he was morphing into a different person. The joy slid from first his face, and then his posture. A defeated and mournful boy took his place.

Jesse's voice caught in his throat, and Symon could hear the pain in his friend's words. "No, I'll cancel. No amount of preening is going to make this worth it."

Thorn slumped her shoulders and gave a warning glare to Symon. The Ennedi could not understand that Jesse was not seeing in the mirror what everyone else did. Too many years at the hands of a monster left Jesse with no sane sense of self worth. Her eyes pleaded with Symon to help her make Jesse see it.

"What do you mean?" Symon asked gently.

Jesse pointed at his face. "You can preen up the rest of me, but I can't fix this!"

"He hates his nose," Thorn replied. "He got it busted when he was twelve, and he didn't have any money to pay the priests, so they just bandaged it up and sent him away. It healed crooked, and has always had a little bump there at the bridge." She turned to Jesse, "I still think it's cute."

"This is a mistake," Jesse turned away. "I'm street trash, a Street Rat. My face is mangled, and I've got nothing to my name. What am I compared to a fucking Prince?!"

Thorn started towards Jesse, but Symon waved her down. He crossed the room in several strides and went to put his hand on Jesse's shoulder. Jesse flinched subtly but turned to Symon. "May I see?" Symon asked gently.

Jesse turned to Symon and put his face between Symon's hands. Symon turned his head a few directions, and then released it and left the room.

"Jes, you have to remember, he asked you out," Thorn cooed from behind them. "Clearly, he knows what he's looking for, and you're it."

"Maybe," Jesse said. "Or maybe when he gets up close, he'll see what a wreck I am."

"No, he'll see what we all see," she said.

"A broken toy?"

"No, a sweet boy, who doesn't know what he truly is."

"Ah ha!" Symon said, returning with a book in hand. "I knew I had read something recently. This is it!"

Jesse and Thorn exchanged glances. Symon had been more and more absorbed with his studies since he discovered his father's library. It was a wealth of knowledge and Symon had spent days there. He had found many books on military strategy, but recently he had discovered his father's extensive medical library.

Symon walked over with a book, opened to a page with a skull drawn on it. Jesse looked Symon in the eye cautiously. "What is that?"

"My father studied a lot about how the body was built. And he has several books on the body of Humans. While you are not exactly Human, you are very close, and I knew that I had read about the nose bones recently."

"Eh, sure," Jesse said hesitantly. "Of course, you would. I'm sure EVERY-ONE reads about nose bones."

"Ha," Symon laughed coarsely.

"So why does that matter?"

"I know why your nose is crooked!"

"So do I, Xerian broke it."

"Yeah, but I know why it did not heal properly."

Jesse shrugged at Thorn. "Because we were poor."

Symon took a step back. "Yes, because the Federation did not care for its most vulnerable. That is a horrible thing. Any magical healing would have set the bones to their natural state. But they did not and so you have scars in the tissue, and your bone has been displaced. The result is this build up there," Symon pointed to the bridge of Jesse's nose. "I would wager that it is also why you snore so loudly."

Jesse spun, "I do not!"

Thorn fell over laughing. "Oh, you do! You always have!"

"You bitch!" Jesse swiped at her playfully. "Why didn't you tell me?"

Thorn laid laughing, "I thought you knew!"

"Well, that's ruttin' awful! And that's it, I'm canceling this date!"

"No," Symon said. "Do not jump to that yet. I think I can fix it."

Jesse and Thorn's laughter stopped abruptly. The silence filled the room and their eyes turned to him in rapt attention.

"Wait! What?" Jesse asked.

"I think I can fix it."

Thorn looked up. "How?"

"If that spur of tissue and cartilage were to be removed, magical healing would put everything back to its natural state."

Jesse looked at Symon in shock. "Are you serious?"

"Yes," Symon confirmed.

"And you can heal something like that?"

"I can. I have been learning a lot about my Gift. It is one of the things that is softening who my father was. It appears he spent as much time learning how to put people back together as he did taking them apart," Symon said resignedly.

"Some fights are unavoidable," Jesse said. "Don't be too hard on him."

"Yes, I suppose," Symon said. "But the point is, I can heal you. I have the ability and it would not be too overly taxing. We would just need to get rid of the scar lump to do it."

"Okay, how do we do that?" Jesse said excitedly.

"I have an idea, but you will not like it."

"Oh, trust me. I'm in!" Jesse said, bouncing on his toes at the thought of having a normal face for the first time in his life.

"It will be... unpleasant," Symon warned.

"Just tell me!" Jesse pleaded.

Symon's fist exploded into speed, striking Jesse directly in the bridge of his nose, breaking it. The snap of bone under his fist sickened him, as did the thud of his friend dropping to his knees on the floor. Jesse bent over, trying to catch his breath from the shock.

"Gods dammit! Thunder licking, grot-thumping, son of a whore!" Jesse yelled, words distorted.

Thorn sat on the floor, eyes agog. "What in the Thirteen Hells, man?!"

"Gods dammit!" Jesse continued. "You hit me in the fucking face!"

"Shh. Shh," Symon consoled. "I told you it would not be pleasant."

"Pleasant? Shit! You broke my nose! Again!"

"I know, I know. Now, come here." Symon grabbed Jesse by the head. "*Todi-see,*" Symon whispered. Jesse stood straight as magical healing energy coursed through his body. Symon looked into his Arcane sight and guided the energy to the broken area. His instincts took over as he let the body reclaim its true form. The bones cracked and snapped into place quickly. The small scar over Jesse's nose disappeared as the healing finished. "There. I am done."

"Wow," Thorn said. "Like, just, wow."

Symon leaned at the desk, catching his breath. "Are you okay?"

"I think so," Jesse said.

Symon turned Jesse to see himself in the mirror. The nose was perfectly natural. The bridge was smooth and slanted gracefully. The crooked divot was gone, now a mere memory to those who knew him. Symon was not sure it made a difference, but the joy in Jesse's eyes told him that it did. The young Isnashi turned and embraced Symon. "You have no idea what this means to me." Tears flooded Jesse's eyes. "Thank you."

"Of course," Symon said. "I just want you to be... you."

Jesse squeezed Symon harder and alternated between crying and laughing repeating "Thank you."

"I love you, my *Rieve* brother," Symon said. "It was my pleasure to help. Now, I must apologize for hitting you in the face. It was dishonorable. A sucker's punch. I am mortified."

"Don't worry," Jesse said. "I'm used to worse. And, if you are going to put me back together like that, you can punch me whenever you want!"

Symon smiled sadly, knowing the sickening truth behind that comment. Everyone had hurt Jesse at some point, now he had joined them. "No, I truly should not have done that. But I was afraid I would not be able to if I warned you it was coming."

Jesse looked at Symon. "I know, but it is okay. Really, I'm fine."

"Still I must make amends. I will buy a dinner outfit. Trousers, a shirt, a proper formal coat, everything you need for your date with the Prince. To pay for my guilt."

"Symon, seriously," Jesse begged. "No. I already owe you for the healing, now."

"It is unlawful to charge for this service in Vargarden," Symon shook his head. "The Federation charges for their skills in Healing. I will never accept money for that. Ever."

Jesse put his hand on Symon's shoulder. "You are certainly not a Federal stooge anymore, are you?"

"No, thanks to you." Symon looked at Thorn. "We are more than we were. And while some of us may return to Highston, we are more together than they would allow us to be. We are family. We are *Rieve.*"

Thorn smiled a toothy grin at Symon. "I must have gotten the looks then."

Symon grabbed his pouch and supplies. "Come on, Jesse. Let's get you a coat. A blue one."

"Blue? Really? Don't you think that's a bit cliche, considering who I'm going to see?"

"Blue will be fine. The Prince will likely consider it a compliment," Symon said, smiling as he walked to the door.

"Maybe," called Jesse after him. "But can we make it a light blue? Leave the dark blues for Caleb!"

"Of course, my friend! Whatever you desire."

Jesse sat in a warm bath, filled with perfumes and balms as the preening continued. The young Isnashi had paid a price when he had asked Thorn's assistance to scrub his back. The little Goblin had a grand time tormenting her buddy with her scrub brush, teasing about "getting in all the cracks and folds", in case the Prince decided to get too handsy with his guest.

"Thorn!" squealed Jesse, laughing and squirming to get away from her and her brush. "You have no need to go digging for my bits and pieces! I can wash myself."

Bath done, Jesse wrapped a towel around his waist, then he and Thorn went out on the balcony. Jesse sat back in a chair, letting the warm early afternoon sun shine down on his bare chest, as he spread his wings wide, letting the moisture wick off of them. Thorn stood behind him, working a brush through his golden hair.

"You've let your hair grow out more than usual," she whispered.

"Yeah, do you like it?"

"I do," Thorn replied. "I'm proud of you, boy."

Jesse purred in response, but was too relaxed to really speak. Instead he reached to grasp her hand and squeezed it affectionately.

"I'm hoping that maybe the Prince might be able to start putting some food in your belly. You're all skin and bones," she said, running a clawed finger across his protruding rib cage. Jesse squirmed slightly at the tickling. Then she added, "But considering he is skinnier than you, that seems unlikely."

"Are 'ya ready?" Moria called from the doorway.

Symon stood by her side, along with Argyle watching him. Jesse shrugged. "I just have to get dressed."

"Well, then," Moria smiled. "Let's hop to."

By the time the four meddlers had gotten Jesse primped, perfumed, brushed, and dressed, he felt like a dress maker's doll. He was pretty sure everyone's hands had been everywhere, and everyone's eyes had seen everything. As much as he appreciated everyone's help, Jesse was quite glad when he was able to say goodbye and get out the door.

Moria walked out with him to the gates of the estate, before joining a

Welengam Patrol of six armed skeletons, decked out in Prince Caleb's personal livery. By the time he made it to the palace, Jesse was feeling nervous. At the entryway to the palace grounds, he was met by a pair of palace attendants, a Gnome and an Ukko.

Moria faded into the corner, taking her ever watchful position as she had since they arrived in Vargarden. The palace attendants dismissed four of the six honor guards after greeting Jesse quite formally. Once the official greeting was out of the way, the two attendants fawned over the poor street thief, complimenting him on his appearance, talking more to one another than they did to him.

Jesse was led into an ornate dining room. Gilt crown moldings ran along the top of the walls, with faux columns built into the corners. The walls were papered a pale burgundy, with gold piping running up and down at seemingly random intervals. The room was so large that no less than eight sets of double doors encircled the room, one at each end and three down each side. The table was at least six feet wide, with ornate gilded chairs at the head and foot. He estimated that twenty or more chairs could be comfortably seated down each side, though all but the two ends were removed.

The pair of attendants ushered him to be seated in the chair at the closest end, giggling and brushing his sleeves as he sat down. Then, as quickly as they had brought him in, they left, the doors closing behind them with a dreadful finality.

The wait for the Prince was terrifying. If he thought he was nervous when he had arrived at the palace, now, he was positively petrified. Jesse's mind raced to calculate the odds on whether he would vomit, run, or pass out. It was a toss of the Dead Man's dice as to which would happen first. Slowly, Jesse attempted to remind himself that he was here by invitation.

He glanced around, scanning the room and taking in the surroundings. Every shuffle he made to straighten his coat, every cough to clear his throat, and every other nervous tick, all echoed in the cavernous room. The tablecloth was glaringly white. The cloth napkins were pressed and the silver gleamed. Jesse was afraid to touch anything.

Time passed. A few minutes or half an hour, Jesse could not tell. Each moment stretched out painfully. His nerves and anxiety were on the highest edge, threatening to cause him to bolt from the room, from the palace, from the city. He picked at a thread on the sleeve of his shirt, feeling more and more unworthy of this room and the man he was here to meet. He kept looking around at all the doors, expecting any moment for them all to open, to release a crowd of nobles into the room, here to laugh at the poor foolish Street Rat.

A heavy thump reverberated through the room as the doors at the far end of the room were opened by a pair of skeletal Eisgeid. Decked out in the Prince's blue tabards, a procession of a half dozen skeletons entered, escorting Prince Caleb. Jesse rose to his feet as Caleb approached, then paused in confusion as the Prince seated himself in the chair at the far end of the table, easily fifty feet away. Jesse waited to see if anything else would happen, and then sat back down.

"I am glad you are able to join me this evening," said the Prince. Even though he was speaking louder than normal, Jesse could barely hear him.

"Thank you for the invitation," answered Jesse, nearly screaming.

Servant after servant entered the room, bringing wine and an opening course. Course after course followed throughout the next few hours, introducing foods Jesse did not know. Conversation barely happened. Speaking over the distance between them was so inconvenient that asking anything less than vital information seemed to not be worth it. Each plate served only a small sampling of the course, but so many courses were served that by the halfway point, he and Caleb were barely picking at anything.

Jesse found himself lost in the space. This was absolutely not what Jesse had been expecting, but there was no way he would be a poor guest. He tried every morsel as it was placed in front of him, trying to be polite. When the third dessert selection had finally been served and then taken away, Jesse's mind began to wander. This intimate evening felt like a failed experiment.

"Jesse?!" Caleb's voice called out.

So lost was Jesse in the space that he missed what the Prince was saying to him, and stammered an apology.

A pair of the Eisgeid mechanically assisted Jesse in standing, and then escorted him to the other end of the table. For the first time all evening he was finally able to see Caleb up close. The Prince seemed as nervous as he felt, the man's hand shaking gently as he took Jesse's arm.

"I was merely asking if you enjoyed the dinner," said Caleb.

"Oh, yeah, sorry," said Jesse. "It was good. I'm not sure I've seen that many different foods in one place though."

Caleb guided him from the room. The adjoining space was an entertaining area of some such, with tall, narrow tables scattered around the space, apparently meant for individuals to stand around. The corners of the room housed groups of imposing armchairs arranged around empty fireplaces. In his mind's eye, Jesse could picture a hundred or more fancy people mingling in this expanse.

Jesse watched as Caleb's fingers fluttered on the surface of his jacket sleeve. The touch was so light he could barely register it. The Prince's fingers were like butterflies, afraid to commit to landing. 'Fitting,' Jesse thought, and smiled. They paired nicely with the butterflies in Jesse's stomach.

"It is good to see you smile," said Caleb. "I was concerned that the dinner was not to your liking."

"I would never be that rude." Jesse chuckled.

"The dinner was not to your satisfaction? Are you too gentlemanly to complain?"

"No!" exclaimed Jesse, taking hold of Caleb's slender wrist as the Prince tried to pull away. "It was, well, it was overwhelming. Like something out of a puppet theater on a high holiday. Getting whisked off to the palace? A banquet with the gorgeous Prince?"

"It was too much, then."

"It was amazing, Caleb, really."

The Prince stared deeply into Jesse's eyes, weighing him with a studious eye. Jesse shifted uncomfortably under the gaze. Caleb frowned. "Jesse, if there is something you want to say, please don't stand on ceremony. Say it plainly."

Jesse took a deep breath, calming his insides. "Look, I like you. You. Not..." Jesse gestured back toward the dining room, "this. Not the Prince who sits in there, surrounded by gold and jewels. Don't get me wrong. I love gold. But I'd choose a simple smile from you over any of the shiny silver trinkets in there."

"My advisors told me to impress you."

"I was already impressed by you. Our walk in the gardens. The magic you shared with me. I don't need any of this. I just need you."

"But you did this for me?" Caleb said, picking at Jesse's sleeve. "Were we not both trying to be the best version of us?"

Jesse looked down at his fancy clothes. Coarse and uncomfortable, they were a false front, too. Just like the dinner. "Yeah, I don't think either of us are being ourselves."

"You truly are amazing, Jesse. Were I free to, I would kiss you."

Jesse smiled. This was his moment. "Fuck protocol," muttered Jesse.

Breathlessly, he threw one arm around Caleb's waist, the other around his neck, and pulled him down into a hungry kiss. The Prince stiffened momentarily, but quickly found himself opening his mouth to accept the kiss from his more aggressive companion. Slowly, the Prince returned the kiss as greedily as Jesse did.

The empty eyes of the skeletal Eisgeid looked on uncaring as the two kissed, mouths searching, hands roaming, moans rising. Jesse pulled back flushed and breathless, not quite ready to make eye contact. The flush once again rose into his cheeks and wings, embarrassment heating him from within. Slightly woozy, he leaned against the wall.

"I'm sorry—"

"My apolog—"

The two of them had started at the same time, cutting off just as quickly. Their eyes met, and both laughed at the absurdity.

Caleb raised a hand to indicate Jesse should allow him to speak. "I have enjoyed your company this evening, as stilted as it has been." The Prince looked at the dining room and frowned. "I propose that we try this again another evening, perhaps in a more relaxed environment. May I call on you again?"

"I would like that."

29

A Forged Legacy

Symon breathed in deeply. The smell of smoke, the deep, dark smell of the coals, wood, and sounds of craftsmen filled the air, making him feel at home. He smiled at his mentor who walked beside him, taking it in.

"Master Zen, thank you for coming with me today."

"Of course," the old man replied.

It had been weeks since the incident that Moria had chided him for his lack of equipment and Symon had finally taken up the idea to go and commission a set of armor. Moria had given him a name. The "Heartstone Armory." It was located across the city in one of the smaller merchant Wards of Vargarden. Upon announcing his intention to shop, Symon had spent half of an hour explaining to Jesse why he couldn't build his own armor as he was a blacksmith, not an armorer. The difference between the two seemed to perplex the young thief, but he had explained that crafting hinges, axles, bindings, and other tools did not provide him with the knowledge of armor design and the complexities of creating such an important piece of equipment.

Jesse had shrugged in defeat and then told Symon that he would be on his own for this trip and went to spend time with Caleb. Moria, much to Symon's disappointment, was occupied with her younger sisters and had taken Argyle to the park to allow the girls to climb and romp on the giant Gargoyle. Thorn had been scarcely to be found, and Symon worried about her greatly. In the end, Symon had found Zenesul to accompany him.

"When do you return to Highston?" Symon asked. "I do not wish to keep you from anything important."

"Fear not, my boy," Zenesul smiled. "I have a bit of time left. Once word reaches of my antics here, I'll be back to ducking the new regime."

"I still cannot believe you betrayed them, master."

"I betrayed no one," Zenesul said, firmly. "The New Nobles are a wretched front of villainy. Paid for by the Bright Guilds, namely Manticore. I serve the people of the Federation, as I always have."

"But how, Master? How did you do it?"

"Simple. The Elysium has always feared what I represent. Their lack of control is petrifying to them. With my reputation as a liaison to Manticore, when the power shift happened, the Magi became desperate to knock on my door and ask for my return. As I needed information, I agreed. For the last few months, I've been cozied up to the breast of the Elysium and watching their movements. All while running the resistance using the secrets I've learned.

"The time for pretense," Zenesul smiled, "has come to an end. It is time to find a way to free ourselves from the grip of the Investurants and Manticore once and for all."

"Caleb may have an idea regarding the Investurants," Symon said. "A key to pacifying them and removing them from the battle."

Zenesul nodded. "I shall inquire from him then. If you believe he would be inclined to share."

"I do."

"Then it shall be one of the last things I have left to do, before I return home. It is best that I leave before the rest of Highston's emissaries arrive."

"I would think so," Symon laughed. Then a wave of melancholy washed over him. Highston, his former home, was still under the grip of the enemies. "How is Highston, master?"

"I won't lie, boy, it's not good," Zenesul said. "The Lord's High Council has all been replaced with the New Nobles. A dozen former members are dead, and the remaining are in hiding throughout the Federation. Investurant patrols are becoming more aggressive by the day. Crime is rampant. It's a dystopia."

"By the Shining Court," Symon whispered.

"Lord Devros... Your former compatriot, Olivar, sits at the top. The heir of House Devros absorbed the place of Lord Montrell shortly after the night Highston fell. He's made quite a spectacle of himself since then. He built a new home in Gaio, a monstrosity of a temple."

"Oh?"

"He built it on the ashes of the Flame Eternal."

Symon's gut clenched. "Why? Master, why does he hate me so much?"

"Only he knows. But do not underestimate him. It will not be the last time he attempts to goad you. It is his deepest desire to drag you back to Highston."

"One day, he may succeed. I cannot ignore him forever."

"Can you not?" Zenesul asked.

"How can I allow him to exert his power upon the people of Highston? To just let him get away with it all? How can I let my enemy take out his anger for me against others?"

"That, my boy, is what he wants you to think," Zenesul said. "He is responsible for these choices, not you. His narcissism is not your fault."

"If you say, Master. But it does not feel like it," Symon sighed heavily. His mind raced through his father's history, his own history with Olivar, the brief encounters with Manticore through Jesse. It was all tangled into one big knot squeezing around Symon, choking him. "I just feel like no matter what I do, it is all on my shoulders. That somehow, I caused all this."

"You are an empathetic man, Symon. You hold too much of other people's choices in your hands. There is no such thing as fate or destiny. Only your choices. None of these events condemn you. It's all in your mind." The old man smiled and waved before them. "In time, maybe you shall see differently. But behold, we have arrived at your destination."

Symon looked at the squat stone building before him. The steeply pitched roof reflected the sunlight. The thick stone chimney stretched into the sky. A small door led into what Symon could only surmise was the shop front. He straightened his jacket and walked inside.

Glancing around the front room, he listened to the ring of the bell behind him fade and as it signaled his entrance. It was so familiar it wrenched his heart and made him miss Highston for a moment. A skeletal servant emerged from the back room with a small chalkboard in its hands. On the slate was written, "One moment, please make yourself at home." Symon exchanged a look with Zenesul and chuckled. The casual display of Necromancy was still, even after all these weeks, taking time to grow accustomed to.

Symon roamed the display racks and examined the works available. It took little time for him to confirm his confidence was well-placed. Moria had said that Heartstone was a generational shop in Vargarden and well-known. Symon could see why.

The pieces shown were immaculate. Plate, half-plate, and even a hybrid plate and scale set adorned the displays. Each piece was designed to show the techniques the smiths would use to build any commissioned set. Symon whistled appreciatively.

"Good morning, friend," a deep voice called out. A burly and broad-shouldered Ennedi walked through the door with his weighted apron still tied around his waist. The man shook his dark black mane, streaked with gray, and brushed his smokey colored fur to shed the dust and ash. Mid-fifties and of good health, the man smiled broadly and his eyes were alight with mirth as he took Symon and Zenesul in. "How can I help?"

"Aye, sir," Symon said. "I am in the market for some armor. Your shop came highly recommended. And with good reason," Symon said. His fingertips brushed the plate in front of him. "Your work is fantastic. The color and purity on this steel is beautiful. The craftsmanship is exquisite. Even thickness across the curves. No thin spots, no lumps..." he paused and turned to the older Ennedi. "And barely a hammer mark to be seen. Quite exquisite."

"High praise," the smith smiled, "Are you a forge rat, too?"

"Yes, sir. Merely a humble blacksmith, not the artisan you are, for sure. I was trained by my fath—" Symon started. "My sire trained me. Worked his shop for many years."

"In the Federation, yes?"

"Aye, sir. How…?"

"We don't get visitors from Khorric lands often. Any we do get, are often not seen outside the palace. Your group has been here for a couple of months and you've stayed. It's quite the news."

"Oh, well," Symon said, shuffling his feet. "Apologies. I would not have wanted to cause a disturbance."

"Not a disturbance," the old smith laughed. "A distraction. A welcome distraction from our bored little lives at that! And a few of us took special notice when you reclaimed the Cyl'Karrick manor."

Symon hesitated, there was still so much history in the name that he had yet to unlock here. "Yes, Kyrn Cyl'Karric was my sire."

"Aye. So we heard."

"Why did you take special notice?" Symon asked.

"Because…" the old smith smiled. "We're kin."

Symon's mind flipped over and his heart soared into his throat. His eyes took in the man before him looking for any physical clues to their shared lineage. Ennedi characteristics were often difficult to connect bloodlines and lineages, but subtle pattern markers within the facial fur were leaning Symon to believe the claim.

"My name is Falearyn Kal'Daren. I'd be a distant cousin," the man said. He laughed heartily. "It's harder to draw the lineage to you because of the havoc Kyrn reeked on the generational balance. You're half my age, but technically I think you're cousins with my patronsire or his sire before him."

"Wow!" Symon breathed. "I am Symon Cyl'Karrick."

"Aye," Falearyn nodded. "I'm glad to meet you." The older Ennedi's eyes softened. A touch of sadness entered his voice as he said, "If it's not too much, may I ask how your sire passed?"

"Oh," Symon said. "Of course."

Zenesul put his hand on Symon's shoulder. "I'll be outside, my boy. Give you a moment to connect to your family."

"Thank you, Master," Symon said. He watched as his old mentor stepped out the door. Turning to Falearyn, Symon said, "Yes, he died in the invasion of Highston. He protected us as we escaped."

"A sad, selfless act, but one I would expect," The smith put his hand on Symon's shoulder. "Any sire would lay his life to protect his children and the legacy of the family. 'New bones, new glory.' That's what I would have done."

"I thought it was 'Old bones, old ways'?" Symon asked.

The booming sound of the smith's laughter echoed through the shop room. "I am assuming your stubborn father said that. Would sound like him!"

Symon stepped back in confusion.

"No, no," Falearyn waved his hands. "No offense. My patronsire told me stories of his cousin Kyrn and the hard head he had. He would have been Nemuku for a few decades by then. Legion through and through."

Symon and Falearyn exchanged stories for an hour. Symon thought of the Heritage Tree and remembered the Kal'Daren branch. Maiya Kal'Khorric had given birth to four children. The eldest was a daughter named Raina who had three sons. Karrick, Daren, and Stanish. While Karrick had only one child, Kyrn, the brothers Daren and Stanish had several children. The Kal'Daren branch was nearly eight generations deep, and Falearyn was the product of that lineage.

"It has been a surprise and an honor to meet you, cousin."

"The honor is mine," Falearyn said at the end. "Mayhaps one day we can sit over a dinner, I can introduce you to my wife and children. Get to know one another more."

Symon smiled and nodded. "That would be amazing."

"We shall make it so. But I assume as you were surprised by our relationship, you did not know who I was before you arrived. If you were not here for a family reunion on this day... What brings you to my shop?"

"Armor," Symon said simply.

Falcaryn smiled broadly, the little fangs peeking down past his lips. "Well, of course, then you are in the right place."

"Lady Moria Yurolindo and Prince Caleb sent me to get armor to protect myself. Apparently running for your life in nothing but a fancy coat is a good way to get stabbed."

"Those are high named recommendations," Falearyn said. "They are right. If you're fighting folks with blades, best to put steel between them and you, not cloth."

Symon smiled as Falearyn asked questions regarding Symon's fighting style and experience in combat. Once satisfied, the smith laid out the work required. "So, we'll propose a blend of new and old. The Cyl'Karrick traditions at work again. The breastplate, shoulders will all be solid plates. As will the bracers and greaves. Your sides, legs, arms, and all joints would be chain to ensure protection, but allow more mobility. I'll have my daughter lay the enchantments into the steel to decrease the weight and then we'll lacquer it. She'll be a beautiful set, for sure."

"It sounds incredible."

Looking at the sword hung on Symon's back he grinned. "You deserve the finest armor to match that sword."

"It was my sire's blade. Now it is mine."

"The legacy will be completed, then. Family blade, family armor. It's so good to have your branch of the family back home," Falearyn laughed. "I would hate to lose it. Let's get you protected. I'll charge you for the weight of the steel, the materials used for the forging. But the enchantment and lacquer I'll be gifting you. Welcome to the family, cousin."

30

Surprisingly Comfortable

Jesse was not a good cook. He knew this. He also didn't like to do it. In the past, Xerian had always fussed whenever the boy took a try at the stew pot. Jesse, however, had always cleaned up the excessive mess that the man made, so occasionally Jesse would be bold enough to try his own hand. Even Thorn, her iron stomach that hardly turned down any meat, grumbled playfully whenever she found Jesse anywhere near a cook fire. The kitchen was a disaster area of Jesse's life.

For the last few days, however, Jesse was finding he either cooked or Symon starved. Still bolstered from his last conversation with the Ennedi, as well as being on an emotional high from his date with the Prince, Jesse was eagerly trying to help, while anxious that it would be "too much." They had run out of several things recently and Jesse hadn't been sure if he should ask Symon for coin to replace it. So, for the third day in a row, Jesse resigned himself to taking a plate of lackluster sandwiches and two bowls of over-seasoned soup up to the library.

"You need to pay better attention to the time, and eat properly," Jesse said as he entered the room.

Symon barely looked up from the current journal he was writing in, halfheartedly saying, "I know. Moria gives me the same complaint."

"Well I'm prettier than her, so you should listen to me more," Jesse quipped.

"Where is she, anyways?"

Symon raised his head fully and a small smile formed on his lips. "At the palace. She's debriefing and planning logistics based on the recent accommodations to the Prince's social schedule."

"Oh?" Jesse blushed and returned the smile.

"Please sit," Symon said. The Ennedi tried moving the journal, only to realize the entire desk was littered with stacks of books, journals, scrolls, and writing implements. Jesse stood there holding the tray, watching him in mock frustration while suppressing a smirk.

"Would you move your damn books? Just throw them in the other chair or something."

"Give me a moment," Symon growled playfully. The man meticulously moved each stack, keeping some form of organization in his head, and made space for Jesse to serve the two of them the meal.

"So, what is all this?" Jesse asked as he sat down. "What are you working on now?"

"Something the Prince said," Symon sighed in frustration. "About the Shard, and the end of the War of Night."

"Okay?"

"Before all..." Symon waved his hand around, "this happened, I was a scholar on the War. It was one of my favorite topics. Ironic, really."

Jesse laughed.

"So, I am attempting to correct and expand information I learned from the Federation's Academy. There, it seemed that no matter how hard I pushed, I could never attain details on what ended the War of Night. The only answer they would provide me was, 'the Battle of Enfeld'."

"Well yeah," said Jesse. "Everybody knows the war ended at Enfeld. Even Street Rats like me know that."

"Correct, but there is almost no documentation of that battle," countered Symon.

"What?" Jesse asked.

"There are statistics. There is a time line. But there are no details or reports.

Now that I am aware of the agenda that Zenesul and Caleb pointed out, it appears that it was all Federal Propaganda. They brokered the deal. They sent both sides home. They took the credit."

"Those fuckers," Jesse sneered.

"So now I am studying the same question from this end. The Legion appears to have the opposite problem." Symon pointed to the stacks of ledgers. "Every officer involved over the months of Enfeld has a report. Just now, I have been able to review Legion documentation on the last few days of the battle."

"And you found all the answers right here, wrapped up in a pretty bow, right?" teased Jesse.

"No," said Symon. "Not exactly."

"Oh, then a good old fashioned waste of time."

"More like a road map to the answer," Symon laughed. "Or at least, a map to the person who may hold the answer." Symon took a spoonful of his soup and his face twisted in disgust. "Did you make this soup in an attempt to push me into cooking tomorrow evening?" He grinned goodnaturedly at Jesse, and added, "If so, it is working."

"Hush, you. Cook it your own self next time then," countered Jesse, finding himself caught between laughing at the joke and being embarrassed over his lack of culinary skill.

"And how old is this bread?" Symon asked, knocking it hard on the desk.

"It's stale, yes. But we're low on food."

Symon frowned. "Oh, I am sorry. I have neglected the house. I will run to the market this afternoon."

"It's okay," Jesse said. Internally, he kicked himself for fretting. He knew Symon would handle it if only asked. "So what is this road map? Or better yet, skip all that and tell me who knows the answer."

"Skip to the end and deprive you of the foundational lessons along the way?" Symon smiled. "Master Zenesul would surely rebuke me for that."

"Cut from the same cloth," Jesse muttered. He couldn't help but laugh at Symon's embracing of the old man's role.

"I found some information while researching the reports of my sire's direct charges. Specifically, first hand accounts of the Deacons that were charged with his crimes."

"I see you have gotten used to saying 'sire' instead of 'father'," interrupted Jesse. "So Moria has gotten onto you about how only The Father is usually referred to with that word? And how everyone seems to take calling your dad 'father' is some kind of a social no-no?"

"Yes, I seem to be getting that habit firmly in hand, thank you."

"Just checking," Jesse smiled. "So, the priests who took the heat for Kyrn?"

"Yes, more than a few... Deacons mentioned that when the armies became fully entrenched at Enfeld and sitting in a protracted siege, my sire packed up and left for a week."

"In the middle of a battle?"

"Yes," Symon nodded. "Only a handful of his advisors knew where he went. But, according to their reports, he visited the Deepland Witch."

"Wait, the 'Witch in the Woods?' The one that you, Hasukawa, and Kiko were talking about when we met them on the road?"

"Yes," said Symon. "Hasukawa said she was real. This confirms it. The problem is, it is still unknown what was discussed. Only that my sire went to see her, and afterward he met with the *Ombramaes*. Then, the Investurant forces departed for their own planar home and he sent the Legion home."

"So how do we find out more about her and what she knows?"

"I have no answers to that, sadly."

"Tell you what," said Jesse animatedly, "I'm meeting up with Caleb tonight for dinner, so maybe I can ask him for something."

Symon dribbled soup from his spoon into the bowl and teased, "Please tell me you are not cooking for him."

"Hush, you!"

Jesse stood before his wardrobe selecting his outfit. He knew nothing about the evening plans other than he was to meet Caleb "before sunset." No information had been given on what the evening would involve, who would be there, or even if it was business or for fun, so Jesse was trying to plan for everything. So he had decided to give himself plenty of time, leaving a bit early, and once again dressed in his newest finery.

As he left the house, Jesse found an Eisgeid dressed in Caleb's livery standing outside the gate. The skeletal servant held out a letter with Jesse's name written in Caleb's tidy handwriting.

"Thank you," Jesse said, taking the letter. As soon as he took the letter, the Eisgeid turned and began walking away, its skeletal feet clacking faintly on the cobblestones. Jesse returned his attention to the parchment, opening it to read.

> *My dearest Jesse,*
>
> *I hope that the day sees you well, and that this missive finds its way to you in time for us to meet by the allotted time. It would please me greatly if you would meet me at the fountain in the main square in front of the Father's Cathedral of the Blessed Soul, just before sunset.*
>
> *Yours in trust, Prince Caleb Cyl'Emptor*

"Well, shit..." Jesse said. He scanned his surroundings and found the street empty. He was talking to no one but himself.

Jesse reread Caleb's note. Given the wording Caleb had used, Jesse wondered how long the bonehead Eisgeid had been standing out here. He had felt that he had left in plenty of time to get to the Palace, but he wasn't sure about the Father's Cathedral.

The Cathedral was the biggest of the churches, one in the center of the city, but he wasn't exactly sure how to get there. At least on foot.

Jesse smiled. His hand traced a moment, weaving a spell and he whispered, "*Hervestoll.*" Jesse disappeared in a blink and one moment of blindness later, he appeared five hundred feet in the air, his outspread wings already catching the evening's thermal updrafts. With the capital city of Vargarden spread below him, he scanned the principal landmarks as they stood out in sharp relief. The skyline was washed in brilliant yellows and oranges, the spring sun hanging low in the sky threatening to kiss the horizon.

Jesse turned towards the Father's Cathedral. It was a towering mass of obsidian granite, all sharp planes, climbing towers, and protruding spikes. The young Ishanshi glided past building after building, weaving his way towards the city center. The landmark remained easy to locate and Jesse made good time as he soared through the sky. He sighed with relief as he spotted the vast open courtyard with a splendid fountain in the center.

From his vantage, Jesse could see, beside the fountain, a small group of priests surrounded by a Welengam Patrol of a dozen skeletons. In the center of the group stood Caleb, accompanied by Reneforte. Jesse banked toward an open area a few dozen yards from the group, coming in wide so as to not alarm any of the guards. He landed lightly, and brushed himself off, straightening his hair as the group parted and Caleb came forward to greet Jesse.

"I am pleased that you arrived in a timely manner," said Caleb. "Not to mention, a spectacular entrance."

"Look at you, speaking all pretty again!" Jesse teased quietly. "Sorry if I kept you waiting. I came as soon as I could." The Ishanshi's eyes scanned the public square, noting a few passersby, but nothing out of the ordinary, other than the functionaries and guards. "So what's up? Why the fountain?"

"You arrived in time. I wanted to show you something," Caleb smiled. "A favorite of mine. But we have a few moments."

"Oh, okay."

"I appreciate your punctuality."

Jesse grinned. "I appreciate the new ability to glide in Vargarden. Hey, if we have a minute... Can I ask you something?"

"Absolutely," said Caleb.

"Right. Symon and I were talking about something earlier today. Do you know much about the Witch in the Woods?"

"Oh," Caleb's eyes raised in surprise. "Not a topic I expected."

"Sorry," Jesse said. "Forget it."

"No," the Prince said. "I am happy to answer. I don't know much, however. Research is relatively limited. From what I know, she's an entity from the Verdant Green, a realm with a relationship not dissimilar to Sainan as the relationship with Mumvuri. She's an entity of great power. Documentation stretches back for quite a bit of time, leading scholars to argue whether she's older than even the Father.

"She's an Oracle of great reputation," Caleb continued. "Her temperament is capricious. Documented encounters with her have reported unexpected prices for the information she provides. It is well regarded as good advice to avoid her if at all possible."

"Oh, yeah," Jesse smiled. "You don't know much at all."

"I will set my researchers on it right away," Caleb replied. "I can gather additional information."

"I'm joking!" Jesse laughed. "You just gave me a minute long description!"

"Oh," Caleb blushed. The tint of his blue cheeks darkened, and he nervously swept his hair back over his ear. "Well, I will still do research. Why do you ask of her?"

"Symon thinks Kyrn went to see her at the end of the war."

"Ah," Caleb's eyebrow raised. "That IS interesting."

"Yeah, well..."

"Thank you, Jesse." The Prince's eyes darted to the horizon. "Oh, here it is!" Caleb stepped forward and grabbed Jesse's hand, tugging him back toward the fountain. "It is spring, so we should stand to the left of the fountain for best effect."

Jesse allowed himself to be led to the appropriate spot, and turned to face the front of the cathedral. It was an imposing and impossibly black mass of a building. His eyes scanned the surface looking for anything of interest, but saw nothing. "What am I looking for?"

"Shh..." Caleb whispered.

The sun inched toward its setting position and their shadows stretched out before them, impossibly long. Jesse fluttered his wings a bit, watching the silhouettes dance and stretch across the paving stones of the courtyard. He craned his neck, glancing behind himself in the stillness and taking in his surroundings. Jesse realized that the buildings facing the opposite side of the square were all of a low, uniform height, allowing maximum access to the brilliant setting sun.

For a moment he wondered what the roofs of those buildings might be made of, for they seemed to catch a harsh reflection of the dying light. As Jesse turned back to look at the shadows at their feet again, he realized that the fountain behind them was casting a much sharper, darker shadow than they were themselves, as the setting sunlight was now being concentrated across the courtyard. Slowly the focused light marched forward as the sun lowered itself nearer to the horizon. Onward the light crept, until it reached the cathedral's foundation.

"Here it comes," whispered Caleb. Jesse felt the Prince squeeze his hand as he leaned over and laid his head on Jesse's shoulder.

The concentrated light hit the black-fronted building and Jesse gasped as the building before him changed. Impenetrable stone now appeared to be minutely transparent, almost like smoke trapped in quartz, or ink diffused in water. As the sunlight played up the buildings facing, it appeared as if the inner material of the stone swirled and flowed around the rays of light. Spectral shapes, almost as if spirits, floated within the building's skin dancing to and fro.

Suddenly, unwantedly, a vision of the flowing, shadowy cloak worn by Rhon flashed through Jesse's mind, causing chills and making him shudder. A word whispered itself in his mind, a name, not just half remembered, but clear and vibrant as if someone was speaking. Rhon. Rhon. Rhon. Then it was gone, and Jesse was left feeling empty and frightened, just as the shadows of the opposite buildings now reached the cathedral, leaving the party without the sun's warmth.

"Are you cold?" Caleb asked.

"No, I'm fine."

"Jesse? I apologize. Please, let us go inside. I have more I would like to show you."

They entered the church and Jesse listened as Caleb spent the next hour giving an impressive tour of the Father's Cathedral. The Prince spent much of the time explaining the history and architecture of the building, as well as the organization of the priesthood. Jesse was rapt as Caleb displayed his knowledge.

Occasionally one of the priests would interject an extra fact, or confirm some point the Prince would make, but for Jesse, only the Prince mattered.

"So, the church exists to serve the Father?" asked Jesse.

"By church, do you mean the Deacons and the organization? Or the Cathedral itself?"

"Oh, uh..." Jesse chuckled. "The Deacons I suppose."

"The church exists to serve the people," one of the priests replied. His tone was off-handed, but not offensive. A tone of a servant who couldn't fathom a difference.

"The church does serve the people, but it exists because of the Father," clarified Caleb. He smiled at Jesse. "The Deacons derive their powers from the Father. He is the source of the Divine and Arcane energy they wield. So the Deacons do worship the Father, if that is what you are asking."

Jesse stared at the iconography and murals carved into the chapel walls. Instead of images of powerful authorities which adorned the Federal Church, he found depictions of supplicating priests and massive crowds of people basking in light. "So different," marveled Jesse, speaking as much to the priest as to Caleb.

"In Highston," Jesse said, turning to the Prince, "the churches are no different than the merchant guilds. They operate for profit, a tithe for everything from attending service, to being blessed, to getting a Healing. Even the orphanages are basically workhouses for the kids sent there. I should know. I nearly got sent to one of them."

"We have discussed the corruption within the Khorric Federation," the Deacon said. Jesse saw instant regret on the woman's face as her eyes turned to the Prince, fearing she had overstepped.

"It is true," Caleb said. "Jesse and Symon have both advised on the failings of the religious institutions within Highston. You may speak your mind."

"It's heresy," the Deacon muttered. "Utter heresy."

"What about the other Gods?" asked Jesse. "Could it be a dogma thing? Alloric, Sand, Gethall, all those? Is it just because the Father is here? Could it be that he's more focused on charity because he has to answer in person? Are there other churches here, are they banned, or what?"

"Easy, Jesse," Caleb said. "One question at a time."

"Sorry."

"But it is complicated," Caleb said. "No Gods are refused worship in Vargarden. We understand the pantheon as well as any, I suppose. None are punished for speaking their names or offering worship. Some small temples exist, and anyone is free to construct their own shrines. Many families do. They are prayed upon for specific interventions within the sphere the Gods are known for.

"However," Caleb continued, "most citizens are quite content to give their devotion to the Father, and to pray at his temples. After all, their lives are surrounded by his works of power, aided by his priests, enriched by his Eisgeid, and protected by his Welgeid."

Caleb paused for a moment. "It may be true that the Father's proximity to his clergy and the people provide him a less detached insight to the needs of his people. But the corruption of the Gods' wills I believe falls fully on the shoulders of the Federal Priests who wield it."

"So, who is the Father?"

"Even I don't know the full story," Caleb said. "But he is a Divine avatar. A being of the God of Death, known by many names around the Realm. Part God, part Mortal, the Father exists in a space between. He guides us. He loves us. And this temple collects the power of his worshippers for him to feed back into the Deacons to serve them. It's a symbiotic relationship."

"Well, that's just..." Jesse stumbled over his words. "I don't know what that is."

"In time," Caleb said, "maybe you will."

Once the tour was completed, Caleb led Jesse back to the entrance of the cathedral, then back out into the square. The sun had fully set by this point, and the square was now bathed in the illumination of hundreds of floating colorful orbs, ranging from vibrant shades of red and pink, into the spectrum of pale blues and purples. None stayed in one place for long, but instead drifted lazily through the air, some floating like moths, while others gathered like flocks of birds. It lent a sense of wonder and mystery to the atmosphere. People had come out of their homes to enjoy the spectacle, children squealing in wonder and excitement, adults proclaiming their appreciation of the entertainment.

"Is this common?" asked Jesse. "I have been out many nights with Thorn, and have not seen this, even from the air."

Caleb took Jesse's hand in his, and began leading him back across the square toward the fountain. As they approached, Jesse could see that a Welengam Patrol had cordoned off a section of the space abutting the fountain, where Reneforte was standing, waiting on them. As they approached the line of skeletons, they could see that a selection of blankets had been laid upon the paving stones, with piles of cushions lining the low wall of the fountain. A picnic basket sat to one side, a meal spread on a half dozen small serving trays. Caleb and Jesse made their way to the cushions, making themselves comfortable.

As Reneforte began serving food and drink, Caleb answered Jesse's question. "This is the Sempiternal Festival. It is a celebration of life and prosperity, held for three days each spring and fall. I thought you might enjoy it with me."

31

Ghosts in the Shadows

The streets of Highston were deadly quiet. The sun had set long ago, and the normally vibrant city was eerily still. So much had changed in the months since the Investurants had seized control.

The Ghost watched carefully, waiting for the patrol he knew was coming. The Vesters were more disciplined than either their Federal or Manticore counterparts, but also predictable. Each night, the same patrol. Each night, the same turns. Each night, the same pattern.

Six blue-skinned warriors turned the corner, marching down the street toward where he waited. They led a small man in chains, the latest prisoner of some bloated charge which would amass to nothing more than an excuse. Just another innocent citizen who had spoken out against the New Nobles, who would be imprisoned and forgotten.

A growl came from the Ghost's stomach. He hadn't been eating well, and he had lost weight. He would have to address it later if he wished to continue his quest. But for now, he reset his focus. The end of the *Sangebula*. The end of the *Ombramaes*.

Silently, the Ghost strode into the street, eyes locked on the squad of Investurant warriors. Their hands went to their weapons as they formed up into a defensive position. The squad leader smiled.

"*La'hemo sesta do'es peran,*" he said, the sinister tone of the Mumvuri language dripping in his voice.

The Ghost replied, "*I've been waiting for you, too.*"

"*You and your arrogance die. Tonight.*"

The Ghost turned as an Investurant Nobleborn approached from the other direction, a squad of six in his wake. They had set an ambush for him. One they were quite confident in. The Ghost simply smiled.

He glanced over the shoulder of the original squad leader, locking eyes with the prisoner. "Duck." The man gave him a quizzical look, but dropped to his knees immediately.

"*Haristodonia,*" the Ghost growled, his hand flicking the last stroke of a spell form. Green light snapped together, forming a horizontal line across the street, severing the torsos of the Investurant squad. His hands went to his short blades, drawing them from his back scabbards and immediately going into motion.

He sprung backwards, twisting in the air, striking left and right before the Nobleborn's squad could react. Three of the warriors fell beneath his blades before the others could even draw their weapons in response.

The high-eared Investurant shoved his companions in front of him, forming a barrier of safety between himself and the Ghost. Whirlwind strikes quickly took down the remaining three soldiers, but provided enough time for the Noble to gather himself and draw his weapons.

The Ghost glared, and growled. "*All I need is a Gateway.*"

"*All you will get is death!*"

The Ghost shrugged and struck quickly. His blades met steel as the azure warrior defended the attack and used his own swords to block and parry. He was a skilled fighter, and the Ghost lost himself into a rhythm of strike, counterstrike.

Suddenly, the Nobleborn phased, his skin going smoky and transparent. Shifting sideways, the warrior poised to strike, waiting for the opportunity to become solid once more. "*Geisfan,*" the Ghost breathed. His blade activated in Quinnar, sliding between the two realms, empowered by the Veil. The Ghost struck, targeting the sword hand of the Investurant, and severed it from his arm.

The Noble crashed to the street, solidifying in shock, laying still in front of the Ghost's feet. The dark shadow of a warrior placed his boot across the neck of the fallen warrior. "*Gateway. Now!*"

The Investurant began tracking the required form, and the Ghost's eyes rose to find the man who had been captured. Cowering in the street, his chains rattled gently.

"Gather your family, and flee the city," the Ghost said. "There are people who will help you escape."

"Who?"

"Look for their signal," the Ghost said. He smiled as the Gateway opened behind him, the Investurant finishing his spell cowering beneath his boot. The Ghost stabbed the warrior through the neck and dove into the portal. As he dove, the Ghost struck a small match across the strike pad on his belt, and tossed it into the street. Lantern oil ignited dancing across the street in a circular insignia.

The sign of the Resistance.

Rhon paced the room that served as the command headquarters, wracking his thoughts in an effort to determine how they could deal with this damnable Ghost. His eyes drifted to the table, filled with papers from their plans against the capital city of Vargarden, to the bulletins regarding hidden Nobles in Eithren, to the last Ghost attack. Each, another report. Each, another failure.

Traps, ambushes, even outright attacks had failed thus far. Every step they made, the Ghost seemed to be aware of and have a counter plan. As much as Rhon hated to admit it, this Ghost was an impressive tactician. As the General of the Investurant armies, Rhon had some of the best military training available, and could appreciate the depth of the Ghost's strategy and planning thus far. But it wouldn't matter. Eventually, Rhon would discover the nature of this Ghost. And destroy it.

So far, their attempts to uncover the identity of the Ghost had also proven futile. Emaly's divinations could not reveal anything on its future plans. In fact, the only thing her magic had disclosed was that the name they had given this monstrosity was apt. This Ghost was invisible to the Veil. According to what Emaly said she had found, this Ghost had no Soul. Not in any way a normal living being would. Whether this being was from Mumvuri or its parallel plane, Sainan, it was an anomaly to both.

Rhon did not consider it to be Undead. He, Emaly, and even their dear *Ombramaes*, had all dealt with the accursed Undead from Vargarden before. Undead Legion troops did not act with the independence, the skillful capability, or even the speed of this being, this "Ghost".

Rhon still could not figure out the end game, however. It was one thing when the Ghost had been ambushing patrols out in the field. Bad enough when on three different occasions it had attacked a military camp, once wiping out all officers in the command tent. But now...

Now the Ghost was in Highston.

They had debated, well, Rhon had insisted, that they take out retribution on the Khorric Federation citizens here in the capital, to add reluctance to any future attacks. But as Emaly had pointed out, this Ghost could just as easily be a defected Investurant officer, in which case the deaths of Sainan peasants may not hold any sway over the Ghost's tactics. Rhon didn't believe he was a traitor. But with no proof, the *Ombramaes* had denied his plans. Damn this Ghost!

"*Lieutenant!*" Rhon roared toward the door. "*Get in here!*"

Almost immediately a younger Investurant stepped into the room. "*Yes, Lord Rhon?*"

The young officer stood before Rhon, shifting his feet and twitching his hands. Rhon often made others uneasy, due to his carefully cultivated reputation. Rhon was determined to ensure that he was instantly and unquestioningly obeyed by anyone, friend or foe. But this officer wouldn't even meet his gaze. Rhon worried that the fear of being near any potential Investurant target of the Ghost was beginning to overshadow the fear of disappointing a member of the *Sangebula*.

Individual preservation was unacceptable within the Investurant army. If this became more prevalent, Rhon feared what it would mean for discipline among the troops. These fools did not realize that all of this was being done for them. To stop these damned Wraiths from wiping out more of the peasant cattle from Mumvuri. They had been selected for service. Given an opportunity to serve their people. Then they had the gall to not even show damned gratitude.

An angry buzzing formed in Rhon's mind as it called forth rage. He wanted to break this young man's spirit. He wanted blood. He made a mental checklist to deliver punishment later.

"Speak! You pathetic excuse for an officer," Rhon growled. *"What has been discovered about this latest attack from the so-called Ghost?"*

"Not enough, Lord Rhon," the officer said quietly. *"We have investigated the scene, but not much was left. We have still been unable to determine the method of entrance or departure. He came and went quickly."*

"It!" Rhon corrected. *"We don't know what it is yet."*

"Of course, my Lord. Arcanist Le'arial is still trying to determine whether the Ghost is walking between planes and if so, how."

"Is she on site?"

"Yes, my lord."

"Very well. Let me know as soon as she—"

Sounds of anguish and pain rang from the hallway beyond the officer, cutting Rhon's words short. The lieutenant spun, his hand already to his blade. *"What in all the Hells is going on out there?"* he cried.

A heavy crunch sounded, a meaty thwack, as one sword blade cut down into his collarbone from behind, another cleaving deep into his skull, the point ending in such a line as to appear to give the young Investurant a new steel nose. Blood sprayed in rainbow arcs into the room as both swords were yanked from the body, which slumped forward, forcing the door open further.

"I hear you're looking for me," the Ghost said, in the common Sainan tongue.

Rhon sprang into action, drawing his twin Kukri in a fluid motion even as he rushed forward. He did not aim for the door, however. Instead he phased to his incorporeal and slid through the wall to the right. He intended not only to ensure his footing would not catch on the corpse of the officer sprawled across the stones in the entry, but to catch the attacker by surprise. Instead, Rhon himself was taken at the disadvantage.

A pair of swords were already bearing down on the spot on the wall exactly where he intended to materialize. The Ghost had spun out of the room and positioned his blades perfectly. The only thing that saved him from what would have been a pair of fatal wounds was the lucky angle that his own blades were sitting at. The attacker's steel pushed back against Rhon's Kukri, one of the tips slicing through the leather of his breastplate and cutting into his chest.

Rhon shoved hard against his assailant, his immaterial feet slipping through the bodies of three other soldiers who had been stationed in the hallway. Rhon snarled as he slipped past the man, he could at least confirm he was male, known as the Ghost.

Rhon paused, his mind connecting and realizing something impossible. Their blades had connected. Rhon was immaterial and yet the Ghost had been able to strike him. Blooded Investurants relied on their ability to phase as an advantage in combat, to cause blades to miss or slide through. The Ghost, already terribly dangerous, had learned a powerful new trick.

Rhon let the rage wash through him. All thoughts of his typical fighting style, of playing with his opponent, were forgotten. The Ghost was not a foe to be taken lightly. Certainly, not one to play with.

The man was bigger than Rhon expected. He was draped in layers of cloaks, and leather armor, his face was masked and only his eyes were truly visible. Rhon's strikes would look true, but would tear away only cloth. The two exchanged a lightning fast flurry of attacks, each striking a hair behind where the other would move to. Rhon used his speed to press the offensive, driving the Ghost back.

Their battle returned into the command room, as the two warriors sought every corner, table, or obstacle to press an advantage. It had been a long time since Rhon had fought someone as skilled as the Ghost. His arms burned with effort and his chest heaved, struggling to catch breath. But he wasn't fighting for victory. He was fighting for time.

The sounds of rushing footsteps thundered up the hall as the cry of alarm could be heard and Investurant soldiers rushed to respond. Sensing the situation, the Ghost's eyes darted around the room, looking for an escape. Rhon smiled, but the man suddenly pressed back on the attack at Rhon, forcing him onto his back foot for just a moment. The Ghost snatched papers from the table and threw them in the face of the Investurant general, then the assailant turned and bolted out the door and down the hallway.

"Oh no you don't, coward!" roared Rhon, immediately giving chase.

The walls blurred by as they ran. They turned corner after corner in the hallway, Rhon only feet behind his target. Coming around the last corner, Rhon smiled. Before them, Emaly Le'arial stood in an open portal. She raised her staff defensively, filling the hallway and flung her hand out towards their foe. "*Pod'obo Os'zatu!*"

Her spell washed over the Ghost, and Rhon watched in startlement as the man bull-rushed through it unaffected. Snarling, their opponent leapt and bounded off the wall of the hallway, flipping over the sorceress. Landing beyond the portal, the Ghost flung a dagger behind him. Rhon dodged it, as did Emaly, but it was enough to break her concentration. The portal slipped from her grasp and shut. The Ghost had escaped yet again.

32

Parting in Sweet Sorrow

The next afternoon found Jesse back in Caleb's apartments, this time joined by all of their friends. Symon, Zenesul, Thorn, Argyle, and Moria reclined on couches, sans Argyle who lounged on the floor, finishing a small lunch that the palace had set out. Caleb had called the meeting, but Jesse still wasn't sure why. He was still trying to figure out Caleb, who bordered between detached and aloof, to coy and mysterious. Soon they were all satisfied, as Reneforte began serving post-meal refreshments.

"So, Symon," Caleb said, "Jesse has informed me of your interest in the Deepland Witch. I've taken some time to consult the library and gathered some information. What do you wish to know?"

"Do you have any indication of what my sire may have spoken to her about?" asked Symon. "There were notes in the Legion libraries from the depositions of his Deacons. Notes that stated he sought her out just before the events at Enfeld. But I have, as of yet, found nothing mentioning the reason."

"Sadly, I have found no more than you," replied Caleb. "That information was not something the Nemuku shared with his advisers. Only the Nemuku knew of the details."

Argyle spoke up, "May I inquire as to what is known about the Witch?"

"Most of the so-called knowledge regarding the Witch is unsubstantiated rumors," Caleb said. "Few are willing to speak about their secrets after visiting her, and many do so with malice because they weren't granted the answers they sought."

"Grendel spoke with the Witch," Argyle said. Jesse leaned forward, intrigued by the bit of history regarding his former employer. "As my Master's plans with the Investurants and their *Ombramaes* were being conceived, Grendel went to consult with the mysterious woman to motivate the Shadow to join his side." Argyle locked eyes with Jesse. "Grendel was a confident man, very sure of himself and afraid of few. Yet Grendel was disturbed by his visit. He would not speak of it other than to repeat her prophecy."

"Prophecy?" Symon asked.

"Yes," Argyle said. "Something regarding the 'Keys to Defeat' and how to collect and nullify them."

"I would be interested to know the question he asked," said Caleb. "Or even the attitude in which he asked it in." Caleb looked to Jesse and smiled. Jesse reached out and took the Prince's hand. Caleb flinched at first, but as Jesse squeezed his hand reassuringly, he relaxed. Social interaction, even amongst friends, was still difficult for Caleb, so Jesse had been taking things slow. The Prince continued, "It is known that the motivation of the question, and the level of respect shown when she is spoken with, can impact her answers."

"I suppose that makes sense," Symon said. "Being more helpful to those who make themselves more pleasant to speak with."

"Not precisely," Caleb replied. "The Witch is a true Fae. From the Verdant Green. Their morals are not the same as ours. I believe the best description of her answers was stated as 'She will always give you enough rope to hang yourself, but that the more respectful you are, the more of the knots she may help you to identify for the unraveling'.

"There is also the matter of ensuring that your questions are respectful of her time," Caleb continued. "Meaning that the question is not one that she would consider petty or obvious. Her spheres of influence are quite capricious and she does not take certain matters kindly. The Council has discussed the possibility of seeking her advice regarding the new attack on the Khorric Federation, but have thus far deemed it too risky to chance it may be beneath her standards."

"Yeah, innocent poor people aren't valuable enough for anyone," Jesse muttered. "What in the Thirteen Hells would she consider important enough then? The sun falling from the sky?"

Caleb took Jesse's hand in his. "I know you are upset regarding the victims of this new 'war,' my friend. No one is saying they are not important. It is more the subject matter itself and the potential consequences of displeasing a powerful being such as she is. The Deepland Witch loathes politics, considering it to be the petty squabbling of petty rulers."

Jesse raised Caleb's hand, kissing it, and said, "Well, I like her already."

"And if she deems the question within the political sphere, she could take offense and provide us answers that could cause greater harm to the innocent people. So, we must determine whether this is an option we wish to pursue," said Caleb. "There is information to be gained, but there is always a cost. It is merely who pays it."

"That sounds ominous," Jesse said.

"It is," Zenesul said, nodding. "It is in what the knowledge tempts the asker to do, as well as in the vagueness of her responses, that prove dangerous. And the more self-serving the seeker, the less she provides. Hoping to limit their power to harm others."

"What do you think she would say to us?" Symon asked. "If our question was not over the rule of the land, but instead the well-being of the people?"

"It is unsure," Zenesul said. "But you would truly have to seek your heart to know if it's what you truly desire to know."

"Grendel certainly was not selfless," Argyle said. "And he survived the contact. I can only surmise that you would as well. However, the risk is too great for an unknown prize. Surely, you would have other, less dangerous options."

"I do not know, Argyle," Symon said. "I am unsure that anyone but my father knows the answer. He refused to tell me. If anyone else in this realm would know, it would be she."

There was a longing in Symon's eyes that Jesse hadn't seen before. Some unanswered question that bore a hole in his friend's heart. It was familiar. Something similar to how he often felt. A loneliness that Jesse hadn't seen in Symon before.

"So, do you wish to go seek her out?" Caleb asked. He turned to Symon. "Is what you are looking for important enough to you?"

"I am willing to take the risk," said Symon. "It is a question which has intrigued and haunted me since I learned of the War of Night, long before I ever knew my sire was even involved." That tone spoke to Jesse, again, of unseen loss.

"We may benefit from me seeking her as well," Caleb said. "I feel that learning, what we can, about this bond between Symon and myself may be worth seeking her knowledge."

"Yeah? Well, I don't need an explanation about this bond that I'M feeling with you," said Jesse, pulling Caleb's hand against his own cheek. "I know what it is. But I'm going with you, whatever the danger."

"These seem like deeply personal benefits," Argyle warned. "Do you truly feel that she will see them as worthy? I advise against this."

"If my sire trusted her," Symon said, "then I must, too. While I know my question is very personal, I fear that it may be relevant to today's troubles."

Jesse frowned at that. There was something Symon wasn't telling anyone. Something his friend had figured out that no one else was aware of. Hesitantly, he asked. "Symon?"

"In time, Jesse. But not yet."

Moria huffed, "We will need a whistle that can summon the guide of the Deepland Witch."

Jesse fished the whistle that Hasukawa had given him out of his pocket. "Got you covered."

"In addition, the Prince will need at least a small military escort," said Moria. "Therefore, I will accompany you."

"And I will accompany you," interjected Zenesul, "but only part way. "Not to the Witch. But to return home. I need to get back to Highston. I have already stayed away longer than I should."

Thorn, who Jesse had noticed had been oddly quiet for the conversation, pointed to Zenesul. Her eyes met Jesse's sadly, but she said firmly. "I'm going back with him."

Symon, Caleb, and Moria all looked at her in surprise, then as one looked to Jesse for his reaction. He smiled sadly, then nodded his approval without saying anything aloud.

"Very well," said Caleb, diplomatically moving the conversation forward. "I will ensure my schedule is cleared for next week. Lady Yurolindo, when can you have a mixed escort prepared to depart, with proper supplies?"

"For my Prince? First light."

Jesse popped up his head, holding up Caleb's hand. "And what about for everyone else's Prince? For Caleb here?"

"I know what we said before, girl," said Jesse. "But are you sure you want to go back?"

The two best friends had pulled one another aside for one last check in. Their companions were making the last minute adjustments to their mounts, typical of such a trip. Moria had gathered quite a squad to escort them. Now that they were preparing to leave, Jesse was struggling to let his friend go.

"I'm not trying to belittle what you've already said. I just..." Jesse trailed off. "I just want you to remember, we can have safety and reliability here. New skills can be learned. We can make new lives." He took both of her hands in his and added, "Lives without people chasing us."

"Jes, sweetums," Thorn said. "People are still chasing you. They're just too scared to come HERE."

Jesse raised his eyes to Zenesul. The old man had caught them up on as much of Highston as he could. Manticore was still after Jesse. The Investurants were still after Jesse. Thorn was right.

"This life isn't for me. You have something real here, and I don't mean your fairy tale Prince, cute as he may be. I mean a REAL life.

"You were never meant for the streets, sweetie. I've always known it." Thorn looked in his eyes and stroked his hand. "Sure you've been great at it, but you've always dreamed of 'respectability.' Much as you hate the nobles, you are smart enough and skilled enough that you could learn their ways, fit right in, and do it better than them. Luckily, Vargarden's nobles aren't like the Khorr. These are good people, and you belong here. Momma's gotta let her baby go."

Jesse had started tearing up as Thorn was talking, and now tried to chuckle, the mix causing him to choke, sending him to coughing. Thorn pounded him on the back, and as Jesse's cough subsided, the two friends ended up in an embrace that was needed, allowing them to release the emotions, love, and trust they had for one another.

"And now, I got to fight to protect you," Thorn said, her voice hardening. "If those grot-licking slimeballs are intent to make your life into the fourteenth layer of the Hells, then it's my job to go stop them. The old man and I will figure out a way."

Jesse hugged his friend tightly. "Love you, girl."

The Isnashi watched as Zenesul placed a hand on Prince Caleb's shoulder. They were a few yards away, so his voice was difficult to hear, but Jesse could make it out. "I know you care for him, my Lord. But I want you to look at that and remember. Always remember what he is sacrificing to be with you. I don't say this to guilt you, my boy, but to remind you how important he already sees you. He is letting go of his best friend for you. Please be worthy of that."

Jesse stood and walked to Symon, who was speaking with Argyle. "Are you of a mind to return to the Federation?"

Argyle chuckled, a deep, rumbling purr, and said, "That life is gone for me, and I wish it good riddance. The Khorric Federation may have freed me from the legal slavery of my homelands, but the Bright Guilds of the Federation enslaved my soul." The Gargoyle laid a massive paw on Symon's wide blacksmith's shoulder. "I have not yet found paid employment here in Vargarden, and I do appreciate the hospitality you have shown me, a former enemy. But I feel at peace here. I feel like I could find opportunities to be appreciated here. I find people drawn to me for interest and curiosity, rather than fear. It is new for me, and I wish to explore this opportunity."

"Of course. You will always find home and hearth with me for as long as you need," said Symon. "Do you still believe going to the Witch is a mistake?"

"Nay, not a mistake, per se, but a risky gambit. A risk I do not agree with. This oracle is a fickle mistress, not to be trusted. Her words could be misinterpreted. With so many eyes on your fate, I do not wish you to become even more paranoid. Jumping at shadows. Her words may provide clarity, or intensify the fear. I would prefer to find my own answers that only the Gods and the Veil may offer."

"We'll be alright, big guy," Jesse said. "Trust us."

"And you," called out Symon, "Master Zenesul. Your thoughts?"

"I debated saying anything earlier," the old wizard paused. He stroked his beard, a look Jesse knew from experience. His former mentor had something he wanted to say, but was making up his mind as to whether to share. Finally he spoke. "She is a risk. While not many visit her, we are considering nearly half a dozen encounters between us."

"Half dozen?" Symon asked.

"Grendel," Zenesul pointed at Argyle, his finger moved to Symon, "your father, the three of you..." The old man smiled as he tapped his chest. "And myself."

"What?!" Jesse said.

"Why did you not tell us sooner?" Symon asked, almost at the same breath.

"Because of the implications," Zenesul said. "A mysterious force who may be mucking about with our lives. I feared that my decision would have undue influence."

"But you saw her?"

"I did, long ago. It was after the War of Night. I was fighting incessantly with my superiors in the Elysium. I was too powerful for them to risk disposing of, yet I was also too politically weak to listen to. I wanted to make the changes that I saw, and still see, needed to be. To help the people. After years of persecution with the Magi, I faltered. So I sought out her advice."

"Shit," Jesse whispered. "What did she say?"

"She told me that my path to change lay not in changing the Federation. It may never change. But to focus instead on impacting the lives of the people who most needed it. That the way to protect the people was to unlock the hearts and minds.

"She said," Zenesul continued. "That if I focused on it, some day, one heart and one mind may save the people of the Federation in ways I wouldn't foresee. So I decided to quit the Elysium and stop fighting."

"The Hells?" said Jesse, "She told you to just give up?"

"In a way," Zenesul said, chuckling softly. "My path to creating the changes I wished to see, it seems, was to stop being an enemy of the Magi, and instead to take on my own students. You, Jesse, and you, Symon, have not been my first covert students taken from the streets and castoffs, and I will be astounded if you are to be my last. I believe that, as she said, one day, one or more of my students will fulfill the goal I long for. Perhaps even one of you."

"So why did you not tell us earlier?" Symon asked again.

"Because," Zenesul said, "while, our history aside, it is rare for people to speak of the encounters with the Witch, it is unheard of for someone to visit her twice. You are going to see her with the knowledge of not one, not two, but now three other visits. If she sees this as a breach of protocol, I fear she may not let you return."

Travel was simple that day, nine figures on horseback, Argyle loping on all fours beside them, and a dozen skeletal guards marching tirelessly in double-step behind. Their passage was noted by all who saw them, many of whom would wave and offer cries of greeting as they passed. Moria and Paulson, a few scouts and a military Deacon rounded out the rest of the party.

Small groups of citizens gathered at various points along the roads leading from the capital city, curious to see the ever popular newcomers from their southern neighbors, and filled with pride at the sight of their Crown Prince.

They were stopped at the edge of the city by another small crowd, this one a mix of civilians and living military. All of the dozen Eisgeid were called forward and met by their living progeny. Each was outfitted in a fine tabard broadcasting the livery of the Father and of the Crown Prince. Each family placed upon their ancestor's bones a motley collection of flower crowns, hand sewn scarves and vests, garlands, ribbons, and prayer scrolls. It was a festive mood, respectful but joyous, not somber. Everyone wished the Prince and his companions well, filled with pride that their ancestors, above all others, had been chosen to protect their Crown Prince.

The group made good time despite the size of their party. They traveled quietly, the somberness of saying goodbye to the friends mixed with the anxiety of the task in front of them. Jesse just stared quietly, watching the countryside roll by on their journey. There were still a few hours of daylight remaining when they arrived at the southernmost village, Roadside.

Jesse was surprised, yet again, by the differences here. A runner had been sent ahead, making arrangements, and Miss Jessie warmly greeted them. Jesse was happy to see her, but worried about the strain on her little inn. That worry was for naught as the Deacon and the Eisgeid began conducting tasks throughout the village. The royal party was showing aid and stewardship, rather than indulgence or privilege of station. The village was at peace and the night was a welcome rejoice.

Everyone was up much earlier the next morning, ready for a longer and more difficult day of travel. They were pleasantly surprised to find that their supplies and horses were ready for them, as was a hot and fresh breakfast, and they found themselves mounted and moving with the sun barely cresting the horizon. They kept a good pace climbing out of the valley, and by the time they were ready to stop for the day were nearing the edge of the Deepland Woods.

It was well known that in order to call the witch's guardian you need to be well within the boundaries of the forest, and the safest place to do that was on the Road of the Dead. Arriving, Jesse looked at Zenesul and Thorn. This would be where they split ways. The two would return to Highston, the rest would brave the forest. Jesse ran to Thorn dropping to his knees and swept her into a hug.

"Girl, I almost wish we had run into some kind of trouble here," he said with a grin. "One last scrap together, side by side."

"One last chance for me to see you knocked on your ass?" Thorn replied, flashing teeth in a wide grin.

"Hey, if that's what it takes," Jesse said, grinning back. "Or just maybe one of us could have taken an oh, so tragic injury and you would have just had to stay behind! With us."

"Tell you what, Why don't you give up the fancy Prince and come back with me."

Jesse's face fell. He was taken aback. "Do you really want me to do that?"

"No! You featherbrained goof!" She smacked him on the shoulder. "I want you to marry that blue skinned rich boy and raise a litter of miscreants!"

Jesse allowed the tears he had been suppressing to rise to the surface and slide down his cheeks. Even as they cut rivulets down his face, his voice was clear, although soft, as he said, "Girl, we've been through everything together. I owe you so much. You've put up with so much because of me."

"You stupid, crazy, fucking insanely loyal boy," she said into his shirt, barely understandable through her own tears. After a moment, she pulled back enough that she could wipe her eyes on her shirtsleeve, and Jesse released her enough that he could do the same. Finally, Thorn took a step back, releasing her hold. She smiled at Jesse as she fought to quell her tears and regain her composure.

"Promise me," she said, voice back under control, "If you come anywhere near the Khorr, you come find me." She yelled out, the next bit. "The rock-head over there," she said, tilting her head in Argyle's direction, "can send out messages over distances. I'm sure your mister high-and-mighty over there can do the same, or find someone who can. You find me, you hear?"

"Hush you," said Jesse, a playful smirk replacing his tears. "A proper bitch like you is easy to find!" But then he dropped the playfulness, and added, "But you have to promise the same. Look after yourself, look in on Mistress Daysleeper, and just like you said, find me if you need me." The grin returned as he said, "After all, I have the resources of a Prince to get me to you, right?"

They each slapped the other playfully on the arm, then Thorn turned away, climbed up to mount her horse, and she took up the reins to follow Zenesul, as they began riding down the road. Jesse watched for just a moment, but then turned away, unwilling to follow her out of sight. For her part, Thorn did not dare look back either.

33

The Playful Price of Pain

Symon put his arm around Jesse, comforting him as much as he could. They stood for a moment and Jesse put his arm around Symon's waist and gave him a squeeze. It was as good a sign as any that his friend would be okay.

"You ready for this?" Symon asked.

"Nope."

"But we will do it anyway?"

"Yep."

Jesse handed Symon the whistle, and Symon blew as hard as he could. As before, a ghostly note began to be faintly heard, as if being produced far off. It grew both in volume and pitch as it passed over the group, a much lower, rumbling sound this time, not as musical as they remembered.

Symon looked at the instrument, puzzled. "I wonder why the difference in notes," said Symon.

"Your set of lungs is certainly bigger than mine," Jesse laughed. "Maybe?"

"Or a different purpose," remarked Caleb who had joined them. "Masuulka was summoned before as a friend, to guide you through the forest. This is more of his true purpose."

"Hmm," said Jesse. "Different people, different purpose, different note, same Masuulka? I have a gut feeling." Jesse took out a thread of vellum and a sliver of charcoal. He carefully wrote a few quick words, then said, "Moria, will you please hold onto this, but don't read it yet?"

She raised her eyebrows but said nothing, taking the scrap and placing it in her belt. Symon chuckled. "So what's the bet?" he asked. "Dinner on you if you are wrong?"

"I'll get in on some o' that," said Moria.

"Bet!" said Jesse. "But if I'm right, it's dinner for me and the Prince!"

Argyle chuckled, asking Jesse, "And when you are incorrect, my boy, how will you afford such a forfeit?"

Jesse laughed loudly. "What? I have a rich roommate and a rich boyfriend! Either way, I get a nice meal!"

"As long as, if I win, you do not cook my meal!" Symon laughed.

"Don't worry," Jesse replied. "IF you win, I'll get Caleb to send a palace chef to the house! Cook you and Moria here a dinner."

Symon's ears flushed and he shook his head, laughing at his friend. Jesse was incorrigible, but there was a look in his eyes. Something that he had figured out, besides Symon's unrequited crush.

They waited, not knowing how long it might take. When Hasukawa had called, it had taken around an hour for him to show. Symon watched as Jesse took the opportunity to drag Caleb behind some trees for a personal moment. Moria rolled her eyes in frustration when she noticed, but her scent was secretly pleased.

It was not quite an hour later when the forest around them began to change. The air became still, and the sounds of the woodland creatures faded away. A sense of power thrummed through the trees, and Symon stood tall, his eyes scanning multiple directions. "Go, get the two love-birds!" Moria pointed at Argyle.

"Hey, we're here!" Jesse said coming out from around a tree. He was grinning like an idiot and his face was flushed. He was tugging his shirt back on, and Caleb came around the other direction, more serene and assembled. Symon saw the flush on his cheeks as well and smiled.

"What is going on?" Caleb asked.

"I think Masuulka is approaching," Symon said.

Roots stirred at his feet. The sounds in the forest changed. The calls of animals and birds that Symon was not familiar with took the place of the traditional sounds they had grown accustomed to. The trees danced and swayed against the wind, yet Symon himself felt no breeze. Mist filled the spaces between and creatures big and small began to take shape within. Glowing eyes stared at them, prowling in circles.

"I do not like this," Symon whispered.

Caleb reached back to take Jesse's hand, when suddenly there was a brief yell, instantly extinguished. Caleb screamed and dove for the ground where Jesse had disappeared. Symon cried out in panic as all four Eisgeid leaped toward the Prince to form a defensive perimeter.

"He was right here!" yelled Caleb. "He was pulled into the ground! There was no warning, no sound, nothing!"

The Prince began scrabbling at the fallen leaves and detritus surrounding the roots at the base of the tree. Symon instantly joined him, but saw the earth was completely undisturbed. Caleb scratched and clawed, the tangles of the roots tearing at the skin around his hands. Symon grabbed Caleb's wrists to stop him.

"Stop! Caleb, do not hurt yourself on these roots!" Symon said. "Nothing has been dug here. This was magic, not burrowing."

Caleb tore away from Symon and dug once again. Symon wrapped his arms around the Prince and stood, pulling him from the ground. He forced the Prince to look up at him. There was clear panic in his green eyes. Caleb's breathing was shallow and his blue skin had turned a sickly shade, almost a sea green. He struggled against Symon's grip murmuring "Jesse" over and over again.

"Caleb!" Symon said, forcing his voice to remain calm. "Jesse will be okay. We need to help him. I need you to help him."

The Prince looked at Symon and for a moment, those eyes cleared. The panic frayed around the edges, but Symon continued.

"Breathe with me," Symon said. He took a deep breath counting to five, and then exhaled counting again. He repeated it until Caleb began to follow him. "Focus on my voice. Look into my eyes. Breathe."

Together, they worked to grasp hold of the panic they both felt. Caleb nodded to Symon, and Symon nodded back.

"Stop thinking physical and consider magical solutions, Prince Caleb."

Caleb paused for just a moment, then began drawing a form in the air. His fingers deftly drew, and Symon could only help but marvel at his skill. Jesse had spoken about the Prince's aptitude for Arcanum, but Symon was still in awe. He had not quite finished when there was a rumble in the earth.

Symon and Caleb looked at one another, while the latter maintained concentration on his arcane form. A few yards away, the ground began to shift, first rising nearly a foot in a wide dome, then dropping down the same into a bowl. It heaved up, then down, several times before expanding like a massive soap bubble of dirt and leaves. The group rushed the area with weapons drawn. Up and up the mound of earth rose, three feet, then six.

When the upheaval grew to more than twice Symon's height, the edges began to fall, dropping dirt and forest debris in a cascading shower. In the remaining center was left a towering form that Symon recognized. Twelve feet tall, and half that wide, the being was made a green and brown mass. Its outer form appeared to be covered with the dirt and leaves, but as it moved and twisted, the detritus shifted so that in areas it was possible to see gaps that showed there was actually no physical form inside.

Masuulka.

The Guardian of the Woods possessed six arms. Two large arms that dragged along the ground, even though it stood to its full height. A smaller set of arms jutting from slightly above its waist. And in its middle set of arms were turned against its torso, and in the crook of its arms sat Jesse, still grinning.

Symon's eyes tightened, and Moria cursed under her breath.

"What in the twisted lining of the Veil's sphincter are you doing?" screamed Caleb, dropping his spell form.

Jesse looked back at the group and his expression changed to concern, then embarrassment. Symon could smell the regret radiating from his friend. He jumped down and ran to Caleb, catching him in a hug. "I'm so sorry," he said. "That was really stupid."

"What did you do?" Caleb, asked. His voice held pain and confusion.

"It was supposed to be funny."

"You planned this?"

"Well, no," Jesse replied. "I just—"

"Could you have stopped it?"

"Well," said Jesse, "I could have warned you that Masuulka was a trickster."

"It wasn't funny."

"I know, I'm sorry." Jesse grabbed Caleb's arm. "I'm so sorry."

"Why was he playing a trick on me?" Caleb looked up at the spirit beast.

"Not on you," said Jesse, pointing over at Symon. "On him."

Symon's lip curled back from his fang in anger. "Why?"

"Let's keep calm," said Moria, her hand on Symon's arm. He looked down at her, and felt his ears flush. "So'en, I'll bite. Why Symon? And how'd 'ya know?" She held up the paper Jesse gave her earlier.

"I didn't know-know. It was a guess." Jesse cleared his throat. "I saw that last time, Masuulka kept eyeing Symon. Knowing how serious and proper our favorite blacksmith is, I figured this old prankster," he hooked a thumb gesturing back toward Masuulka, "had picked him as an easy mark."

"So that's part one," said Moria, holding up the vellum. "But this says, 'Scare us – attack me to scare Symon.' Did he try to jump you that first time?"

"Oh, no!" Jesse tried to laugh nervously, but Symon and the rest of the group remained silent. The Isnashi swallowed and continued, "The first time was a completely different whistle sound, and when he showed, it was less a display of power. There was still wind, moaning, and mist and such, but not like this one.

"I figured," Jesse said, "that since this time the whistling was very serious and simple, it meant more of a call to work. The Deepland Witch is very big on not wasting her time. So, I figured her guardian here would be the same. Thus a tune for work, and a tune for visiting, that I bet not too many people know."

"And this display of power would dissuade those who took this lightly?" Symon asked, at last.

"Why would he prank on a work whistle, and show off power for a visitation call? Should it not be the other way around?" Caleb asked.

"I would hazard two possible reasons for that, my Prince," said Argyle. "First, right now he just initiated a test against us. Had we reacted in a way that displeased him, he would have had the opportunity to dissuade us from seeking his services."

"Nailed it in one!" chirped Jesse. "And your second reason? Can you go two for two?"

"Certainly," responded Argyle, "and it is the more likely of the two. He recognized many of us from our prior introduction. In our first meeting, he seemed to take quite a liking to our young winged friend, and a playful dislike to our furred friend."

Symon bristled at that. "He dislikes me?"

"Playfully dislikes. As young Jesse stated, he found you stoic and too easy a mark, as opposed to a comrade in deviousness. Which, I would hazard a guess, is why Jesse assumed he would feign an attack on Jesse, on the assumption that Jesse would gladly participate, as he certainly did."

"Absolutely," said Jesse.

"How did you know all this?" Moria asked.

"It's a street thing," Jesse said. "Taking the wind out of people's sails is often the best option we have."

Symon was reminded of the first true spar that Jesse and he shared. It had been similar. An attack on his pride rather than his person.

"I don't like practical jokes," Caleb said, flatly.

"Nor do I," Symon said, as well.

"Yeah," Jesse said. "I'm sorry. I see that now."

"Poor timin' or not," Moria looked at Symon, teasingly holding out the note. "Looks like we owe the boys dinner!"

"To palace standards, of course," said the Prince. "My offended nerves were apparently at your expense, Symon."

"Joy to me," Symon grumbled.

Jesse followed Masuulka, leading the rest of the group into the heart of the Deepland Woods. Paulson and four of the Eisgeid were left with the horses, which would be useless in the dense forest, to await their return. He did not seem happy with this duty, but answered with a "Yes, Osi," and left it with nothing more.

Jesse tried not to dwell on the blunder he had made. Joking about danger and death had been a coping mechanism for so long, that he didn't think anything of it. Thorn and he had often played games like it. Now, seeing Symon, Caleb, Hells, even Moria's reaction, he realized that it could come across as juvenile. He was sure that there would be conversations regarding it with Caleb, and he hoped it would be something they could get past. Instead of losing himself in the guilt, he focused on the journey.

Their guide looked like a solid, giant creature, but moved more like a ghost or a spirit. He gave every appearance of walking, his thick legs taking steps, all of his arms swinging to his gait. However, Jesse noticed how as he moved, Masuulka was constantly shedding leaves and debris, while adding more local items to maintain his form. The forest creature also had a tendency to drift into the ground at times, especially when the forest floor was uneven. A few times he would even separate slightly to flow around trees, especially saplings, that the others would have to step around.

They had been traveling for several hours, when Masuulka stopped the group. He turned to face his charges, holding up two of his hands, palms forward, in a 'stop' motion. He lifted all six of his arms, spreading them all palms up, toward each of the living individuals. They watched as in each palm, a small yellow and brown mushroom magically sprouted and grew, in only seconds, each a bit more than an inch tall. Masuulka nudged his hands forward, gesturing toward the group.

"What is he doing?" Symon asked.

Jesse started to say something, but held his tongue.

"Is he offering us the mushrooms?"

The spirit solemnly extended a hand a bit further towards Symon. The Ennedi reached forward, wrapping his fingers around the stem of the mushroom in the hand closest to him. Gingerly, Symon plucked the mushroom. Instantly, Masuulka yanked his hand back, waving it up and down and shaking his head in pain.

Symon jumped back as he dropped the mushroom, and Jesse fought to hide a smile. Completely bewildered, ears turned back in alarm, the smith growled. Watching the faces of his companions turn from concern to mirth, Symon looked back at the guardian, who was now bobbing his head up and down in silent, yet unmistakable, merriment.

"He got 'ya again," whispered Moria.

Masuulka offered his palms once again, and the others took their mushrooms.

Symon grabbed his mushroom from the ground, and Jesse heard him mutter, "It is not funny anymore."

"Hey, big guy!" Jesse said to Masuulka. "Let's cut him a break, eh?"

Jesse could feel Masuulka grin, even though he had no face, and nodded back.

"So, do we eat them, or...?" Jesse asked

"We are to inhale the spores," said Argyle. "He may be of something similar to a Mycenoid, who 'speak' mentally through sharing spores, rather than by sound, even though he seems to understand our spoken speech quite effectively. It is similar to what was required of Grendel."

Jesse inhaled the spores deeply. His nose tickled, and he sneezed, but otherwise nothing seemed to happen. Then gradually, he heard a musical humming sound in his head. The humming grew slightly louder, and he could make out a melody. Subtle voices, all intermingling and meshing, grew in volume, overtaking the melody.

>*It is good to see you, my friends. For those of you who have interest in Sephistos, I shall take you to her,*< the voices said. Jesse shivered at hearing the Witch's name outloud. Something in the words felt magical. Not Arcane, not Divine, but something else. A mysterious connection through the power of a name. >*For those of you without worthy business, you may go no farther. Be warned, if you do not have acceptable questions and continue further, there will be difficulties.*

>*Your safety will be ensured,*< the voices spoke in their minds. >*Only your questions and the answers of Sephistos may harm you while you are in my keep.*

And only the living, with questions, may proceed.<

Jesse scanned the group and watched as the Deacon and Argyle stood aside with the Eisgeid. Moria, Caleb, Symon and himself stood before Masuulka. "Well," Jesse said. "Guess that's us."

>*Those who wish to accompany me to see Sephistos, come forward to me, one at a time.*<

Symon stepped forward first. Masuulka held out two arms, beckoning him closer. Once the Ennedi stood within only a few feet of the forest spirit, the creature raised his arms, two above his head, two near his shoulders, and the large pair to either side of Symon's waist. A cascade of spores shot from the limbs and chest of Masuulka, drifting over Symon. As they fell, however, none stuck to his skin or fur, but instead seemed to be repelled, to fall to the ground around his feet.

>*You have valid questions,*< they all heard, as Masuulka nodded down at Symon. >*And no, there is no jest in me at this time. You are safe, the Son.*<

Caleb came forward, standing where Symon had been. Again the arms encompassed the potential visitor. The cloud of spores once again released, and as with Symon, were repelled, drifting harmlessly to the ground.

>*You also may pass, the Son.*<

Caleb stepped out of Masuulka's embrace and moved to join Symon, while Moria stepped forward. This time, however, as the cloud of spores poured over her, Jesse watched in horror as they stuck to her skin, acting almost as if attracted to her.

Patches of moss began growing on her skin, springing forward where the spores had collected. She began scratching and clawing at the areas. She cried out, "What in 'tha Thirteen Hells? This shit burns!"

In the areas where her fingernails scraped away the moss, Jesse could see that roots had already dug into the skin, tearing and drawing small amounts of blood as the roots had been ripped from beneath. Where blood dribbled, mushrooms began sprouting from the broken flesh, the wounds becoming surrounded by patchy mold, spreading in dusty browns and sickly greens.

"Stop it!" she screamed.

Symon and Caleb immediately rushed to her side, easing her to the ground.

Jesse slipped his sight into the Arcane. He could see a film of arcane energy encasing her body. Caleb began weaving a form in the air and the Arcane form melted like wax or honey, flowing down onto her body. Where Caleb's energy encountered the spore's energy, both were eaten away and cleared.

"What were you doing?" Symon asked.

"It's'n my duty to protect the Prince," Moria said, voice hoarse. "And 'ya."

Symon turned to Masuulka. "That absolutely was atrocious. You could have just said 'no'."

>*You speak as if this is personal,*< the voices replied. >*The Child has no business with Sephistos. I do not judge, the Child. I merely inform.*<

Jesse saw the rage in Symon's eyes. Masuulka had pushed the man too far. Defiantly, Jesse strode forward toward forest spirit.

Caleb stepped forward and grabbed Jesse's arm. "Please, Jesse," Caleb whispered. "You already said you have no questions for the witch. There is no need to prove yourself."

"Oh, I have thousands of questions," Jesse smiled. "Just don't know if any of them are worthy."

"Please, don't," Caleb said.

Jesse turned to the Prince and took his head in gently in both of his hands, and pulled him down to kiss his forehead. "Besides, I promised you I would go with you. And I owe you for Masuulka's prank. Now, I owe Symon. Let's find out."

"You owe me nothing."

"Then perhaps I owe myself something," said Jesse.

34

Witch in the Woods

Trusting in their guide, the three men continued off into the woods, following Masuulka. The late afternoon sunlight was beginning to cast long shadows through the trees, playing with their depth perception and making distance occasionally difficult to judge. Masuulka seemed to vary his pace, sometimes drifting lazily, yet often breezing through areas the other three had to struggle to scramble through. For the most part, they kept their thoughts to themselves, solemnly following the forest spirit and focused on their goal.

Jesse and Caleb came to a stop ahead of Symon, and he heard Caleb mutter a curse. Coming to the edge of a clearing, the smith could see why. "Oh, no."

Before them was an open area where the canopy no longer provided the shade they had been experiencing. The evening sun shone brighter here, yet the sight did not offer the encouragement it may have in other circumstances. The ground sunk into an area of swamp. The trees were stunted and stripped of much of their vegetation by overpowering vines and creepers. Thick, sticky mud became standing water as the ground sloped down to become lost beneath the surface. The scent of decay and rot filled Symon's nostrils from still, stagnant water with insects playing across the surface. His eyes locked on a small gurgling ripple that came and went as something moved just beneath the surface.

>*You must follow me*< said Masuulka's voice in their head. >*Ensure that you follow precisely the path I create. As long as you do so, not even the attention of a mosquito shall disturb you.*<

The ominous tone of disobeying the instruction filled the space. Symon glanced at Caleb and Jesse. The forest spirit walked out into the swamp. With each step, bits of dirt and leaves were left behind, leaving a path two feet wide that sat on the surface, dry and unsinking.

"Single file it is, then," said Jesse, as he stepped out onto the offered path. He did not sink at all, his weight being supported as if he walked on stone. As the others joined him and they continued walking, Jesse turned back enough to ask, "Does this seem weird to you? I'm a city boy, but even still, this seems out of place."

"It is unusual," Symon responded.

"I think we're changing realms," Caleb said, simply.

"What?!" Symon and Jesse said simultaneously.

"Is it possible this is not even our realm, but a glimpse of the Verdant Green. That might explain why she can never be found without the guide, and does not seem to be located in a consistent place. Also notice that the boundary is too tidy. The transition is too rapid and too even a line."

The setting sun had disappeared into a colorless ashy white fog. Occasionally something would approach the path, only to turn away at the last moment, and as promised, the multitude of insects could be seen and heard, but not felt. It also became apparent that as they traveled, Masuulka became smaller. Not in proportion, more like slices melted away as he walked, first his feet, then his knees, then up his legs, as he used the materials of his form to create the pathway. His speed never slowed.

A mound came into view, rising well over forty feet into the air and likely half again that from side to side. As they approached, Symon was able to distinguish squared off and perfectly straight tree roots running down the sides of the mound. Like the poles of a cage, evenly spaced geometrically grown offshoots connected the support pillars to form bars. Inside was a mixture of dirt, clay, mud, and all manner of other soil, but it was pure, without debris of either plant or animal.

Rising above them, a massive tree, fifty feet in diameter, stretching high into what little sky could be seen loomed above the boys. Masuulka had eroded down to his waist by the time he reached the odd earthen formation. He turned to address the trio.

>You first, the Thief. Step forward.<

"Well, that's fucking great," muttered Jesse as he looked at the other two. "He called Moria 'the Child' and both of you 'the Son', but I'm 'a Thief'?" He chuckled a bit, but Symon could smell the annoyance. "Should I be offended?"

"I'm sure it means nothing," Caleb said as he stepped forward and gave Jesse a quick hug. "Don't let it trouble you."

"No, seriously, Caleb?" Jesse said. "Why do you guys get to be called by your family positions, and I only get called by my dirty street job? I was someone's son, too."

"I have no answers," Caleb said.

"That is not you anymore, Jesse," Symon said. "Do you hear me? Whatever this means, we shall get to the bottom of it. Now get up there, so we can get what we came for, and not get murdered by Moria for being late."

Jesse gave a sarcastic mock salute, said, "Yes, Osi."

Caleb looked to Symon. "I understood that you were not taking up your Sire's military legacy?"

Jesse deadpanned, "It's a joke. I'm not seriously calling him an officer."

Symon watched as Jesse turned to go to Masuulka. As the boy approached, the spirit melted completely into a raised disk floating just above the path. Jesse stepped onto the circle and it rose higher, quickly enough that Jesse flexed his wings for balance, until it reached the top of the caged mound. The circular area then lowered, calling for first Caleb, then eventually Symon.

The top of the mound was nearly flat, rather than domed, but the ground was uneven. Exposed roots, like on the sides of the mound, formed straight lines and angles, in patterned designs and in no way natural. Symon tentatively tested the ground between the roots, and found it to be solid, easily supporting his weight.

All of the main roots led like spokes to the impossibly large tree. As he and the group examined closer, they realized that the bark of the tree was swarming with dozens of creatures, perhaps hundreds. They were small humanoids, no bigger than ten to twelve inches tall, and something akin to a Pixie, but with the limbs and tail of a lizard or a salamander. Their colorations ran through the spectrum of greens and blues, all with translucent wings and long pink or green hair on their tiny heads.

Around them, the forest came alive with voices. Dozens of overlapping, high-pitched cries formed a chaotic chorus delivering a broken message. "Welcome! Welcome! Welcome! Find the the find door find find door the the answers answers the door!"

"Cute? Funny? Or creepy?" asked Jesse with a smirk.

"Why why not not not all not all three three all not three?" the voices replied, unexpectedly.

"Creepy," Jesse said. "Got it."

"Find the door, find the answers?" Symon asked.

"Worth a try."

"I might like this lady," Jesse said, chuckling. They all looked at one another, and Jesse laughed fully. Kissing Caleb on the cheek, he said, "Let's go find this door."

Symon circled the tree, scanning for anything. He spied a small hollow in the trunk. Upon first glance, it seemed narrow, but upon closer inspection it was actually quite large, possibly wide enough that Argyle could have squeezed through, had he been with them.

"Jesse! Caleb!" Symon said. "Think this is it?"

The voices responded, "Yes yes enter yes go enter inside yes inside go enter."

"Thanks! He was talking to us!" Jesse quipped.

"Jesse," Caleb chided. "Let's try not to anger the mysterious spirits."

"Oh, my bad," Jesse grinned. "Keep up the good work, mystery ladies!"

Symon shook his head. "I suppose we go in,?"

Jesse shrugged and Caleb nodded, so Symon worked his way towards the gap. While wide, the fissure ducked back and forth, like a mountain switchback, and he turned his shoulders to and fro. Caleb and Jesse followed behind, and they emerged into an interior chamber.

Consisting of a single circular room, walled with paneled wood and a hard-wood-slatted floor laid with throw rugs, piles of cushions, and small tables, it was an unexpected find. Arranged around the space in haphazard fashion were a collection of wooden chairs, all draped in crocheted blankets. While the ceiling was tall, perhaps two dozen feet in height, nearly half of it, above their heads, was filled with hundreds upon hundreds of fireflies. Their light filled the room with a yellow-green glow, augmented by a cozy brick fireplace set into the opposite wall, its light silhouetting a figure sitting in a large wooden rocking chair. Soft clicking sounds came from the figure as they were able to make out a pair of hands delicately working a set of knitting needles in their lap.

"Please, come in and be seated," said their host.

As their eyes adjusted to the lighting, details emerged showing the woman regarded as the "Witch of the Woods." Dressed in a pastel floral dress, like that of the quintessential grandmother, an apron, and a shawl, she looked mostly humanoid, yet was covered in red chitinous scales. She had black, claw-like fingers, thin horns that curled and spiraled back like a ram's, and hair that was more like loose, sagging tentacles. Her face bore a mouth that was circular and open, with no lips to cover the rows of tiny teeth that spiraled back into her throat. The wall around the fireplace swarmed with even more of the small Pixie-like beings, who flitted back and forth from the wall to also crawl in and around the clothing of the witch, as well, although they seemed to know to avoid interfering with her knitting.

"Come, now, my dears, don't be rude," she said at their hesitation. Her speech was odd, yet perfectly understandable. The fact that she seemed to have no jaw, in addition to having no lips, caused her syllables to be formed by contracting the muscles of her mouth and tongue. Her words were more forceful and controlled, and the hollow echo was disconcerting.

Symon and Jesse started to sit in one of the chairs, but Caleb quickly intervened. "We will show respect, and allow our host to sit above us." The Prince gestured to the pillows and cushions around the floor. "These are laid out for us, let us be gracious and accept them."

Quietly, Symon and the couple took their seats and faced the Witch.

"So," the Witch said, gazing at them critically. "Who shall address their questions first?"

"Yes! Yes! Yes!" called out the chorus of small beings. "Who who is who brave is who enough brave is to is to risk to risk going brave going first going first?"

The three men exchanged glances with one another. When it became clear that none of them seemed eager to begin, Caleb nodded. Speaking clearly to the Witch, he said, "I suppose I shall begin."

The witch continued her knitting, but turned her gaze to the Prince. "Ask your question. What answers can I provide the Son?"

"My dear lady, I seek information regarding this bond between myself and Symon Cyl'Karick. I feel a connection between us, and he with me. It has eluded the greatest Arcanists in Vargarden. Do you know its origin? Do you know the truth of it? If it is not physical, Arcane, nor Divine, how does it exist? Is it dangerous?"

"So so so many many so many many too many questions questions! Too too so many many too many questions questions!" The cacophony of voices filled the chamber, resonating angrily throughout the chamber.

Symon worried for their safety. Caleb had inadvertently asked four questions. A breach in protocol like this could spell disaster if the Witch took offense. The pixies buzzed around the room, their lips snarled and exposing their tiny sharp teeth. All, but one, that stood serenely on the shoulder of the woman in the chair.

"Be still, my sisters," the Witch said. The pixie chorus obeyed immediately, their voices returning to the same soft sing-song buzzing as before. "Many questions, but only to seek the one truth." Symon felt her gaze fall over them. The weight of their motivations was being read by her mystic powers. Symon watched carefully as the Witch's eyes took them in, and the tiny pixie nodded. "I see no reason to limit the questions of these young men. They are well intentioned. I shall permit them to speak freely.

"To answer your questions, the Son," she continued. "There is no longer danger to your bond. The bond stood merely as a barrier between you and the Thief." Symon saw Jesse shift uncomfortably at that word. A wash of irritation flooded his nose from Jesse's scent as the ire of those words sunk into his friend. "The two of you have overcome that threat, and are within the next phase of your destiny. We wait, now, for the unlocking of your heart."

"Oh," Caleb said.

"As to its origin..." the Witch said. "It was a price paid for interventions I made years ago."

"If I may?" Caleb asked, hesitantly. "What does that mean?"

"I would answer now, but it shall come later... in time."

Symon began to speak, but hesitated. His instinct told him that the truth should be spoken, but he feared to risk offending this powerful being. An unnatural sensation filled his mind. Fractures of conversations echoed through his thoughts, both with or without his words. Seeing more good than harm, he spoke. "Madam," he addressed the Witch in the rocking chair, "May I please have your name?"

The room became utterly silent.

Jesse and Caleb glanced over at him in confusion, as the Witch's eyes turned to a dread, fateful stare. "Why do you ask this question?" she replied, her voice cold and distant.

"I mean no offense," Symon said. "I know that Masuulka referred to the Oracle as Sephistos, but you are not she." Symon's eyes turned to the small pixie perched upon her shoulder. "Madam Sephistos, you are seen. I appreciate your power. But this dear lady has been acting as your proxy for us. May I be honored with her name as well?"

"Very clever, the Son," Sephistos, the pixie laughed. Her voice was a soft, bright, and twinkling sound. "Much like the General. Not many bother to realize the true situation. Her name is Adonaise, and she is one of my dearest friends."

"Thank you, Madam Sephistos," said Symon.

"You know, to the deepest corner of the Thirteenth Layer of Hell with it all!" interrupted Jesse in anger. "I can burn there, too, for all I care. I'm sick of this." Caleb grabbed Jesse's arm in alarm, while Symon merely stared at his friend with concern.

"Yes?" Sephistos said, eyeing Jesse with interest.

"What's with all this codename nonsense? Caleb's is 'the Son.' Symon is 'the Son,' too. Why in the Hells do all of them get the 'Son' while I get stuck with being called a 'thief'? My mom may be dead, but I was a son, too. Thief? I'm not a thief anymore! You want to call me a liar, too?"

Sephistos flitted from Adonaise's shoulder. Slowly, she flew to Jesse, who sat staring at her defiantly. She landed softly on his crossed legs, reaching up to stroke his cheeks and slowly reached up on her tip-toes to kiss his nose.

"My dear Thief," she said, softly. "You have my apologies. While you have grown much this last year, there is still a long road ahead. It is, quite likely, that you will have another job or two before you. I cannot and will not corrupt the truth to assuage your feelings, or the guilt of your past or future."

"No!" Jesse said, tears in his eyes. "They get to be the sons. I'm done being a thief. Why can't I be done?"

"That is not the question you wish to ask."

Jesse's shoulders sagged and his chest heaved with a sob. "Why am I so unimportant? Why can't I be worthy?"

"My boy," laughed the witch, "You are quite worthy. And quite important." Sephistos turned to Caleb and smiled. "You see, I told you the answer to your question would come in time." Sephistos returned to the shoulder of her companion and spoke plainly. "This conflict has tendrils that have stretched on nearly in time as much as it has in impact. It has been curious to see how many of the 'Key' individuals have sought my insights.

"The bond they feel is because they are not sons. They are the Son!" Sephistos looked away from Jesse, her head turning to give her attention to Symon and Caleb. "You are not born as two beings, you were created as such. The progeny to be the potential end of this conflict."

Symon sat stunned. His words would not form, and he glanced at Caleb and Jesse who looked as pole-axed as he.

"Many decades ago, the General, the Nemuku of Vargarden, came to me. He sought merely the keys to defeating his enemy. To end the War of Night. Little did he know, the Mother of Shadows had come to me as well." A sinister grin appeared on the pixie's face. "I warned them that there would be a personal cost. They agreed to the consequences, unknown as they were. I crafted a love spell, and opened their eyes against the hatred brought by military conflict. From that moment on, neither had a taste for war."

"This explains so much of my sire, and why he left Vargarden. There, he could only have been a military general." Symon murmured.

"So, how did this create us?" Caleb asked. Symon could hear the hesitant confusion in his voice.

"The General and the Mother of Shadows stayed the course and stayed together. They had progeny of their own. However, the father was of one reality, while the mother was of another. The children's physical forms were fractured hybrids, belonging to both realms, Sainan and Mumvuri. The physical form, however, may only exist in one place at a time and the strain it placed on them was great. After two lost offspring, they came to see me again, this time together. They wanted a child who would be free.

"Again, I warned that there would be a cost," she said, sadly. "I aided them in conceiving a new child. The Son."

The three young men could scarcely breathe. What she was saying made little sense. Two children. The Son. Symon was unsure of how to process the implications.

"However, in order to allow the Son to exist properly, I took everything of him that was the blood of the Mother of Shadows, of the other realm, and gave it one form, the other was purely of the General. One form was given to the General and Mother to raise, the other bequeathed to the Father of Vargarden. It is this bond that connects you. You two are the Son. Two bodies, one Soul."

The three looked at one another in shock. None of them seemed capable of speech. His sire, Kyrn Cyl'Karrick and the Mother of Shadows were his parents. Caleb and Symon were something akin to twins. Everything made sense, but also none of it did. His mind swam. Symon struggled to gather questions or thoughts. His tongue felt huge in his mouth, unable to form words.

"Well... shit," Jesse whispered.

"You are saying that..." Symon paused. "That Caleb and I are brothers? The same Soul in two bodies? And that the *Ombramaes* is our mother?"

"Shit," Jesse whispered again.

"The *Ombramaes* is a meaningless, political name. It is barely within my foresight. The *Ombramaes* was your mother, the *Ombramaes* is now your enemy. I instead stick to the roles I have assigned them in this tale.

"The Master of Shadows discovered the truth. She has vowed to kill both of these halves that comprised this one Soul." Sephistos pointed at Symon and Caleb. "Your Soul."

"Why?" Symon asked. "I do not understand."

"Because," she smiled. "You have been identified as the 'Keys to Defeat.'"

"What does this mean, my Lady?" Caleb asked.

"The Master of Shadows and the Manticore were self-serving in their requests. They wished only to know what would stop them upon their paths. I advised them accordingly."

Symon's mind raced once again. It was his turn to seek answers, but there were too many questions left. He still did not know why they were being hounded by the Shadow. Or by Manticore. Sephistos referred to the Master as a different being of the Mother of Shadows. The question of who his mother was still remained unanswered. He struggled to start.

Then, her words struck him. Important words that he had almost missed. Focus on the goal, not the obstacles. "What can we do to end this for good? How can we oppose the current conflict, and save lives?"

Sephistos laughed in delight, her voice high and pure. "Oh, so much like the General. Always the Nemuku!"

"We seem to be destined to play a part," Symon said. "I just want to do my best."

"Ah, yes," the Witch smiled. "I can speak truly. For one part of this battle, the Son must not only lock the door between realms, but break the Key. For the second part, the Son must engage the Father and rid the world of an unknown Shadow of an ancient evil. You can do this many, many ways."

"Why us?" Caleb asked. "Why is this task not able to be handled by those more versed in the world?"

"Ah, my young friends," Sephistos smiled. "I see you are not 'heroes' rushing off to save the world. It is true, there are many paths before you. This conflict can be shaped in many ways. Many lead to a desirable end. Many more lead to catastrophe. You could turn away from this conflict. In fact, I would advise you to do so. If you can accept the cost."

"Cost?"

"Along the path, I see a point where a grand choice must be made. To accept the Loss of the Son, or to not."

Jesse put his arm around Caleb, then his other around Symon. "No! Not happening."

"I can tell you this. The only way that you should enter the conflict is if the conflict is brought to you. Go home, live your lives, and ignore this grossly ignorant war. Only defend what is yours, and fight only that which threatens you. If you do, the loss will be minimal. If you rush to involve yourselves otherwise... death awaits. Many deaths."

No one spoke for several minutes. "Jesse, you have one more question."

"Oh," said Jesse quietly. "You mean the age old question everyone asks when difficulty comes knocking. 'Why me?'"

"Actually, yes," Sephistos nodded, satisfied. "Jesse, you asked why you were important. Why could you not be worthy? I wish for you to be at peace as you leave. When the Manticore asked, I told him. The Thief is the Key to the Son, the Son is the Key to the Father. The Father is the Key to Defeat. Many would believe your task is done, but it is not. You are here to lose your Heart as a cost to gain your Soul. Your actions will shape this conflict as it unfolds. Wear that responsibility well. For when next I see you, I shall call you Priest." And with that, Sephistos leaped from the shoulder of Adonaise and was immediately lost in the swarm of her fellow beings.

Caleb immediately hugged Jesse. "Are you okay?"

"I think so," said Jesse. "But she is gone. I guess that means we are done." Symon rose to his feet and said, "Farewell, Sephistos. We thank you for your time and your wisdom, and will endeavor to take what you have told us to heart."

The trio left. As they walked, the forest spirit stalked silently behind them, gathering himself back up as they went, until by the time they reached the forest he stood back at his original towering height. The boundary was even more disconcerting this time, for as they stepped from the mire back to solid ground, the sky transitioned instantly from the pale ash white of fog, to clear night sky. While their view was mostly blocked by the tree canopy, they could see that the moon had not yet risen.

Symon glanced around the forest trying to spot the path they had come from, but it faded from memory. The night around them was dark as pitch, but Masuulka was filled with phosphorescent moss, and his surface flitted with hundreds of fireflies. His form cast a gentle yellow-green glow that reminded them of something, although Symon could not recall what. Perhaps a dream.

As they walked, Caleb remarked, "It is odd, is it not, that we could all go to visit the Deepland Witch, gain the knowledge of her answers, and yet none showed the courtesy of asking her name?"

Symon paused, trying to recall it. He knew that she had given it, Masuulka had given it. But the name was no longer there. "Curious, but I suppose you are correct. I recall the conversation, yet I do not recall even her visage."

"You got to be kidding me!" Jesse laughed. "Of course she had a name and a form. She was... She was..." Jesse grin faded. "Oh, shit." He shook his head, then said with a grin, "Well, I guess she was the Deepland Witch. Scary as all the combined Hells, but she told us what we needed to know. Right?!"

35

Monsters of the Future

Symon sat in front of the campfire staring at Jesse and Caleb. Moria and the others sat aside, allowing the three men privacy to deal with the information received from the Witch. They had wanted to ask questions, but the crestfallen look of the trio had dissuaded them, for now.

It was a numbness. A disconnection of the memories of what had just happened from the emotional reality that it signified. The words he could recall, but the meaning seemed to stretch into the corners of his mind and fracture into endless conversations and possibilities.

"Does anyone else feel like their mind is broken?" Jesse asked. "Like the next few days are all being lived at the same time, but we don't know what they're doing yet?"

"Yes," Caleb said. "It could be a temporal effect of the encounter with the Witch. Being that close to Time itself, seems to have had an unpleasant effect."

Symon grabbed his wineskin and drained it in a single pull. The journey had been taxing on them all, in different ways, but each of them were trying to deal with what they needed to.

It was all about his family. The war, this new conflict, even the Manticore connection, all pointed back to him. It was a twisted wreck of lies and secrets that had become a problem for everyone. Symon was at a loss as to what to do about it anymore. He was unsure of how much more he could take.

"Symon?" Jesse asked. "You okay?"

"No," Symon replied. "No, I am not okay."

"It'll be alright."

"No it won't!" Symon roared. "I should be happy! I should be rejoicing in the fact that I have a brother! That Caleb and I are twins and were separated at birth only to find one another again."

Moria and Argyle glanced his way, a look of quizzical interest. Symon lowered his voice, trying desperately to restrain his emotions.

"First, my sire, the man who was but a humble blacksmith in Highston, was instead the legendary Nemuku. A man feared by the Investurants, despised by the Federation, and treasured by Vargarden. He lied to me for my entire life, and yet... I cannot be angry with him because I am still grieving his loss!

"Next, I find out about my secret brother!" Symon growled. "My literal other half. Mystically created by some unknown Magicks and kept safe in the homeland I should have been raised in. And do I get to enjoy this news? Do I have a moment to accept it and learn what it means? No! We get hit with another punch to the gut!"

"Symon—" Caleb started.

"No, Caleb," Symon shook his head. "You should feel the same way. We learn about each other, and in the same breath we find that our mother is the thrice-damned, Hellspawned, goat fucking *Ombramaes!*"

Jesse stepped back, and Symon clenched his fists tightly trying to regain control. "This woman has tried not only to kill me," Symon pointed his finger to Jesse, "and Jesse," shifting his finger to Caleb he jabbed in emphasis, "but you as well. And she did kill my sire. Not to mention the untold lives she has destroyed along the way. We are bred of monsters.

"And like monsters," Symon's voice hardened. "We deserve to die." Caleb and Jesse flinched at his words. Symon's anger fueled his thoughts, holding back a wash of other emotions. He was on the verge of collapse. "You heard the

Witch," he said. "To end this conflict. To protect the people. The Son must die."

Symon's shoulders started to heave. The weight of his thoughts crashed down and overwhelmed him. His composure broke and he began to sob. It was too much. It was unbearable. He was unable to breathe, unable to think, and completely vulnerable. He wanted to give up.

"Shit!" Jesse cried. Jesse leapt from the small log he had perched on and quickly ran across the campsite. Leaping over the stone that Symon used as his chair, Jesse wrapped the larger Ennedi in his arms. "Shh.. Shh... it's okay."

"I am so sorry, Jesse. I am."

Jesse stroked Symon's mane and said, "No. There's nothing to be sorry about. You're okay."

"I don't want to hurt you, or Caleb. I hate this. I will do it. I will die if it means you all will live."

"You aren't hurting anyone. It's okay." Jesse looked to the Prince, his eyes also wet. They reflected the pain his friend was in. "Isn't that right, Caleb?"

"Symon," Caleb said. "Brother. We will figure it out together."

"No, this is all my fault. My father, my mother, all of it."

"Our mother. Our father," Caleb repeated.

"Shh," Jesse whispered. "It's not your fault. It's okay."

Symon continued to weep in his friend's arms. He could feel Caleb put his arm around his shoulders hesitantly as well. The three sat quietly for moments, allowing each other the time needed. "Maybe, I am cursed," Symon whispered. "Maybe we all are. You guys don't deserve this."

"Not a curse," Caleb said. "Just misfortune. Until now."

"What do you mean?" Symon asked.

"I have been pondering the Witch's words, for as much as I can remember them," Caleb smiled. Symon nodded in understanding. In almost every conversation, Symon could recall accurately the exact words people said. It was a talent he had often used to his advantage. The Witch's words seemed vague in his mind. Clouded away from his impeccable memory. "The Witch sees Time at a level that we do not.

"Many call it prophecy, or fate," Caleb said. "It is not, however. It is merely the vision to see the outcomes of choices and predicting the most likely outcomes." Caleb straightened and locked eyes with Symon. "Like any educated guess, there are always variables. Changes to the equation that renders that prediction invalid. We are not destined. We control our own fates."

"I just do not know what to do anymore," Symon said.

"Neither do we," Jesse comforted.

"We heed the Witch's advice," Caleb said` simply. Jesse and Symon exchanged a confused glance. "Her last words were to walk away. To deny this conflict and live our lives. The Council must decide if Vargarden will be pulled into this insurgency within the Khorric Federation. They must decide if a treatise with the Investurants and the return of the Shadow Shard would have the desired impact. I believe, as the Witch said, we should allow them to make those decisions and move on."

"But what about Zen?" Jesse asked. "Thorn?"

"We can convey this information to your friends, Jesse," Caleb said. "But ultimately, it will be on them to make those decisions as well. We know the impact of our involvement, and the personal toll it could take. It is for us to heed this warning and act accordingly."

Jesse hugged Symon's shoulder tighter. It was a choice. To let go of the guilt and responsibility and place that burden on others or to wear the mantle of a hero and risk it all to save them. Symon felt like a coward.

"What about the *Ombramaes*?" Symon asked. "She is not the responsibility of others."

"No, but while her vendetta is personal, it cannot touch us unless we allow it. We are protected here," Caleb added. "Far from her grasp. She's not my concern. You two are."

Symon shook his head, "But if it is me they are after, I can just go."

Caleb placed his hand on Symon's shoulder. "Not you. Us."

Symon listened to the Prince, his brother, and allowed those words to sink in. Caleb was right. Symon was shouldering the burden alone. Selfishly. His brother, and his best friend were here attempting to lift the load, if only he would allow them. "Thank you."

"So?" Jesse asked. "What do we actually do?"

"What do you desire to do, Jesse?" the Prince asked.

"Honestly," Jesse smiled. "I just want to go back home to Vargarden. Take a week to sleep, and then try to see what I can do to make the Witch's words about loving you be true."

"I agree to this plan," Caleb said. "For me, I want to go back to the Palace and begin researching. There are potential ramifications to learning about being a Cyl'Karrick. What it means to my adoption, the royal authority, as well as Symon's inheritance claims. Revealing this information to the courts must be done delicately, as to not upturn the apple carts. So to speak."

Symon stood slowly and turned to the group. "I am sorry, everyone."

"Do not worry, Symon," Caleb replied. "I will think on this. We do not need to solve the world's problems tonight. Only to plan how we shall live our lives from this point forward."

"Yeah," Jesse said. "So, Symon... what do you want?"

Symon's eyes rested across the camp and fell on Moria. He wanted to go home. He wanted to go back to being a blacksmith. He wanted to live a simple life and be the type of parent that his sire had been, or pretended to be. He wanted to be himself and let go of the problems of the past.

"I am not sure I am strong enough to admit it," Symon said at last. "At least not yet."

36

Cry of Caged Wings

"*Y*ou keep spoiling me like this," cooed Jesse, "and I might fall in love with you."

It had been over a month since they had returned from their visit to the Deepland Woods. Caleb had steadily traversed a series of meetings with Council advisors, Arcanists, and Deacons avoiding detailing the information he had received. For the first time in his life, Caleb was holding onto secrets that were deeply personal. He wasn't ready to reveal his family or love interests at this time. Not for political dissection.

Caleb sat in his usual position, legs pretzeled beneath himself, his back nestled in the corner of the couch. The Prince had been overly formal. His attempts to court Jesse in the traditional ways. The remnants of a light afternoon snack littered the table waiting for Reneforte to dispose of.

Caleb fumbled nervously, trying to find a way to snuggle Jesse into himself. His anxiety levels were through the roof as he calculated his next words. The lack of a public setting had something to do with it. Caleb knew how to be "The Prince." Being in public, with an audience, his expectations were clear. The things to say were pre-planned. He had the required skills. How to entertain, how to hold court, how to comport himself properly, how to speak and what to say.

Here in private, however, he wasn't acting a part. Caleb had to be Caleb. And it made him uncomfortable.

Jesse, who obviously had no such issue, took his cue and laid his head on Caleb's shoulder. He lazily ran his fingers through the fabric of the robes covering Caleb's belly. Caleb felt his body tense at the unexpected touch, struggling to respond "properly."

"Promises, promises," whispered Caleb. It was a phrase Jesse was fond of. Repeating it by rote, Caleb willed himself to relax. He awkwardly reached up to play with Jesse's hair. Focusing on the texture, so fine and silky compared to his own thicker black hair, he counted silently the strokes.

"What should we talk about?" Caleb asked.

"Ooh," Jesse smiled. "We've talked about Arcana. We've talked about Vargarden. What other interests should we explore?"

"I was thinking something more..." Caleb hesitated. "Personal."

"Oh, yes," Jesse said surprised. "Gladly, I want to learn all about you." The Isnashi gave him a smile. "Tell me about your first boyfriend."

Caleb winced and his eyes tightened. "I've never had a boyfriend."

"Girlfriend, then?"

"No, no girlfriends, either."

"Oh, come on," said Jesse. Caleb felt him shift against his torso, and looking down, saw that Jesse was looking up at him, smiling encouragingly. "You are going to try to tell me that you have never had a romance?"

"No," Caleb admitted. "I've regarded some applications, but have never acted on any."

"Applications?"

"For royal suitors."

"Well, I can have Symon submit my paperwork, I suppose," Jesse winked.

"Not necessary," Caleb said, smiling down to Jesse. "I have handled it already."

Jesse looked up at him in surprise, and Caleb smiled as best he could. It was a joke. Jesse laughed and pushed the Prince's shoulder lightly. "Funny! But seriously, you've never had a crush? Or tried anything?"

"Crushes are another thing entirely," Caleb said. "And yes. I believe I could speak on one.”

“Ooh! Tell, tell!” Jesse said, sitting up a bit to better give Caleb his attention.

“His name was Caereno. He was a Societies tutor from up north in the Caleigh Free States. A very gorgeous Alvan man.”

“An older elf,” teased Jesse. “Nice.”

Caleb looked down at Jesse and grinned. “I was also thirteen. For weeks I was smitten. I failed my studies and wasn’t able to proceed.”

“So what happened?”

“He was with us perhaps half a year,” Caleb said, whistfully, “And then returned to his homeland.”

“How sad,” said Jesse, laying his head down on Caleb’s chest.

“A mere childhood crush,” Caleb said. “Nothing more.”

The two were quiet for a few minutes. Caleb rested his arm on Jesse’s back, stroking his feathers and marveling at the feeling. He cleared his throat, focusing on his next compliment. “Your wings are quite soft. It’s like running my fingers through a cloud.”

“Mmm,” Jesse purred into Caleb’s chest. “Erin used to say something similar. He always said my wing feathers felt like air, made solid.”

“Erin was a past boyfriend?” Caleb asked. “Tell me about him.”

“I guess it’s my turn,” giggled Jesse. “He was a lieutenant with Beckoning, one of the Bright Guilds in Highston. He was an Orthrus. Have you ever met one of them?”

“A Canid race from farther west. Rare in the Khorric Federation. I have not met one here, either.”

“Yes, he had a kind of a long snout, fine, short, dark fur, triangular tufted ears. All black and brown. He was like a hunting dog standing on its hind legs. Adorable, really.”

“Sounds like it,” said Caleb.

“He was high up in his Bright Guild, so he had money. Had nice clothes, fancy apartments, all the finery of a right Prince.” Jesse grinned and looked up a bit, adding, “Or I thought so, before I saw what a real Prince could have!”

Caleb shifted uncomfortably. An attraction to money wasn’t something uncommon. "So, he was rich?"

"Oh, no!" Jesse laughed. "I mean to a kid like me who had nothing, he seemed like it, but he was once just a Street Rat like me." Jesse gazed in Caleb's eyes and the Prince could see earnestness in his eyes. "I didn't even know who he was when I first met him. But, I had a silly, crazy crush on him from the start.

"We met at a party," Jesse hid his face in Caleb's robes, but he could hear the smile in Jesse's words. "I was working, and by the end of the night he had his tongue halfway down my throat. That's no exaggeration, either! Gods, that man had a tongue that could do such things."

"Oh," Caleb said. His cheeks flushed and his fingers stopped their trailing. "I see."

Jesse glanced up and Caleb tried to avert his gaze. The young Isnashi giggled nervously, and Caleb could see the color rise into his cheeks as well. "Sorry, too much."

"No, proceed," Caleb said. "How long ago was this?"

"Eh, around two years ago I guess. I wasn't quite sixteen yet."

"It seems like it was an intense relationship. How long did it last?"

"Intense?" Jesse smiled. "That man worked me hard! I can't think of a position he didn't take me in. He had a body to die for, very endowed, and proved many times over that he knew how to use it. Taught me all sorts of things!"

"Oh, I see," said Caleb, taken aback.

"Don't worry. Erin's gone," Jesse said, a touch of sadness in his eyes. "You've got nothing to be jealous about." A touch of color was in Jesse's face, indicating that he was embarrassed by his bluntness as well. But instead of retreating, the young Isnashi snuggled closer into Caleb's lap. "Besides, from what I am feeling down here, I'm sure you have plenty to compete with in the pleasure department."

Caleb tensed, his body blushing when he realized what Jesse was referring to. He was surprised at how casually Jesse could be at describing a former lover. He was so much bolder than Caleb had been at such an age.

Jesse's fingers had worked their way through the folds of his robe and were now touching the bare skin of his stomach. Caleb shivered slightly at the alien contact against his skin.

"Um, Jesse?"

"Hush," whispered Jesse huskily. "I've got you."

Caleb wasn't unaccustomed to Jesse taking the lead. But this felt different. It felt... more.

The young man slid gracefully from Caleb's side to straddling him, face to face. As Jesse leaned in to meet Caleb's mouth with his own, Caleb felt Jesse's hand begin to slide deeper inside his robes. That palm rubbed up Caleb's stomach and then his chest, sliding smoothly over his skin.

Jesse worked his tongue into Caleb's mouth as his hand simultaneously worked to spread open the top of his robes. Caleb wrapped his arms around Jesse's waist, rubbing his back as he matched the energy in the other's kiss. He could feel himself growing firm beneath the man on his lap.

Jesse pulled back from their kiss, breaking it off suddenly and confusing Caleb. But before the Prince could react, Jesse immediately moved down and began attacking his neck, kissing, sucking, and nibbling at his tender flesh. The sensations were close to being too much. Caleb found himself giving something between a moan and a cry, brain turning to mush as he fought to process all the new sensations.

"By the Father," Caleb managed to get out, body tensing as taut as a bowstring.

Jesse relented. Whether he had sensed that Caleb was in overload, or had other intentions, the Isnashi pulled back and sat upright. Jesse wrapped his hands around Caleb's sides, beneath the robes, and leaned his body against Caleb's chest, melting into him. He very gently kissed Caleb's lips, before settling his head against his shoulder, resting for the moment.

"That was..." Caleb said, searching for the words. "Very pleasant."

Jesse laughed. "Pleasant?"

"Incredible," the Prince replied. He wanted to convey his adoration for Jesse and the wonders of their intimacy. He couldn't recall any words to express it, however. He had studied the bards of old, but he had no practical experience in tying the words to his feelings.

"Better," Jesse laughed. "Besides, you heard the Witch. I am going to be here for a while. Best I start trying to unlock your heart, right?"

"Yes," Caleb said, smiling. The three of them had agreed that until anything changed, they would no longer focus on the conflict in the Federation and instead set their intentions on building their lives here in Vargarden. Caleb had committed to helping them adjust to the culture, as well as finding the remaining resources they would require. "I shall endeavor to protect you, my winged wonder."

"That was terrible," Jesse smiled. "Try again."

"Oh," Caleb said. "I want you to know how infatuated I am becoming. That you are precious to me."

"I know. It's cute."

"Yes. Cute is what I'm aiming for."

"My Prince," purred Jesse, "my delectable, tasty Prince. I could kiss you all day. See?"

"Ah. As I could you," Caleb hesitated looking for another nickname he could try. "I could stay with you forever, my bird. My precious little bird."

Jesse stiffened against Caleb, motionless. The young man pushed himself off the Prince, standing up and staring down at Caleb with such a dead expression that it was difficult to determine if he were seeing Caleb, or looking right through him. "No, no, no." Jesse murmured.

"What's wrong?" asked Caleb, confusion whelming him. "Jesse? What's wrong?"

Jesse continued to back away, shaking his head. He quickly gathered his things and turned away. His wings wrapped around his frame like a cloak, or even a shield. Jesse did not speak. He merely left.

Each step was quicker than the last, so that once he reached the double doors to the Prince's chambers, he burst through them violently, shoulder first, at a run. Caleb was left devastated, utterly confused, his robes dangling as open as his stupefied heart.

37

Lara

Symon wandered the palace, listening to the people he passed by, as he wondered what the day would bring. He came here from time to time, and listened to the gossip regarding the council's discussions on Highston and the Federation. While they had agreed to leave the details of the invasion to the politicians, Symon could not help but to worry about his former home.

The palace was alive with personnel. Messengers and clerical pages ran on errands constantly. Combined with the consistent drumming of the Welgeid, it was an intricate dance of government efficiency. Symon watched them run and settled on going to the main library. He would often go there and look over healing manuals that were present. From what he could determine, healing was rare in Necromancy. His father had been something of a legend and what little material available often cited Nemuku Cyl'Karrick as an anomaly.

Vargarden had been complicated for the group. Jesse and Caleb had been finding their way, although Jesse had come home the previous night upset. Symon was still trying to find the courage to court Moria, but hesitated to risk the delicate friendship they had formed. He was constantly finding himself balancing the needs of his friends and his own, trying to focus on the right things. The Witch had changed his perspective on the war, and what it meant. Heeding the words of the

Witch, he looked to start his life here in the city and find a service that satisfied him.

He had great concern for Argyle. The Genbu were barely referred to in academic literature. Gargoyles were rare in the Khorric Federation, actually quite rare in Sainan, from what Symon could find, and the details of their culture were scarce. Since Argyle had chosen to stay with the group in Vargarden, Symon was trying to help establish connections that may be able to put Argyle in a good position. Symon knew that speciesism was frowned upon in society, but the Federation had proven often that the nobility could twist the definition of "worth" the way they saw fit. Justifications could be made. Symon did not want his friend to face undue hardships simply for his unique heritage.

Symon heard Caleb's voice from around the corner as he neared the library. Caleb was surrounded by an attaché and some other aides, as they slowly made their way down the hall. Symon hesitated, not knowing how to approach Caleb if he was conducting business with dignitaries, but that hesitation was unheeded as Caleb spotted Symon in the hall and waved for him.

Caleb smiled politely as he approached, and Symon caught a scent in the air behind the Prince. A familiar scent. "Symon!" the Prince called. "It is good to see you. I was hoping that you may be here today!"

"Oh, of course. I was heading to the library."

"Ah, the library, yes. Could I persuade you to diverge from your task?"

"What can I do for you, Prince Caleb?" Symon asked. His eyes scanned the envoy of aides and saw their approval. Symon had addressed the position, not his friend.

"We received guests of the Federation last night. Dignitaries, as we expected, and they have spent much of the morning discussing the situation in the Khorric Federation with the council."

"Yes, of course, my Lord," Symon nodded. "What do you need from me?"

"Nothing official," Caleb smiled. "However, I was escorting the lady to her chambers before I take these aides back to the council to draft up a formal report on our proceedings.

"As we talked, the Lady asked after you. It appears that she may know you."

Caleb said. He gestured behind him and the aides stepped to the side. As they did, the smell of orange and incense hit Symon fully. A scent nearly forgotten. "May I present to you Lara Devros, representative of the New Nobles of the Khorric Federation."

Symon could scarcely believe it. Before him stood a woman he had not seen in nearly a year. Lara was dressed in a regal golden gown, her blond hair tied up tightly. She was adorned in fine jewels, and her brown eyes glistened under the light of the hall's lanterns. She smiled shyly and licked her lips. "Hello, Symon."

He didn't remember her being so small. Lara was slender, almost too much so, and her gown draped over her in angles. Her pale skin looked like porcelain. She looked delicate. Fragile.

"Lara," Symon said. "It has been some time."

"Yes, it has," she said. "Will you escort me as the Prince requested?"

"Of course." Symon looked to Caleb. "I will take her from here, my Prince."

Caleb nodded and motioned to the rest of the group. "Let us return. The lady is in fine hands."

Symon and Lara watched quietly as the group walked away. When everyone was out of earshot, she turned to Symon and said, "I am so happy to see you, Symon."

"What are you doing here?"

"I had to pull some strings, but I convinced Olivar to let me take this run. We've been on a campaign to settle things in Highston, and an emissary to Vargarden was needed. There were rumors you had run here after the invasion, so I hoped to see if it was true."

"Rumors?"

"Yes, but it's not important. You ARE here. That is what matters!"

Symon shook his head. Lara had been a hard loss in his old life. For months, he had dwelled on the break up with her. Olivar had intentionally gone after him personally and Lara had been the finishing blow. Olivar had targeted everything precious in Symon's life and reclaimed it. Yet, here she was, standing in front of him. Then, dread hit him.

"Is Olivar here with you?"

"No," she smiled. "I convinced him to stay behind. There is still much to do in the Lord's High Council."

"Good," Symon said. He tried to keep his voice calm, but the relief of not dealing with his Alvan bully was prevalent in his tone, unwilling to be hidden. "So, are you staying, here in the palace?"

"Oh, Symon!" she laughed coyly. "Are you trying to take me to my bedroom?"

Symon's ears turned pink and he choked, coughing hoarsely. Lara had never been so bold when they had been courtly, and her joke was unexpected. She had a scent of something dark. A sinister intent lurking behind her sweet exterior. He stammered, "No... No, of course not."

"Ah, that's unfortunate," she said, winking. "I'm staying in the west wing."

"Lara, I do not wish to give you the wrong impression."

"Relax, Symon," she said. "I know what I'm here for."

"What do you mean?"

"I didn't come here only for Highston. I came here for me. For you."

"But you are with Olivar."

"Symon, he's horrible," she said. "He is doing what he promised, funding my projects and letting me start additional education facilities, but there's no relationship there."

"So he is not... cruel?"

She smiled sadly. "Not to me, no. He's got a mean streak, but he and I have our arrangements."

"Arrangements?"

"Yes, he's got 'unusual' needs that I'm not comfortable with, so I pretend to not notice he runs out to address those with paid women, and he keeps me bedazzled with gifts and things."

"So you do not love each other?"

"Of course not. We love ourselves enough. It's a start."

"That sounds sad." Symon looked at Lara, and could see the lines around her eyes. The past few months had strained her for sure, and those lines were forming from hard stares and a stern face. "You deserve better."

"I don't want your pity, Symon."

"No, of course not."

"I want you! I want you to come home and save me."

"Lara, I cannot," Symon flinched. "My life is here. Not to mention, you are a married woman. If you were to divorce your marriage, defect from Highston. You could build a life here. I could help you with contacts, as could the Prince. But I cannot save you from Olivar. Only you can do that for yourself."

"But, surely you miss home. Just come with me. I could keep my position on the Council. I could clear your name." She smiled, "You and I could do so much good."

"Lara..." Symon stuttered. "Clear my name?"

"Olivar still hates you intensely. It was very hard to talk him out of coming here. He wanted to demand you be arrested and brought back in chains."

"Arrested, for what?"

"Some trumped-up charges, I presented them to Vargarden to send you home with me. They dismissed them out of hand."

"And you want me to return with you? To be..."

"Yes," she said. "I can get them dismissed. It will irritate Olivar greatly, and I'm hoping it will rattle him enough that I can get my way on my next argument with him. He's been blocking an idea of mine, and if I can get him to lose focus, I can get it through." She smiled deviously and Symon could see that sharp mind that she had always possessed now had an edge.

"But you don't want to come home, do you?" she asked. They reached her door, and she turned to him. "That's okay. I think I have something I know will unsettle him enough for many arguments to come. And you don't have to go any-where."

Symon looked at her dubiously. He could smell danger in this conversation, and was becoming rapidly uncomfortable. She leaned against him, snuggling deep against his chest. The familiar scent of her perfume wafted into his nose. He felt sick to his stomach. The once sweet smell was now cloyingly overwhelming.

"You and I could go to the other side of this door and have the moment that we never had. I could love you like you always wanted. We could be what we were meant to be."

"No," Symon said.

"What do you mean, 'no'?" Lara sneered. "This is your chance! I know you wanted me. Take me."

"You are a married woman."

"I'm married to a man who cares about himself and his title more than anything else. You and I would be the only two who would ever know. Well, except him," she smiled, a dark light in her eye. "But he'll never be able to do anything about it, and he would never, *ever* admit it to anyone else."

"You cannot be serious, Lara."

"Oh, but I can."

Symon shook his head. "This is not you. You are better than this."

"You are still as naive as ever, Symon. This is why Olivar beat you."

"Because I have honor? Because I have values?"

"Yes. Your integrity makes you vulnerable. It weakens you."

"No, it does not."

"You fool. I could give you everything you ever wanted. In one night in my bed, I could give you my body and a way to get revenge on Olivar! How can you say no?"

"I can say 'no' because I do not want revenge. I was not angry that he attacked me, I was angry because I lost my friend. I lost you. I was alone!"

"Then come to me. I can be here with you now!"

"No, you cannot. You are still Olivar's wife. You would never be fully mine. You would never be my wife."

"Marriage is merely law. It's nothing. You and I can have everything else. This is what we were made for, Symon. I loved you, too."

"I would not share you with anyone. I certainly would not share you with Olivar."

Lara slapped him. "You greedy *larg-thrumper*. How dare you presume to own me?!"

"That is not what I meant."

"I can see why Olivar tired of you. You've always been chasing us, and you think you are owed what we have. You want our lives, but you're not willing to get your hands dirty. To do what it takes to succeed!"

Symon stood tall and glared at Lara. His ears pinned back, and he was seething with rage. "Lara, I do not know what has happened to you, but you are wrong. I never wanted any wealth or power, I just wanted to have a happy life. I thought you wanted the same. But clearly not."

"You foolish imbecile!" Lara screamed. "This isn't over!"

She continued to rant at him, as Symon opened the door and gently pressed her inside. "Lara, I hope that you and Olivar are everything you ever expected to be. I can honestly say no two individuals were ever designed to be with each other more."

Symon had stormed home, directly from the palace. His fur still bristled, his arms, tail, and ears still shaking off the anger. His mind raced, trying to figure out what had just happened. She was not the woman he thought he had known. He wondered if he had ever known her. Lara had been a bastion in the sea of vitriol that was the upper class of Highston. To see that she was just another one of them was horribly disappointing. It was clearer than ever before. His life in Highston was over.

He burst through the door still seething. He stood before his Heritage Tree and willed himself to calm down. A growl formed inside his chest filling itself with Symon's rage and begging to be released. He arched back and roared at the ceiling.

"Symon?" Moria asked from the dining area. Symon had not seen her as he entered. A small plate of fruits and nuts were on the table.

"I am sorry," Symon said, embarrassed. "I did not mean to disturb you."

"Tis okay. Just weren't expectin' 'ya back so soon."

"I know. I just couldn't stay at the palace any longer."

"You're upset," she said. "What happened?"

"I would rather not talk about it."

"Okay."

Moria began collecting her lunch remains and prepared to head to the kitchen. Symon's heart fell into his stomach. He did not want her to leave. "Moria, don't go."

"What's wrong, Symon?"

"I ran into someone from my past."

"One o' tha deligates?"

"Yes, an emissary. Lara Devros." Symon paced the small room, his tail still twitching in frustration. "The wife of Olivar Devros."

"Oh," Moria's eyebrows rose in recognition. Symon had told her about Olivar's plots against him and the repercussions. She had been a friendly ear for many months. "Tha woman 'ya were in love with? The one you told me about?"

"Yes, that same one."

"Oof," Moria said. "Takin' it didn't go well."

"No, it did not."

"Too many old feelin's?"

Symon growled softly. "No. I thought there would be. But…"

"Not the woman 'ya remembered?"

"Not at all," Symon said. "I thought she was different, you know? I just thought she was different. But she was one of them. This whole time."

"One of…?"

"The ones that Jesse always complains about. Those who take from everyone and are never satisfied."

"Aye, they seem to be the base of the Federation."

"I just remember her from before. Or the idea of her, at least." Symon tested his thoughts carefully, trying to form the words. "She was my first real relationship. I thought she was special. I thought she was…purer."

"Virgin?"

"No," Symon said, quickly. "Not like that. Just not corrupted. Not like the rest of the Nobles. I just can not see why I did not see it before."

Moria stood and walked to Symon, putting her hand on his shoulder. "Ya' were bred into that life. 'Tis all you knew. She played 'ya. Made 'ya see what she wanted 'ya to see."

"She's horrible."

"Aye, sound as such. What'd she say to ya'?"

"She tried to seduce me."

"Oh, shit!" Moria laughed. Symon's face tensed, and she recovered the best she could. "I'm sorry, I just didn't 'spect that." He had to forgive her. It was absurd.

"I told her no, obviously."

"Obviously," Moria smiled. "And she took it poorly?"

"Very."

"Aye, sounds 'bout right."

"Why are women so complicated?" Symon asked.

"We're not. Ya' just haven't figured us out yet."

"Well, I suppose I shall never do so." Symon shrugged.

"Givin' up?"

"No, she gave up on me. She gave up on herself."

"So she gave up on 'ya, and so you give up on love? Is this how you love? So temporary?" Moria was goading him. "Is this what you are?"

"Of course not," Symon said. "I know it was not love. I was just a kid. A stupid child, apparently, who fell for someone who took advantage of me. 'My integrity makes me vulnerable.'"

"She said that?"

"Yes, her voice, her words. Olivar and her are truly the same now."

"Olivar again?"

"I think he is why I was in love with the idea of her. Of the life she could give me. Maybe they are right. Maybe I was always chasing them."

"No, they told ya' that was what ya' wanted. They made ya' believe it." Moria smiled up at him. "Think careful, now. What do *you* want?"

Symon stared at her. Moria was so unlike Lara it was jarring. That dark hair, slicked back and pinned by steel barrettes. A simple sundress hung from tiny straps supported by her strong shoulders. A powerful, yet elegant, grace of a warrior woman who would be a partner, not a dependent.

"I want someone who will be my friend, someone who shares my goals, my troubles, and my happiness."

"And..." she said.

Symon took a step towards her. "I want someone who knows me."

"Someone who shares your honor, who knows your secrets, knows your family. Someone who has watched you grow into a man here in Vargarden?"

"Yes, someone who wants me to build a life here. And share it with me."

"Sounds 'bout right," Moria smiled.

Symon took a final step towards her. He looked down upon her, he was still a head taller than she. "I want someone like you."

"Like me?"

"No," Symon smiled. "I want you."

"'Tis what I've wanted as well. I've just been waiting on 'ya to give up on your past. I din't want to share you with it."

Symon stared at her. She stared back, looking directly into his eyes. He weighed her words carefully, making sure he had truly heard what he had thought he heard. That she shared his feelings.

"You should be kissing me, you fool," she whispered.

"Yes, I should."

Symon pulled her in and kissed her passionately, and the world lost focus. All thoughts of the past evaporated, and he leaned into her with all his being. He had felt magic before, but this was a power beyond anything he knew.

38

Smoothing Ruffled Feathers

Caleb replayed the previous day's events back in his mind, over and over. It had taken some time before Caleb had been able to collect himself. Jesse's departure had rattled him. Caleb had not a clue as to what had occurred, or what to do about it. All he could do was hope that Jesse would return, or perhaps that he could visit with Symon or Argyle to attempt to gain insight. Whatever happened, he did not wish for it to ever happen again. He desperately hoped that he had not just ended their chance at being together.

But all too soon afterward, the Prince's free time came to an end and he was called to council duties. Escorting dignitaries, meeting with emissaries and advocates, all mundane tasks that normally put the Prince in comfort. It didn't do any good. Caleb was just as distracted and despondent as he had been in his apartments. Nothing said in his presence was heard. Nothing was given his full attention. Instead, he just thought of Jesse.

Over and over the conversation replayed in his mind as Caleb attempted to deduce what he could possibly have done to have upset Jesse and make him leave. They had been attempting nick-names. "Winged wonder", followed by "delectable Prince", followed by "precious little bird". While none of them seemed particularly clever or creative, none could be deemed offensive. Or at least he hadn't thought so. Admittedly they had been caught up in the euphoria of one another's company, but surely he had not said anything else.

Over and over the thoughts played in his head, he attempted to analyze the event and conversation from every angle. None of it made sense. And yet Jesse, while passionate, did not strike Caleb as someone taken by random bouts of emotion. There had to be something to it.

"My Lord, do you have any opinion at all on this matter?"

"Huh?" Caleb looked up, hardly realizing what room he was in. Over two dozen councilors and aides sat looking down the table at him. The gentle lady currently speaking was one of the lesser councilors, and Caleb could see that less than half the council was represented here, so the matter could not be terribly important. He hoped. Nevertheless, he waved the councilor off, shaking his head.

"My Lord," the woman said, "are you unwell?"

Caleb sat up straighter in his seat, knowing that he owed these men and women his courtesy, if not his attention. "My apologies, truly," he stated to the group at large. "I have an issue pressing on my attention, and this is causing me to become discourteous to you. Please forgive my lapse of attention."

At this, the High Councilor leaned forward to address Caleb. "My Prince, if this is a matter the council might assist with, please let us know. In any case, think nothing of it. The council can easily handle the matter at hand. Would you prefer to retire at this time?"

"I appreciate your solicitousness, Master Magran," said Caleb. "I will stay, and I shall endeavor to better handle my duty to our council."

A side door opened, admitting a palace runner into the room. A few eyes watched the boy, to see who his message might be for. The young Gnome approached the Prince, and Caleb took the small parchment from the page. Four simple words. But words which lit a fire in the eyes of the Prince.

Master Olben is here.

Caleb stood immediately and addressed the table. "I do apologize. It seems that I am needed immediately elsewhere," he said. He then grinned and added,

"It seems, Master Magran, that my discourtesy must stand."

With that, Caleb made haste to leave the room, pulling the messenger from the room with him. Once in the adjoining chamber, Caleb turned on the boy who had brought him the message. "Where is he?" he anxiously asked.

"Who, my Lord?"

"My guest. This message speaks of an Isnashi guest who is waiting to see me. Where is he currently?"

"Oh, my apologies, my Lord," he answered nervously. "I did not read the message. But the guest you speak of is nearby. I can take you to him. This way, please."

Caleb trailed behind the messenger, hope and anxiety building within him in equal measures. As they approached his apartments, Caleb paused to gather his thoughts. His mind fractured the conversation into its potential possibilities. If Jesse was here for conflict, the Isnashi would have furrowed eyebrows, a frown or stern mouth. It would require that Caleb defend himself or apologise. If not, and Jesse was hurt but willing to talk, Caleb would need to ask questions and determine the trauma source.

Caleb's mind ran faster and faster, anxiously working out all the possible ways he might delicately ask what had caused the issue. He struggled to predict Jesse's behavior, so hundreds of scripted responses were possible. His stomach knotted. This conflict had taught him something he hadn't realized fully. He needed Jesse.

He had known he liked Jesse. He found him interesting, intelligent, entertaining, and amazingly attractive, but until this issue, he hadn't realized how much he was becoming attached to him. How much he was becoming accustomed to having the sweet young man around. How much it had changed Caleb.

The messenger asked, quietly "Do you require anything else, my Lord?"

"No," said the Prince. "Thank you for your assistance." At last he pushed open the door.

"Oh, thank the Gods!" cried out Jesse as Caleb entered the room. The Isnashi rushed up from the seat he had been in, charged across the room, and wrapped his arms around Caleb's waist. "I'm so sorry," he squealed. "I'm so glad you still wanted to see me."

Caleb stood there motionless as his abdomen was squeezed tight. He once again went through his checklist of responses, trying to find an appropriate one. None came to mind. Jesse mumbled words of apology into his shirt. None of Caleb's scenarios had considered that Jesse would take blame for the incident. He pulled Jesse back from himself slightly, and the young man looked up into his eyes.

"I am very happy to see you, Jesse," said Caleb. "I will always be glad of your company. Before anything else is said, however, please accept my deepest apologies for whatever I said or did to offend you last time."

"No," Jesse said. "I'm sorry. I shouldn't have left you. Or I should have come back sooner. I'm sorry."

"Jesse," Caleb said, plainly. "I just need to know what I did so that I may never repeat the offense."

"Oh, no!" Jesse emphatically cried. "I was a moron and completely overreacted." He embraced Caleb again, once again speaking into the Prince's chest, "I'm so sorry I worried you. I probably ruined your whole day. I'm so sorry. I'm such an idiot." This and more was repeated, a mumble turning into a mantra.

"Jesse, I just wish to talk," Caleb said. "Please, Jesse. Let us set aside faults from either side. I said something that upset you. You reacted poorly." Jesse scoffed at this, clearly considering that to be a minor description. "Can you tell me, what was the offense?"

Jesse pulled back from Caleb enough that he could wipe his eyes on his sleeve. They took seats on the sofas, and each took a moment to collect themselves. After a bit, Jesse nodded, took a fortifying sip of his drink, clearly stalling, and finally said, "My little bird."

Caleb sat stoically. He had known it had been a bad nickname. But he wasn't sure as to why. He patiently waited for Jesse to continue.

"You called me 'my little bird'," Jesse's voice caught on the words. "He always called me that, especially when he wanted to get my attention."

"Who?" Caleb asked.

"He!" he cried out, "He! Xerian! Xerian always called me that. Usually after he got finished teaching me a lesson."

The tone in Jesse's words insinuated that 'teaching a lesson' was not a mentorship phrase. He had read about abuse, and studied psychological documents, but he didn't have any experience with it. Caleb made sure his voice stayed calm, looking to give Jesse a baseline energy level to return to.

"Who is Xerian?" Caleb asked. "I do not recall you or your friends mentioning him before." Caleb harshly felt the intensity of the mood and desperately wanted to look away, but forced himself to maintain eye contact in support. Instead, it was Jesse who could not stand to keep his eyes away from his lap as he began to speak.

"You know I grew up on the streets, right? I told you my mom died when I was a kid?" Jesse asked.

Caleb nodded, and then realizing that Jesse could not see his response, replied, "Yes."

"Well, Xerian is who took me in. He kept me alive. He fed me, bought me clothes, taught me the streets. A year ago, I would have told you that I owed him everything." Jesse sighed.

Caleb looked around. This wasn't the first time that Jesse had spoken about the material gifts provided to him by others. He was beginning to see that people in Jesse's life used it as a dependency and had warped the young man's sense of worth.

"Now?" Jesse continued. "Now, I think I'm ready to admit that Xerian was an asshole. He always insisted he needed to teach me lessons 'for my own good'. But really it just came down to his lessons ending in black eyes and broken bones. I'd say about half got healed by a priest. The rest were left for me to heal naturally as best I could."

"Oh Jesse," whispered Caleb. Trying to display comfort, he reached out and squeezed Jesse's hand. "I hope you know I could never do that to you."

"Oh no!" exclaimed Jesse. His eyes raised quickly and Jesse looked up determinedly at Caleb's face, but his hands pulled away. "I would never think that! I wasn't trying to compare you or anything. It just completely caught me off guard."

Caleb's insides gnarled as he thought of the pain that this man had caused Jesse. Rage twisted inside him, and his voice went cold. "This man, Xerian, sounds atrocious. It is likely best that I never meet him."

"Oh, damn!" said Jesse. Caleb saw fear in the young man's eyes. Not fear OF Caleb, but fear FOR Caleb. "I hope you never, ever have to meet him."

"For his sake, yes."

Jesse's eyes widened in surprise at that. Then he broke into a very familiar, impish grin. "Well, I have some things to make up for. Is there any chance we could pick up where we left off from before?"

Caleb sat back as Jesse climbed atop him. He wasn't prepared for how to move forward. Again, his checklist was failing him for any response. "Can I still call you 'my angel'?" He asked.

"Hmm," smirked Jesse, straddling his lap. "Only if I can call you my bitch." Before Caleb could respond, Jesse pressed their lips together, beginning with a passionate yet closed kiss.

Caleb pulled away from Jesse's lips long enough to breathe out, "I want each of us to make the other a promise, if you are willing, of course."

"Anything," Jesse answered as he moved down to begin kissing Caleb's neck. "Anything you want."

"I want us to promise one another that we shall be open, and tell one another when we are upset, and why."

"Of course," nodded Jesse before immediately going back to the meal he was making of Caleb's neck.

Caleb pulled him back, needing Jesse to hear him. "I'm serious, my angel. I never want to hurt you, but I would rather a thousand stinging complaints than to feel the guilt and uncertainty I experienced from this incident."

"I'll never make you do it again," Jesse giggled like a child. There was a sadness to it. A familiar rhythm in Jesse's words.

Caleb squirmed at how the assault on his neck tickled. Soon his body began to respond. His mind and heart were confused, but it was clear that Jesse wanted intimacy. They resumed kissing, hands roaming across one another's upper bodies.

He first worried it would be awkward, but soon found himself so invigorated by the pleasant noises he was able to draw from Jesse. All thought of concern left him. Caleb allowed himself to explore, both with his mouth and his fingers, and the more he did so, the more Jesse let him. Caleb went to remove Jesse's shirt first. Normally, the Isnashi did this himself, and it took Caleb a moment to deduce how it was fastened around Jesse's wings. The young man laughed and squirmed as Caleb fumbled. Quickly, the Prince treated it as an Arcane glyph, reversing movements in his mind and snapping the clasps in quick succession.

Once he had finally released Jesse from his tunic and shirt, Caleb was able to marvel at the physique of his new partner. A life of hard living combined with the light build required for flight left a body that was toned but wiry, slender and beautiful. Caleb noticed various scars, some faint, others more pronounced. He ran his fingers over several of them, enjoying the tactile differences to them, yet also thinking of what their stories might be. He worried those tales may have more unintended consequences on their relationship.

Jesse lifted up, and stood to beckon Caleb. He then led them to Caleb's bedroom, eyes teasing and dancing lasciviously. Caleb tried to pull Jesse in for a kiss, but was surprised when instead Jesse pushed him back onto the bed and began kissing down his chest to his belly. Jesse's deft fingers began working at the ties to the Prince's exposing himself to Jesse fully for the first time.

"Wow," grinned Jesse as he took Caleb's hardened shaft in his hand.

Caleb gasped at the feeling of someone else's hand on his genitals for the first time. It felt so amazing, so unique and personal. He reached for the buckles on Jesse's pants, but his hands were slapped away.

"Soon, my soul," said Jesse, reaching out to lick Caleb. "Right now I owe you, and I plan to make things right. Don't worry, I was right. You could give Xerian and Erin both a run for their money!"

It felt like being dowsed in cold water. Caleb's entire body shut down in shock. "Owe me?" said Caleb in confusion. "You don't owe me, love."

Jesse ignored him, trying to get Caleb to rise again. Caleb reached down to make Jesse look up at him. "Jesse, please stop. You don't owe me."

"But I have to make things up to you. I can do this for you. I promise I'm good!"

"No, Jesse, not like this."

Jesse looked at Caleb in confusion. "You don't want to make love to me?"

"I absolutely do," said Caleb. "But if you are pleasuring me out of some sense of 'owing me', that isn't making love." He kissed the top of Jesse's head. "You aren't going to make me happy like some transaction. That's not what I want."

"But I fucked up," Jesse said quietly into Caleb's chest. "I need to make it right, right?"

Caleb understood. Everyone in Jesse's life had made it an exchange. Please them, or suffer. This detachment was too familiar. Caleb hadn't been abused, but he knew isolation. He knew what it felt like to "go through the motions".

"You will never owe me sex. Never. No matter what anyone else has ever told you." Caleb could feel Jesse's quiet tears against his skin. His heart broke for what this sweet boy must have been put through. "If, and when, we disagree, we shall talk it out. We shall fix it, like we did this, and move on. But you shall never 'owe' me."

Jesse squeezed Caleb's torso, holding tight. "I'm really fucked up, aren't I?"

"You aren't fucked up."

"I hate Xerian. I hate that he broke me."

"You aren't broken. You aren't less, soiled, damaged, or anything else your head may be telling you." Caleb swallowed hard, looking for the words. He decided to speak plainly. "I think I love you. And I want you, all of you. If we are patient, we can teach one another how to love. How to truly love."

39

Victorious Hearts

Jesse had been in the kitchen eating breakfast when Symon had found him and convinced Jesse to join the Ennedi outside. Jesse was anxious to share some time with his friend. After a rough start to the week, the rest of the days had flown by. Jesse had barely been home, and during those brief times, Symon hadn't been available. There was something brewing. Jesse was curious.

Jesse had walked into the courtyard and spotted Moria was sitting on the bench to the side of the arena, and Argyle was lounging in the sun; stretching his legs and vast body across the lawn. The Isnashi smiled and strode to the center, his training blade in hand and stretching his shoulders. It felt like old times.

"Before we begin," Symon's voice called from the dark of the hallway beyond the door. "You are not holding any grudges or grievances that may break forth during our workout to the detriment of my bodily health, are you?" Symon's voice made the joke clear, and Jesse couldn't help but appreciate it.

"No," Jesse said laughing. "I think I've made clear all the ways you continue to piss me off. Nothing new added to the list..." he smiled, "yet."

"Well, that is good. But just in case, I decided to protect myself against any potential such outlets, in case you felt the need to expend your frustrations on my ribs again."

Symon stepped out of the shadows into the sunlight, and the air left Jesse's lungs in a low whistle. The Ennedi was clad from head to toe in steel plate armor, lacquered as black as night. The blue of the sky reflected purple and highlighted the edges of the chest plate and pauldrons. Jesse examined closer and realized that the scales down Symon's sides were merely a dark, deep grey. The "v-shaped" effect made Symon's shoulders, massive as they already were, appear wider and more intimidating. A small half cape hung from his left side, bearing the insignia of house Cyl'Karrick. The armor was a breathtaking display of power and presence that reminded him of when he had seen Kyrn burst through the flames so long ago.

"Shiiiitt..." Jesse said.

Symon made a twirl around to display the armor in its entirety. "Do you like it?"

"Fuck yeah!" Jesse cried. "That's badass! Is that what you went to go get a few weeks ago?"

"Yes, this is the armor my cousin made for me."

"Well..." Jesse smiled. "You were right. There's no way you could have made that."

Symon gasped in mock insult, then his face split in a wide grin. "I told you armor smithing is a different art." Symon walked to the center of the ring, his training blade twirling steadily in one hand. "You want to help me give it a try?"

"Yeah!" Jesse said. He danced on his toes. "Aren't you worried about the weight? I mean, at some time you're gonna hit your 'big boy' limit and be the slow oaf we all know you want to be."

Symon smiled at Jesse, "Yes, I was worried about the extra bulk of a set of plate. But I believe my cousin has resolved those concerns admirably."

Jesse couldn't stop smiling. It was nice to see the old Symon again. Whatever had been heavy on Symon's mind seemed to have eased, and there was a bounce in his step. Jesse could feel the walls between them breaking down again.

Jesse stepped up to the center and jokingly whispered, "'Resolved your concerns admirably.' You pompous ass."

"Easy there, your gutter rat is showing."

"Yeah, yeah."

The two young men hefted their blades in a salute and nodded at each other. "Let us begin."

Symon settled into his familiar steady stance. The stance of defense and evaluation. His weight was evenly transferred, and the blade was positioned so that its weight was being held by his shoulders and back, rather than his arms. Jesse knew he could react to any movement and could hold it indefinitely. It was the first step to a well-known dance between them.

"You never learn, do you, big guy?" Jesse sprang forward and went into butterfly strikes. Four quick successive strikes, high to low and low to high, reversing then going low to high and high to low.

Symon shifted his blade back and forth to block the actual intended strikes, turning Jesse's blade away with ease. Instead of retreating and turning with the pace, the larger man stepped forwards into Jesse's inner reach and forced the Isnashi's swings to narrow, reducing the angles that Jesse could create.

Jesse spun on his heel with a reverse strike, engaging Symon's block, and then lunged backwards to disengage. He strolled around the ring watching Symon, who settled quickly and easily into that motionless statue of defense once again. Jesse had to admit that whatever Symon had been doing for these past few months, he was a much better fighter than before. "So, it's like that, is it?"

Symon nodded at Jesse with his small little fangs peeking out from his broad smile. "So it is."

"Well, then. Let's see who's learned more. 'Cause you ain't the only one who's been training."

Argyle growled from the side of the show. "I am hearing a great deal of bravado, and seeing far too little actions that are worthy of such impudence. Fight already."

Jesse made an obscene gesture to Argyle and grinned. "You want a piece, too, bitch?"

"You would not handle this, bird boy. If I took a piece, I would take it all." Argyle waved Jesse to Symon. "Handle the kitty cat, and then you may have what it takes to come at me."

"Please," Jesse said, mockingly. He turned back to Symon and his stride took the edge of battle once again. "Okay, big guy. You wanted it, come get it."

Jesse startled as Symon exploded into motion, rushing directly at him. Symon's thrust his blade towards Jesse's shoulder with his leading hand and Jesse parried quickly. Symon redirected the momentum of the block and spun his grip, and took the blade into a low arc which Jesse jumped up and over.

As Jesse landed, he saw the ploy too late. Symon's off hand was already drafting a quick spell form that Jesse knew all too well. With a quick little gesture and a small whisper "*Sival*", Symon cast and sent a small bolt of force into Jesse's back foot, taking his heel out from under him. Symon swung his blade high to pull Jesse's defense and shift his mass upwards and finished the maneuver with a quick kick to Jesse's side.

Jesse fell onto his hip and he swept his wings forward to propel himself across the cobbles. He rolled backwards and took his feet, blade at the ready. His breath was uneven from a combination of effort and laughter. "You fucking cheater!"

"Learned from the best."

Jesse bowed deeply. "Thank you."

"Of course."

"Still didn't get me," Jesse said.

Symon shrugged his shoulders. "Worth a try, though."

"Yes, it was."

Jesse kept moving, watching for another surprise. Whatever had gotten into Symon, the man was looser and more impulsive. Jesse could only keep Symon turning, and hoped that it would delay him enough that Jesse could react. "So the armor? Not slowing you down at all, is it?"

"No," Symon said. "I requested they enchant it to reduce the weight. The scales provide flexibility, and it feels pretty good."

"Yeah, that tracks," Jesse smirked. "You're so predictable."

"You do know me well."

"It's still not fair to be built like a damn wall, but still be—"

"As fast as you?"

Jesse smirked. "You're not that fast."

Symon started to say something but Jesse rushed him, his blade a blur of motion, as he struck several times in rapid succession. Symon turned the attacks aside using both his blade and new bracers, and the spar began in earnest.

Exchange after exchange, Symon and Jesse tested each other, displaying strikes and counters that they had been practicing with their personal trainers. Moria's calls of "good form" and "well struck" punctuated the clack of their training blades against each other, making the song of combat complete.

The strikes became sharper and faster, each of them circling. The boys pressed harder and harder as they warmed up. The spar stretched out to a minute, then two, then three, as each of them tried to gain an edge that wasn't there.

"Are you two ready to call this a draw?" Argyle asked.

Symon called back, "No, I have a bit left in me."

"Same here," Jesse said.

Symon's training blade outweighed Jesse's by more than half. Symon pressed the attack, and each blow fell heavier and Jesse's hands stung from the vibrations. The larger Ennedi was lulling Jesse into a pattern, and Jesse knew it, but the blows were taking everything he had to resist, and he couldn't escape the trap. Jesse watched as Symon's muscles coiled and with a violent spring, exploded into that sideways viper strike.

Jesse tried to block, but the powerful strike took the blade from his hand. End over end, it toppled across the stone blocks with a rattle. Symon smiled as his opponent was defenseless and went in for the "kill." Jesse dove towards Symon's feet and tumbled past him. With quickness and precision, he drew a spell form and called out, "*Osival!*" Moria's practice blade staff magically lifted off the bench beside her and flew into Jesse's outstretched hand.

Jesse took two steps at Symon, who had recovered from the dodge, and planted the butt of the staff into the ground. His wings flapped downwards as he leapt, using the force of the staff as leverage and propelling him twenty feet into the air. The blade arced downwards and Symon threw a hard block upwards to defend it, sending Jesse into a backflip.

Dust scattered as Jesse used his wings to right himself and landed in a three point stance. Jesse pointed at Symon and whispered, "*Essevoy*" flinging a web.

"Not this time," Symon said, smiling as he ducked.

Jesse took off into another wing-powered leap and Symon tried to turn and follow him. His support foot however wouldn't budge, and he looked down to find it glued in place by webbing.

"You little trickster," he growled up at Jesse.

Jesse felt Symon grab his ankle and arrest his momentum. With a mighty tug, he threw Jesse crosswise back to the ground in front of him. Jesse watched as the large smith pulled hard until the webbing released, gossamer tearing loose and floating in the wind.

With one final effort, Jesse engaged, spinning the blade staff in wide arcs using its reach to keep Symon's bulk at bay. Three spinning blows delivered one after another served to unbalance the big cat. Jesse caught the staff in both hands, in a horizontal grip, using his shoulders to put power behind his grip. He shoved both hands forward, catching Symon's hilt crosswise and pushed it above his head. Another shove threw the staff across the bridge of Symon's nose, stunning the big man.

Jesse spun the staff and made an attempt to drive the blade into Symon's abdomen. Symon instinctively stepped to the side, eyes still blurry and grappled Jesse into a bear hug. Jesse fought as his grip on the staff was lost and it clattered to the ground. He thrashed against Symon's large arms kicking and laughing.

"Yield," Symon said, squeezing softly.

"Alright, alright. I yield!" squealed Jesse delightedly.

The boys collapsed to the ground together. Symon's arms still wrapped around Jesse. The hug of battle, became a relaxed friendly embrace as they laughed and rolled to their backs, weak with exertion. The sun warmed their faces as they stared at the sky, smiles as radiant as the orb of light above them.

"That was fun," Symon said, at last.

Jesse reached over and punched Symon's arm playfully. "Fuck fun! That was awesome!"

Symon tousled Jesse's hair and pulled him back in for another hug. "I love you, man."

"Love you, too," Jesse said. He pushed up from the ground and reached down to help Symon up.

"You have learned that staff well."

"Yeah, Paulson has been drilling me relentlessly."

"It has paid off, my friend."

Jesse nodded. "You aren't half bad either. Now that you fight to win, you're even more of a beast than you were before. Fucking relentless!"

Symon ducked his head in embarrassment. "I have still far to go before I would be worthy of such praise."

"And throwing spells... in combat... for shame!"

"Ah, well. It seems to be the trendy thing to do. You know I am all about fancy trends." Jesse smirked at him, knowing that it was a far cry from the boy he had met a year ago. "I am still a clumsy caster, though."

"Ya' not that bad. Still got a way to go and shake off the Khorr habits," Moria said as she came to stand by them. Her hand gently brushed Symon's as she smiled at both of them. "Nice bout boys."

Jesse swept up her blade staff and tossed it to her. Moria caught it with a deft hand and spun it behind her into a resting position with a flourish. Jesse still marveled at her skill in weaponry. Paulson and he had conversations about her techniques and the men who had trained with her admired her. "Thanks for the loan, my lady."

"O'course," she said. "Nice, improv' there."

"Yep." Jesse turned to look at Argyle. "And a fat lot of help you were! Just laying there soaking in rays. Thorn would have thrown me a bone, or a stone, or something."

"I will endeavor to be more mindful of your fake peril in the future," Argyle dipped his head in mock shame.

"Damn, I needed this," Jesse said. "It's been tense, you know. We needed a break."

"Yes, I agree," Symon nodded. "I hoped it would help. I needed it, too."

Jesse wiped his brow, sweating in the sun. "Well, it was fun, but I should go clean up. I'm hoping to run over to the palace later and see Caleb, if he's not mucked up with Prince duties."

"So things are going well?" Symon asked.

Jesse winked. "Very well."

Moria wrapped her arm around Symon's waist. "He sh'ld be done with the Feds later today. It may be early evenin' before he can catch a moment for himself."

Jesse looked at her relaxed stance and how she sided up to Symon. His eyes flicked back and forth between the two, reading their body language like an open book. The mountain of tension of the unknown had seemed to disappear. There was an ease of two people who had solved a mystery that only they had known about, an air of satisfaction and contentment that they now shared together. Then suddenly, it hit Jesse like a bolt of lightning.

"You two..." he started. "No, you didn't..."

"Gentlemen would not speak of such things..." Symon started.

Moria smiled slyly. "Aye, we did. And he's better at that dance than he is at this one." She waved at the arena.

"For your sake, I hope so!" Jesse jested.

Symon gasped. "Hey!"

"I'm just messing with you. Let's go get a drink! We've got things to talk about."

Jesse grabbed Symon's hand and started out of the courtyard. Moria smiled gently to Argyle as she gathered her things to head back into the manor. "Ugh... y're all the same."

40

Lavendar and Smoke

Symon laid on the bed listening to the comforting sounds of water falling like rain in the small bathing chamber adjacent to his bedroom. Steam rolled out of the door, carrying the scents of lavender and rose, as Moria had her evening wash. She had been shadowing Jesse at the palace all day and was home for the evening.

As the sound of the water faded, Symon could hear Moria saying something about her day. She often attempted to talk to Symon while bathing, but even with his hearing, he could not make out her words over the sound of the water sloshing about. He had not found the heart to tell her, so he would often strain to keep up with the conversation as she went, building a story from context.

Finaly, her words were clear and he heard her say, "...'Tis just tha' they're so fuckin' cute!"

Symon chortled. While Moria was one of the toughest individuals he had ever met, she was also a hopeless romantic. Moments where she let her guard down and peek out were precious to him.

"Jesse would never believe me if I told him the things you say here alone."

Moria poked her head around the door frame. "Don't 'ya dare tell him. Do you'n know how hard it would be to stare daggers at him if he knew? I can't yell at him for being a bad 'fluence on the Prince if he knows how much I like him!"

Symon laughed from his belly. "You all spend so much time trying to out maneuver each other in the strangest arenas. It is dear to watch."

As Moria pulled back into the washing room, Symon could catch her eyes roll in amusement. They had easily settled into a healthy routine, and this little banter was only the first part of it.

"So they are cute, you say?" Symon asked.

"Aye, they're adorable. They just stare at each other trying to figure out who will start first."

"Jesse has had a rough life, I do not think he has ever truly known romance or love."

"Same 't be said 'bout the Prince. He's been surrounded by folk his whole life, but I think he's always been alone. 'Ya know?"

"Yes, I do," Symon said. He remembered back on his life in Highston, trying desperately to fit in and match his life to what he thought people expected of him. He had several companions, but no true friends. Even Lara and the girls he courted before her were always distant. Jesse, Thorn, Zenesul, and now Moria had changed that.

"A'sides, we don't want t'push 'em too much. Skittish as they are."

"No, they will come into their own in their own time. But I know Jesse is happy, and that is a great thing."

"Same with Prince Caleb. All the aides and his personal guard want this to work. So we'll keep settin' up good things for them to do together, as we can."

"You all talk about them?" Symon asked.

"Jesse's right!" Moria laughed from the other room. "While 'ya weren't raised noble, you certainly seem to forget the servants are folk, just like us."

Symon blushed with embarrassment. He had tried to be more conscious of those who helped around the house, but still struggled to think much about their lives outside of these walls. They were people, and, of course, they would talk to each other. They had watched the Prince grow up over two decades. It would only make sense that they would be invested in his happiness. "I am sorry. I try."

"We know you do," she said, consolation in her voice. "At least you're not an ass about it."

"Yes, there is that."

"Jesse's a good kid, but sure'n he puzzled us for a bit. He don't act like anyone we've ever seen with the Prince." Moria paused for a moment, just long enough for Symon to wonder about what she was doing, a slight humming audible as she concentrated on something. Just as he was about to ask, she continued, "Matter o' fact, he's the opposite. It's like every time the Prince gets fancy or tries to lavish Jesse, he pulls away."

"Jesse has hated nobility and the rich for a very, very long time. It has been his experience that most of them use their wealth and privilege to keep those without under their boot."

"Aye, that fits. For as much as he jokes 'bout havin' a rich boyfriend, he barely accepts any gifts. Mainly just books and trinkets."

"Jesse hates things given to him. He only trusts what he earns with his own hands. Thorn and he raised each other on the streets and feel that whatever can be given can be taken away."

"They ain't wrong."

"I miss her." Symon said. "Through all her prickles, Thorn was a good woman. She was *rieve.*"

"Aye, I miss her, too. She was a ball o' fun! Made my guards nervous. Kept their edge."

"I hope she is doing well. She was so adamant to go home to Highston. I worry that the war will swallow her." Symon mused.

"You should get a 'Distant Message' spell. I can pick up the scrolls from the shop down the street. Shouldn't take 'ya more than a week's time to learn. Then you could check on her and Zenesul."

"That is a fantastic idea!"

Moria clicked her tongue in amusement. "I'll grab one tomorrow."

Symon smiled and laid his head back deeper into the pillows. It would be nice to reach out to his old mentor and his friend. He had been so worried about them, that he failed to consider a spell like the one Moria described. She was that practical balance to all his idealism, and without her, he feared he would be lost again.

"So, anyways, you're right. Jesse doesn't want anything. They'll just sit and talk for hours about magic, and history, and pranks they've played. They're just fuckin' cute is all."

"Yes, dear. I, too, hope that they will work out."

"Just got to keep after my liege, 'ya know?!"

"Is that all?"

Moria came around the door dressed for bed and wearing a smile, lace, and little else. "No, I'm a romantic and want to see a charming love story."

Symon's breath caught as she stood bathed in the light of the candles of the room. Her beauty continued to stun him, and the lace nightgown was sheer enough to have left nothing to the imagination. "So, we are not sleeping much tonight?"

"Why would we? I'm off duty t'morrow and we've got the night. Let's make the most of it."

Symon leapt off the bed with a playful growl and bounded across the room towards Moria. She laughed musically as she danced outside of his grasp. She twirled around, flaring the lace skirt of the gown high up her legs temptingly.

"Do you like?"

A low growl escaped Symon as he grinned mischievously. "Yes, indeed."

She looked at him, and he realized that his robe had come undone, exposing the soft thin fur on his stomach. The fur was thinnest here and not nearly thick enough to hide the excitement that he was feeling. A small, sly grin of her own appeared on Moria's face. "I can see."

"Where do you even obtain such scandalous clothing?"

"The ways of womanly seduction aren't for the minds of men. You let me worry about that."

"Yes, dear."

She slowly reached up into his mane and pulled his head down so she could kiss him. Her lips brushed his, and his mind went blank as he fell into bliss. Suddenly, he felt his entire body weight get thrown into the air as she leveraged his arm and ducked under his hip, exploiting his higher center of gravity. He tumbled over and landed on his back, caught by the soft bed. And gracefully, she flipped back and landed on him, pinning him down.

"Got'cha," she said.

A low, content purr rumbled through Symon's chest. "Take me, then. I am yours."

"Do you think we are rushing into things?" Symon asked. The bedside candle had burned low, so Symon reached into the nightstand door to grab another. He transferred the flame and laid back. The evening had blurred as the two made love for hours.

"I think it's a bit late to be askin' that," Moria said, her voice muffled once again by the wash water. The same scent of lavender and roses that had begun the night was drifting from the washroom once again.

"I know, it is just that I have not felt this strongly for anyone, and we have only known each other a short time."

"We've lived under the same roof for half o'year now. We've laughed together, we've cried together, and I was there when you found out Prince Caleb was your Soul kin. I think we've gotten to know each other pretty well.

"Now'n we got peace. I'd like 'ta not waste time."

"But we just started..." Symon said.

"Sleepin' together is the least o'what we've been doin'."

"Truth," Symon said. "I just worry that folk will talk."

"Let 'em. None of their concern."

"But what of our reputations?"

"Bah!" Moria snorted. "There's nothin' to it. I spoke with my parents shortly after you arrived in Vargarden. I had fallen for you in the first few weeks. It was merely a matter of time."

"Really?"

"Aye, you have a way about you. I knew pretty instantly."

"But you never said anything to me. Why would you wait?"

"Your heart was here, and I knew you had eyes for me. But your head was still in your past. Needed 'ya to be complete first."

"Oh, well, that makes sense."

"Plus, you kept us busy. With the Vester attack, the Witch, and your bookish nose stuck in the library... you were pretty hard to get to."

"Well," Symon huffed jokingly. "I do not think it was that bad."

Moria crawled back into bed with him and snuggled her head into his chest. "Nah, but you're cute when you get flustered."

He playfully smacked her with a pillow and she giggled into his fur. "But to the serious point. Now that we are courting, is it proper that you still act as caretaker?"

Again, her musical laugh filled his ears. "For all the Federation's claims of being advanced, y'all still have some archaic beliefs. 'Courting' me? You big lunk!"

"Well, I just..."

"'Sides, I stopped acting as your caretaker weeks ago. Been stayin' here to be close to 'ya. That's all."

"Then more is my concern. I do not wish to besmirch your honor."

"My honor is fine. And 'sides, young folk here test their lives by livin' together all the time. Not all o' the older families are fond of it, but quite a few are. We're barely noticeable in the gossip circles."

"But it was you that said 'Two unmarried kids staying together all alone. People will talk.' Was it not?"

"I was just makin' you work for me. 'Sides you didn't know our culture yet, didn't want to scare 'ya off."

"Oh, well, then good, I suppose," Symon said. "So you have talked about our relationship with your parents?"

"Aye, and they are fond of 'ya. They feel you're a good match. A solid anchor for me to come home to when on campaign, if it were to occur."

"And what about my choices? Does it bother you that I do not want to follow in my sire's footsteps?"

"But 'ya are. As the blacksmith he was as you knew him, not as the Nemuku that I did from his books. The Ward will love 'ya as much as I do."

"Love?" Symon asked.

"Aye," Moria stared at him. "And?"

"Just caught me off guard."

"And?"

Symon searched his feelings. She was right. Even though they had only been intimate for a few weeks, he had grown close to her over the months. She was the one he came home to. The one he confided in. Moria was there as his equal. He smiled, "I love you, too."

"Of course, if 'ya are truly troubled about folks spinnin' rumors, you could just make us honest," she said smiling.

"You mean marry you?" Symon asked, his voice unable to conceal his surprise.

"Aye."

"So that would be us 'not rushing things'?"

"I'm serious," Moria said, sitting up on the bed and folding her legs underneath her. She turned and looked Symon directly in the eyes and he felt that sensation of being weighed. "We're both buildin' our careers and lives. We both know who we want to be. The only question is, do 'ya want to do it together? Are 'ya ready?"

Symon could not think of anything he wanted more. She was his center point. His days and nights were filled with thoughts of her and what they would experience that day. It surprised him a little that he had no hesitation in his answer. She was right. Now that Jesse and he had chosen to step aside from the conflict, there was nothing more to do than to build their lives. Together. "Yes, I truly am."

"Well then, there 'ya have it."

"So, do you wish to get married? To me?"

"Aye."

"Then I shall speak with your parents immediately and gain their blessing," Symon said.

She jested, "So traditional."

"Yes. And I shall not budge on this. I will speak with your parents, and then I shall get you a marriage band, and we shall celebrate our engagement with a dinner and dancing."

"I would fight 'ya on this, but it sounds quite nice," Moria said. "I accept."

"So we are to be wed?"

"Aye, I s'pose we will."

41

Problems of the Soul

The palace was in chaos.

Alarms rang through the halls, filling the air with a siren's scream. Symon had been sitting in a meeting room waiting to give the news to Jesse and Caleb when skeletal Welgeid flooded the halls, barricading entryways. It was another attack. Symon rushed off and attempted to make his way to Caleb's chambers. If he was correct, Jesse and Caleb would be there, and probably in danger.

Symon spied two Investurant soldiers advancing down the hallway. He broke his peace tie and freed his sword from its scabbard. Green flames came alive in his hand, and the soldiers paused to consider him. Symon remembered the night in front of the Flame Eternal, where he had lost Kyrn. These were the same type of soldiers. More elite. More deadly.

The Investurant on the left placed his hand on the jewel hanging around his neck and said something in Mumvuri. Moria had been teaching him the language of the Shadow, but Symon had little time to get any phrases committed to memory or understanding.

The two warriors approached quickly and in perfectly synchronized motion. Symon kept his blade centered and flicked it back and forth between the two swords, keeping each at bay. Over the last few months here in Vargarden, Moria's training had honed his reflexes and strengthened his stance. His father's blade was also lighter than his old sword and easier to handle. Even still, they were pressing him hard, and he was doing everything he could to stave them off.

One of the Investurants spun a spell form and cast a beam of dark purple energy at Symon. He ducked to the side, but the spell clipped his hip. While his new armor had turned away their blade strikes, this spell was not deterred. Entropic energy sapped the strength from his leg as he fell to one knee, screaming in agony. Symon called upon his Gift and channelled Healing energy into the wound. He raised his blade and studied his enemy. He hoped that he could hold them off enough for someone to intervene.

Words spoken many times in Moria's voice filled his head. "In battle, you c'n only rely on what you have at hand. If y're prayin' for salvation, you've already lost."

Symon gritted his teeth and a deep growl emanated from his chest. He spun his shoulders and delivered a powerful sideways swing. The warriors leaped back, dodging the blow with ease, but gave Symon space. Green fire sparkled in his eyes as he stared them down.

"What do you want?!" Symon roared. "Why will you not leave us in peace?!"

The pair glanced over his shoulder and stepped back as Symon called out. With no words, the two turned on their heels and darted into another hallway, pursuing a new goal. Symon shook his head. They had the advantage, retreat made little sense to him at all. Then Symon saw her.

A squad trailing in her wake, the leader of the Investurant armies swept down the hallway, her blade cutting foes like a scythe through wheat. Her twin swords blurred, striking down skeletal soldiers left and right as her gaze fell upon Symon.

The *Ombramaes.*

His blood went cold with fright. He scanned the area around him looking for an escape. The hall he had come from would be of little service, as it ran directly to the library and would dead end there. There was a branch a few yards in front of him, but with his leg, she would reach it before he did. The windows to his left were glass paned and would shatter easily, however, the three-story drop would break his bones just the same.

Symon dashed to the branching side hallway, hoping against everything that he could make it. It was the best of his bad options.

The *Ombramaes'* eyes were locked on him, and with the mask, he couldn't see her expression, just a dead-eyed stare of hate. With a quick motion, she stabbed her blade into the eye socket of the skeleton in front of her, released the handle and spun. Through that spin, she drew a dagger and launched it at Symon, slicing his cheek as he barely ducked out of the way. Without slowing, she grasped her sword and pulled it from the collapsing skeleton as she stepped forward, filling the hallway before the exit.

Symon scrambled on the tile, stopping short of her.

"Don't run from me, Symon!" she screamed.

Again, the ice ran through his veins as terror threatened to take him. "What do you want from me?"

"Oh, the same thing I've always wanted. You to suffer."

"Why?"

She pulled her mask back, and revealed her face. Underneath was actually a quite beautiful woman. Her blue skin, bright violet eyes, tall ears, and a smile that was slightly fierce with four little pointed fangs, like a canine or Ennedi would have. Her face appeared younger than Symon had imagined. She appeared to be somewhere in her middle years. But with her reputation and the original war, even knowing that the Mumvuri were a bit longer lived than mere Humans or Ennedi, he expected a bit more age. Maybe she had tapped into something like Symon's sire. Just the thought of that scared him to his core.

"Because I hate your very existence," she spat. "It surprised me to find you in Highston. I hadn't seen you since you were a mere babe. When Kyrn took you and Taryk away from me."

"What do you mean?"

"Taryk was at least useful," the *Ombramaes* said. "You were an abomination. Kyrn stole you. I told Kyrn to leave. I warned him that if he interfered, I would kill him. The two of you were mine, and I would handle it. You would be my last sacrifice, and with it, your brother and I would have enough power to finish this war once and for all! But Kyrn stole you. Stole you both!"

Taryk's name sounded wrong in her mouth. It was inhuman, monstrous even. Symon was convinced she was lying. "We would never betray our sire. And our sire would not betray us."

"Oh, you're right," she laughed, mirthlessly. "He betrayed me. Stole you and ran off! I searched for years, but never in my life would I have thought that he would return to the center of it all. To that Gods-forsaken den of corruption known as Highston. He was much bolder than I ever believed possible."

"So you were just going to kill me? An innocent child?"

"I told you. You were a mistake. An aberration. But since you were born, there was no reason not to take your Soul, and channel it into something useful."

"You are psychotic."

"You're naive."

"What do you want from me now?" Symon growled. "Are you here to finish the job?"

"Nothing would please me more! But I grow tired. You were barely worth the effort then, you haven't made it any better since." The Ombramaes sneered at him. "I'll make you the same deal that I made Kyrn. Leave. Give me your brother, hand over the Stone, and I'll let you live."

"You can take the Shard for all I care!' Symon replied. "But I do not know where my brother is, nor would I ever give him to you."

"LIAR!" she screamed. "Give him to me, or I will destroy you and take him!"

Symon roared back, "I don't know where he is!"

Her eyes tightened and that cold gaze fell upon him once again. "You are just like Kyrn. You are pathetic and I've had enough of you."

"Why do you hate us so? Your own children?"

The *Ombramaes* raised an eye at the comment, a touch of confusion on her face.

"*Silokoval!*"

She was blasted to the side as a crack of force struck her and the echo of Jesse's words rang through the chamber. Symon could see Caleb and Jesse standing there in the hallway to his right. Caleb had brought another Welengam with him. He stood straighter than normal and summoned power into his voice. "You are unwelcome in my home, Master of Shadows. Leave now."

The *Ombramaes* snarled and gestured her squad forward. Chaos erupted as the skeleton warriors and the Investurant soldiers clashed. Swords clanged, flesh was rent, and bones broke in a violent symphony. All the time, the *Ombramaes* kept her eyes on Symon.

The Eneedi marvelled as Jesse drafted the form for a daylight globe. The spell was quick for him and Jesse's deft fingers spun through it effortlessly. As he completed, the Master flung a spell from her hand striking Jesse's own form. All of the energy he had drafted into the form was sucked up and dissipated. The bracing form, devoid of power, broke open and washed away with no effect.

"What the fuck was that?" Jesse asked, shock riding through his voice.

Caleb said from behind him, "That was our sign to leave."

Symon scrambled to his friends and they backed away.

"*Ombramaes!*" a voice called out. A soldier appeared from down the hall. The soldier and the Master exchanged quick words, and then she turned. "You get another chance at life, it seems. If I come back. I expect your brother returned to me, heed my words. Or I shall kill you then."

A portal opened behind her, and the squad stepped through. Symon could see them stepping through and dropping out of sight. The shadow gate snapped shut behind the Master and the threat seemed to be over. But the adrenaline was still pumping through them.

Jesse's eyes were still wide. He turned to Caleb and asked, "What did she do to me?"

"I believe that was a counter-spell. I have heard of them, but I have never seen anyone cast one."

"Counter spells?"

"Yes, spells intended to do exactly what she did. Diffuse your spell before it could form. Negate the magic entirely."

"And that's a thing?" Jesse asked. "We can just fuck with someone's spell like that?"

"Apparently," Caleb said. "It takes skill, to absorb the Essence and break the structure without causing an ill advised effect."

"Zenesul had taught us to Interrupt. To break a caster's concentration, but it relied on them not having drawn from the Arcane. It would be mad to do otherwise," Symon added.

"Yes, this is very dangerous if not done properly. She's a much stronger caster than we realized."

"Or I'm just a shit caster," Jesse said, dejected.

"No, that was on her skill alone," Caleb said.

"Could she have countered you?"

Caleb thought about that, his eyes replaying the scene. "I'm not sure. You've gotten very good at that spell, but I'm still faster at it. It would have been close."

Jesse turned away, "Right."

Caleb put his hand on Jesse's shoulder. Jesse reached up and held his hand and slowly turned back. "I know. I'm just letting it get to me. I just want to be better than I am."

"You've gotten very good. But there will always be people out there better than us."

"Better than me."

"No, better than us. I have had masters from Asoterra who trained me. Their form of Arcana is still outside of my skills. And the Father makes them pale in comparison." Caleb looked at Jesse. "All you can do is be better tomorrow than you are today."

"Those are words that my sire said to me often," Symon said.

Caleb smiled, "It's a common saying here. Family members are masters of their craft and pass it to the next generation. Be it smithing or Arcana, it is the same."

"Can I say how fucked up it is that we are having a philosophical discussion after we just survived a fucking attack?!" Jesse asked.

The three all looked at each other, and the reality of it hit them. Finally, Symon said, "Apparently we are just getting used to it." Nervous laughter escaped them, and they shook their heads.

"So, what did she want from you?" Jesse asked Symon. "You seemed to be in the thick of things."

"She wanted my brother. Taryk."

"Your dead brother?"

"She called him by name. She seemed to believe he was with us."

"My friend," Jesse said, "that is fucked up."

"Yes, it is. But she said that he belonged with her."

"So, it's true," Caleb said. "She is our mother?"

"I do not know" Symon said, remembering the look of question on her face. "I am not sure what she is. But I am afraid. I am very afraid." Symon's ears dropped and his shoulders shook. Jesse realized his friend was crying and ran to hold him. Caleb came around and put his arms around Symon's waist and the three stood there, letting him break. Symon finally lifted his head from Jesse's shoulder and looked at him. "I do not know what to do."

"Nothing changes," Caleb said. "We avoid this as best we can. They wanted the Shard, and from the words of her officer, now they have it. If she returns, we will defend you. But I cannot see it being worth the risk again."

Symon watched Caleb and Jesse as they stood in front of him. Their arms linked and their shoulders close. They had grown together quite quickly in the short time they had been seeing each other, and seemed happy. He could only smile at that. With all the terror, he had to think of the little joys or risk breaking down again. His embarrassment tinged his ears and finger pads pink. He knew he shouldn't be, but he was. They expected him to be strong, so he would be.

>*Symon. She hunts me. We must talk.*< Symon's head rang. The voice was everywhere at once, overwhelming his senses. Even speaking with the spirits, he had never had someone speak to his mind like this.

"Who are you?" he called out.

Caleb and Jesse turned to him. "What?"

>*You know me, brother. I am Taryk. I am here.*<

"Where are you?"

The two other boys looked puzzled. "Who are you talking to?"

>*Long ago. Trapped in blade. Tried to speak. Like father. Your will is strong.*<

"My brother. Someone trapped him in my sword." Symon said to Caleb and

Jesse with a question in his voice. "Caleb?"

"Other than a Soulbound weapon from the Investurants, I have nothing," the young mage said. "I'll ask the Father and the Council about anything like this. And if not, we'll start looking for it in the library. I know it seems overwhelming, but we'll get through this, Symon. I promise."

>*We must talk soon.*<

"Symon?" Jesse asked.

"The 'how' is not important," he said, ignoring the voice. "I will deal with my brother myself. This is all attached to the conflict. Irrelevant. We move on, as we promised."

"You sure we can?"

"I am not," Symon said. "But we will try."

"Agreed," Caleb said.

Jesse shrugged. "Alright. If you two say so."

42

Delicate Balance of Life

Jesse followed Symon as they walked into the common room of a tavern held within the ward they called home. Symon was being cagey, but Jesse let him guide them. His friend had said that he had intended to do this earlier, but the attack at the palace had thrown a stick in the cogs. There was joy in the Ennedi's eyes, but also a touch of fear. Jesse knew Symon well enough that it meant the big guy had a secret he wanted to reveal. Jesse was just giving him time.

"Master Cyl'Karrick!" a Gnomish tavern keeper cried out. The bar was shorter than many Jesse had visited, being that the vast majority of the patrons were Gnomes or Ukko. Jesse scanned the room and saw meals served from a full kitchen, and one of the best selection of wines and ales in the area.

"Nice," Jesse whispered.

The Gnome smiled, "I have your room prepared, it's right this way."

"Master Kin'Garo, I have asked that you call me Symon."

The Gnome smiled, "And yet, you continue to call me 'Master' the same. When you call me by my name, I shall call you by yours."

"Of course," Symon said. "Parin, please lead the way."

"My pleasure, Master Cyl'Karrick," Parin said with a wink. Jesse laughed and punched Symon in the shoulder. The barkeep leapt down from the raised platform behind the bar. "Just down the hall here, my lads."

"They'll always get you!" Jesse teased his friend. "You always fall for it."

Symon chuckled, and said, "Yes, but I will continue to try."

Jesse smiled at the exchange, seeming to endlessly be pleased by Symon's continuing struggle with over formal exchanges. Parin led the two down a lengthy hallway panelled in well burnished oak. He opened the farthest door on the right, and waved them in. The two entered a small private dining chamber with two high-backed, cushioned chairs and a tall polished wood table. A silver platter with wine, water, meats, and cheeses laid out before them as a welcoming snack.

It reminded Jesse of one of the private nooks back at the Duck and Tackle. Mistress Daysleeper prided herself on being a host for secret conversations held between anonymous parties. A flood of nostalgic memories washed over Jesse and he smiled once again.

"Master Parin, this is quite nice, thank you," Symon said.

The gnome bowed quickly and smiled at Symon. "You are quite welcome. I will begin the feast straight away, and shall bring you the first course completed shortly."

Jesse plopped into a chair, while Symon sat opposite of him. The Isnashi kicked his feet up on the table. "What's with all the fanciness, big guy?"

Symon shifted uncomfortably. "I am not trying to put on airs, but I wanted to invite you out to a nice dinner. Parin has a wonderful chef here at the Silver Lantern. It is a special night for me, and I wanted to share it with you."

"Well, I've been eating fancier since we got here. So, I guess a bit more practice won't hurt." Jesse laughed but his friend sat scratching nervously at his jacket cuffs. "I'm kidding. What's so special?"

Symon sat quietly for a moment. He reached over and poured a small glass of wine from the pitcher and took a sizable swig. "Well, I am not sure where to begin."

"Just say it, man. If it's special, it should be easy to say it. What's got your tongue?"

"It is just my nerves are getting the best of me. I fear that if I say it out loud, it will end up being a dream or fade away. I barely believe that it is possible, and I am so excited."

Jesse's boots hit the floor as he leaned towards the table. "Shit, Symon! Now you got me all wondering. What is it?"

"Moria and I are to be wed."

Jesse's eyes widened in surprise and he spit a small piece of cheese out of his mouth. "Are you shitting me?"

"No. No jest. We agreed that it was what we both wanted. We cannot see any reason why we should not act on our wishes." Symon hesitated, and Jesse saw his nostrils flare. That subtle sign that Symon was testing Jesse's scent for his true feelings.

Jesse smiled. "Thirteen Hells! That's amazing!"

"Really?"

"Fuck yeah!" Jesse laughed. "She's amazing! Scary as all get out from time to time, but amazing! And better than you deserve!"

Symon beamed and laughed heartily. "Thank you, my friend. I hoped you would approve."

"Of course I approve. What'd you do? Did you knock her up? Are you marrying her for her money? Is she marrying you for your money? How'd you close the deal?"

"Are you saying that I could not turn her heart on my own?" Symon asked sarcastically.

"That's exactly what I am saying!"

Jesse grabbed the pitcher and refilled their drinks. Parin came in and set down the first plate, an array of baked meat pies with several tins of sauces for dipping.

Jesse snatched a pie and took a bite. He looked to Symon. "So, spill. What happened?"

"She is just different. We love each other greatly. I have been with other women, and I thought I had known love before. Not like this. It is different with Moria."

"You're really smitten aren't you?"

"Indeed." The Ennedi sighed heavily in relief. Jesse reached out and stroked his hand. Symon stared at Jesse and continued, "I was truly concerned that it would upset you."

"Why?"

"I just did not want to put any undue pressure on you. Considering that Moria and I did not form our relations until after you and Prince Caleb had started courting each other, I did not want to rush you."

"Oh," Jesse said. He smiled warmly at the large lion-like man. "You're something else. I didn't even think about that."

"So, you are good?"

"We're fine," Jesse said. "I love you, man."

"So, the prince and you?"

"Yeah, we've been having a great time. He took me out to see the Black Yards and he showed me where all the Deacons do the Raisings. And he's really good at..." Jesse paused. "You know, I'll just say, we're good."

"So the attack on the palace did not disrupt you?" Symon asked.

"Oh, Hells yes!" Jesse grinned. "But it kinda helped, too. Caleb was really busy for a few days after it all happened, but he said it made things easier. They don't have to decide what to do with the Shard, and Highston made its bed, so it can lay in it."

"It is crazy to think of. Everything we have been through that led us here. To have someone who I have viewed as a brother, who I trust with everything, to form a relationship with the unknown actual brother who I never knew. It is just a magical circumstance."

"It's fucking crazy!"

"Yes. Yes, it is."

"But it's REAL nice," Jesse smirked. "You know, I'm really glad you came in and wrecked my life."

"I still sometimes feel guilty about it," Symon replied.

Jesse put his hand on Symon's and comforted him. "No, it's cool. It got me here and gave me Caleb. It really worked out."

"I am glad of that. Do you miss Highston?"

"Yeah, it's fucked up, but I do, from time to time. You?"

"Sort of," Symon smiled. "Mainly, I miss Thorn and Master Zenesul."

"You said it!" Jesse laughed. "I miss them, too! But man, she hated it here. She's always going to enjoy being a criminal, and this place is too... nice."

"I was trying to help you both, but I did not realize I was trying to force her into something she was not. I see that now."

"Don't feel bad. We both were. I didn't even know what she was missing back home." Jesse shook his head, remembering the shame of his neglect. "I never even asked. But I'm glad she's gone home."

"Yes. And they are doing okay."

"You've been checking in on them? Getting word from Highston?"

"I have obtained a spell to allow me to communicate with them."

"Oh, Distant Message? Argyle and I used to use that all the time."

Symon smirked, "It appears that everyone remembered this spell but I."

"Moria remind you?"

"Yes," Symon threw a bread roll at Jesse, who caught it deftly. "She purchased the spell for me. It took me a few days to pin down the details, but it is not too dissimilar to how I speak with the dead. Other than it is a Mental connection, not a Soul connection. Now that I have learned it, it is not terribly taxing."

"Nice!" Jesse said. The Isnashi remembered how boring the form had been when he had seen it. "Argyle tried to show it to me a few years back, but I couldn't get the hang of it. But they're okay?"

"Indeed," Symon nodded. "Zenesul has based himself right in the thick of things. He is sneaking refugees out of Highston through the underground. He says that with some of the younger representatives allied with the Shadow, they are stamping out any who would resist the new regime.

"Thorn says she is back to work," Symon continued, "and with Zenesul tapping into the Bright Guilds, she has been able to gain influence with some of the smaller street gangs and organize them. With time, they may become a Guild of their own."

"That devious little bitch!" Jesse laughed. "She always said she would run her own crew one day. But that was fast!"

"She says that the chaos is exactly what was needed."

"Sounds right." Jesse took a deep drink of his wine and leaned back in his chair. "She always is, eventually." He looked at Symon and thought about how significant the changes in their lives had been over the last year. Jesse barely recognized himself. "So, we just stay here. We live our lives, be happy with our new lovers. And the world just keeps going on?"

"For now, that would seem prudent." Symon sipped his wine. "It does not help with the feeling of guilt, though."

"Welcome to my life, big guy. I'm finally happy, and it feels like I shouldn't be."

"Well, my friend, I say... fuck it. We deserve our happiness. Let the world manage its own troubles. '*If a leader spends his energy attempting to manage the intangible factors of battle beyond his control in an attempt to ensure victory, he instead shall lose the ability to control the factors within his grasp and find defeat*.'"

"Well, that's cheery," Jesse deadpanned.

"Yes, my sire's library is full of tactical wisdom such as that." Symon reached out and held his goblet before Jesse. "A toast. To us. To our achievements of happiness. And to my sire's tactics, that shall let us enjoy what we have worked so hard to obtain."

"Well, shit. If it's tactics, I can't argue with your dad." Jesse clinked his goblet to Symon's, and they both drank deeply. He smirked again and slyly looked at Symon. "So, Moria? Are you sure you ain't tricking her?"

Symon waited until Jesse started another sip before he said. "Well, she is pregnant, that is true."

Wine sprayed across the table as Jesse sputtered and coughed. "What?!" He wiped his chin with a napkin and dried the front of his tunic. "Do you just wait for me to do that?"

"Yes, I do, actually. It is amusing."

Jesse threw the napkin at Symon's face and Symon snatched it from the air. "You asshole! She's not really pregnant... Is she?"

"I think she may be. Her smell has changed. She does not know yet, but based on my medical books, she exhibits all of the early signs. I do not wish to put her on edge, so I will let her discover it naturally, as she should. But, yes, I may be a sire myself soon."

"I was just fucking joking man!"

"I know, but it is possible. It is not the reason for our marriage. Again, the marriage was her idea, and she is still unaware."

"Wait. She asked you?"

"Well," Symon smiled. "I would say we asked each other, but it was her idea first. I did meet all the formal requirements that I desired. I spoke with her parents, I presented her a marriage band, the whole deal."

Jesse giggled. "You're so formal!"

Symon shrugged. "Old bones, old ways."

Symon passed the guards on his way through the palace and down the now familiar hallway leading to Caleb's chambers. He paused at the door and Caleb's personal Welgeid stepped out to greet him "Oh, wonderful!" Caleb's voice said cheerily through the glowing control gem. "You're here, please come in."

The doors swung open and Symon thanked the skeletal soldier as he strode into the chamber. Symon examined the room, taking in the sea of marvelous blue decorations. His imagination took over, as it often did on his visits, as Symon thought of all the stories behind the trinkets and treasures adorning Caleb's shelves. Symon also noticed the two additional Welgeid stationed inside his door chamber.

"Heed them no mind, Symon," Caleb greeted.

"Good morning, Caleb,." Symon said. "Thank you for the invitation. I have been trying to arrange an audience with you, but your schedule has been intense."

"It has been," Caleb agreed. "Things are still on higher alert, but I still strive to make some time. I apologize for the early hour, but was afraid that if I didn't call on you now, the day would escape me once again." Caleb was still dressed in his night clothes, a pair of black silk pants, and a bluish-purple robe. Symon made a mental note to barb Jesse with some vivacious comments when he got home.

"I understand."

"Can I offer you anything to eat?"

"No, I ate before you called. I would not say no to a refresher, if it were offered."

Caleb pointed to a silver pitcher which was chilled and beaded with condensation. "Help yourself."

Symon spied Reneforte in the corner, and knew that Caleb was appeasing one of Symon's former requests and appreciated it. Ever since Jesse and Moria had mentioned it, Symon had paid more attention to servants, both living and undead, and preferred to take care of common tasks himself, if possible. Caleb would traditionally dismiss his servants during their visits to ease Symon's discomfort.

"I have a topic to discuss with you, but you also requested an audience. Who would you prefer to go first?" Caleb asked.

"I am sure your topic is more valuable than mine, but mine will take little time," Symon said. "If you would allow, I can get mine out of the way first."

"Of course."

"Moria and I have agreed to be wed. We will be planning a wedding soon."

"My sincerest congratulations."

Symon blushed, the insides of his ears exposing the reddened flesh as he was overcome with joy. "Thank you."

"You're welcome. Please let me know what I can do to help make the day special for the two of you."

"Much appreciated, but Moria and I hope to keep it simple."

"I wish you luck. I imagine it will become a grand event before you know it, and I stand ready to assist when you need me." Caleb allowed a small smirk to cross his lips. "But no matter, whatever the event, big or small, I wish you two the best."

"And you will be there?"

"If I am invited to be, of course."

"Of course you are invited!" Symon said excitedly. "You're special to both of us. And Jesse. It would not be the same without you."

Symon saw small tears in Caleb's eyes, and the light of the morning sun sparkled at the corners of them. The Prince's voice trembled as he said, "Thank you. It is so wonderful to have ACTUAL friends."

"Yes, it is. I am still getting used to it as well," Symon agreed. "So, what did you need from me?"

"Jesse, well it started with Jesse, but it's something that I wanted to talk to you about."

"An issue with Jesse and me?"

"No, no, it is not that at all," Caleb said, frowning.

"I apologize," Symon said. "I do not mean to interrupt. Please continue."

"Yes, Jesse and I have been sharing stories of our lives with one another. He told me of many events and a story of the night he showed you his wings for the first time."

"Ah," said Symon, nodding. "Yes, that was an interesting series of events."

"Is it true that you saved his life?"

"Well, to a certain point."

"Explain," Caleb said.

"The Hunter, Hasukawa, diverted the attacker, Rhon, and used a Soul Binding Arcana to hold Jesse's Soul and spare him from the finality of death." Symon recalled the night clearly. It was the first time he had nearly lost his friend. "Afterwards, I merely healed the wounds he had suffered at that villain's hands."

Caleb shook his head. "It was dangerous."

"There was little choice."

"Yes, but even with your Gift, you must know that Arcana has a price. That is what I brought you here to discuss. I needed to speak with you about the dangers that Healing can be. The nature of your Gift means bypassing safety guards that structured spells provide."

"Oh, yes. The Soul Reaping. I know."

Caleb's eyes went wide in surprise. "You know?"

"I do," Symon said, his ears twitching for a moment with mild embarrassment. "It was one of the first things I looked for in my sire's library."

"Fascinating. How did you figure it out?"

"I had a suspicion that something was going on before I left the Federation. It was not any one thing, it was, in fact, a series of things that led me to my concerns."

Caleb sat up and turned his full attention to Symon. He poured a glass of water from the pitcher which was flavored with lemons and berries, and nodded to Symon to continue.

"The first time I exposed my Gift, it was to heal a stonemason who had taken a horrid fall from scaffolding. His head had struck the pavers of the street and cracked open.

"I could tell the wound was fatal," Symon recalled, "and something inside me awoke. I just knew how to fix it. It was something I talked to Master Zenesul about at great length, no spell form, just an instinctive casting that pulled his Life force back into his Body and made him whole again.

"For days afterwards, I had splitting headaches and fatigue. But I wrote it off as having never touched my Gift before."

"A reasonable, if incorrect assumption."

Symon smiled at Caleb, "Yes. I know that now."

"Go on."

"Well, as you may know, Master Zenesul laid down the foundations of spell theory with me, as well as Jesse over the next few months. I struggled with the complexities of casting forms and the speed of spell work, but I never had a physical reaction again. So I started to look more into the balance of Essence."

"Yes, each spell exacts a price from the Material realm. To accommodate for introducing Arcane energy into reality, something must be lost."

"Exactly. But I still could not determine how to calculate it. With spell forms, it is easy to see the formula. Unless of course, you are Jesse and seem to cheat at everything."

Both Caleb and Symon smiled at each other, and Caleb responded, "Yes, he's innovative."

"Indeed. So, the night you spoke of with Jesse was the second Healing. It was where I understood the cost of Healing. Jesse had been in bad shape. His wounds were severe enough that without help he would pass away. I was concerned he was beyond my powers. With Hasukawa's encouragement, I called my Gift and pushed his body back to whole.

"When he breathed again..." Symon smiled. "I was so happy and so relieved. But the following day, I could barely breathe. The impact of his wounds, the scope of damage took a toll on my own Life force. The recoil of energy had snapped one of my ribs. I was not able to leave my bed for nearly a day. It became obvious at that moment that I needed to learn more about the Balance of Essence before I inadvertently put myself into the same danger that I seemed to be trying to avoid for others."

Caleb frowned. "Jesse did not tell me about that."

"He does not know."

"Why?"

Symon smiled at Caleb's concern. "I know he would hold himself accountable. The guilt would weigh on him greatly and he would not forgive himself." Symon growled softly. "It is not his fault that a madman had struck him down, and it was my decision to risk myself out there to heal him. There was no need to burden him with those dark details while they were outside of his influence."

"That's a remarkable insight, brother."

Symon's ears turned red, and his eyes turned down. "No, no."

"You truly are an honorable man. It is nothing to shy away from." Caleb paused, letting the emotion of the memories and trauma fade away for Symon. "So all of this led you to your sire's library?"

"Yes, yes it did." Symon reached out and poured another glass for himself and took a sip. "That and Deacon Baktu. The pain of the injuries I sustained while Healing were obviously lesser than the wounds of the victims, so I figured there was a ratio of transference that could be found."

Symon smiled slyly, "And I supposed that if Jesse could cheat the balance on minor spells, then there must be a similar way for me to cheat at this as well."

Caleb laughed, his normally meek voice taking a musical quality as it rang in the chamber. "He's such a bad influence on us."

Symon laughed as well, "He is."

The two men sat for a moment sipping their drinks as Symon collected his thoughts. The next part of the explanation, the things he had discovered in Kyrn's journals, would border on heretical in Vargarden culture. He thought that Caleb might appreciate the spellcraft, so he chose to proceed.

"As I expected, once I found my sire's journals, the balance was clear. The fact that he was a studied Necromantic Healer, instead of a Gifted, actually was a blessing for this. Seeing the healing spell forms drawn out showed the transference in a way that I am not sure that I would have ever seen, otherwise."

"If I remember, the influx of your Life energy to shape the spell, then it drafts the Life of the subject of your casting. The larger the gap, the more Life the form requires. If there's not enough…"

Symon nodded, "The bridging of the Veil with the caster's Soul Essence. Tapping into the Veil and using your own Soul to guide the Life energy into the body and reestablish the connection between Body, Life, and Soul so that the subject lives naturally."

"And the damage to your Life force and your Soul must be recovered at the correct rate, or you will do irreparable harm."

"Which is where my sire's idea might surprise you."

"Oh?"

Symon stood up and walked to the center of the room. He drew a small Light Essence shape, and then filled a Spell Brace form to draw in the air. It was far more inelegant than Caleb's ability to draw spells in the visible spectrum, but it would serve the purpose he needed.

Symon drew a shape he had studied many times allowing the Light to fill it. Caleb joined him and ducked under his arms to stand with his back to Symon's chest, crouching slightly to keep Symon's eye line clear.

Symon finished the form quickly and stepped back allowing Caleb to stand taller and examine the form. Caleb's shoulders hunched and Symon walked around to watch his brother. "Inconceivable!" Caleb cried, waving his hand through the form and dissolving the display.

"Yes, I thought as much."

"Such a casting would be at the cost of your own Soul!"

"Yes, but my power resonance would increase. I would be able to Heal more severe wounds without the recoil.”

“But the Reaping will mean that you may lose your Soul in the Veil when you yourself pass. You would be unreachable by Necromantic magic. Your Soul could be consumed to whatever is beyond the Veil.”

“My soul was already threadbare after pulling Jesse back. It was far more damaging than I believed. Deacon Baktu confirmed that it would be years before the damage would recover and I would be free to Heal again. Trading Soul for Life force is a stronger balance.

“I refuse to let the fear of the unknown restrict my will to help those I do know.”

Caleb shook his head slowly. “You are so much like the Nemukku. He was a brilliant mind, and he was willing to break any traditions needed to achieve his goals. A dangerous, but ultimately brilliant mind.”

“I am only trying to help those I can.”

“And that is why you succeed. I am beyond impressed, but it is still hard for me to set aside millennia of traditions.”

“Well, I cannot speak to my sire’s ability to do that, but for me,” Symon smiled. “I never knew enough about the traditions to worry about breaking them.”

“Remember when I called you a rule-breaker and Jesse laughed?”

“He can never know.”

“He wouldn’t believe us anyway!” Caleb laughed. “And Lady Moria?”

“Yes. She knows it all.”

“How did she react to it?”

“It was easier for her,” Symon said. “With everything she knew about Kyrn, she already knew what the situation could be. ‘What is done is done.’ Her military discipline allowed her to accept the reality of the losses I already faced.”

“But she’s not going to let it go so easily.”

“No, of course not. She is already plotting trips to Asoterra and other regions of study to see if there are alternatives we could use to overcome this.”

“Well, let me and Jesse know. We will join you on your journeys.”

“As a honeymoon?”

“With boundaries, of course,” Caleb said smiling. “So is the Soul transference how Kyrn extended his life?"

"Yes, when one no longer concerns themselves with the longevity of their post-life existence, one is no longer bound by the limitations of protecting it. So he focused on protecting his Life instead. With effort, he figured out a way to extend his life by ten times its traditional span."

"Regeneration?" Caleb asked.

"Nearly. A constant stream of Healing to repair the damage of age. Eventually, the Body will break down, but as Alvan and Ukko have taught us, the Body can survive for centuries if given the appropriate chance."

"Genius."

Symon smiled. "Kyrn really was a talented Healer. If he hadn't been forced to war, I imagine he would have pushed many more limits."

"Tell me more."

43

Spirit of Celebration

Symon sat with Argyle and watched Caleb, Moria, and her mother dismiss the final guests. The evening had been a long affair of feasting and celebrations. The large dining hall was elegantly decorated with celebratory beads and flowers, and lit by thousands of candles. With the last of the attendees on their way, Moria smiled and waved goodbye to Symon. They had decided she would stay with her family until the wedding.

"It was a spectacular affair," Argyle said. "The palace provided a grand contribution. Very well organized, as is all they do."

"It is all thanks to the Prince. He put this together for Moria and me. Allowing our families to meet and celebrate." Symon glanced around at the tables still laid out. "It is still fascinating to think that my family is considered small by Vargarden standards. There must have been thirty of my relatives here."

"Yes, and it seems that while spousal members vary, the Ennedi blood runs strongest in your lineage."

"I am still researching why certain bloodlines mix and provide hybrid offspring, like Nymphs, Alvas, and others, while certain bloods, such as Ennedi, seem to stray towards a dominant child. It is a fascinating subject."

"Was this a topic your father's books have information on? It is a curious subject matter."

"No," Symon smiled. "This seems to be an interest I alone have. It is nice to have my own identity again and deviate from my sire in that arena."

Jesse sauntered up to the table and grabbed a chair. He had dressed immaculately, wearing a silver and white tunic, with trousers that were striped in bright greens and blues, that brought out subtle highlights of his wing's current molt. "What we talking about?"

"Interspecies reproductive probability theory and the inheritance of racial traits," Symon said with a dry smile.

Jesse exchanged an exasperated look with Argyle. He glared at Symon. "Well, it's a good thing I showed up to end that."

"You asked," Symon said. "It is a fascinating subject."

"No, it's really not, Symon. I'm sorry." Jesse looked at him with a wry grin. "I swear, sometimes, you want to bore me to death, then raise me from the dead and bore me all over again."

Symon shook his mane out in mock frustration. "I attempt to expand your limits and enlighten you on theoretical topics and you spurn me. you simple hedonist."

Jesse drained his goblet and smiled. "You know it. Ugh!" He laughed, mockingly. "What does Moria see in you?"

"I have it on good authority that I am 'a sexy beast.' Is that not what Thorn said you called me?"

Jesse tossed a flower from the table at Symon and giggled. "You don't forget a thing said to you, do you? Remind me to murder that bitch the next time I see her."

"Do not blame the lady Thorn for your words," Argyle said, chuckling.

"And my mind merely remembers notable things," Symon said. "And that seemed appropriately notable."

"It is a damn good thing you're cute. Because you are dull, bitch."

The two stared at each other hard, each daring the other to break. Finally, Symon could not hold it together any longer and lost himself in a roar of laughter. Reached over to Jesse and pulled him into an embrace. "Thank you, my friend.

This evening has been most excellent."

"Well, you have to thank Caleb. He's the one that set it all up."

"I know, and I shall thank him properly," Symon said. "But I thank you, because you are the best friend I have ever had, and you being here tonight means everything to me."

"Aw, shit. You're going to make me blush."

"I mean it, Jesse. I love you. Thank you for everything."

Jesse wiped a small tear from his eye and hugged Symon again. "You're the best."

"And thank you for agreeing to stand for me at the wedding. It will be nice to be up there with my brother."

"Brothers," Jesse corrected. "Caleb will be there with us, too."

"Brothers, then."

Symon pulled Jesse into a hug and squeezed him tightly. He held his friend for a moment, allowing himself to feel the quiet peace of their friendship.

"Symon, you have a tendency to bring everyone to a sober mentality and create an existential state of being when you arrive. Are you aware of this?" Argyle asked.

"I do?"

"Ha!" Jesse laughed. "You do. You're kind of a killjoy."

"Oh, I never noticed," Symon said, flatly.

"Come on, let's go have some fun!" Jesse laughed.

"Yes. Let us go," Symon said. "Grab Prince Caleb, and we'll head to the Silver Lantern."

"Fuck yes!" Jesse cried.

The four sat in the corner booth of the common room of the Silver Lantern, and Jesse kicked back smiling. The tavernkeeper had scrambled to accommodate them, but was placated by Caleb and Symon so quickly that Jesse still marveled.

Offers of a private room were politely declined. The Prince's Welengam took positions around the interior and exterior of the bar, but were unobtrusive. Even the Deacons that escorted them had procured a table and were enjoying a meal. After the mild shock, the tavern once again resumed its state of revelry.

The remnants of that revelry laid on the table before them. Half-filled goblets of wine, empty tumbler glasses that had once contained hard spirits, and vacant trays covered in the crumbs of meat pies had collected over the two hours they had spent relaxing in the establishment.

Jesse couldn't remember ever actually seeing Symon drunk. But he had been drinking freely since they had arrived and was well into things. He seemed to be the same polite and orderly person he normally was, but just more open. Jesse sipped on his watered-down wine and smiled.

"So, you big lunk!" Jesse asked. "First girl you've ever been with... and you marry her? Well done."

"What?" Symon asked. "No, no. I have been with plenty of other women. Moria is just special."

"Wait! You've been with other girls?"

"Yes! Of course! Why would you think otherwise?" Symon asked. His words were a touch slurred, but those eyes still sparkled.

"Well... because..." Jesse hesitated.

"You have presented yourself as such a traditionalist in many ways, Master Cylkas," Argyle grinned. "It is inconsistent that your decorum would be broken in this way considering your more conservative approach to life."

"Oh?" Symon raised an eyebrow.

Jesse laughed. "What he's saying is, you've got a stick slammed up your rear end and I didn't expect it had ever come out!"

Symon pushed Jesse's shoulder playfully, nearly spilling him from the chair. "Bah! I courted a young woman when I started my apprenticeship. We had gotten pretty serious, but then her family moved to Strongwald and we were unable to keep the relationship.

"Then I courted Lara." Symon reached over to the prince's shoulder, squeezing it gently. "Caleb, you met her."

"Yes," Caleb nodded. "The young liaison from the Federation."

"Yes," Symon nodded. "She was from a more traditional family and wanted to wait until we were married to consummate the relationship. But there were pleasurable things that could be done, even beyond that limitation.

"I had been courting her for nearly a year, when I met you, Jesse. She was the one that Olivar stole from me." Symon shook his head. "It was unfortunate. She was sweet, once."

"She seemed spiteful and bitter..." Caleb trailed off, and Jesse saw a touch of blush in his cheeks as he realized his words could be taken as an insult. "To me, of course."

"Oh, that bitch you told me about?" Jesse said, taking the heat from Caleb.

"Jesse," Caleb chided.

"No," Symon smiled. "She was certainly that."

"She was a detestable woman of ill-merit," Argyle replied.

"You met her?" Jesse and Symon asked together.

"I had the misfortune of being at an orphanage within the old ward she had decided to visit. While she showed the Deacons and Housemothers a pleasant smile, any deviation from their attention revealed a puckered face of vile judgement and appraisal. I would advise not to trust her."

"Oh, great," Symon said, flatly.

"Are you aware she made accusations of misconduct against you, brother?"

"You didn't tell me that!" Jesse turned to Caleb in shock. "Symon?!"

Symon put his hands up, in protest,as he spoke. "It is not true! I did nothing inappropriate. These accusations are false."

"Of course they were," Caleb replied. "We saw the Scry of the Welgeid outside her door and witnessed the whole exchange. You were completely innocent, and it proved her to be a liar.

"I sent her on her way back to the Federation," Caleb smiled, "without fanfare or aplomb. The only thing endangered was her reputation and the requests she had presented."

Symon sighed, relief pouring out. "Thank you, Prince Caleb."

"So, you monitor the activities within the place through your Welgeid?"

Argyle asked.

"Yes, of course," Caleb said. "A network of Arcana that allows us to review any incidents that occur."

"Intriguing," the Genbu mused. "Is this an indefinite window? That seems like powerful spell craft."

"It is complex, but not indefinite. Normally, ten to twelve hours are reserved at a time. The Deacons handle the majority of it."

"Nice," Jesse laughed. He swirled his drink and leaned in to lighten the mood. "So, your only experience is a puppy love romance that took your virginity, and a crazy girl who would only let you 'pet' her, and the woman you're going to marry? Are you sure you don't want to live a bit more first?"

"Throwing stones in the past relationship arena seems a dangerous gambit, my young winged friend," Argyle said casually.

"Good point," Jesse said, immediately regretting the choice. "But still... it is a quick engagement."

Symon shrugged. "When you know, you know."

"I guess so," Jesse shrugged. "But hey, you're happy. And that's all that matters, right?!"

"Indeed," Caleb said. He raised a glass and called, "To Symon."

The four toasted and drank deeply. Jesse caught a twinkle in Symon's eye as he watched Jesse waiting for the glass to be on his lips. "Besides, I did have several experiences at the Brothels in Altazio."

Jesse caught himself and took a hard swallow of the wine before he sprayed it across the table. He gave a dark glare to Symon. "Damn you! I'm never drinking around you again."

Symon roared with laughter and caught the eyes of several patrons. Several of them raised their glasses to what was an obvious celebration. Symon raised his own in return.

Jesse smiled and leaned back. They drank another round and joked some more. He didn't want to press the issue, but he was curious about the wedding and Symon's family in general. "So, Moria will have her mother and sire there? Have you decided what to do?"

"I will not hide from my past. My sire died protecting us. Prior to that, he served Vargarden well. I will stand with my brothers at the front of the temple and be proud of the family that I have," Symon said, his head coming up high.

"Does that mean you have figured out what your dad was about?" Jesse asked. "Not the monster you thought?"

Caleb glanced at Jesse with a small look of disapproval, "Jesse."

"I know, I know. It's not polite, but was he?"

"No, Caleb, it is okay," Symon shook his head. "I have read nearly everything I can find, both about him and from him. The war reports, his previous journals, historical accounts, and everything else I could get a copy of. From what I can see, he made hard choices. But they were always to serve Vargarden.

"I think I understand him more now. There are still dark things I have to deal with, both from him and myself. Hard choices that I understand more clearly," Jesse saw Caleb and Symon exchange a knowing glance. "When we escaped Highston, I struggled with killing that Brownie thug. The one that was going to kill you."

Jesse nodded, "I remember. But it was her or me, Symon. And you chose me."

"Yes," Symon said. He punched Jesse in the arm playfully, "and on most days, it was the right choice."

"Bitch," Jesse said, laughing.

"But honestly, looking back, I did not struggle with the fact that I killed her. I struggle with the fact that I did not hesitate." He looked into the distance, gathering his thoughts. "I knew it was us or her, just like the half dozen other Investurant scouts I killed before her. And when faced with the odds, I did not falter. Even slightly.

"I knew they had to die, and I made it happen. That terrifies me. The fact I can coldly end life, because it is the correct thing to do in the moment without hesitation scares me. I think that is what my sire was struggling with, too. But instead of one life, or a half dozen scouts... it was thousands."

"Shit," Jesse said. "I guess I never had to think about it. I've always lived in a survival mode. But yeah, that's a lot of souls to hang on your shoulders."

"I think Master Yurolinto said it true when I first arrived," Symon said. "He told me 'there are many good men, but not a lot of great men. Kyrn was a great man, who grew to be a good one'."

"Then to your dad," Jesse said, raising a glass.

The quad toasted somberly and drank deeply.

"Enough of this," Caleb said, attempting to lighten the mood. "We came to this establishment to revel in joy, not the darkness of the past."

"This time it was your fault," Symon said as he pointed at Jesse.

"My bad."

"And also," Symon said. "Would you two please just sit next to each other? You keep reaching for each other and are too far apart for it to be comfortable. Just snuggle next to each other, for my sake."

Jesse grinned and slid over to the bench next to Caleb. He placed his head on Caleb's shoulder. Caleb slowly put his arm around Jesse's shoulder as if waiting for something to stop them. As they settled in, he smiled at Symon. "I guess it is just too new."

"Yes, but it is wonderful!" Symon smiled. "Not to bring him right back up, but I just wish that my sire could be here to see this night. We spent so much time alone in Highston, separated from true friendships by a secret he could not face.

"If he could see me here, with my *rieve*, I am sure he would be elated."

Caleb laughed. "*Rieve*? You know this term?"

"Of course," Symon said. "It is Ennedi. For clan."

"It is in the Ennedi language," Caleb said. "But it is a Vargarden word."

"It is?" Jesse asked.

"Yes," Caleb nodded. "It was introduced by Maiya Kal'Khorric when she first came to Vargarden. A term she used for her two husbands, as she established her lineage here. It was quite the popular fashion for nearly a century. But they have not used it much in the last two hundred years. It is quaint."

"Then we truly are home," Symon said, nodding to his friends.

"What is old is new," Argyle said. "Traditions die hard, and the Cyl'Karric family seems to stand firm in their ways."

Caleb and Symon smiled again. "Yes, we do."

"You know you're my soul, right?" said Jesse as he slumped onto the couch next to Caleb. "Totally my soul. That's what the witch said."

"You are drunk, my angel," said Caleb, trying to take Jesse's goblet.

Jesse waved the goblet around, keeping it from Caleb and nearly spilling its contents. "I am not THAT drunk! I've only had two glasses."

"That is your third, and it is nearly empty."

"So why would that make me dru- drunk?"

"One, you drank only watered down wine at the tavern," Caleb chuckled. "Two, this is really good wine, stronger than you're used to drinking. And three, we ate nearly five hours ago." Caleb smiled shyly. "And you weigh as much as a sparrow!"

The Prince reached for the goblet, anticipating that Jesse would move it away, which allowed Reneforte to smoothly remove it from Jesse's hand. Jesse looked first one direction for his cup, then the other. "Hey!" he cried out when he couldn't find it. "Fine. If I can't have my wine, I'll drink of my soul!"

With that, Jesse leaned in and began kissing Caleb, who made no effort to stop him. The kissing was short lived, as Jesse became distracted by a worry that had gnawed at him all evening. "Caleb?"

"Yes, my angel?"

"What's going to happen to me?"

"What do you mean? Nothing is going to happen to you. We are all safe."

"No, I mean, where will I live? What will I do for money?" Jesse said, sadly. "Symon's going to want to have the house. He'll kick me out. I've got nowhere to go. I don't wanna go back to being a thief no more."

"Don't worry, my angel," smiled Caleb.

"No, really," said Jesse seriously, "I da' wanna be a Street Rat no more."

"Jesse, being a thief, or a Street Rat as known in Highston, was what you had to do to survive," Caleb said. He hugged Jesse and comforted him. "Those identities were never who you were. You are, and always were, my angel. And there is no need for that life any longer."

"But who will trust me?"

"We all trust you."

"You're not mad at me? Mad at me for stealing stuff?"

"I wish it had not been necessary for you, my angel," Caleb replied. "But no, I do not begrudge you doing what was required."

"You're talking pretty again," Jesse grinned. He touched the end of Caleb's nose with his forefinger. "'Cause you're pretty."

"Pretty, am I?" said Caleb, amused.

"Yup! And you're mine!"

With that, Jesse leaped onto Caleb, aggressively kissing his cheek and neck, pulling the front of his shirt open, and working his way down the prince's chest. Caleb made no complaints, but rather vocal sounds of satisfaction. Jesse had been very eager to show Caleb skills his past had given him. As he took Caleb into his mouth, he felt the Prince give in. Jesse felt a moment of pure joy and relief. An echo of positive benefits from Jesse's experiences, even at the hands of Xerian, reminded him that he was worthy, at last.

After Caleb was spent they laid side by side, smiling. He felt safe.

"Caleb? I'm curious about something," Jesse said. "Now that you know your parentage, what does this do to your position? Are you still the prince?"

"Why should it change anything?" Caleb asked. "I am still who I was a month ago, before we knew this. It will have more impact on the Cyl'Karrick house than the palace."

"Do you think your sire, um, the Father, knows about this?"

"I have not spoken with him directly about this matter."

"Oh," Jesse replied.

"I fail to see how he could have taken me in as an infant and not have known something of my origins."

"Oh yeah?" said Jesse, grinning, "If he knew, then why didn't they let YOU stand in for Kyrn Cyl'Karrick so they could have cleared those charges years ago?"

"I don't know," Caleb mused. "That is a very insightful question, oh angel of mine," said Caleb. Hesitantly, Jesse felt Caleb reach over to pull him into a kiss.

"Uh uh," said Jesse. "Not the couch again," Jesse stood and walked towards Caleb's room. "Bedroom."

Jesse squealed and broke out in giggles as Caleb stood suddenly and spun him around, ducked the swirling wings, and dipped him back, only to catch him and lift him in his arms.

"Bitch!" cried out Jesse with laughter. "Warn a guy when you are going to do that!"

Caleb just smiled and walked to the bedroom. "It is my turn to give you pleasure. You will not deny me this."

"But—"

"No, it is your turn." Caleb replied. "I desire to please you."

Caleb removed Jesse's pants, and mirrored what Jesse had performed earlier in the night. While he may not have the experience of Jesse, he was an apt student, and Jesse leaned back.

"Is this alright, my love?" Caleb asked.

"Of course." Jesse realized he had started softly crying. He wiped the tears from his eyes and stared upon his prince. "Of course it is."

"What's wrong, my angel?"

Caleb laid on the bed next to Jesse and took him into his arms. Jesse released whatever emotions he had pent up had finally boiled up to the surface. After a few minutes Jesse was able to calm his crying, and rolled over to face Caleb, giving him a soft yet heartfelt kiss.

Jesse said, "I'm sorry, I just got a little worked up."

"You know that I am here for you, in whatever you need."

"That's it," said Jesse softly, snuggling his face into Caleb's chest and sighing contentedly. "You are here for me. You are the first time—" The rest was cut off in unintelligible muffles.

"My love, can you repeat that please?"

Jesse met Caleb's gaze, his eyes full of affection. "I said, you silly, lovely, perfect man of my soul, that you are the first time someone has wanted to..." Jesse's face began to turn pink, his ears glowing, "to love me, and not just fuck me."

"Oh!" Caleb said.

"I'm just not used to it. And I love you more for it."

"My angel," said Caleb, squeezing Jesse against him, "We have so much to make up for. My goal in life is now to ensure that every sad memory that you may have is overshadowed by a joyous memory of me. And I wish that you will fill my life with new opportunities that I have been sheltered from before."

"Bard?"

"Paraphrased," Caleb smiled. "But true, nonetheless."

"The witch was right, wasn't she? You really are here, trying to be my soul."

"Merely trying?" grinned Caleb. It was a practiced grin, but Jesse could see warmth and comfort in it. Slowly, the real man behind the prince was breaking through.

"Succeeding, and you know it!"

Several minutes passed, as they lay there just embracing one another and rejoicing in the comfort they derived. After a time, Jesse mustered his courage once more. "What do you think the witch meant by the other half? You know, about me losing my heart?"

"I don't know, my angel," Caleb said. "Her words were unclear, but also pointed. She said to gain your soul. That seems to refer to me, or perhaps Symon and myself, as we are one. Have you paid a price with your heart?"

"I don't think so," Jesse said. "I haven't lost anything that I'm aware of."

"Then we shall watch and wait. Whatever it is, we shall handle it together."

"It better not be you," said Jesse, determination in his voice, "I'd better not lose you."

"You won't lose me, my angel."

"Promise?"

Caleb hugged him close. "I promise. I am not going anywhere, without you."

"Good," Jesse said as Caleb ruffled Jesse's hair. "Should we discuss the wedding?"

"Wedding? Are we getting married?" Jesse held his hand to his chest, filling his voice with drama. "But sir, how can we possibly marry, when I have yet to meet your family? It's so sudden! Entirely too soon!"

"Sir, you wound me!" cried Caleb, surprisingly playing along, "You have the advantage on me, having met my true sire, the Nemuku, when I myself have not!"

"Well, I'd meet the Father, if I could," Jesse said. "If he's real."

"Of course, he's real," Caleb said, frowning. "Do you doubt it?"

"Sometimes I have trouble telling if the Father is a real person, or just an idol of power, like the Gods in the Khorr. There's not a lot to work with."

"He's a bit of both, I suppose," Caleb smiled. Then he leaned in and nibbled Jesse's ear, whispering, "Are you truly implying that you would turn me down if I were to ask for your hand?"

Jesse shuddered at the sensation against his earlobe being chewed upon but was otherwise silent.

Caleb noticed the shift in Jesse's mood and his words became serious. "What is it, my angel?" he asked gently. "What has you thinking so hard?"

"You joke about marriage, but really, I wish we could."

"Why couldn't we, my angel?"

"But I'm me, and you are you." When Caleb looked confused, Jesse continued, "Look, whether you are the crown prince, or a son of the Cyl'Karrick house, you are still a noble. You have family lineage, money, responsibility, a high position in society. I'm, well, I'm just a former street thief with no skills above that former station, no family, no resources, and nothing to offer you."

"Oh, Jesse. I don't need anything from you except your love and your company."

"That's not good enough, don't you see? I have to have something to offer you, or I'm cheating you. Cheating everyone."

"Angel, look at me." Caleb waited for Jesse to turn around and look. After a moment, he nudged Jesse's shoulder, turning him over so that he could see Jesse's face. "We are not like your past. I am not like them."

Jesse started to look away, but then kept his eye contact. "I thought I loved Erin. I really did. I was fifteen, and I thought he was rescuing me. But I've felt real love now, here, with you. I would've been a kept boy, a trophy, a plaything for Erin to have sex with at his say-so. I thought he made me feel wanted. Does that make sense? Instead, you have made me want to prove myself worthy of you."

Caleb started to say something, but Jesse put a finger to his lips and continued, "I know what you are going to say, that I don't have to prove anything to you or to anyone. And you are right! I don't HAVE to prove anything. Your love makes me WANT to prove myself. To you. To anyone who might doubt us. But especially... I want to prove it to myself. I need, really need, to make myself something other than a Street Rat." Jesse finally looked away, saying, "Otherwise there will always be the possibility that I was nothing but a thieving Street Rat who got picked up by the Prince."

They sat in silence for a moment, then Caleb finally said quietly, "I think I understand. I can't promise that I will fully be able to see things from your perspective, but I will trust that you mean what you say, and will do my utmost to aid you in fulfilling this desire."

"I will hold you to that favor, my love, my soul," said Jesse. "But for now, can I ask a more immediate favor?"

"Anything, my angel."

"Can I please feel you inside me?" Jesse asked.

44

The Wedding

Symon stood in his chambers and pulled out the outfit that had been selected for the first ceremony. The schedule had been laid before him for the first of two days that would comprise his wedding. He had a list of the ceremonies that would be performed, and some assistive directions from his cousin, Falcaryn, and from Caleb as well, but whenever he asked about what to expect, everyone would just smile politely and nod at him. They told him it was best experienced firsthand and would say little more.

The whirlwind of events and emotions swirled within. Nearly one year ago, the fall of Highston had stripped his life bare. His group had arrived in Vargarden merely ten months ago, and so much had happened since then. To see the changes in his life was, at times, overwhelming.

Here he stood in his sire's house, ready to add to the legacy of his family. Symon felt closer to his sire than ever. After months of reading his journals, living in this house, Symon felt like he had a more solid identity than ever before.

He wished he could talk to Kyrn again. To tell him how much he understood now, and that he had forgiven him. To beg for his sire's forgiveness as well. All attempts to reach out to his Soul in the Veil, however, had failed.

Without a body to work with, Symon had no luck in finding his sire's Soul.

With the Soul Reaping, Symon wondered if he ever would. Kyrn could be lost beyond the Veil.

He had also attempted to reach out to his brother's Soul. Something in the way the spell structure bonded him to his sire's sword changed the path to the Veil. Whatever barrier had come down during the attack was back in place and Symon was unable to breach it. His family was there, he knew it. His inability to locate them was agony.

Symon wiped away the tear that formed in his eye and refocused. He grabbed the larger brush and began to work on his mane. He smoothed it out, rubbed oil in it to keep it darkened, and tied it behind his neck. He moved on to the smaller brush and began to methodically turn down his body's fur. The meticulous care needed was soothing to his mind, allowing him to focus on each task. Brush after brush, oil after oil, he straightened and scented himself to prepare for the day.

He pulled on his jacket, a dark violet, and some drab olive pants. Everything was trimmed in a bronze thread, all selected by Moria's mother. His family colors, violet, green, and bronze, had been selected as his personal theme for the upcoming ceremonies. Symon was just glad that they looked good on everyone.

Symon took one last glance in the mirror, made sure everything was perfect, and then walked down the hall. Argyle and Jesse were already waiting for him in the front room. Jesse was dressed in violet robes, tapered and cut to show around his wings. Argyle wore violet beads and flowers, worked into a garland draped over his neck and shoulders. He smiled at the two as he approached. "Good morning, my friends."

"Good morning..." Jesse said, a smile formed in the corner of his lips, "brother."

Symon smiled broadly and grabbed Jesse into a massive hug. "I am so glad you are here."

"So," Jesse laughed, "I'm supposed to 'stand' for you?"

"Yes," Symon nodded. "That's what I was told. That you would stand for me as I speak to the families. That you would be my patron."

"Yes," Argyle said. Argyle stood by the door and placed his giant paw on the handle. It was rare that quadrupedal Genbu came into the house, due to his size, but today was a special occasion. "From what I have heard, you need to petition the families for their approval. Jesse shall act as your patron and speak to your intentions and your value to the Yurolinto family."

"What if the families say 'No?' What do you do then?" Jesse asked.

Symon's gut twisted and he looked sideways to his friend. "I have no idea. I hope that will not happen."

"I'm just playing with you," Jesse laughed, punching Symon in the shoulder. "Of course they will say yes, you big lunk."

"Are you ready, Symon?" Argyle asked.

"Nope," Symon said.

Jesse grinned. "We gonna do it anyway?"

"Yes."

The Genbu swung the door open and Symon strode into the courtyard with his friends. Steamers, garlands, and banners of violet, green, and bronze, with flowers and paper lanterns hung between the trees and lantern posts, decorating the front of the house from wall to wall.

A dozen of his ancestors, raised as Eisgeid, were prepared, draped in violets and greens. At their head was his Grandmother's skeleton next to the Ukko priest, Baktu, who served this district. She had raised this contingent of skeletons and controlled it. It was she that would lead the procession.

"Master Cyl'Karric! You look so handsome!" the Ukko beamed. Her voice was gentle and warm. "And Masters Jesse and Argyle, you two are dashing as well."

"Thank you, Madam," Symon said, his ears flushing pink.

"Up you go!" Baktu said. She pointed to a small palanquin held by four of his ancestral Eisgeid members. Symon stepped onto a small stool in front of it and lifted Jesse onto the platform. Argyle would lope behind them, due to his massive frame, part of the ceremonial party.

"Let us begin!" Baktu cried.

The progression began its march across the city. Down every street the group walked down, people were lined up cheering and wishing good luck to Symon and the family. As instructed, Symon tossed out small candies and paper wrapped petite cakes, as an offering to the community and accepting their blessings in this union. Children ran forward and scooped up the treats with brilliant smiles and laughter.

"Wow!" Jesse breathed. "You're famous here! Look at all these people! This is kinda awesome!"

"I agree, it is awesome, but it is not because of anything special about me," Symon replied. "It is our new home. Our community. They show up like this for all. Lady Pietra's daughter was wed just two weeks ago, and they did the same thing. The entire district was out in the streets watching the parade and cheering just as loudly.

"The only difference, I suppose, is that my ceremony is stretched across multiple wards and they all celebrate."

"It's just everyone here is so happy. It's still weird, 'ya know?"

"Yes, but wonderfully so," Symon said.

"Yeah," Jesse smiled. "It is."

Symon continued to toss treats and wave to the crowds as they crossed the city. Jesse joined in as well, taking care to aim for groups of smaller children that could be missed. Argyle playfully swiped and tossed things to the children as well, laughing. Slowly, they crossed from ward to ward as they proceeded to the military churchyards, where Symon and Moria's wedding ceremonies would take place.

As they pulled up to the cathedral, the escort formed a small half circle and Eisgeid placed the palanquin at the foot of the stairs. As Symon climbed out, Argyle and Jesse took their ceremonial positions at Symon's side, while Baktu took the head of the procession, with Symon's grandmother.

Entering the church, Symon gazed at the large aisleway between split rows of pews, sitting side by side. The chamber was filled with hundreds of figures dressed in dark gray robes, sitting silently. On a raised stage behind the altar, he saw the woman who would become his bride.

Moria was dressed in a bright orange gown, her face veiled in white lace, and stood next to her mother, who was dressed in the same grey robes as the attendees.

In near unison, the heads of those gathered turned to watch the newcomers walk down the aisle. A somber tone permeated the room, contrasting starkly with the vibrant celebrations they had left behind. Symon hesitated, unsure of what to do, his nerves clenching his muscles and freezing his legs in place.

Baktu stepped onto the dais and whispered "*Tsamautu,*" casting the spell form to raise her voice. She turned to the crowd and spoke clearly to all in the room. "Honored members of the Cyl'Karrick and Yorulinto families, thank you for gathering here today. I present Master Symon Cyl'Karrick who has come to seek your blessing to unite your families with the marriage of Moria Yorulinto, daughter of Rakar and Escheila.

"Speaking for Master Cyl'Karrick is Jesse Olben," she continued. Jesse winked at Symon and joined the Deacon. "Please hear the words of Master Olben, *rieve* of Master Cyl'Karrick, and friend of Vargarden."

Jesse pulled a small scroll from his belt pouch and turned to the crowd. The Isnashi smiled and his eyes lit with the bravado and boldness that was his personality. Symon, however, could smell his friend's discomfort. Together they had faced many threats and dangers, but Symon could see that standing in front of this many eyes was a challenge that brought out an unfaced fear in Jesse. Symon considered himself lucky to have such a friend.

"Eh, hello everyone," Jesse started, his eyes drifting to the scroll in his hand. "We are here that Symon may seek the blessing of both families to marry Moria. I stand here, in his colors, to show you that I already bless this union. Moria and Symon have shown me that they have become one already. They are servants of Vargarden, they are servants of their families, and in this union, they will be servants of each other as well."

Symon could hear Caleb's influence in the words. The Ennedi scanned the crowd to see if he could find the prince, but was unable to locate any familiar faces in the sea of gray.

"While he was raised in Highston," Jesse continued, "looking at him, I see that Vargarden has been with him the entire time. When I met Symon, we were separated greatly by social classes. While, according to the customs of the Khorric Federation, we should not be friends, Symon looked beyond such limitations. He saw me as an equal, welcomed me to his side, and through tragedy and terror, we have been by each other.

"His sire, Kyrn, instilled the values of Vargarden and servitude into him and it was untouched by the ways of his surroundings. And while his sire cannot be here today, I speak as his *rieve* to express his deeds in proving his servitude to the community and the ways of Vargarden." Jesse waved to the crowd giving them a sheepish smile. "Thank you."

A small murmur swept through the room and in the back of the crowd a few members on each side of the aisle rose to their feet slowly. In a single synchronized movement, each person standing pulled back their gray robes, exposing bright colored vestments underneath. Community members of each family, violet and green on Symon's side, orange and green on Moria's, showed those colors as signs of their approval and remained standing.

A lone figure in gray stepped away the front-row of Symon's side and approached Jesse. The figure placed a flower in Jesse's hand and said in a deep voice, "I give you this as my acceptance of your words, and honor your request. Please pass this to the groom."

Jesse stepped before Symon and placed the flower in his mane, tucking it behind his ear. Symon hugged his friend tightly and the Isnashi whispered into his ear, "That was terrifying."

"I know, and I love you, brother. Thank you."

"We're not done, yet," Jesse laughed. The Isnashi's eyes darted to the side of the room, and Symon followed his gaze. Standing in a small, tucked away chamber, Rakar, dressed in orange vestments, stood next to a weatherworn and shadowed figure with twin swords on his back. Rakar whispered something to the man, gave him a hug, and then entered the cathedral proper.

"Over there," Jesse whispered, pointing. Symon's eyes turned to the opposite wall, and from a similar chamber, Caleb dressed in violet, emerged as well. The two strode to the front of the altar, each taking their place and nodded to one another.

Rakar cleared his throat. "My fam'ly has watched over the Cyl'Karrick grounds since the Khorr' campaign. When Symon came home, t'was a great joy. And since that day, the boy ain't done nothin' but pour over his his'try and books.

"When not there, he's been with my kin," Rakar said. His voice was tight, his words clipped and short. Public speaking was not his forte, either. "He has been a student of his fam'ly since comin' home. He's learnin' our ways, and makin' strides to become one of us. I stand here, in his colors, to show you I already bless this union."

"I, too, speak to Symon's dedication to learning the ways of his heritage," Caleb said smiling. He placed his hand on Rakar's shoulder and stepped forward on the dais. His voice was clear and comfortable. "When Symon arrived, he agreed to inherit the legacy of the Cyl'Karrick family, both good and bad. While I don't believe he truly understood the ramifications at that moment, his decision spoke clearly of his character.

"Symon is a man who thinks of others," Caleb said. "He spoke first of his companions, and how they would be treated. He has responded to threats against our nation, placing himself in harm's way to protect others. He embodies the values of self-sacrifice, inheritance, and long-term well being as we do. Through each moment, he proves himself to be a model of Vargarden tradition. I would share with you one of those moments.

"Together, Symon and I learned of a secret. This secret means as much to our community as it does to us. His place as the patriarch of the Cyl'Karric house was tested with this secret, but he did not flinch. Instead, he trusted in our bond. He trusted me to handle the details and speak to its place in our home.

"So, today," Caleb smiled. "In addition to standing here in his colors to show I have already blessed this union, I am also welcoming before you, my brother. Both of us born of Kyrn Cyl'Karrick, we grow as a family today!"

Instead of murmurs, the crowd erupted in gasps and awestruck conversation, more so on Symon's side. The shock of this news rippled throughout the congregation as the impact of what they heard settled in. The news of the Crown Prince being part of the Cyl'Karrick family had been hidden, and the casual manner in which Caleb had said it hit everyone with shock. Dozens of members from both families stood, revealing their colors, like a field of flowers blooming.

At the front, the lone figure in gray stood once again and walked to Caleb and Rakar. He handed them flowers and in that deep voice, "I give you this as an acceptance of your words, and honor your choice. Please pass this to the groom."

Caleb and Rakar placed their flowers in Symon's mane. Rakar embraced

Symon. "Ya' sire would be so proud."

"Thank you," Symon replied.

Caleb smiled, and patted Symon's face. "I am proud of you, too, brother."

Symon held Caleb and held back the tears that threatened to form. "Thank you, so much. I cannot ask for more than you have given me."

Symon watched as the two men returned to their seats. Symon's eye strayed to the side chamber, but the shadowed figure that was there had already gone. The deep voiced gray figure stepped to the altar and was joined by Moria's mother, Escheila. "Symon," she said gently, holding her hand out to him. Symon approached slowly, remembering the words that were given to him. A few nights ago, this petite Nymph woman coached him on everything he needed with a loving smile. That smile was not visible today.

As he neared, he finally could identify the figure with the deep voice. Still two generations younger than Symon in the heritage tree, he was the eldest of the Kal'Khorric, therefore the Cyl'Karrick, bloodline in Vargarden. A wizened grey Ennedi, slender but powerful, he was the best representative of the family, per traditions.

"Symon," Escheila announced. "While your family is the eldest of those present today, your youth here in Vargarden is known. You are also the youngest of the two who have requested union. For this, you have been deemed the supplicant of this betrothal. As such, it is your burden to prove that this marriage is best for the community, the families, and my daughter. How do you speak?"

Symon stood tall and recited the words he had memorized. "Jesse and Caleb, my seconds, as well as your husband, stand with me today, my lady. Jesse has spoken to how I embrace the values of community and build family.

"His words are true. I dedicate myself to Vargarden and her traditions," Symon said. A small applause sounded behind him. He continued, "Rakar and my brother, Caleb, speak to how I honor my family, and strive to serve it as the patriarch the best I can.

"Their words are true. While I came in ignorance, I dedicate myself to learning and improving each day to honor my sire, and his parents before him." A louder applause signaled behind him and he glanced over his shoulder. Robes were being shed and nearly half of the audience was brightly colored.

Symon gathered himself and spoke loudly. "While, by my own eyes, I am still unworthy of Moria's affection and shall always be, I dedicate myself to proving my love and devotion to her until my last breath. *Sacrificar, el brav quaendis un-dollo.*

"With my family's honor, I seek your daughter's hand, if she will have me, and shall serve her, and you, for all eternity. In this life, and beyond, I will be hers."

The Elder Ennedi turned to Moria, his deep voice rumbling from beneath his cloak. "And you, Moria Yurolinto? Do you accept this supplication, knowing all he stands for? Knowing what the Cyl'Karrick family stands for? Do you agree to give honor to our family, combine our strengths, protect our weaknesses, and hold this bond as ancestors to the generations to come?"

Moria stood slowly, and drew back her veil. "Honored mother, honored grandfather... With the blessings of our families, if you accept his supplication, so shall I."

The two family elders faced each other and nodded. They slowly drew back their robes and revealed their family colors beneath. They embraced one another and turned to the crowd. As one they spoke. "We, the family, stand here in our colors, to show you that we bless this union!"

The audience exploded in applause and the remaining gray robes were tossed back and flew into the air. Colors bloomed throughout the chamber as the Supplication ceremony closed, and the Garden of Life event began. Symon's eyes teared up at the beauty.

"One more day to go, big guy," Jesse said to him.

He hugged Jesse tightly with one arm. "Thank you, brother. This meant everything to me."

Jesse looked over at Caleb, "Maybe you'll pay me back someday?"

"It would be my honor."

Symon stood at the head of the aisleway the following day, in the same cathedral. Dressed in a white and gold robe, he stared over the gathered crowd, centering himself and calming his nerves. He listened to the rain drumming against the windows and rooftop and watched the colors dance on the wall above the altar as muted sunlight streamed through the stained glass. Slow, even, measured breaths formed a delicate rhythm as he waited anxiously for the start of the ceremony.

Today was the day.

Across the church, at the altar, Moria waited for him. She was dressed in her ceremonial armor, also draped in white and gold, and her nut colored skin shone radiantly against the platinum metal. A small Arcanum had removed the black inks and her hair was brightened to its natural vibrant green, pulled up and adorned with flowers and lace, along with a long bonnet that draped across her shoulders.

Symon's keen eyes spied the silk handkerchief that she had taken from his sire's wardrobe. It was sewn into the bonnet and, as Vargarden tradition, would be passed on to their child.

His knees trembled and he scanned the crowd for familiar faces. Jesse and Caleb sat up front, and smiled at him. He gathered his strength and nodded.

"Let us begin!" Baktu's voice called from the altar.

Symon took ten steps down the aisle towards his bride when a bell sounded. One of Moria's sisters emerged from the crowd and stood in front of him, halting his progress. She raised her hand before him, and Symon took a knee so that she could reach his forehead as he had been instructed. The girl dipped her fingers in a small jar of white powder made from lotus flowers that grew around the Black Yards and stroked his forehead, staining his fur with the powder in three small circles.

"I anoint you with the *kissac* powder, blessed by the Deacons of the Father, to bring you luck and good fortune," she said. "May the spirits of our ancestors forever bless your days"

She kissed his cheek, and Symon rose. He took ten more steps and listened as a bell rang out once again. Moria's other sister took her place before him. She presented a small white bowl, filled with a carved slice of hard pink fruit, its darkened rind still visible, sitting in a pinkish white milk.

"I present you the *gauv* fruit, its meat and milk to signify fertility. With this gift, may the blessings of your family give you strength so that you may sire many strong children to gift our ancestral families new members and honor for generations to come."

Symon took a bite from the fruit, and she wiped the juices from his chin. With a small kiss to his cheek, Symon rose once more. Ten more steps, and the final bell. Escheila stood before him, dressed resplendantly, and held a black bowl in her hands. She kneeled, placing the bowl, rim down, on the floor in front of him and draped a small cloth over it.

"This life will place obstacles in your path. But together, as a community, we shall overcome any that stand before us." Gently, she placed his foot upon the bowl, Bracing herself on his shoulders, she pressed her foot down on his, and the bowl shattered beneath them. Escheila kissed his cheek and said, "May the blessings of the Vargarden and the Father guide your hands for years to come. Now, join me and approach your bride, knowing that we have equipped you with everything you need for a successful life together."

Symon took her arm and began his walk down the aisle. Escheila was barely above four feet tall, snuggled up to Symon's waist as she guided him to the front of the cathedral. They ascended the stairs to the raised platform and she positioned him before his bride. Symon smiled down at Escheila and whispered "Thank you, dear mother."

"Thank you, dear boy," she said. Her eyes were shiny with tears, as she smiled up at him. "You have made us all so happy."

Symon turned to Moria. Like a beacon, she stood strong and radiant. The colored light that poured in from the windows, muted even by the rain, reflected off her armor. Her smile and eyes were lit with joy. Symon smiled at her, and she nodded subtly.

Tratesi Erdo, the Gnomish magistrate who Symon had not seen since his trial, had taken the raised pedestal next to Baktu. Their stout forms were now elevated putting their eyes at level with Moria, but still below Symon's. The two officiants watched carefully as the couple prepared for the rituals.

"Honored families," Deacon Baktu began, "we have gathered here today to unite your lineages through this holy ceremony in the eyes of the Father, and to be recognized throughout Vargarden and her servants wherever you may be.

"With the Supplication accepted, your families provided their consent and blessed this union. I have witnessed the Supplication and decree that these two have achieved all obligations. Let us begin."

The Ukko Deacon stepped toward the table and placed her hands on the top of a large golden goblet, encrusted in precious stones. To each side, a set of smaller cups were arrayed for both Symon and Moria. Baktu's deep voice rang clear and said, "Under my eyes, you must announce your commitment to the union of these families. What say you?"

Symon took the smallest of the chalices in his hand and raised it as he watched Moria do the same. Together, they said, "I am grateful for my ancestors who raised me and for my past. I honor their memory with my love to thee." They each drank a sip of wine and poured the remainder into the large goblet still held by Baktu.

They both reached for their second cup, slightly larger than the first and raised each of theirs before themselves. "I am grateful for the person in front of me and the love they have shown me. I honor that love and aspire to marry this person. To work together for the good of our community, and the good of our families." Each of them took another sip of the wine and poured the remains into the large goblet once again.

Moria and Symon stepped to Baktu and placed their hands on the large be-jewelled goblet. They smiled and said as one, "I am grateful for our future and the opportunity it provides. I honor that future, and desire to build our happy family. With this, I pledge my eternal love." Symon drank deeply from the goblet and held it to Moria. She drank deeply and smiled at him. Baktu took it from them and Symon grasped Moria's hands in his.

Tratesi Erdo clapped his hands together and cleared his throat. "Moshka Kal'Daren, you were the eldest member of the Kal'Khorric lineage represented in our lands before Symon Cyl'Karric returned. Without his presence, you assumed the mantle of leadership. All names within your family and the responsibility for all decisions for the Cyl'Karrick family were yours. By yesterday's light, you accepted the Supplication of this couple to join. Today, we must decide as one, if they shall bear the Cyl'Karrick name, or if they shall bear the Yorulinto name. To achieve this goal, I ask you to bear witness and stake your vote, which shall be honored by Priestess Baktu and I before commitment to the history books."

The grey Ennedi stood and turned to face the family gathered behind him. "My family," he started. His deep voice rumbled over the crowd and commanded attention. "This young man has come a great way to be with us here today. Just over three seasons ago, he came to us as a refugee, fleeing from the lands he once called home. As he embraced the responsibilities of his sire, he has walked in the footsteps of his ancestors, and with that time he has become a true Cyl'Karrick. And now, he has anchored his life here with the selection of a fine woman from an honored family to build upon the generations of our history.

"For the honor of our family, I beg that my great uncle Symon retains the mantle of Cyl'Karrick. To honor his sire, Kyrn Cyl'Karrick and claim the title and deeds so deserved. Our blood is one, our honor is strong, and with my heart of hearts, I vote. Does my family agree?"

Symon's side of the cathedral shouted loudly, hoots and cries of glee caused an explosion of joyful noise. The din stretched out for many moments until he placed his hand in the air to quiet them. Moshka turned back to Erdo and smiled. "My vote and the vote of my family has been cast."

Erdo nodded and turned to Escheila. "As the eldest of the Yorulinto lineage, you speak for your family. The Cyl'Karrick hand awaits your decision. By yesterday's light, you accepted the Supplication of this couple to join. Today, we must decide as one, if they shall bear the Cyl'Karrick name, or if they shall bear the Yorulinto name. To achieve this goal, I ask you to bear witness and stake your vote, which shall be honored by Priestess Baktu and I before commitment to the history books."

"Thank you, Matron Baktu," Escheila said. "I have prepared a *beru'nokier* as tradition dictates."

A murmur of surprise rippled through the crowd as Baktu brought forth a large oaken box, nearly two feet in length and a foot wide. "The matriarch has produced a gift, to please families, honor the Magistrate, and display her intentions.

"My family," Escheila announced. "For her entire adult life, my daughter Moria has had her hand on the Cyl'Karrick estate. She has tended its history and preserved its honor while it sat dormant here in our homeland.

"Today, I look at this man before us and realize that it was all for this moment. He represents everything that his sire before him upheld, and he strengthens us with this union. The Kal'Khorric line, through Symon Cyl'Karrick, shall hold our honor from this day forth.

"Our blood will mix with his," Escheila continued, "and generations to come shall convey our greatness with each deed. I give my daughter to the Cyl'Karrick name, and add our names to their tree and their name to ours. It is our tradition to knit this shawl, emblazoned with their family crest, when their intentions to marry was announced. With the suddenness of that announcement mere three months ago, and the rush of preparations for the ceremonies today, my gift is more humble than I would wish."

Escheila pulled an ornate brocaded shawl woven in violet and bejeweled with emeralds and citrine gems.

"With this humble gift, I drape my daughter in our choice and Moria Yorulinto shall become Moria Cyl'Karrick on this day. We look to the day where their kin bear their name." She draped the shawl into a triangle over the back of Moria and tied it across her chest. Escheila kissed her daughter's cheeks and turned her to face the audience.

Both the Kal'Khorric and Yorulinto families cried out at that moment, their joyful voices forming a celebration. Rakar turned to Erdo and spoke, "Our d'cision made and the vote of our fam'ly has been cast."

Escheila approached Symon and hugged him tightly. He hugged her back. "Thank you," he said, his eyes straying to the shawl. "That is beautiful work."

The motherly Nymph reached up and brought Symon's head down to whisper in his ear. "You're lucky I began that shawl the night my daughter came back from meeting you nine months ago. Two months isn't enough to make that shawl. I would have had to wait until your child was born to complete it if I hadn't known my girl so well."

Symon looked at her in shock. "You knew?"

"Of course I knew," She laughed and whispered back. "And I know of your youngling. I've known everything. You silly kids!"

Erdo smiled and brought his hands to the shoulders of Moria and Symon. "Then I shall decree you Cyl'Karrick by laws and rights of Vargarden."

"And I," Baktu said, "shall consecrate this union by the eyes of the Father." Erdo and Baktu draped the couple with a large garland of flowers and beads, wrapping it first around Moria, then around Symon, forming a loop that entwined them both. Once the garland was completed, a small Arcanum bound the ends together, making it whole.

"So we shall begin," Erdo and Baktu said together.

Symon, thankfully, had been prepared for this portion of the ceremony. For nearly two hours, the Deacon and the Magistrate performed blessing rituals. It was not a mere ceremony, but a ritual with both Arcane and Divine spells unrecognizable to Symon. He felt his Body, Life, and Soul being fused to Moria's, her warmth a guiding light to him.

With the ritual complete, Baktu presented them one last time. "Honored family members, standing before you I present Moria and Symon Cyl'Karrick, long may their names be held!"

Once again, the crowd erupted in cheers and celebration. Symon took his moment to grab Moria into his arms and kiss her passionately. He was hers now, and he had trouble finding any words to say that would express what he felt. He hesitated as he looked deep into her eyes. She cocked her head to the side and squinted at him in mock disapproval. She whispered, "I love you. I believe those are the words y're looking for, you fool."

"I love you, dearest," Symon said. "Thank you for bringing me home."

"They're waitin' on us to say somethin', 'ya know."

Symon glanced up at the crowd, who were indeed waiting in anticipation. He looked down again at Moria smiling broadly. "Together?"

She nodded and he brought her back upright.

"Friends, family," they said together. "We feast!" A new eruption of cheers filled the room.

Symon yelped as he was rushed and grabbed by a dozen hands. The crew of Moria's soldiers dragged him towards the feast hall doors. He glanced over his shoulder and saw his new wife standing, one hand on her hip, with a wry smile upon her face. Before her stood a squad sergeant arms crossed and a mischievous look in his eyes. "You know the drill, Osi. You want him, you got to prove to us you are strong enough to keep him."

"I thought I told 'ya to skip this part of the tradition," she said to her sire.

Rakar laughed, "I'm retired, don'a look at me."

She patted her mother's arm. "We best get the good kegs, these boys will need something to numb the pain." Symon smiled as she exploded into action and properly thumped her men, freeing him quickly from their "capture."

The families filled the rest of the night with equally ludicrous tasks and deeds for each of Moria and Symon, challenging their ability to prove their love to the community and family members. Symon spied Argyle standing off to the side with that telltale head tilt, once again lost in thought. Rakar and Escheila were deep in conversation with his great-nephew Moska. Symon thought he spied the mysterious stranger, the one with the twin swords, but the figure had quickly disappeared like a ghost in the night.

Symon smiled as he saw Jesse and Caleb snuggled in the corner. He watched as his family, his *rieve,* danced and drank in celebration. Memories of everything they had been through in this last year faded away in an instant. He raised his glass to Jesse, and Jesse raised his back. They smiled and drained their cups. They were no longer alone. They were home.

45

The Crown Job

Argyle was quite content in Vargarden. More so than he thought he may have been. He had enjoyed his time with the children. It brought him a level of contentment to see the joy on their faces as they climbed atop his form, playing Man of the Mountain, or Slay the Beast. At first, some of the adults had taken offense to that last one, fearful that he might take it as an insult. But Argyle had been called much worse and knew that he was merely a stand-in. The children did not truly think him a monster.

In many ways, the orphanages felt familiar. They reminded him of Highston. It was how many of Manticore's recruits had been found. It had been how Xerian found Jesse and introduced the boy to Argyle.

However, while unfamiliar, the months he had spent in Vargarden had been illuminating. Jesse's time with the Prince had been of special attention. The wedding had been enjoyable, a grand opportunity to see another culture in action. Little by little he learned about this place. The kingdom of Vargarden. It was so different from the Khorric Federation. Life moved at a different pace, more methodical, more contemplative.

It was comfortable for Argyle.

It fit his patient nature.

Even the events leading up to the ceremony had been enlightening. Argyle had found himself surprisingly pleased when Symon had insisted that Argyle be a part of the celebrations. It made him realize how much Grendel had underestimated the two blacksmiths, both father and son, and their commitment to their friends and family.

"Argyle?" came the tentative voice of one of the boys near his ear. "Doyle said you prolly won't roar for me?"

"Oh did he now, little one?"

"Ple-ease?" said the boy with a look of trepidation, "Doyle said I'm not brave enough to ask you."

"Very well, Seff. Run behind me now, so that my roar is not too much for your ears."

The Genbu then let loose a mighty roar from deep in his chest. The children scattered, yelling in delight at the attention. Argyle tracked his green haired target, giving chase as he ran to the side. Even though the boy was older than many of the others, Argyle was too large, his limbs too long, for the boy to get far. He was quickly able to tackle his target to the ground, doing it in such a way that he controlled the boy's fall, making it more of a roll that had little chance of causing any harm worse than some grass stains.

"Doyle," growled Argyle menacingly. "I hear you have little faith in the boy, Seff. You wouldn't be his bully, by any chance?"

"He's my cousin," Doyle laughed. "I wouldn't never pick on 'im!"

"It is well that you answer such," said Argyle, his face low to the boy. "He had the courage to approach me, and he is under my protection. If you are on his side, you are thus also protected."

"I have heard of your antics with the children from the others," Prince Caleb's voice called from the edge of the courtyard. Argyle glanced up and saw the Prince standing with a small Welengham, not more than a half dozen, and Paulson, the Isnashi who had been instructing Jesse.

"Good morning, my Prince," Argyle replied.

"Your roar is an impressive sight."

"Thank you, my prince," said Argyle. "I can see that our man Paulson here thinks differently."

"I do not disagree with the Prince," Paulson said with a scowl. "It's just good that you are on our side. I would hate to have to fight you."

"Do not fear, Lieutenant. On my honor, you will never need to face me on any field of battle."

Argyle turned his attention back to the prince. "I am somewhat surprised that you have come from the palace with no Deacons, especially considering events of the past."

"Don't worry, friend," the Prince said. "As you know, the Deacon's eyes are upon us." The Prince gestured to the control gems of the Welengham. "Now, what do you wish to discuss?"

"Yes, my Lord. It is known that you have spent some time with Jesse. That he has become enamored with you since our arrival in your fair city. While he has been open with you about his past, I fear that there are still things to discover. Something that I fear could cause complications to Vargarden."

"That sounds serious," Prince Caleb said.

"I fear that it may be. Can we speak somewhere private?"

"Of course. If you would please lead the way?"

"There is a warehouse just down this street that I use as a place of refuge. A few of the children introduced me to the discovery, no doubt attempting to curry favor." Argyle pointed ahead and said, "If it pleases you, it is just ahead."

"That sounds acceptable," the Prince replied.

Argyle led them down the street. It was an unremarkable building in an unremarkable stretch of road. Nearly no landmarks were discernable. The warehouse was a sanctuary of anonymity.

As they reached the door, Paulson stepped forward. "My Lord? If I may?" he asked, motioning toward the door. The prince nodded and Paulson pushed open the doors to the building. After glancing inside, the Lieutenant allowed two of the Welgeid to step inside. Paulson then entered behind them and after a moment, his voice called out, "It appears unoccupied, my Lord."

"As expected," the Prince said flatly.

"Do not fault your man for caution," Argyle said.

The remaining skeletons entered the building, taking their positions as guard. The prince gestured for Argyle to precede him inside and Argyle led him into the warehouse's cavernous interior. Much of the space was empty, with the right and rear walls stacked with crates of various sizes and construction. "This way, just ahead."

Prince Caleb stepped ahead, flanked by four Welgeid. "*Farroos,*" he whispered, shedding an area of light from his hand. "This is your den, Argyle?" asked Caleb. "Perhaps you can come and show me where we are headed?"

"Yes, Caleb, it is certainly time to show you,"

The flat deadpan tone of Argyle's voice alerted both his quarry and the guard. Argyle smiled deeply. It was too late.

"*Te'Jaman'ela!*" Argyle yelled out, snapping a pre-structured Arcane spell rod. A purplish blast of energy exploded, filling the warehouse from corner to corner. The Welgeid dropped to the dirt floor as if puppets with cut strings. Their once animated forms were now piles of ordinary bones.

Argyle swiped his paw stoically at Paulson before the Isnashi could clear his blade staff from the scabbard. A violent ribbon of blood sprayed the wall as Argyle's blow took off most of the man's face. With a leap, Argyle took Paulson into his grip, his back foot raking, tearing the warrior's torso. Pinning him to the ground, Argyle twisted mechanically and heard the satisfying snap of Paulson's neck as it broke.

Caleb's eyes were wide with terror. His hands turned quickly, drafting a spell form, but there was no Arcana to fill it. The prince's eyes darted around trying to understand what was happening. The inanimate skeletons around him, his Light spell extinguished, the sudden realization of anti-magic filled the eyes of Argyle's quarry.

"It is no good, my Lord," Argyle said, sinisterly. "I have played this scenario in my mind many, many times. I have everything accounted for."

"What are you doing?" Caleb asked.

"It took me so long to get you alone," Argyle said in his deep, calm voice. "Please, don't fight me. There really is no point, and it would just end with you sustaining injuries."

"I don't understand."

He noticed the prince staring at the body of the Isnashi soldier. Argyle wiped his foot smearing blood into the dirt. "I did not lie. I swore an oath that he would not have to fight me."

"You're a murderer."

"Always have been."

"Why are you doing this? What has changed?"

"Changed?" asked Argyle as he finished cleaning his claws, "There was nothing changed. This has always been the plan. The only question was always when, not if."

"You have been among us for nearly a year," the prince said in anger.

"Yes. Patience in all things."

"But why? Why so long?"

"I was in need of several things," said Argyle. "I needed to learn from your Deacons how your Undead worked. I needed to study defenses. I had to plan a way to leave the city undetected. And most importantly, I needed the tools that Lady Lara Devros delivered. She provided me with the Anti-magic trap so that I would have a way to keep you from your Arcane abilities."

"She's working with you?"

"The Devros family has long been an ally of Manticore."

"You bastard!"

"For someone with such a sordid family history, those words may wound me less than you desire," Argyle said, mockingly. He snatched the Prince by the shoulder and delivered a punch to his gut. The young man vomited on the floor. Caleb feebly punched Argyle, but the blows were barely felt through his rocky exterior. The Genbu lifted Caleb up to stare at him directly in the eyes. "Caleb, Prince of Vargarden," he said in a menacing growl, "do not fight me, and I will ensure you a safe and tolerable journey."

Caleb flailed in Argyle's grip and the Genbu laughed. More feeble punches landed about his forearms and shoulders. The Prince placed his foot on Argyle's chest and attempted to kick himself free.

"I warned you," Argyle said, flatly. The Genbu launched the prince, sending him flying. With a crash, Caleb collided with a crate and tumbled across the dirt floor. The prince was barely conscious when Argyle grabbed him by a handful of robes and began dragging him toward the back. "This could have been much easier."

Argyle bound Caleb's arms sharply behind his back, each of his hands encased in thin wooden boxes that left all joints below the wrist held firmly in place, a protocol against casters. A gag had been placed in the boy's mouth, a blindfold across his eyes, and a leather hood around his head. His ankles were similarly bound, and he had been carefully wrapped in a roll of burlap, bound with sturdy hempen rope.

Argyle took a long sheet of bark from a pouch, braced himself, and shoved it into his mouth. Heartmoss, he was told it was named. He had taken it once before, but was still unprepared for the adrenaline that flooded through his body. His muscles screamed to move. His senses were on fire. The narcotic coursed through him, demanding action.

Argyle grabbed his supply pack and his captive, strapping them to his back. He began a loping run on all four legs, his drug-fueled state allowing him to cover the ground at half again the speed of a galloping horse, a pace he kept for many hours. His plan had gone off without a hitch. Unseen, unsuspected, he disappeared from Vargarden with his prize in hand. When he finally came down from his intense high, he was miles into the Road of the Dead and on his way back to Highston.

46

Darkness Lies Behind

The front door of the estate burst open. The bells of the city could be heard outside as Welgeid poured into the foyer. A Gnome Deacon, black robes flowing, entered behind them, stopped in the center of the room, closing his eyes in concentration.

Symon and Moria emerged from their bedroom, eyes bleary with sleep.

"What's going on?" Moria asked.

"Osi," the Gnome replied. "We have urgent news. There's been an—"

"Guy's what in the Thirteen Hells is going on?" asked Jesse, entering the foyer. "What's with all the ruckus?"

Symon saw the Gnome glance at Moria. There was silence for a moment, then Moria nodded for the Gnome to proceed. "Yes, Osi. There's been another attack. Something has happened to the Prince. Paulson is dead."

Symon stood transfixed. The words were clear, but the meaning was slow to come. Jesse's legs went out, and he collapsed near Symon, his eyes vacant and expressionless.

"Details," Moria said, firmly.

"Lieutenant Paulson was part of a contingent escorting Prince Caleb with Argyle in the western side of the city this afternoon. Six Welgeid were dispatched.

We lost connection with the unit, and when we were able to locate the scene, we found Paulson's body and signs of a struggle."

"Argyle? Is he alright?" Symon asked.

"Why such a small contingent?" Moria asked over top of him.

"Argyle said it was a 'personal' matter, Osi. The Prince insisted on privacy," the Gnome hesitated. "Based on the wounds the Lieutenant sustained, we should have been more steadfast."

"What are 'ya sayin'?"

"Osi," the Gnome replied. "We believe Argyle killed Paulson and abducted the Prince."

Symon's gut twisted into a knot and he nearly vomited. A wail escaped Jesse, and Symon knelt to hold his friend. The young Isnashi clutched onto him tightly. Together, they rocked upon the floor trying to find any sort of comfort in the chaos.

Moria growled. Her orders fired at them. "Raise the Black Yards. Send Messages to the outposts and close the roads out of Vargarden's borders. Scour the valley. If he is within any kind of a distance, we will find him, we will catch him, and we will return our Prince."

"Already done, Osi."

"Good," she said. She turned to Symon, her eyes full of pain. "Symon?"

"Go, my love," Symon reached up and took her hand. "Do what you need to do."

Jesse pushed against Symon, his face full of tears. "How in all the Hells did this happen? Caleb is the most powerful mage I know. Plus, he can't even step into the palace gardens with me, without half a dozen people watching us! How could this happen? How?!"

"It was a well-planned attack," the officer spoke. "By the time we could identify the scene, Argyle was long gone. We found the remnants of an Anti-magic spell construct. We let our defenses down because we believed Argyle to be a friend. There's no excuse."

"Tha' time for review can wait 'til after our Prince is home," Moria said sternly. "We don'na have much time."

Symon smelled burning air. The sizzling sensation of the Veil being pulled back for Arcana. The Gnome's eyebrow raised as well. "Osi?"

"Gather the Legion and—"

"Osi!" the Gnome yelled.

Symon dove towards Moria knocking her to the ground as a crackle of energy ripped a tear in reality before them.

Weapons were drawn all around, from every skeleton, and by the Deacon. Symon's hand went to his hip, but found nothing, still dressed in his bed linens. "This makes no sense," said Moria to the little Gnome. "Did the Church not bolster the aether?! Weren't you supposed to protect us against Arcane intrusion?"

"We did, Osi. And yet..."

The tear transformed into a shimmer in the air, a nearly invisible line in space, hanging perpendicular to the ground, perhaps four to five feet tall.

The sound of a whip crack reverberated through the air, causing them to jump, as a point of violet light appeared at the top of the disturbance. It began as a small prick of light, no larger than a firefly, but grew in both size and intensity, until it appeared to be a blade of pale purple energy piercing the air.

Slowly, the blade slid lower along the shimmering line. As it did, it was as if the air itself fell aside like cloth, revealing an Investurant woman holding a staff.

"There, that's better," she said. The woman regarded them, slightly breathless from the physical exertion of breaching reality. She was a slight woman, dressed in Arcanist's robes, not quite black, yet not quite blue or purple. The edges of the cloth were lined in glowing script, and her entire appearance spoke of power. "That was quite the barrier that you enacted. I have been trying to find you for days. I only pray I am not too late."

Symon recognized her from the night Highston fell. She had been with Rhon and the *Ombramaes.* She was one of them.

"You!" cried out Jesse. "What in the unholy fuck are you doing here? What have you done? Now? Of all days?"

"Of all days?" she said softly. "*Kash ak'sai,* does this mean I am too late?"

"Like you don't fucking know!" screamed Jesse. "Are you going to stand there and play dumb?"

"Careful how you speak to me," she said, coldly.

"You dare?" Symon growled. He stepped forward, allowing the rage to fill him. "You kidnap my brother and dare to come here, into my home, and threaten us?!"

"I am not here to harm you. In fact, your Arcane barrier is preventing me from being able to step through the portal. I am strong enough only to open it and speak with you. I came to warn you about the prince."

"Fat lot o' good that does," Moria spat.

"This is what I was working to avoid." the woman sighed in disappointment. "We were warned years ago that the Son would be one of the most damaging individuals to our struggle. I have advised the Ombramaes and Rhon that there was no cause for this, but they refused to listen.

"Manticore's words, particularly Grendel's words, still convince them," she said. "I came to warn you to prepare, but I was unable to do so."

"So, is Argyle working for you? Or against you?" asked Symon.

"I know not," she replied. "I fear what this act will mean. It is stupid and antagonistic against an enemy we should not wish to face again. We have captured the Betrayer's Stone from your palace here. We had our objective. There was no need for this. And yet, Rhon is rogue, overcome with nearly blind rage at your world, and I fear that my Kyora, the *Ombramaes*, is becoming mad."

Symon felt the world tilt again. The name was not what he expected. "Aida is the *Ombramaes.*"

"Oh, child," Emaly said sadly. "She was, during the first assault for the Betrayer's Stone. Her eldest daughter, Kyora, took that title from her, along with her life. The former *Ombramaes* betrayed her position and her people by making peace with your father without fulfilling our goal of safety for the Mumvurii. Now my wife, your sister, stands as the Avatar of the *Sangebula*. Kyora is the *Ombramaes.*"

Symon stood there in shock. Waves of nausea overtook him once again, threatening to spill his guts to the floor. His hand fell from Jesse's shoulder, and Jesse took up the conversation in his stead.

"So, you are now worried that either Rhon or Kyora has gone behind your back and ordered Argyle to kidnap Caleb?" Jesse asked.

"Yes." Emaly said simply.

"What does this mean?" Moria asked.

"I don't know," she said. "I'm sorry. My chorus has been unable to see much past this event. But what they could see was a detriment to us all."

"So help us! Where would he have taken Caleb?"

"Argyle will likely take the Son to Highston. I wish you luck."

"Wait!" Symon asked. "Who are you?"

"Emaly Le'arial. I do not wish to be your friend. But I do not wish to be your enemy, either." She smiled. "I do, however, wish you luck in returning your prince. For all our sake."

With that, the Investurant Arcanist swiped at the air with her staff, releasing her spell. The portal closed with a snap. There was silence for several minutes as everyone looked at one another, trying to process what just happened.

"Osi?" the Gnome spoke, finally.

"Leave half the Welengam. Go to the palace and report this breach. Don't try and save my sensibilities. Report it all."

"Yes, Osi." he said, and then turned and left.

"What in all the Thirteen Hells just happened?" asked Jesse quietly.

"The secrets of my family continue to give," Symon replied.

Moria whispered. "Your sister?"

"I don't know," Symon said, shaking his head.

"What do we do?"

"We get our prince back."

Symon held Jesse and Moria, and looked towards the door to his home. Mere weeks ago, he had vowed that the conflict would stay behind him. The words of the Witch echoed in his head. She had told them to turn away from it all, if they could accept the cost. Symon was unable to accept the loss of Caleb. Jesse's eyes stared up at him, helpless. Symon was unable to accept his friend's pain. He growled at the door, knowing that beyond lies the path to vengeance. The path back to Highston.

--Continued in Book Three—

"Son of Night, Son of Light"

APPENDIX

Appendix I
Characters

Argyle (Genbu)   A Lieutenant with the Bright Guild Manticore who serves Grendel. A member of an enigmatic species of wingless Gargoyles, Argyle was brought **into** the Khorric Federation many years ago, as a personal slave to a foreign merchant.

Caleb Cyl'Emptor (Mumvurii) The Crown Prince of Vargarden
Prince Caleb is the adopted son of the Father, acting as an advising leader to the Council of Vargarden and a diplomatic representative to visiting dignitaries.

Deacon Bakta (Gnome) A priestess of the Father
Baktu is a healer who Symon begins studying under.

Emaly Le'arial (Mumvurii) The Sorceress of the Investurants.
She follows the instructions of the Ombramaes, and is seen leading Investurant forces.

Erin Sasa (Orthrus) A lieutenant with the Bright Guild Beckoning.
Was once a love interest of Jesse but was killed.

Falearyn Kal'Daren (Ennedi) A Vargarden armorsmith
A distant cousin of Symon who later stands for Symon as a family representative. Falearyn makes a suit of commissioned armor for Symon.

Lord Grendel Montrell (Human with Giant blood) Once the leader of the Bright Guild Manticore.

A master manipulator with as many stories of his past, as those he had told it to. A political tactician. Killed by the Ombramaes during the fall of Highston.

Hasukawa Nakama (Arktos) A Deacon of Vargarden.

He appears to be hunting Rhon. Hasukawa gives advice to the travelers, and has an unusual meeting with the Ghost.

Jesse Olben (Isnashi) A teenage Street Rat

Striving for a life above the streets where he is forced to live. Often hired freelance by the Bright Guild Manticore. Once in Vargarden, he struggles to find a place to fit in.

Kiko Nakama (Tellervo) Husband to the Deacon Hasukawa.

A small, white Felinoid, Kiko dresses in a wide hat and long coat. In a manner unusual for Vargarden, he fights with a pair of Skyfallen Blasters.

Kyrn Cylkas (Ennedi) Former owner and Master of the smithy, the Flame Eternal. The father of Symon, Kyrn arrived in the capital city of Highston with a one year old son and a quiet determination. Once a refugee, he has built a solid business on his reputation as a stern, honest, and fair man. Fell to the Investurants during the fall of Highston

Lara Hopesinger (Human) A student at the Federal Academy.

A fellow student and romantic interest with Symon. Her family comes from money, with a wealthy mother and a merchant father. Now the wife of Olivar Devros, she visits Vargarden as a representative of the New Nobles from the Khorric Federation.

Magistrate Jurdanus (Gnome) A judicial officiant of Vargarden

This is the man who arrests Symon upon entering Vargarden.

Masuulka (Fae, not from Sainan) A protector and guide in the Deepland Woods

The spirit forest guardian that acts as a protector of the Deepland Witch, and guide to those who wish to speak with her.

Miss Dodonna (Karhu) Partner to Mistress Daysleeper.

Co-owner and barkeep of the Duck and Tackle, she hides her true personality behind a gruff and demanding exterior.

Miss Jessie (Gnome) Matron of the inn at the outskirts of Vargarden

An elderly woman that gives Jesse, Symon, and their companions a surprising greeting as they enter the Kingdom of the Dead.

Mistress Daysleeper (Tellevero) The cultured and composed owner of the Duck and Tackle bar. Dressing well above her station, this exotic and mysterious woman opens her establishment to Thorn and Jesse, while also hosting the city's powerful above her popular gaming tables.

Moria Yurolinto (Human/Nymph mixed blood) Rakar's daughter

Caretaker of the Cyl'Karrick Estate and an officer in the Vargarden military. She becomes a friend and ally of Symon and his companions.

Olivar Devros (Alva) The leader of Symon's group of friends.

The leader of his social circles, Olivar relishes the prestige brought by his family's wealth and power.

Ombramaes (Mumvurii) The fierce leader of the Investurants.

This enigmatic woman, also known as the Master, or Master of Shadows, is the spiritual and military leader of the Investurant army. The Ombramaes is a title, yes, but much more. As the head of the Sangebula, the elite ruling class of the Investurants, the Ombramaes is actually a step above the nobility she leads. The position of Ombramaes is one of bloodline, enabling them to be the current physical manifestation of their god.

Paulson (Isnashi) A lieutenant with the Vargarden military

Paulson is brought in at the Council's order to train Jesse in combat. While gruff, he becomes something of a mentor to Jesse.

Rakar Yurolinto (Human) A scout in the army of Vargarden.

An older human that has experience in scouting and torture. He is an old friend of Kyrn, helping Symon come to understand who his father was.

Reginald Grenthana (Raiju) A member of Symon's group of friends.

The son of a Trade Guild Master. A pacifist at heart, but clever and quick. An aristocrat and gentleman in the truest sense, his family is one of the oldest and most stable of the Nobles.

Rhon (Mumvurii) A principal agent of the Investurants operating in Highston.

Appears to be a premier fighter, and has a keen interest in Jesse.

Sephistos (Fae, not from Sainan) A powerful Oracle known to be as tricky as she is accurate.

Better known as the Deepland Witch, or the Witch of the Woods. She is a very old power, considering herself above the politics and dealings of civilized mortals. Sephistos has prophetic powers, but can be capricious with the answers she gives, especially to those who come to her in arrogance.

Symon Cylkis (Ennedi) The son of a prominent blacksmith.

A middle class young adult struggling to fit into the extravagant lifestyles of his friends. Often questions his family's ultimate purpose and legacy. Finds new connections to his father and his legacy in Vargarden.

The Father (Unknown) The leader and figurehead of the Kingdom of Vargarden

Rumored to be an Avatar of the God of Death and thousands of years old. He is the center of the religion in the Undead Kingdom, bestowing power on his Deacons and his people.

The Ghost (Unknown) A plague on the Investurants.

> This unknown being harasses and disrupts Investurant military groups, killing all he comes across. General Rhon becomes obsessed with him, yet Hasukawa seems to know him.

Thorn Daass (Hiisi Goblin) Jesse's best friend and fellow Street Rat.

> She serves as a mentor to Jesse and often accompanies him on jobs. Their symbiotic relationship allows her to take advantage of Jesse's charm, while providing her experience to him.

Xerian Luran (Lindorm) A foot soldier in the Bright Guild Manticore.

> Jesse was one of several Street Rats Xerian has given a home and training to over the years, though at a cost.

Zenesul A'Dynell (Human) An enigmatic teacher of the Arcane.

> An old man offering scribing services in a poorer section of the city of Highston and acts as an initial envoy to Vargarden.

Appendix II
Species

Overview

While many worlds offer few, or impossibly only one, sentient species, Sainan is host to approximately fifty native, and hosted, sentient species. This world sits at a thin section of the Veil, the barrier between mortal reality and the realm of the infinitely possible. Therefore the Gods have had a larger hand in the development of Sainan than most worlds.

Many fantasy worlds may include non-Human species, but Humanity still seems to hold half or more of the population. In Sainan, Humans are but one of many species. While one or two species may hold a population majority in one city or region, globally the species are equally balanced. While debates are held on if there is a majority population of the world, there is no realistic way to determine it.

Regional terrain, climate, sociological conditions, and other factors have often led to different varieties to skin, hair, and other external conditions. Just as how Humans from different regions of Earth have different external features, so might an Ennedi from one region have different fur coloration, or even a different average build.

Breeding

Perhaps due to the nature of the Divine intervention into the formation of the world of Sainan, many sentient species are able to cross breed without mixing genetics. Rather, most pairings will prove one of the bloodlines dominant to the other. Therefore, children will typically take on the full-blooded racial heritage of one of their two parents. Occasionally, one of the bloodlines of a grandparent will emerge, although this is more rare.

A few species have the potential to blend parentage if interbred with certain other species. Even this potential is spontaneous, not always occurring, and no explanation has been discovered. Species known to have this trait include the Alva, Nymphs, Humans, Orcs, and Giants. Even when these bloodlines are mixed, one heritage typically takes genetic dominance. Future generations often return to one of the pure species in time, shedding their blended traits. No predictable pattern of dominance has been successfully determined. Again, no one knows why this is.

Additionally, there are species families which cannot interbreed. For example, the Florum species can only interbreed with others of their same species. Non-native species, such as Skyfallen, even after seven centuries, have not adapted a way to share genetic material with native Sainan bloodlines.

Families

Biologically, different species are grouped into families, based on shared characteristics. The identifying traits of the various families are as follows:

Carnivid— A collection of Humanoids sharing unique dietary traits of being pure carnivores. Unable to gain sustenance from non-meat sources, they have stronger digestive systems providing protection from spoiled or rotted meat. This means they are even able to digest carrion, and have a reputation as cannibals, as even the meat of sentient species is often not overlooked.

Draconic— Due to the magic of Sainan, many intelligent species draw their blood lines from the ancient Dragons of Sainan, and their magic. Each species shares general attributes taken from this heritage, such as tough, scaly hide, tails, or additional limbs.

Dwarven— A collection of species combining a shorter stature with a stronger build. It is believed these attributes come from millennia of living underground.

Faunic— A variety of species with anthropomorphic animal traits. Some have heightened senses that serve them as well as their sight. A consistent feature is full body fur.

Fae— Varieties of bloodlines purported to have origins steeped in magic. Unusual aspects such as long lifespans, innate magic, pointed ears, and other traits are common in many of these species.

Florem— Sainan is host to several sentient plant-based Humanoids. Feeding via photosynthesis, members can become unhealthy and wither if underground for a week or longer.

Humanid— Mostly hairless Humanoids, spanning a variety of heights.

Reptilian— Scaled, hairless collection of species with variations on Humanoid reptiles. While there are a variety of body types, most are coldblooded.

Non-Native— Sentient species stranded on Sainan after the catastrophic events of the Devastation, seven centuries prior.

Species

Carnivid

Hiisi Goblin — A smaller species, typically averaging two and a half to three feet in height. Known to be more intelligent and cunning than their cousins, the Nisse.

Nisse Goblin — Similar to Hiisi in size, they often have larger ears and more gangly features. Members of this race are often of lower intelligence and seen as nuisances rather than threats.

Orc — A larger race, typically averaging more than seven feet in height, Orcs are brutish and culturally prone to tribal warfare. Perceived by more civilized races as "savage," Orcs are often dangerous fighters and mercenaries.

Draconic

Gargoyle— With thick, stone-like skin and large, heavy wings, this is one of the few species with true flight.

Genbu— A larger, wingless variant of Gargoyles, they walk on four limbs like a dog or a bear, though with fully functional hands on their front limbs. Genbu also have the toughest hide of all the Draconic species, but due to their build as not being Humanoid, they have a reputation as one of the least intelligent sentient species.

Lindorm– Reptilian skin and bipedal, with four equally sized upper arms. Average height of six and half to seven feet. Some unusual races have frills or even limited head hair.

Taniwha– Human-size bipedal Dragon Humanoids. Often considered half Dragon, half Alva.

Dwarven

Gnome– Small Dwarven Humanoids standing two and a half to three feet in height, with a preternatural affinity for gems and metals.

Ukko– While their cousins, the Svartal, continued evolving below ground, this race of Dwarves has adapted to life on the surface. Typically four to four and a half feet tall on average.

Svartal– Shorter and stouter Dwarven race, born and bred to live, mine and build in their underground halls. Typically three and a half to four feet tall.

Faunic

Arktos– A Humanoid polar bear, averaging seven to eight feet tall. Their shorter legs are adapted to walking upright, or dropping to all fours for sprinting.

Ennedi– A feline species of lion-like Humanoids. Typically the strongest and largest of the feline species.

Karhu– Brown bear Humanoids averaging six to seven feet tall. Similar to their Arktos counterparts, they adapt to bi-pedal or quadrupedal transportations.

Orthrus– Canid Doberman Humanoid, short furred, no tail. Typically slightly taller than Humans.

Raiju– Fox-like Humanoids known for their speed and heightened senses.

Tellervo– A feline species of panther-like Humanoids. Often about average Human height of five to five and a half feet.

Fey

Alva— The Elves of Sainan. One of the oldest and longest-lived races. Human height, but averaging a third less their mass, with long, slender limbs.

Ajatar— Shorter Alvan cousins, averaging three and a half to four feet tall. Tend to have stronger builds, more body hair reminiscent of a Human. Often with animalistic traits such as sharp teeth or claw-like nails.

Nymph— Humanoids standing five to six feet, seeming to be a blend of Alva and plant.

Menninkainan— Diminutive cousins of the Alva, more slender than the Ajatar. Known for their darker skin tones and uniform black hair.

Pixie— Humanoids averaging only a foot tall, yet magically hold the strength of the average full size species. Have wings and are capable of flight.

Florem

Briarborn— Shorter wooden-limbed Humanoids, three and a half to four feet tall. Briarborns do not display bark, branches, or leaves in their features, rather, they appear to be made of smoothed wood, animated via magic.

Parthalon— Tall, thick-limbed Treemen. Standing eight to nine feet tall, with an external bark as skin, their shoulders and head often have offshoot branches and even leaves.

Humanid

Giant — While similar proportions to Humans, Giants average a height of twenty to twenty-five feet.

Human — Bipedal Humanoids without fur, but with sporadic hair, particularly on the head.

Isnashi — These appear to be Humans with wings. One of the rare species capable of flight, they have more frail bodies with hollow bird-like bones.

Vaettir — Proportionate Humans with an average height of two and a half to three feet.

Reptilian

Naga — Reptilian Humanoids with the upper body of a bipedal, but the lower body of a large snake. The lower body is strong enough to allow upright movement.

Ophisi — Taur-like beings, with six limbs on a long, sinuous body. The bottom pair of limbs are shorter, causing them to move lower to the ground. The middle limbs usually act as feet, although they do have the capability of limited dexterity when standing on two legs.

Skink — Diminutive lizard-like Humanoids, typically two and a half to three feet tall, with long balancing tails allowing for quick, balanced movement. Something about their origin gives their species an affinity for the Arcane.

Non-native

Coleope— An insectoid, ant-like species, uniformly approximately four feet tall, separate abdomen and thorax, with a large central third set of limbs that are able to be used for four legged movement, or to assist in lifting when moving in a bipedal fashion. Capable of independent, sentient thought when alone, though their personality is subsumed into a hive-like group mind when in proximity with a large number of other Coleope.

Gauch— Human-size Bipedals, completely hairless with long, thin limbs, rounded triangular heads, ashy gray skin, and large solid black eyes. The Gauch were the engineers and technologists of the warring races from the Devastation. They tend to stay with their own kind, and have some kind of genetic memory of the Skyfallen technology that arrived with them.

Mumvurii— While not technically a Skyfallen species abandoned on Sainan during the Devastation, the Investurant forces are alien to this world. Mumvuri is their name for a shadowy alternate world, overlaying Sainan as a parallel dimension. Through their unknown abilities, they are able to travel between their home and this plane of existence.

Ogre— Former slave foot soldiers of the battling forces during the Devastation. Standing eight feet tall, they are each four hundred pounds or more of dimwitted, brutish ferocity. They travel the world in floating Sky-cities, using their Skyfallen teleportation Gates to launch assaults on unsuspecting civilized regions of the land.

Appendix III
Magic and Spellcraft

Magic is an intrinsic force that shapes the very fabric of existence.In the realm of Sainan, there are distinct forms of magic which define how a practitioner can access magic, and what can be performed: Divine and Arcane. While both magics are sourced from the Realm beyond the Veil, they differ in their uses and methodologies. While both magics are prominent throughout the realm of Sainan, laws and culture greatly influence the way magic is viewed.Such influence creates a diverse landscape of magical practices within the world of Sainan.

I. Divine Magic:

Divine magic derives its power from higher beings, celestial entities, or other divine sources. It is channeled through prayer, faith, or devotion to these higher powers. Users of divine magic act as conduits for the divine energy, manifesting miraculous effects and wielding potent blessings or curses.

Source: Divine magic originates from gods, goddesses, spirits, or other divine entities worshiped by the inhabitants of Sainan. Each deity or divine entity governs specific domains or aspects of existence, granting their followers access to corresponding magical abilities.

Practitioners: Divine magic is predominantly wielded by the Friars within the Khorric Federation. These priests have formed connections with the divine beings. Their abilities often align with their deity's dogma and tenets, allowing them to perform acts of Healing, Protection, Divination, and righteous judgment. There are many Gods outside the Federation that provide similar power, but Federation law prohibits the worship of deities unapproved by the Federal Church.

Access: The Friars serve the citizens of the Khorric Federation. In more rural areas, Federal Friars are often seen as town leaders, advisors, or esteemed persons within their communities. However, in some cities, government influence results in Friars focusing their services on the citizens of the city that pay taxes, and often neglect the poorer communities.

II. Arcane Magic:

Arcane magic draws its power from the raw energies that permeate the cosmos, manipulating these energies through sheer will and knowledge of arcane principles. Within the realm of Arcane magic, there exist two distinct subsections: Gifted and Structured.

A. Gifted Arcane Magic:

Gifted Arcane magic is an innate ability possessed by certain individuals, often referred to as sorcerers or innate spellcasters. Unlike structured magic, which requires rigorous study and adherence to predefined rules, gifted arcane magic flows naturally through the veins of its practitioners.

Source: The origins of gifted arcane magic remain shrouded in mystery. Some attribute it to ancestral lineage, while others believe it is a random manifestation of magical potential within individuals. Regardless of its source, gifted arcane magic is deeply personal and often tied to the sorcerer's emotions or life experiences.

Practitioners: Sorcerers are the primary practitioners of gifted arcane magic. They wield their powers instinctively, relying on intuition and raw talent rather than academic learning. Gifted sorcerers often exhibit unique abilities, with their magical prowess reflecting their individuality and personal journey.

B. Structured Arcane Magic:

Structured (or Learned) Arcane magic, in contrast to its Gifted counterpart, is a disciplined and systematic approach to magic. It requires rigorous study, adherence to established principles, and mastery of arcane techniques.

Within the confines of Structured Arcane magic, the Magi hold considerable influence, regulating its usage and ensuring its responsible application.

Source: Structured Arcane magic draws upon ancient texts, arcane rituals, and scholarly knowledge passed down through generations. It is a product of meticulous research, experimentation, and refinement by scholars, wizards, and other learned practitioners.

Practitioners: Wizards, Magi, and scholars dedicated to the pursuit of magical knowledge are the primary practitioners of structured arcane magic. They undergo extensive training, often within prestigious institutions or under the tutelage of experienced mentors, to unlock the secrets of arcane lore. These practitioners adhere to strict codes of conduct and are subject to oversight by the Magi, who enforce regulations governing the responsible use of structured magic.

III. Prophecy Magic

Similar to Arcane magic, the magic of prophecy involves manipulating the Sphere of Time. This magic practice is too strong for performance by a single individual practitioner or a simple structural form. Instead, the magic of prophecy relies on a complex ritual performed by a group of spell casters, often known as a "Chorus."

Together, the Chorus views all possible time streams that stretch into the future, as well as the previous time streams that lead to the present. Evaluating the decisions of the past, the group estimates the likelyhood of similar decisions and the most likely outcomes of key moments of an individual, entity, or region and the decisions that would be available.

Source: Not many Sainan sources of prophecy are known. The biggest source of prophecy is the Witch in the Woods, widely regarded as a fey monster.

Access: Access to prophecy is strictly guarded. The cost of knowing the future is a terrible burden and not to be disregarded. It is a well known parable that asks "If the Witch can tell you your future, are you willing to pay the cost?" Because of this, visits to the Witch are rare and considered only by those in the most dire of circumstances.

IV. Regulation by the Magi:

Within the Khorric Federation, Structured Arcane magic is the only acceptable form of magic, and its practice is closely regulated by the Magi of the Elysium. These Arcane authorities oversee the training, licensing, and ethical conduct of all Arcane practitioners, ensuring that magic is wielded responsibly and in accordance with established laws and protocols.

Enforcement: The Magi enforce strict regulations to prevent misuse of Arcane magic, including prohibitions on forbidden spells, unauthorized experimentation, and unauthorized use of spells in public spaces. Violations of these regulations can result in severe penalties, ranging from fines and reprimands to expulsion from magical institutions or imprisonment.

Education and Training: As guardians of Arcane knowledge, the Magi over see the education and training of aspiring wizards. They establish curricula, administer examinations, and grant licenses to individuals deemed competent and trustworthy to practice structured arcane magic.

V. Magic Outside the Khorric Federation:

In some ways, the people of Mumvuri and those from Vargarden are tied together, polar opposites, Yin and Yang. Long ago, a Priestess from the Shadow Realm and a Necromancer from Sainan formed a pact, an alliance, to mutually aid one another's people, to explore both lands, and to share resources. The Goddess Amarant saw what knew the intent of these two leaders, and blessed their endeavor.

Amarant is a God of Death. She is not a heartless reaper of Souls, but rather a balance, a protector of the divide between life and death, loss and renewal. Looking upon both peoples, she bestowed her blessing in the way she felt would best give each society what they needed most.

A. Mumvuri

Amarant saw the heart of the leader of the Mumvurii people and knew that she did not want the burden she carried. Rather, she wished to shed her rule, free to explore untamed lands. Therefore she poured her blessing into the woman's blood. Once her daughter came of age, she became the Master, a Divine representative of Amarant. The Master was able to lift up her chosen friends and lieutenants, imbuing their blood with this power, thus forming the Sangebula, the ruling class of the Mumvurii people.

Due to the land in which they live, the Mumvurii share a different spiritual physiology. Their Souls reside closer to the Veil separating the Mortal from the Immaterial. Powers such as Astral Projection, Divination, and becoming Immaterial are vastly easier to achieve. In addition, much of their magic, both Divine and Arcane, is centered around the Soul. The Mumvurii, and especially the Sangebula, can aid a person's mind, heal one's body, and empower the senses, all through manipulation of the Soul.

Naturally, this includes their aggressive combat abilities as well. As the people of this land have much better control over their Soul, with even the weakest able to perform limited manipulation and protection, attacks against the Soul are considered commonplace. When brought to another realm like Sainan, the Sangebula found they had a decided advantage over a populace who were decidedly weak when it came to their connection to the Veil.

Their one weakness has come during the few times the Mumvurii have crossed swords with the Necromancers of Vargarden. After all, the Undead have no souls.

B. Vargarden

To the representative from Sainan, she made the Necromancer her Avatar, seeing his heart to know that he would use his power to provide benevolent rule to as many people as he could reach. He became the Father of Vargarden, creating a kingdom that has lasted longer than some civilizations. His political power and influence have waxed and waned over the centuries, at times stretching to the very corners of their continent, at others, such as now, retreating to the encased valley which holds his Undead city.

Being a demigod in his own right, half Deity and half Mortal, the Father holds some of the powers of a God. The Deacons of his church derive divine magic from their worship, and his Undead city has unique protections. Even when his political influence is not expansive, very few risk tempting the Necromancers to march out of their borders.

The wielders of magic in Vargarden are Necromancers first and foremost. Some wield the Arcane, others the Divine. Both are Deacons of the Father. In some ways, the form the magic comes through from the Father blends the two branches, though most remain purely in one branch.

VI. Structured Arcane Magic Mechanics:

Structured Arcane magic operates on a unique system that involves the manipulation of two fundamental forms: the Aether Form and the Structural Form.

Aether Form: The Aether Form represents the raw essence of magic drawn from the surrounding environment. It is shaped and infused with intent by the practitioner to resonate with a specific Sphere of magic, defining the elemental or thematic nature of the spell. For example, drawing upon the Fire Aether Form imbues the spell with the essence of flames, while drawing upon the Ice Aether Form imbues it with the chilling power of frost.

Structural (or Brace) Form: The Structural Form determines the shape and manifestation of the spell's effect. It acts as the framework through which the magical energy is channeled and directed towards a desired outcome. Wizards and mages select from a variety of Structural Forms to craft spells tailored to their needs or preferences. For instance, the Bolt Structural Form may shape the magical energy into a concentrated projectile, while the Barrier Structural Form may create a protective shield or barrier.

Example of Spellcasting:

Combining the Aether and Structural Forms allows practitioners to cast a diverse array of spells. For instance, if a wizard draws upon the Ice Aether

Form and pairs it with the Bolt Structural Form, they cast an Ice Blast—a projectile of freezing energy capable of immobilizing or damaging their target.

VII. Key Terminology:

In the study and practice of magic within the Khorric Federation, as in much of Sainan, several terms hold significant importance, defining the very essence of Arcane knowledge and its application. Understanding these terms is essential for navigating the intricate landscape of magical lore and spellcasting techniques.

Arcana: The term "Arcana" refers to the field of arcane magic itself, encompassing the vast body of knowledge, rituals, and practices that constitute the study of magic. It serves as a broad term for all things magical, encompassing both theoretical understanding and practical application. Within scholarly circles and mystical traditions, the pursuit of Arcana is revered as a noble endeavor, seeking to unravel the mysteries of magic and unlock its boundless potential.

Arcane: As an adjective, "Arcane" denotes qualities or aspects related to magic. It is used to describe phenomena, objects, or abilities imbued with magical properties or derived from arcane sources. For example, the term "Arcane arts" may refer to the various disciplines and techniques employed by practitioners of magic, while "Arcane ward" signifies a protective barrier infused with magical energy to repel or deflect threats.

Arcanum: The term "Arcanum" specifically refers to the energy utilized by spellcasters to fuel their magical spells. It represents the raw, unbridled power of the Arcane, harnessed and shaped by the will of the practitioner to enact mystical effects. Arcanum is the fundamental essence that permeates all magical phenomena, serving as the catalyst for spellcasting and the conduit through which magical energies are channeled and manipulated.

Spell Commands:

Creosilo -- A small blast of frost.

Essevoy -- A spell that creates a small patch of spider webs.

Ferrelius -- A brilliant flash of pure daylight.

Farroos -- A spell that illuminates an object or body part. Can be directed as a beam with creative casting.

Halsivatio -- A sweeping barrier protecting an entire side of the caster. A one-hundred and eighty degree arc of shielding.

Harsitodanio -- A barrier of souls drawn from the Veil. A wall of deathly energy separating mortals.

Harsival -- A spell that creates a standing shield barrier that can be handed off. Lasts for a short time, but is solid for the duration of the spell.

Hasil -- A temporary ward of protective energy that can deflect an incoming attack. Instantaneous, but quickly able to be memorized and cast.

Osival -- An ability to telekinetically grab an item and pull it to your hand.

Selives -- A spell of revealing, allows the caster enhanced senses to spot hidden compartments or panels.

Silokoval -- An arcane whip spell that creates a sharp damaging blast.

Sival -- A small spell of quickly bound force that can be targeted. Enough to snag or trip an individual.

Todvedoblum -- A spell known as the Withering Flower. A decaying spell that eats its target.

Todisee -- A moderate healing spell able to heal minor wounds.

Todiselive -- A powerful healing spell that can heal mortal wounds.

Todisomatis -- A spell that allows the caster to reach out to the soul of a being through their mortal remains.

Tsamautu -- A voice amplification spell, typically used to speak with large crowds.

Appendix IV
The History of the Khorric Federation

History

The year the alien war was fought in the skies of Sainan is remembered by everyone. Such were the fundamental changes of the event that there is no corner, whether physically, socially, or spiritually, left untainted. This year of upheaval became known to all as the Clade.

Regardless of what names denizens had formerly given to the land, over the next century the name Sainan, Elven for catastrophe or disaster, became the universal word for their world. New technologies and new understanding of the laws of physics allowed vast regions to make contact, and the name spread, along with the start date of a new universal calendar. A common language and writing spread, allowing for more uniformity in thought and communication.

By the new calendar, it is now the year 690 ST (Sainan Toshi or "Year of the Calamity"), and has been close to seven centuries since the events of the great war. There are still a few persons alive who personally experienced the Clade and tell stories of the world before, but for most, the new world is all they've known. New magics, interaction with divine beings, travel to alternate planes of existence, alien technologies, and alien species have become a woven part of life on Sainan.

The Aspiring Federation

In the early years after the Clade, at an event known as the Holy Conclave, the various leaderships of one particular region surrounding three crash-sites met and decided to ally themselves, both for protection and to take advantage of the new resources now available. The rulers of this time agreed to share certain powers across all their lands, coordinated their forces to one purpose, and over the course of four tumultuous years, took all parts of their land under one shared government, forming the Aspiring Federation. All kingdoms, fiefdoms, and clans within the new borders were approached, and either surrendered to be part of this new rulership, or were overrun in short order.

The Khorric Empire

For over two centuries, the Aspiring Federation was ruled by a council, called Governors. In 233 ST, Vess Khorric, known to history as "the Betrayer" emerged. An Ennedi noble and the son of the Governor of Tennhel, he strove for more influence, and manipulated the political system to seize military power. Through the threat of war, and many real battles, Vess took power, disbanded the Council, and declared himself Emperor.

He ruled for fifteen years, before he died and his son, Chronn, took up the mantle in 248 ST. Chronn renamed the region the Khorric Federation, and spent the next forty years fighting off rebellions. He managed to die a feared and respected ruler.

His daughter, Ellana Khorric, only fourteen at the time of her father's death, took control of the Federation in 289 ST. Many members of the Federation believed it would be a natural time to take control. Regents and leaders positioned themselves behind the scenes to grab for power or begin a revolution. In her first two years on the throne, no less than a dozen regents died or resigned, including Elanna's mother, who retired away from court.

On her seventeenth birthday, Elanna had herself crowned as Empress. Historians have pieced together that Elanna had spent those first two years creating a network of spies, agents, and enforcers to do her bidding and secure her rule. Soon after her coronation, a sort of secret police were formed, an organization called Briarwood, which infiltrated and quelled rebellions, silenced political dissidents, and ruthlessly forestalled any trouble to the Federation.

For those in the nobility, it was an age of strife and paranoia, but for the majority of the citizenry, it began an age of prosperity and enlightenment.

Religion flourished, trade abounded, and both craftsmen and the arts received vast patronage from the elite and the government. Empress Elanna Khorric's rule proved to be the saving point of her grandfather's upheaval.

And it continued. And continued.

While Ennedi are known to have a natural lifespan of seventy to eighty years, and elite members of society have access to magics and technology that can extend that life an additional thirty years, nothing explained Elanna Khorric's unnatural reign. Elanna Khorric remained Empress for just over two centuries, finally passing in the year 492 ST. Over the course of her rule, she married and lost three husbands, and had another four consorts. She raised and outlived sixteen children, and had two living elderly children at the time of her death.

It is said that at the time of her death the Empress still retained her appearance of being in her mid thirties. The details and method of her death are unknown, but it was not of old age, nor did she meet a violent death. It is recorded that she was merely found one morning to have died seemingly peacefully in her sleep. The reaction of Briarwood over the next year, simultaneously investigating her death and fighting to seize control, nearly destroyed the Federation.

The Khorric Federation

In 494 ST, the nobility managed to regain control of the Federation, convened a new Holy Conclave, and reinstated a new Council. After two and a half centuries under a single rule, however, many of the old kingdom borders from the old Federation had merged, and rather than trying to redefine those old borders, the Federation was divided into eight governing Provinces, with each Province holding a hereditary Governor, and an appointed Council Lord. Briarwood was disbanded and run underground by the noble families. There were several attempts to declare Briarwood illegal, but they held too much positive folklore with the commoners. So too failed any attempts to change the name of the Khorric Federation. The memory of Empress Elanna Khorric's rule proved to be too beloved.

Over the last two hundred years, the Council has maintained control of the Khorric Federation. Although there have been several attempts to wrest control from within and to change the nature of the government, the Federation is considered too big and powerful to be attacked from without. It helps that two of the eight Council Lords are old enough to have been involved in reforming the government after the death of the Empress, one a Taniwha and the other an Alva. Only the name Briarwood still publicly exists, with its current incarnation that of a Hunters Guild.

The War of Night

In the year 607 ST, the Khorric Federation was rocked by a surprise invasion of an unknown species of people, the Investurants. The blue-skinned Humanoids were armed with an intimate grasp of shadowy Arcane abilities, magic that attacks the soul directly. The Arcanists of the Federation's Elysium had no counter to this foreign attack, and took horrific losses. As the Investurants never attacked in great numbers, the Khorric Federation suffered four decades of a hit-and-run gorilla war they never developed a strategy to combat. In the end, the Khorric Federation swallowed their pride and revulsion, and accepted the help of their dreaded neighbors to the north. The Undead Legions of the Necromancers of Vargarden had no souls to be lost to the magic of the Investurants, and within two years, the long war was, at last, ended in 649 ST.

The Second War of Night

In the spring of 689 ST, rumors began to stir that the Investurants from the Shadow Plane of Mumvuri had been seen harrying patrols and communities in the extreme northern edges of the Khorric Federation. By the spring of the following year, they were heard to be harassing patrols in the eastern provinces of Strongwald and Highlock. It was unknown what their goal was, but the leadership of the Federation and its Nobles were concerned that things were moving toward another war.

The Khorric Federation was caught unaware when in the spring of 691

ST, the bulk of the Investurant forces began appearing through Shadow Gates all throughout the capital city of Highston, right within their very walls. The Lightning Cult scouting parties which had been harassing the outer provinces for the last year and a half had been doing so in order to pull the Federation's army of the Praetorian Guard away from the center of the Federation. Away from the capital.

Within months of invading the capital city of Highston, the true intention of the Investurants was revealed. The Investurants stepped aside in order to support a coup within the local government. This group, called the New Nobles, were a mix of a small part of the children of some of the older families, but even moreso by new families raised up to bring the leadership of the Khorric Federation in a new direction.

Highston

Highston is the capital city of the Khorric Federation, and is not considered to be a part of any of the eight provinces. The Council resides and rules from here over the Federation, while the city itself is run by a ninth Governor.

The Provinces of the Khorric Federation

Anadre

This is the province known for its mountain folk, providing mined materials, both minerals and metals, as well as some of the finest smithing craftsmanship known throughout the Federation. Some say that the weapons coming out of the Dwarven Smithies of the Undercity of Eastwall are among the best in the known world. Eastwall is also popular for housing one of the three Skyfallen Gates in the Federation.

Bethel

This province, situated in the northeast corner of the Federation, deals heavily in the skins and animals trapped and hunted from both the Deepland Forest to the north, and the Yyalesken Jungle to the east. This region is also the primary trade route for goods brought in from Ahnk-hass on the eastern coast.

Eithren

Eithren is widely considered the breadbasket of the Federation, housing vast tracts of farmland and dairy ranches. The fertile grasslands of this region provide ideal growing conditions, and so is known for its grains, cheeses, and produce.

Highloch

Stretching into the Decaying Wastes to the northwest, this province has little to offer in the way of crops and farmland. Instead, it has become a stronghold against the aggressive forces of the Northern Plain States. In that capacity, Highloch has come to host the training grounds and barracks of the Praetorian Guard that defend the borders of the Khorric Federation.

Parth

Lacking a coastal port city of its own, this Province acts in that capacity as it is the hub for all imports and exports with the coastal city of Shrikesport. Additionally, Parth is home to the mountain monastery of Arlingminster Heights, a regionally famous spiritual location.

Strongwald

Located the furthest west, Strongwald receives the goods imported from the Dorne Empire down the Hinbalt River to the southwest. As the bulk of the province encroaches into the desert of the Moaning Expanse, the principal reason the Khorric Federation has fought so hard to keep this stretch of land within its grasp is the city of Vogfaldur, the site of another Skyfallen Gate.

Tennhel

Despite being the ancestral seat of the Khorric family and a powerful kingdom before the Federation was formed, the Empress neither raised nor diminished this region during her reign. In fact, she hardly visited her family's lands, preferring to stay to the Federation capital city of Highston. In modern times, Tennhel has a primarily agricultural role in the Federation. The grains from this region also make this province highly regarded for its beers and ales.

Tollorheim

With the forges of Redmont Stronghold to the south providing the weapons and armor for the Praetorian Guard, the vast grazing pastures of the east and north housing the bulk of the livestock to the Federation, and the vineyards shared with Strongwald in the west, Tollorhaim is often seen as one of the wealthiest of the Khorric provinces. Naryn is lauded as the fashion center of the Federation's Nobility.

Neighboring Kingdoms

Shrikesport

To the southeast lies Shrikesport, a large port city ruled by a collection of merchant families. With the Khorric Federation having no ports of their own, much of their imports are forced to come through this kingdom, and both sides know it. Relations are sometimes strained, tempers can sometimes run high, politics run rampant, and embargos can oftentimes be threatened by both sides.

Ahnk-haas

Located far to the east, this coastal city stands on its own, separated from their closest neighbors by the Yyalesken Jungle. They do not interact much with the Khorric Federation, except during those times when Shrikesport chooses to to embargo the landlocked region.

Vargarden

This kingdom lies to the north of the Federation, led by a High King. This High King is a Lich Lord, raising the dead of his mortal subjects to act as his own standing army. The Necromantic priests of Vargarden are the subject of horror stories in the Khorric Federation. Tales of their silent armies marching beside the Praetorian Guard are still told around campfires and bars to this day.

Dornish Empire

Most members of the Khorric Federation do not understand the size of this vast empire to their southwest. While trade is encouraged, particularly for the exotic Dornish spices and woods, politically they retain a grudging stalemate that has, at times, threatened war.

The Caleigh Free States

So named because of their break from oppressive kingdoms to the north, this small collection of city-states take pride in their large groups of freelance mercenaries, and the ancient, powerful families that control their cities.

Appendix V
Politics and Organizations

The Khorric Federation is a society of Guilds and unions. Everyone from the lowliest chimney sweeper to the highest Noble takes their worth and their livelihood from the organizations to which they belong.

I. Government

Every Province has its own governor and ruling council, each with similar positions such as the Master of Goods, overseeing merchants, pricing, and disputes, the Master of Wheels, overseeing intercity trade, or the Master of Swords, monitoring the city guard. Each city also has a Council of Lords, overseeing the ruling class of Nobles and keeping guard over their concerns.

Highston, as the capital of the Khorric Federation, has a slightly different ruling structure.Highston's ruling council is called the Council of Commons, staffed with prominent non-Nobles promoted from the various guild members associated with their various trades.

Highston has its own Lords High Council. However, the Highston council oversees the Councils of Lords of all the cities of the Khorric Federation, making decisions not only for Highston, but the entire realm.

With the second War of Night, many of the old, corrupt Noble houses were overthrown in a coup. The New Nobles were formed in order to bring new leadership to the Khorric Federation, backed by the Inversterant forces and several of the Bright Guilds, primarily Highston's branch of Manticore.

II. Law enforcement & National army

Each Province, and within, each city, is responsible for maintaining law and order within its own borders. This also means that while laws as a whole apply to the entire Federation, the strength at which those laws are upheld are determined by the ruling Lord's Councils of the various Provinces. Overarching laws such as the abolishment of slavery are universally supported and ruthlessly enforced, but assault, theft, and other criminal charges can vary widely, based on the station and status of the victim and perpetrator.

While internal order is handled by each Province and each city, protection of the Realm from external enemies is handled by the Praetorian Guard. The Generals and military leadership answer directly to the Lords High Council in Highston. Individual Provinces are not allowed their own individual military, but as a further separation of powers, the Praetorians have no authority within city walls, save for in a state of declared war.

III. Criminal Elements

As with the Federation at large, the criminal underworld is divided into Guilds as well. These organizations are called Bright Guilds, rumored to come from a story of a Guild lieutenant claimed that:

> *"Our guilds, our fine organizations, bring the bright light of free thought, and free action, to all the people of the Khorric Federation. We bring the bright light of freedom to the dark, tyrannical bureaucracy of the government of this otherwise fine nation."*

While started as an ironic joke, this quickly became the mantra among thieves and vagabonds looking for a means to excuse their criminal activities. Among the government, these organizations are called Crime Guilds, or Crime Syndicates.

Not every Bright Guild is represented in every Khorric city, and there is some debate as to which guilds are the largest. Each Bright Guild is self-governed, some with a council, others with an unopposed leader.

Manticore is one of the largest, some claiming it to be the largest. It has certainly seen its stars rise within recent years. Even with the loss of their leader, Grendel, Manticore was able to use the Investurant invasion to grow even larger in power, enabling them to operate even further in the open.

IV. Independent Adventurers

The Khorric Federation offers an official line between those in law enforcement and military, and the criminals in the underworld. Official organizations called Hunters Guilds hire and train mercenaries, singly and in groups. The Hunter Squads are the only way to operate in a legal capacity as a bounty hunter, hired guard, or monster hunter. The cities of Faegento and Esterwitch host the largest schools for Hunters Guilds.

V. Trade

As with the law and crimes, when it comes to trade, Federal laws and regulations trump Province or City rules, assuming the injured party has the resources to bring the details to someone that will enforce the difference. However, in matters of trade, the ultimate power comes from the Merchant Guilds, and the Nobles that they often answer to. The Guild you belong to holds more sway over your business practices than the Province you work in. The various councils oversee any disputes between Guilds, but actually spend more time governing trade with other nations, leaving the inter-city trade to the Guilds to deal with.

VI. The Church

The churches are many and varied, as numerous as the Gods of the Pantheon and the combinations that can be made between them. There are a few that are officially sponsored by the government in exchange for the support they give to the Nobility, but all but the most chaotic and anarchic are welcomed within the nation.

VII. Education

By law, all children of the Khorric Federation are given a basic education at one of the schools run by the Academy. Since this practice is upheld for "citizens" of the Federation, Street Rats and other less fortunate members of society fall through the cracks, often barred from the hallowed halls of learning. Reading and writing are common throughout the Federation, at all levels of life, and through magic and machinery, books and paper are common and well used.

All knowledge is controlled by the Academy, and through them, by the Nobles of the Federation. Everything from history to the Arcane is curated and dictated, ostensibly for the benefit of peace and prosperity.

Basic Arcane forms are taught by the Academy, for a nominal fee, in addition to being for sale in bookshops in every city. Spells beyond the most basic forms, however, are carefully controlled by the government and their Nobles. To access these spells, one would need to be accepted to the ranks of the Magi, taught exclusively at the elite Elysium.

Appendix VI
The History of Vargarden

The Father of Vargarden

The current calendar begins at the Devastation, or Sainan Toshi. The calendar before this ended and gave way to the new calendar in the year it called 6260. The foundations and prehistory of this older calendar has been lost to myth. Some attribute it to the Gods, some to the beginning of a great civilization or a religious event.

According to the teachings of the Church of the Father, by the time of the Devastation, the being known as the Father of Vargarden was already approximately eleven centuries old. Their teachings and doctrines confirm that the Father had performed the dark rites necessary to become a Lich, a being that foreswore their Mortal form to embrace Undeath in exchange for Arcane power and a longer existence.

Arcane tomes advise that the final step in becoming a Lich is for the Arcanist to place their Soul within a Reliquary, an object or container intended to house and protect the Lich's essence. If the Reliquary is broken or corrupted, the Lich will be ended as well. Therefore the choice of what to use as a Reliquary is of the utmost importance. For clear reasons, the Father's reliquary selection, nor its location, has been disclosed to anyone or any recordings.

As troubling as this is to many Federation scholars, and the Federation Church as a whole, the details of the Father's status as a Lich has additional points of concern. Alva and Ukko are the longest living beings on Sainan. Members of their species can live as long as 700 years. Beings who become a Lich can survive much longer. The process tends to add between five and seven additional centuries to their time on Sainan, meaning some Alvan Liches, while rare, can live for nearly 1400 years. By this accounting, even with the most generous scenario, the Father's time should have come to an end. By the legends told by the Church, skeptics are not taking into account that the Father is also a divine avatar of the Goddess of Death.

The Founding of the City of Vargarden

According to the church, one of the first actions of the Father, after his fall to Lichdom, was to revisit his home village, in the valley that would eventually become Vargarden. The families there became his first Deacons, with their bloodlines still being passed down in the kingdom to this day. The Father marched an army of the Undead into the valley from the west, He laid down a protection over the valley, ringing the entire area in a massive line of skeletons. They were left to an uninterrupted watch in his stead as he once again left the kingdom for unknown reasons. This clear show of macabre power, defense, and control gave rise to the earliest reputation of the valley of Vargarden being a "dark, evil kingdom".

Per Vargarden histories, a century later the Father returned to the valley, recently imbued as a divine Avatar of Amarant and erected a shrine to the Goddess of Death. This church became the foundation for the Father's worship and centralized power structure of his Deacons. The village became a town, and over the centuries grew to become a city. As the city grew, the Father stayed busy with his business out in the world. Every few decades he would return, each time teaching his Deacons and sharing with them his power. His church ruled Vargarden as a theocracy. As the power of the Deacons grew, the Father handed more and more control of the protective Undead surrounding the valley's perimeter to them.

When the Skyfallen battle of the Clade occurred, the Father withdrew back to his kingdom. With him came a second army of the Undead, this time several hundred Jotun, Human-like beings ranging eighteen to twenty feet in height. These new Undead were immediately put to work, along with half the skeleton army already within Vargarden. With their untiring efforts, a massive palace was constructed at the northern side of the city, with cleared area for the city to grow around it. Working to quiet the kingdom's reputation with the surrounding lands, the Undead army was pulled back from the valley's border, to instead be laid to rest in the area known as the Black Yards.

The Church of the Father

By the teachings of the Church of the Father, from the beginning the Father's mission was to aid the powers of the world in eliminating the Undead being used for evil, as well as any roaming the world unchecked. He held a fascination with the razor's edge that was the event horizon between life and death, and took the step from an intellectual curiosity to an active experience. However, he always kept a hard discipline about ensuring he never fell to abusing his new position, even as he used his Necromancy to fight fire with fire.

After gaining the attention of Amarant and the increase in power she gave, the Father began teaching others, Deacons, who spread throughout the region, not to proselytize or to gain power, but to teach others how to fight and control the Undead. It took experimentation and force of will to navigate the politics and religions of the different nations. Some attempts succeeded, others failed. In some kingdoms, temples to the Father still stand, acknowledging what he and his Deacons have done throughout the centuries. In other areas, he is looked on as Evil Incarnate, vilified for his methods without regard for results.

The reach and influence of the Father and his church have waxed and waned over the years, sometimes aiding on a continental scale, while at others pulling back nearly to Vargarden itself. In the current age, there are a few areas that still harbor a temple, usually dedicated to Amarant, rather than to the Father directly. Many of these temples are actually the home to various sects of a priesthood that follow the original intention of the Father. Rather than merely following the teachings of the Father and reactively protecting the Living from the Dead, these Deacons train to aggressively hunt the Undead, both wild and those controlled by those who would do evil. These Deacons are not well known, but nevertheless still operate behind the scenes.

Vargarden Terminology

Eisgeid

Vargarden term for servant or manual use skeletons, as opposed to armed, fighting style Undead. These work in single units, able to follow limited, simple voice commands given by anyone who has been voice-assigned by a priest.

Welgeid

Vargarden term for military and/or guard skeletons, as opposed to servant style Undead. These work in linked groups, where a priest can control a certain number of skeletons to guide them through combat or city patrol interactions.

Welengam

Vargarden term for a collection of Welgeid. A ***Disordered Welengam*** would be a random or hastily raised group. A ***Welengam Squad*** would be a group of a dozen or less. A ***Patrol*** would be Welgeid used in civilian areas, such as city guard.

The Legion

Informal name given to the standing army of Welgeid at any current time. Officially, this is the organizational name, used in recordkeeping, but informally it is used for the troops as a whole, as well.

The Ordered (Welengam)

These are the actual companies of Undead armies currently in use. The term "Welengam" may be dropped in casual use. For example, one might refer to the Ordered 12th, as opposed to the official name of the Ordered Welengam 12th. This would include the attached living command leadership and all assigned Necromantic Priests.

SON OF NIGHT
SON OF LIGHT

It was supposed to be a peaceful honeymoon. The warm night air provided a tranquil atmosphere over the Cyl'Karrick Estate, mirroring in sharp contrast the cold devastation which had befallen the occupants of this hard earned, peaceful home. A slim quarter moon, mostly hidden by the overcast sky, did little to light the landscape, which only drew attention to how dark much of the house's windows were. The lights and sounds of a vibrant cityscape sprawled to the west of the estate, not quite intruding on the quiet grounds. One of the few lit windows opened into the ground floor library, where the home's occupants could be seen in talks. The temperature of their discussion was announced with the sharp explosion of shattering glass.

Symon narrowly ducked the brass skull that would have caved in his own, had his feline reflexes not avoided the missile hurled by his best friend. He looked back at the impressive dent put in the bookcase behind him, before turning back to Jesse.

"Is there an option here that does not resort in violence?" he asked, fighting his desire to raise his voice.

"Fuck you, fuck the council, fuck this whole place! It's been two fucking days, and we haven't left the house, much less the fucking city!" screamed Jesse.

The advisor from the council had just left. Symon, his new wife Moria, and Jesse were in the library, their typical locale for thinking and studying. Today, it was their place of arguing.

"Jesse, you need'n to calm right down," snapped Moria, "before I put you ov'r my knee."

"Not helping," muttered Symon quietly, placing a hand on her shoulder. Then, in a normal tone, he said, "I get it, Jesse, I really do. We understand your frustration. Yes, it has been two days since Argyle left with Caleb, and you are correct that we have not been able to do much yet. The Legion are searching the valley of Vargarden, and the Road of the Dead all the way through to the Khorric Federation. We have not yet found them."

"So for all we know," spat out Jesse," Caleb could be fucking dead and buried in the Deepland Forest!"

"No," said Moria, standing to face Jesse, sighing as she kept her mounting frustration out of her voice, "Reneforte is still going mad."

"The unholy fuck does Reneforte have to do with Caleb right now?" yelled Jesse.

Moria glanced over at Symon, a look that he clearly understood to mean, 'You deal with this in your way, or I will deal with him in mine', before looking back at Jesse. "The Eisgeid is soul-linked to the prince. It operates by his will. Were he dead, it would fall to pieces. Were he calm, it would be still."

"So, you are saying he is insane? In pain?" Jesse turned from anger to panic in an instant. "Is Caleb being tortured? Is that why Reneforte is going crazy?"

Moria realized she was making things worse here, and reached out her hands, palms forward, in a supplicating gesture. "No, no. More likely he is drugged and asleep, his unconscious lashing out, that is causing the Eisgeid to act out." She turned to address her husband. "Least wise, that's what the priest earlier was saying is most likely, right, Symon?"

"This is correct. Prince Caleb is most assuredly alive," said Symon. "And we are going to find him."

"So why haven't we left yet? Have we suddenly lost all the maps to Highston?"

"Jesse, please, we need calm right now," said Symon, "You know why we have not left yet. We need to wait for the council. We are going to need more help than just the two of us."

"The council," muttered Jesse sarcastically. "You know, I'd get it if I was the one kidnapped, and it was Caleb asking for help to come get me. But this is their prince! Do they seriously not give a shit?"

"Course they do," said Moria. "But ya just said it. T'were you, or Symon, or even me who was gone, t'would be easier to figure out. There's no politics involved if we were missing. However, it is nothing *but* politics when it is the crown-damned-prince!"

Jesse started pacing like a caged animal. Symon and Moria spent a few minutes bouncing between watching him and glancing at one another. When Jesse passed by Symon's desk, he let out an almighty scream of frustration and reached forward to sweep its entire contents in one angry rush. Symon and Moria both jumped as stacks of papers went flying, journals hit the floor, and ink splattered everywhere. For the briefest of moments, Jesse paused as if he was surprised by what he had done, but after that small pause, he just grunted and went back to pacing.

"I'm really trying to be understanding here and keep some slack in your rope, Jesse," growled Symon, "but if you disrespect my sire's journals again, you are going to hang yourself."

Jesse stopped mid-stride, his shoulders tensed. Slowly, he turned to look angrily at Symon, his entire body strung tighter than a bow. "When I'm holding Caleb's hand, I'll fucking apologize."

Moria hopped up from her seat, clearly about to charge the impetuous teen, when Symon gripped her shoulder, attempting to keep her seated. For a second, she acted like she was going to shrug off his hand, but then she slumped back into her chair and looked away.

"I am letting this slide for now, but-" Symon barely started speaking before, not even looking back, Jesse strode to the door, opened it, and flipped a crude hand gesture before exiting the room with a slammed door.

Follow Us On Social Media

facebook.com/sainanbooks

@sainanbooks

@sainanbooks

SAINAN
Books

www.sainanbooks.com

About the Authors

Greyson Black is the nom de plume for one half of Sainan Books. Born an army brat in Germany, he attended 3 Elementary schools, 3 middle schools, 2 high schools, and 3 colleges before finally ignoring all education to set out on the impossible task of becoming a professional author.

Wherever he tries to move to, Huntsville, AL is the leash that always tugs him back home, where he lives with his roommates: Me, Myself, and I. When not transmuting coffee into ink, he is typically found painting miniatures, researching the etymology of his latest distracting phrase, or telling really bad jokes.

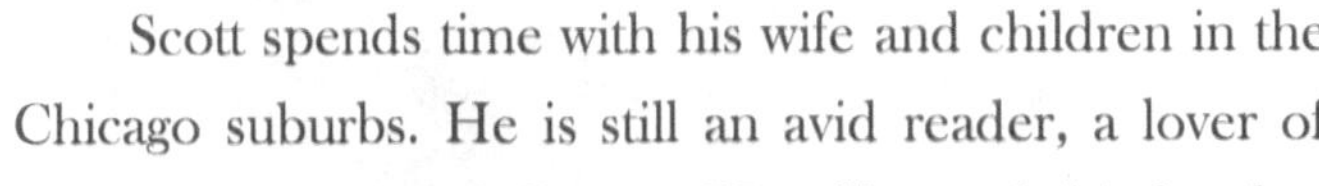

Nestled in the serene suburbs of Chicago, the other half of Sainan Books, E. Scott Clevenger draws inspiration from the extraordinary bonds that shape his life. As a son, a devoted husband, and father of two boys, Scott's tales are woven with the threads of family love and the magical moments that define his characters.

Scott spends time with his wife and children in the Chicago suburbs. He is still an avid reader, a lover of RPGs, and stories of all types. He still attends his Sunday and Tuesday night game sessions, and loves to annoy the table with pop-culture references and broken song lyrics.

MORE FROM SAINAN BOOKS

THE MANTICORE'S SHADOW
EPIC FOUR BOOK SERIES

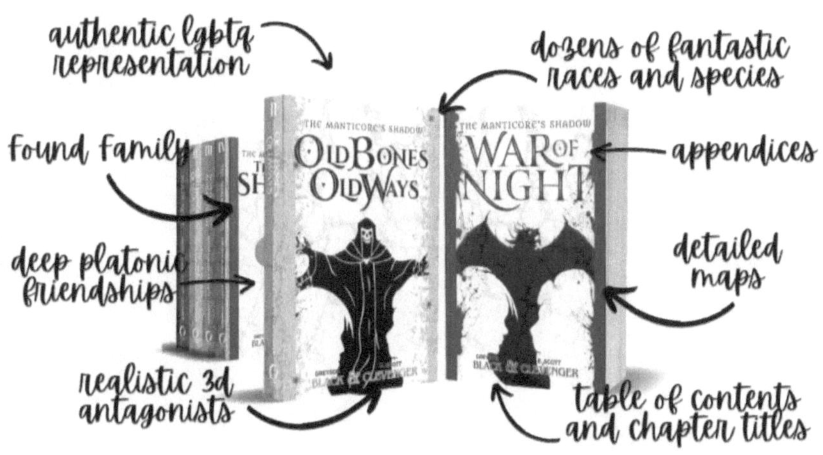

**What do you get when beings from the Shadow Plane
go to war with the Land of the Dead...
and your home is caught in between?**

The middle class meets a lack of class when street thief Jesse encounters blacksmith apprentice Symon on the streets of Highston. Jesse's criminal cohorts intersect with Symon's political enemies as the two youths turn to each other in their hopes of navigating a maze of betrayal and lies towards a brighter future.

This fresh take on epic fantasy storytelling strives to bridge the old and new, bringing a modern fantasy voice to the classic world building elements of days past. A bold new world and concepts, blended with traditional elements.

SAINAN
Books

www.sainanbooks.com